PENGUIN BOOKS

THE OLD DEVILS

Kingsley Amis, who was born in South London in 1922, was educated at the City of London School and St John's College, Oxford. At one time he was a university lecturer, a keen reader of science fiction and a jazz enthusiast. His novels include *Lucky Jim* (1954), *Take a Girl Like You* (1960), *The Anti-Death League* (1966), *Ending Up* (1974), *The Alteration* (1976, winner of the John W. Campbell Memorial Award), *Jake's Thing* (1978), *Russian Hide-and-Seek* (1980) and *Stanley and the Women* (1984). Among his other publications are *New Maps of Hell*, a survey of science fiction (1960), *The James Bond Dossier* (1965), *Colonel Sun*, a James Bond adventure (1968, under the pseudonym of Robert Markham), *Rudyard Kipling and His World* (1975) and *The Golden Age of Science Fiction* (1981). He published his *Collected Poems* in 1979 and his *Collected Short Stories* in 1980 (revised edition 1987). Many of his books are published in Penguin. He has written ephemerally on politics, education, language, films, television, restaurants and drink. Kingsley Amis was awarded the CBE in 1981.

The Old Devils was the winner of the 1986 Booker Prize.

Kingsley Amis

The Old Devils

Penguin Books

Penguin Books Ltd, Harmondsworth, Middlesex, England
Viking Penguin Inc., 40 West 23rd Street, New York, New York 10010, U.S.A.
Penguin Books Australia Ltd, Ringwood, Victoria, Australia
Penguin Books Canada Limited, 2801 John Street, Markham, Ontario, Canada L3R 1B4
Penguin Books (N.Z.) Ltd, 182–190 Wairau Road, Auckland 10, New Zealand

First published by Hutchinson, an imprint of Century Hutchinson 1986
Published in Penguin Books 1987

Made and printed in Great Britain by
Cox & Wyman Ltd, Reading, Berks
Typeset in 10/12½pt Linotron 202 Plantin by
Rowland Phototypesetting Ltd, Bury St Edmunds, Suffolk

Author's Note

Many real places are referred to in this novel (Carmarthen, Cowbridge) and many fictitious ones too (Birdarthur, Caerhays). Lower Glamorgan corresponds to no county division. The fictitious places are not real ones in disguise or under pseudonyms: anybody trying to go from the coast of South Wales to Courcey Island, for instance, would soon find himself in the Bristol Channel. Courcey and the others have no more actual existence than any of the characters here portrayed.

K.A.
Swansea: London

Contents

To Louis and Jacob

One – Malcolm, Charlie, Peter and Others

1

'If you want my opinion,' said Gwen Cellan-Davies, 'the old boy's a terrifically distinguished citizen of Wales. Or at any rate what passes for one these days.'

Her husband was cutting the crusts off a slice of toast. 'Well, I should say that's generally accepted.'

'And Reg Burroughs is another after his thirty years of pen-pushing in first City Hall and later County Hall, for which he was duly honoured.'

'That's altogether too dismissive a view. By any reckoning Alun has done some good things. Come on now, fair play.'

'Good things for himself certainly: *Brydan's Wales* and that selection, whatever it's called. Both still selling nicely after all these years. Without Brydan and the Brydan industry, Alun would be nothing. Including especially his own work – those poems are all sub-Brydan.'

'Following that trail isn't such a bad –'

'Goes down a treat with the Americans and the English, you bet. But . . .' Gwen put her head on one side and gave the little frowning smile she used when she was putting something to someone, often a possible negative view of a third party, 'wouldn't you have to agree that he follows

Brydan at, er, an altogether lower level of imagination and craftsmanship?'

'I agree that compared with Brydan at his best, he doesn't –'

'You know what I mean.'

In this case Malcolm Cellan-Davies did indeed know. He got up and refilled the teapot, then his cup, adding a touch of skimmed milk and one of the new sweeteners that were supposed to leave no aftertaste. Back in his seat at the breakfast-table he placed between his left molars a small prepared triangle of toast and diabetic honey and began crunching it gently but firmly. He had not bitten anything with his front teeth since losing a top middle crown on a slice of liver-sausage six years earlier, and the right-hand side of his mouth was a no-go area, what with a hole in the lower lot where stuff was always apt to stick and a funny piece of gum that seemed to have got detached from something and waved disconcertingly about whenever it saw the chance. As his jaws operated, his eyes slid off to the *Western Mail* and a report of the Neath – Llanelli game.

After lighting a cigarette Gwen went on in the same quirky style as before, 'I don't remember you as a great believer in the integrity of Alun Weaver as an embodiment of the Welsh consciousness?'

'Well, I suppose in some ways, all the television and so on, he is a bit of a charlatan, yes, maybe.'

'Maybe! Christ Almighty. Of course he's a charlatan and good luck to him. Who cares? He's good fun and he's unstuffy. We could do with a dozen like him in these parts to strike the fear of God into them. We need a few fakes to put a dent in all that bloody authenticity.'

'Not everybody's going to be glad to have him around,' said Malcolm, giving another section of toast the standard treatment.

'Well, that's splendid news. Who are you thinking of?'

'Peter for one. Funnily enough the subject came up yesterday. He was very bitter, I was quite surprised. Very bitter.'

Malcolm spoke not in any regretful way but as if he understood the bitterness, even perhaps felt a touch of it on his own part. Gwen looked at him assessingly through the light-brownish lenses of her square-topped glasses. Then she made a series of small noises and movements of the kind that meant it was time to be up and away. But she sat on and, perhaps idly, reached out to the letter that had started their conversation and fingered it as it lay in front of her.

'It'll be, er, fun seeing Rhiannon again,' she said.

'M'm.'

'Been a long time, hasn't it? What, ten years?'

'At least that. More like fifteen.'

'She never came down with Alun on any of his trips after whenever it was. Just that once, or twice was it?'

'She used to come down to see her mother at Broughton, and then the old girl died about that long ago, so she probably . . .'

'I dare say you'd remember. I just thought it was funny she never really kept up with her college friends or anyone else as far as I know.'

Malcolm said nothing to that. He swayed from side to side in his chair as a way of suggesting that life held many such small puzzles.

'Well, she'll have plenty of time from now on, or rather from next month. I hope she doesn't find it too slow for her in these parts after London.'

'A lot of the people she knew will still be here.'

'That's the whole trouble,' said Gwen, laughing slightly. She looked at her husband for a moment, smiling and lowering her eyelids, and went on, 'It must have come as a bit of a shock, the idea of, er, Rhiannon coming and settling down here after everything.'

'Call it a surprise. I haven't thought of her since God knows when. It's a long time ago.'

'Plenty of that, isn't there, nowadays? Well, this won't do. All right if I take first crack at the bathroom?'

'You go ahead,' he said, as he said every morning.

He waited till he heard a creak or so from the floor above, then gave a deep sigh with a sniff in the middle. When you thought about it, Gwen had given him an easy ride over Rhiannon, not forgetting naturally that it had been no more than Instalment 1 (a). A bit of luck he had been down first and had had a couple of minutes to recover from some of the shock – rightly so called – of seeing that handwriting on the envelope, unchanged and unmistakable after thirty-five years. Gwen had left the letter on the table. With a brief glance towards the ceiling he picked it up and reread it, or parts of it. 'Much love to you both' seemed not a hell of a lot to brag about in the way of a reference to himself, but there being no other he would have to make the best of it. Perhaps she had simply forgotten. After all, plenty had happened to her in between.

Finishing his tea, he lit his first and only cigarette of the day. He had never greatly enjoyed smoking, and it was well over the five years since he had followed his doctor's advice and given it up, all but this solitary one after breakfast which could do no measurable harm and which, so he believed, helped to get his insides going. Again as always he filled in time by clearing the table; it was good for him to be on the move. His bran flakes and Gwen's chunky marmalade enriched with whisky went into the wall-cupboard, the stones of his unsweetened stewed plums and the shells of her two boiled eggs into the black bag inside the bin. He thought briefly of eggs, the soft explosion as spoon penetrated yolk, the way its flavour spread over your mouth in a second. His last egg, certainly his last boiled egg, went back at least as far as his last full smoking day. By common knowledge the things tended to be binding, not very of course, perhaps only a shade, but still enough to steer clear of. Finally the crocks went into the dishwasher and at the touch of a button a red light came on, flickering rather, and a savage humming immediately filled the kitchen.

It was not a very grand or efficient dishwasher and not at all a nice kitchen. At Werneth Avenue, more precisely at the house there that the Cellan-Davieses had lived in until 1978, the kitchen had been quite splendid, with a long oak table you could get fourteen round with no trouble at all and a fine Welsh dresser hung with colourful mugs and jugs. Here there was nothing that could not have been found in a million cramped little places up and down the country, lino tiles, plastic tops, metal sink and, instead of the massive Rayburn that had warmed the whole ground floor at Werneth Avenue, an oval-shaped two-bar electric fire hanging on the wall. Most mornings at about this time Malcolm wondered if he had not cut down a bit too far by moving out here, but no point in fretting about that now, or later either.

There came a faint stirring in his entrails. He picked up the *Western Mail* and without hurrying – quite important as a matter of fact – made his way to the slant-ceilinged lavatory or cloakroom under the stairs. The old sequence duly extended itself: not trying at all because that was the healthy, natural way, trying a certain amount because that could have no real adverse effect, trying like a lunatic because why? – because that was all there was to do. Success was finally attained, though of a limited degree.

No blood to speak of, to be conscientiously classified as between slight and very slight. This was the signal for him to sit to attention and snap a salute.

In the bedroom Gwen was at her dressing-table putting the foundation on her face. Malcolm came round the door in his silent, looming way and caught sight of her in the glass. Something about the angle or the light made him look at her more closely than usual. She had always been a soft, rounded, fluffy sort of creature, not ineffectual but yielding in her appearance and movements. That had not changed; at sixty-one – his age too – her cheeks and jaws held their shape and the skin under her eyes was remarkably supple. But now those deep-set eyes of hers had an expression he thought he had not noticed before, intent, almost hard, and her mouth likewise was firmly set as she smoothed the sides of her nose. Probably just the concentration – in a second she saw him and relaxed, a comfortable young-elderly woman with gently tinted light-brown hair and wearing a blue-and-white check trouser-suit you might have expected on someone slightly more juvenile, but not at all ridiculous on her.

To get her voice as much as anything he said, 'More social life? No letting up?'

'Just coffee at Sophie's,' she said in her tone of innocent animation.

'Just coffee, eh? There's a change now. You know it's extraordinary, I've just realized I haven't seen Sophie for almost a year. One just doesn't. Well. You'll be taking the car, will you?'

'If that's okay. You going along to the Bible?'

'I thought I might sort of look in.' He went along to the Bible every day of his life. 'Don't worry, I'll get the bus.'

A pause followed. Gwen spread blusher – called rouge once upon a time – over her cheekbones. After a moment she dropped her hands into her lap and just sat. Then she speeded up. 'Well, and how are you this morning, good boy?'

'Perfectly all right, thank you.' Malcolm spoke more abruptly than he meant. He had prepared himself for a return to the topic of Rhiannon and the query about his bodily functions, though usual and expressed much as usual, caught him off balance. 'Quite all right,' he added on a milder note.

'Nothing . . .'

'No. Absolutely not.'

As he had known she would, she shook her head slowly. 'Why you just can't deal with it, an intelligent man like you. The stuff that's on the market nowdays.'

'I don't hold with laxatives. Never have. As you very well know.'

'Laxatives. Christ, I'm not talking about senna pods, California Syrup of Figs. Carefully prepared formulae, tried and tested. It's not gunpowder drops any more.'

'Anything like that, it interferes with the body's equilibrium. Distorts the existing picture. With chemicals.'

'I thought that was what you were after, Malcolm, honestly, distorting what you've got. And what about all those plums you go in for? Aren't they meant to distort you?'

'They're natural. Obviously.'

'How do you think they work? Just chemicals in another form.'

'Natural chemicals. Chemicals naturally occurring.'

'How do you think your guts distinguish between a bit of chemical in a plum and a bit of the same chemical in a pill or a capsule?'

'I don't know, love,' said Malcolm rather helplessly. He thought it was a bit thick for a man not to be able to win an argument about his own insides, even one with his wife. 'But then I haven't got to know.'

'Don't take my word for it – fix up to see Dewi. Yes yes, you don't hold with doctors either, and why do I have to go on at you. Because you're foolish, that's why, you won't help yourself. Unteachable. You know sometimes I'd almost take you for a bloody Welshman?'

'There's nothing to see Dewi about. There's nothing wrong with me. No sign, no sign of anything.'

'Just ask him for a prescription, that's all. Two minutes.'

Malcolm shook his head and there was more silence. In a moment he said, 'Can I go now?'

They embraced lightly and carefully while Gwen made another set of little sounds. This lot meant that although she still thought her husband was silly about himself she would let it go for the time being. There was affection there as well, if not of an over-respectful order.

As often before, Malcolm could see strength in the case against ever having mentioned his defecations in the first place. He had never intended more than an occasional appeal for reassurance and so on. As an apparently irremovable part of the daily agenda the subject had its drawbacks, while remaining streets ahead of his shortcomings as a man, a husband, an understander of women, a provider and other popular items dimly remembered from the past.

In the bathroom across the landing he cleaned his teeth, first the twenty or so surviving in his head in one form or another and then the seven on his upper-jaw partial. This was such a tight fit that putting it back was always a tense moment; bending his knees and moving them in and out seemed to help. What with the five crowns in front, of varying manufacture and recency, the ensemble was a bit of a colour atlas, but at least no one was going to mistake it for snappers top and bottom. They would have to come some day – which meant not now, bless it. The thought of having a tooth extracted, loose as nearly all of his had become, bothered him in a way he thought he had outgrown many years before.

The face surrounding these teeth was in fair trim, considering. In shape it was rather long, especially between the end of the nose and the point of the chin, but the features themselves were good and he was aware without vanity that, with his height and erect bearing and his thatch of what had become reddish-grey hair, people usually found him presentable enough. At the same time he had noticed that now and then a stranger, usually a man, would glance at him in a way that always puzzled him rather, not quite hostile but with something unfavourable about it, something cold.

He had seen a good deal of that sort of glance at school, where he had been bullied more than his fair share for a boy not undersized, foreign or feeble, and he remembered asking Fatty Watkins, one of his leading persecutors, why this was so. Without thinking about it, Fatty had told him that he looked the type, whatever that might have meant. Twice in later life, once down Street's End on a Saturday night and then again on a train coming back from an international at Cardiff Arms Park, just minding his own business both times, he had been picked out of a group of mates and set upon without preamble by an unknown ruffian. Perhaps without intending it he sometimes took on an expression people misinterpreted as snooty or something.

Whatever the ins and outs of his face he was going to have to shave it. He hated the whole caboodle – teeth, shave, bath, hair, clothes – so much that he often felt he was approaching the point of jacking it all in completely and going round in just pyjamas and dressing-gown all day.

But for Gwen he would probably have got there long ago. She kept on at him to play himself through with the portable wireless and he still tried it occasionally, but he cared for chatter about as much as he cared for modern music, and that was about all there seemed to be apart from Radio Cymru, which was obviously just the thing if you were set on improving your Welsh. The trouble was they talked so fast.

Welsh came up again and in a more substantial form when, having heard Gwen drive away, he settled in his study to put in a bit of time there before going along to the Bible. This, the study, was on the first floor, a small, smudgy room where water-pipes clanked. Its dominant feature was a walnut bookcase that had not looked oversized at Werneth Avenue but had needed the window taking out to be installed here. One shelf was all poetry: a fair selection of the English classics, some rather battered, a few Welsh texts, all in excellent condition, and a couple of dozen volumes of English verse by twentieth-century Welshmen. One of these, not painfully slim, had on it Malcolm's name and the imprint of a small press in what was now Upper Glamorgan. On taking early retirement from the Royal Cambrian he had intended to set about a successor, completing poems left half done for years and years, writing others that had only been in his head or nowhere at all. He ought to have had the sense to know that intentions alone were no good in a case like this. Not a line had turned up in all that time. But some day one might, and meanwhile he must practise, exercise, try to get his hand back in. Hence the Welsh.

Among the books on his table there was a publication of the Early Welsh Text Society – to give its English designation: the poems and poetical fragments of Llywelyn Bach ab yr Ynad Coch (*fl.* 1310), open at his funeral-song for Cadwaladr, quite a substantial affair, three hundred lines odd. Malcolm's translation of the first two sections was there too, a lightly corrected manuscript, also a pamphlet containing the only other translation he knew of, done and published by a Carmarthen schoolmaster in the Twenties but in the style of fifty years earlier. Never mind – whatever it lacked as a piece of poetry it came in bloody handy as a crib.

Moving at half speed, Malcolm opened the pamphlet now at the beginning. His glance shifted to and fro between the Welsh original of this passage and the two English versions, picking out words and phrases in either language that he felt he had never seen before: the tomb of the regal chieftain . . . red stallions . . . ye warriors of Gwynedd . . . I the singer, the minstrel . . . heaps of Saxon slain . . . chaplet . . . hart . . . buckler . . . mead . . .

Malcolm jerked upright at the table. A great God-given flood of boredom and hatred went coursing through him. That, that stuff, fiddling about with stuff like that was not living, was not life, was nothing at all. Not after today's news. No indeed, poems were not made out of intentions. But perhaps they could come from hope.

He made to tear up his manuscript, but held his hand at the thought of the hours that had gone into it, and the other thought that he would go back to it another day and transform it, make something wonderful of it. For now, he could not sit still. Yet if he left the house now he would be much too early, or rather a good deal, a certain amount too early. Well, he could get off the bus at Beaufoy and walk the rest of the way. On more of the same reasoning he went and gave his shoes a thorough polish; not much point hereabouts, agreed, but virtuous.

When he finally went out it was overcast with a bit of black, damp already, mild though, with a gentle breeze clearing the mist, typical Welsh weather. If you can see Cil Point it means rain later; if not, rain now. As he started down the hill he could see it, just, a dark-grey snout between the ranks of black slate roofs shining with moisture. Soon the bay began to open out below him, the sweep round to the west where coal had once been mined on the shore and inland along the coastal plain, and steel and tin-plate were still worked and oil refined, for the moment anyway, and behind all this, indistinct through the murk, the squarish mass of Mynydd Tywyll, second-highest peak in South Wales.

It was mid-morning in the week, and yet the pavements were crowded with people darting in and out of shops or just strolling along like holiday-makers – here, in February? Children and dogs ran from side to side almost underfoot. Crossing the road was no joke with all the cars and the motor-cycles nipping about. There was a queue at the 24 stop but, even so, nothing showed for a long time. Staff shortages, they said, recruitment down since the automatic-payment system had meant good-bye to days of plenty, when the conductor fiddled half the fare-money on the out-of-town part of the route and handed over half of it, or nearly, to the driver when they got to the garage. To save going round the end of the queue, youngsters on their way to the opposite corner kept breaking through it, always as if by pre-arrangement just in front of Malcolm.

The bus came. While he was climbing the litter-strewn steps his left ball gave a sharp twinge, on and off like a light-switch, then again after he had sat down. Nothing. Just one of the aches and pains that come and go. No significance. He would not always have taken such a summary line, in fact at one stage cancer of them, or one of them, had been among his leading special dreads, distinguished as it was by its very personal site and alleged virulence. There had even been the time when, after a day and most of a night of just about unremitting twinges on both sides, he had spent the dawn hours compiling in his head a draft list of books to take into hospital: mainly English poetry with one or two descriptive works about Wales, in English naturally. The following morning, by one of the most rapid and complete recoveries in medical history, the affection had vanished. So far so good, no further. But then he had read in the *Guardian* that recent advances had put the survival rate for testicular tumours up to or above ninety per cent, and for the rest of that day he had felt twenty, thirty years younger, and something of that had never been quite lost.

Reflecting on this and related matters took him past his stop and almost into Dinedor itself. With an air of transparent innocence that luckily escaped remark he got off by Paolo's Trattoria. Just round the corner was the Bible, more fully the Bible and Crown, the only pub of that name in the whole of Wales. According to local antiquarians the reference was to a Cavalier toast, though research had failed to come up with a date earlier than 1920, some time after it had become safe to proclaim loyalty to the King's party in any or all of his dominions, even this one.

On the way in Malcolm's spirits lifted, as they always did at the prospect of an hour or more spent not thinking about being ill and things to do with being ill. It was still early, but not enough to notice.

2

'But uglier still is the hump that we get from not having enough to do. You know who said that?'

'No.'

23

'Kipling. Joseph Rudyard Kipling. He was usually right, you know. Had a way of being right. No use sitting about, he said, or frowsting by the fire with a book. Wonderful word, frowst, isn't it? Wonder what it comes from. Well anyway, the thing is, get out in the fresh air and take a bit of exercise. A brisk walk, two miles minimum, three preferable. No need for any of your sleeping pills after that. I haven't taken a sleeping pill since . . . Guess when I last took a sleeping pill.'

'No idea.'

'1949. That's when I last took a sleeping pill. 1949. Morning, Malcolm. Another early bird.'

'Morning, Garth. Morning, Charlie. Now what can I get you?'

The two had nearly full glasses and declined, but the offer was standard arrivals' etiquette. Malcolm went and got himself a half of Troeth bitter at the hatch in the corridor, the nearest place. During his absence, Garth Pumphrey let Charlie Norris know more about the benefits of exercise and the dispensability of sleeping pills. Charlie followed Garth's talk with only half his attention, if that, but he found it comforting. He knew that nothing Garth said would surprise him, and as he felt at the moment, which was very much how he felt every morning of his life at this hour, even a pleasant surprise, whatever that might be, would have been better postponed. He flinched a little when Malcolm reappeared more abruptly than he had bargained for.

'Ah, here we are,' said Garth cordially, holding out an arm by way of showing Malcolm to the chair at his side. 'There. I've been treating young Charlie to a highly authoritative lecture on the subject of health, physical and mental. My number one rule is never sit over a meal. Breakfast least of all.'

It was amazing, thought Malcolm to himself, how invariably and completely he forgot Garth when looking forward to or otherwise weighing up a visit to the Bible. Forgetting things like that was probably one of Nature's ways of seeing to it that life carried on. Like the maternal instinct.

'Of course, you know Angharad says I'm turning into a real old health bore – a notorious pitfall of age, she says.' In the ensuing silence Garth took a good pull at his drink, which looked like a rather heavy vin rosé but was really gin and Angostura. Then he shaped up to Malcolm in a businesslike way. 'You were quite a performer in days gone by, Malcolm, weren't you? Sorry, with the old racquet. Oh, I was saying earlier, I remember the way you used to bash that ball. Give it a devil of a pasting, you would. That serve of yours. Famous. Deservedly so.'

'Many years ago now, Garth.'

'Not so many as the world goes in our time. November 1971, that's when the old place finally closed its doors.' Garth referred to the Dinedor Squash Racquets Club, of which all three had been members since youth. 'The end of an era. You know you and I had a game in the last week very nearly. I took a proper clobbering as usual. You were really seeing them that evening. Then we had a drink after with poor Roger Andrews. Do you remember?'

'Yes,' said Malcolm, though he had forgotten that part, and Charlie nodded to show that he was still in the conversation.

'He seemed so full of life that time. And then what could it have been, six weeks after we started coming in here, eight at the outside, off he goes. Like that. Sitting just where you are now, Charlie.'

Malcolm remembered that part all right. So did Charlie. Roger Andrews had been nothing out of the way, a building

25

contractor of no more than average corruption, not even much of a good fellow, but his fatal collapse in the so-called saloon lounge of the Bible had had a durable effect, confirming the tendency of a group of ex-members of the defunct squash club to drop in regularly midday and in the early evening. Over the years the room had become a kind of relic or descendant of that club, its walls hung with inherited photographs of forgotten champions, teams, presentations, dinners, its tables bearing a couple of ugly old ashtrays that had escaped being sold or stolen when the effects of the DSRC were disposed of. The habitués had even acquired something of a prescriptive right to keep out intruders. The landlord of the Bible made no objection, in fact it suited him well enough to have up to a dozen or so comparatively well-behaved drinkers perpetually occupying the least convenient and agreeable corner of his premises. From time to time the old boys complained among themselves about the discomfort, but there they were, the dump was almost next door to the Club building, which was what had drawn them there in the first place, and in winter the genial host actually let them have the benefit of a small electric fire at no extra charge.

After a moment of reverie or premeditation Garth Pumphrey again turned his face on Malcolm, a dark serious lined face with a hint of subdued passion, an actor's face some might have called it. 'What exercise do you take these days, Malcolm?' he asked.

'Just about zero, I'm afraid.'

'Just about zero? A fellow of your physique. A natural athlete like you. Dear, dear.'

'Ex-natural athlete. I'm not going to start going on cross-country runs at my age.'

'I should hope not indeed, it's altogether too late for that.' Garth whistled breathily to himself and moved his

26

hand crabwise along the table in front of him. Then he said, 'Do you find you fancy your food all right? I hope you don't mind me asking, we're all old friends here.'

Charlie thought a distinction could be drawn between Garth's boasting about his own insides if he had to and his involvement with others', but he was not the man to put it into words. His second large Scotch and dry ginger was beginning to get to him and already he could turn his head without thinking it over first. Soon it might cease to be one of those days that made you sorry to be alive.

'No, that's all right, Garth,' Malcolm was saying gamely. 'No, my trouble's all the other way. Keeping myself down to size.'

'Good, good.' Garth's small figure was huddled up in the cracked rexine chair, turned away from Charlie. He smiled and nodded. 'And, er . . .' His eyebrows were raised.

In a flash Malcolm knew or as good as knew that the next second Garth was going to ask him about his bowel movements. He felt he would do, must do, anything at all to prevent that, and mentioned what he had not even considered mentioning, not there, not yet, not until he had hugged it to himself as long as he could. 'Alun and Rhiannon are moving down here in a couple of months,' he said quickly. 'Coming back to Wales to live.'

That did the trick. It took quite some time for Garth's incredulity to be mollified, likewise his craving for information. When that was done he explained that, what with being stuck out at Capel Mererid and so on, he had not known the couple in early years, but had met Alun many times on trips to these parts and anyway, he finished strongly, 'the bloke is a national figure, let's face it.'

'You face it,' said Charlie, who had reasons of his own to feel less than overjoyed at Malcolm's news. 'I realize

27

he's on television quite a lot, though we don't usually get it in Wales, and when anyone wants a colourful kind of stage-Taffy view on this and that then of course they go to him. With a bit of eloquent sob-stuff thrown in at Christmas or when it's dogs or the poor. He's the up-market media Welshman. Fine. I can take him in that role, just about. But as for Alun Weaver the writer, especially the poet . . . I'm sorry.'

'Well, I'm no literary critic,' announced Garth. 'I'm just going by the general acclaim. I'm told they think highly of him in America. But we've got a writer here now.'

'Oh, no,' said Malcolm, embarrassed. 'Not in that sense. Well, what can I say? It's true that a lot of his work falls under Brydan's shadow, but I see nothing very shameful in that. And there's more than that in it. I'm not saying he didn't get quite a bit from Brydan, but they were also both drawing on a common stock to rather different effect. Something like that.'

Charlie said with a bland look, 'Everything you say may well be true – it cuts no ice with me. Brydan, Alun, you can stick the lot. Take it away. Forget it.'

'Oh, Charlie,' Garth pleaded. 'Not Brydan. Not *Tales from the Undergrowth*. Known and loved all over the world as it is.'

'That in particular. Write about your own people by all means, don't be soft on them, turn them into figures of fun if you must, but don't patronize them, don't sell them short and above all don't lay them out on display like quaint objects in a souvenir shop.'

'I didn't realize you felt that strongly,' said Malcolm after a silence.

'I don't, I don't feel strongly at all. Not my field. But I do think if a chap decides to make a living out of being

Welsh he'd better do it in a show on the telly. Which I think Alun realizes part of the time.'

'Oh dear.' Malcolm too seemed quite cast down. 'And you see that in the poetry, in Brydan's poetry too, do you?'

'Yes I do. What's that stuff about, er, the man in the mask and the man in the iron street. All he'd done was juggle two phrases about and had the Americans going on about childlike Welsh vision. Stark too it was, boyo. It's not serious enough, that kind of thing.'

Malcolm set about considering the justice of parts of this in his conscientious way. Soon Garth, who had been looking anxiously from face to face, made a permission-to-speak noise. Charlie nodded encouragingly at him.

'I was just going to say, what about, what about her? I have met her, of course I have, but I think only the once and long ago.'

'Well, what about her?' said Charlie. 'Just a very pleasant –'

'Rhiannon Rhys, as she was when I first met her,' said Malcolm fluently, raising himself in his seat like a panellist answering a question from the audience, 'was one of the most stunning-looking girls I've ever seen in my life. Tall, fair, graceful, beautiful complexion, grey eyes with just a hint of blue. An English rose, really. And a lovely nature – modest, unassuming. She made no attempt to be the centre of attraction, but she was, in any company. No, I haven't seen her for a long time either, and she may look a bit different now, but there are some things that don't change, not in thirty years. I'm glad she's coming back to Wales.'

Malcolm believed that he had on the whole said this in a conversational, down-to-earth way. Garth paid close attention. Charlie drained his glass for the second time, sucking fiercely to get the last couple of drops.

'Well, er,' said Garth, 'that sounds absolutely marvellous. Thank you, Malcolm. I'll look forward to renewing my acquaintance with, with Mrs Weaver.'

Before he had finished Charlie was urging Malcolm to have a real drink, assuring him that what he had before him was piss and getting up from the table. This was not as straightforward a procedure as might be thought, in view of the table itself and his chair and their respective legs, and his own bulk and state. On the way out of the room he gave a muffled cry of shock when the side of his heel bumped against the door-frame. By standing quite still for a moment and concentrating, however, he successfully avoided the hazard in the passage floor where for some years most of a tile had been missing. His shoulder grazed but did not dislodge a framed photograph on the wall showing a row of men in hats standing outside a thatched cottage in Ireland or some such place.

As he waited at the hatch for Doris to finish giving change for a couple of twenty-pound notes in the bar, Charlie thought about Malcolm's speech just now. Almost every phrase in it had been all right in itself, would have been, at least, if said in a different voice or eked out with a few oaths or perhaps seen written. It was the way the silly sod had looked and sounded so pleased with himself for having had no false shame about coming out with it – that was what had called for a frantic personal exit head-first through the closed window or, more prosaically, overturning the table in his lap. And that clear holy-man's gaze . . .

Doris ambled along and Charlie ordered a large pink gin, mentioning Garth's name, and three large Scotches and water. Down went one of the Scotches in its entirety while Doris was ringing up and right away the old feather duster twirled at the back of his throat and he was coughing his heart to bits, right there at maximum first go, roaring, bellowing like an imitation, in a crouch with his fists shoved into his guts, tears pouring down his face. A silence fell widely round him. When he tried to look he thought he saw somebody, several people, hobbledehoys, leaning over the bar to peer. Doris gave him a glass of water and he sipped and breathed, then drank. With a great exhalation he straightened up and mopped his eyes, feeling now quite proud of himself, as if his well-known toughness and grit had got him through another testing external assault.

He had not yet touched the tray of drinks when the door banged at the end of the passage and a large lumpish figure creaked towards him through the gloom, recognizable after a moment as Peter Thomas, runner-up in the open tournament of the DSRC a couple of times in the 1940s but more of a golf man. Neither one nor the other these days, of course.

'Hallo, Peter. Early for you.'

'No, not really. Yes, I'll have a gin and slimline tonic.'

If Charlie Norris had ever been thought of as big and fat and red-faced, and some such description was hard to avoid, a revision of terminology might have been called for at the sight of his friend. Charlie's backside pushed the tail of his tweed jacket into two divergent halves, true, and his paunch forced the waistband of his trousers half-way down to his crotch, but Peter could have given him a couple of stone and still been the heftier, not so obviously from front or back where the cut of his suit tended to camouflage him, but to be seen in anything like profile as even thicker through than wide. And Charlie's cheeks and forehead were no more than ruddy compared with Peter's rich colouring. Their faces in general were different: Charlie's round and pug-nosed, with the look of a battered school-boy, Peter's fine-featured, almost distinguished between the bulges and pouches. At the moment Charlie was smiling, Peter not.

'Well, how are you today?' asked Charlie. A duff question on second thoughts.

'How do you think? But as you see I can get out of the house. Who's in there?'

'Just Garth and Malcolm.'

Peter nodded and sighed, accepting it. His massive, bottom-heavy head turned sharply at a burst of laughter and jocular shouting from inside the bar. The voices sounded youthful. Frowning, he limped to the hatch and stuck his head round.

'According to Malcolm,' began Charlie, but stopped when the other turned back, speaking as he moved.

'I thought we were supposed to be in the middle of a depression. Have you looked in there? Three-quarters full, at this hour.' It was all coming out as if freshly minted. 'Most of them in their twenties or younger. Unemployed school-leavers, no doubt. Who'd be anything else these days if he had the chance, eh? What happens if we ever have a boom? They'll be falling down drunk from morning till night, presumably. Like the eighteenth century. You know, Hogarth.'

Charlie wanted to grin when Doris put the slimline on the tray next to the (large) gin. Talk about a drop in the ocean. Like an elephant going short of a banana, he thought. He also thought Peter looked distinctly fatter since he had last seen him, though admittedly this was doubtful after no more than a couple of days. Nor did he appear well. He had been breathing hard when he arrived and seemed to be sweating, though it was far from hot outdoors or in. High blood-pressure. Not good.

Still talking, he preceded Charlie down the passage. 'You should see the old bags coming out of the supermarkets with the goodies piled up on their trolleys like Christmas.' His hip thumped considerably into a table against the wall, agitating the leaves of the flowerless pot-plant that sprawled there. 'And I don't mean in the middle of town, I'm talking about wretched holes like Greenhill or Emanuel.' He opened the door of the lounge. 'And the point is you can't tell anybody. Nobody wants to know.'

Peter Thomas had to hold the door open because an ancient shoddiness of workmanship would have made it swing shut in a few seconds, and Charlie was much occupied with the tray after a pair of speedy over-corrections had nearly sent the stuff piling over opposite edges. At last they were in and settled and Garth had finished welcoming Peter.

A glance at Peter showed there was no more to come from that direction for the moment. Half to provoke him, Charlie said, 'Anybody happened to go by St Paul's recently? They're having fun there.'

Malcolm said, 'Are we talking about St Paul's Cathedral in London?'

'No, no, the church off the Strand here. Old what-was-he-called, old Joe Craddock's church.'

'Used to wear a green tweed cap with his dog-collar.'

'That's the fellow. Well, he should see it now. So should you, it seems. Sex cinema is what it is now. You couldn't invent that, could you? You wouldn't dare. Nobody would.'

'Come on, Charlie,' said Garth right on cue, 'you don't mean to sit there and –'

'I bloody do, mate. Adult movies on Screens 1 and 2. In the nave and chancel respectively, I presume. "Come Play with Me" and another witticism.'

'I dare say they exerted themselves to deconsecrate the building,' said Peter.

You fat old hypocritical Welsh cunt, thought Charlie. 'It would have appealed to Joe, anyway,' he said, and added for Garth's benefit, 'Used to fuck anything that moved, old Joe did. Bloody marvel, he was. Pulled in an enormous congregation too. Very tough on drink. Of course, I'm talking now about twenty years ago.'

'I didn't know that,' said Malcolm, trying not to sound shocked. 'I mean about his activities.'

'No, well . . .' Again Charlie kept to himself what he thought. Still grinning, he met Peter's eye, only for a second, but quite long enough to be sure that Peter was trying not to join in an admiring, part-horrified laugh in reminiscence, something he would certainly have done up until more recently than twenty years ago. 'Amazingly lucky with the horses as well, Joe was. He said he used to count on five to six hundred a year, which in those days was all right. You never ran into anyone who reckoned that was fair.'

Another silence followed. Silences were a great feature of these Bible sessions. Peter sat on with his hands spread on his bulky thighs, sniffing and groaning quietly, perhaps trying to think of something that summed up what he felt about the fate of St Paul's, if so failing. Finally Garth said in his eager, quacking voice, 'Malcolm was telling us, Alun and Rhiannon Weaver are coming back down here to live. They –'

Peter swung himself round almost fiercely on Charlie. 'Had you heard this? Well, you didn't mention it to me just now.'

'You didn't give me much of a chance.'

'Down here to live, you say.'

'Apparently. Yes,' said Charlie, signalling with his face to Malcolm to come in, and after no great delay Malcolm started explaining that the Weavers had rented a house in

Pedwarsaint to look round from and things like that while Peter stared at him or in his direction through his thick glasses and Garth listened as if every fact were new to him.

Malcolm did not disclose that, while Peter had been a young lecturer at the local university and Rhiannon in her second year as a student, they had had an affair, and she had got pregnant and had had an abortion performed on her at his expense by a doctor in Harriston, a man incidentally struck off the medical register soon afterwards for another of the same and now long dead. This had been a remarkable train of events in the South Wales of 1947–8; more remarkably still, Peter had not been thrown out of his job at the university, in fact nothing official was ever said on the matter. What counted, after all, not only in South Wales, was not what you knew but who could prove you knew it. Quite soon, however, Peter had given up a promising career in academic chemical engineering for a different sort in the real thing not far away, a few miles along the coast to the west in Port Holder. Rhiannon had promptly vanished to London, where after an obscure interval she had got a job as a receptionist at the BBC, where in turn a year or two later she had met Alun Weaver.

That was, of course, not all that had happened. Just about when Rhiannon had become pregnant, Peter had shifted his attentions to another female, someone outside the university, and after another few months had turned out to be engaged, presumably to this other. His fiancée was a certain Muriel Smorthwaite, the daughter of one of the managers at the tin-plate mill he now worked at. In those days Peter had been considered rather lucky, given his record, to be engaged to anyone at all west of Offa's Dyke, for although the Smorthwaites were from Yorkshire originally, not local, some conscientious neighbour must surely have passed the word. But the two had got married, living in Port Holder for a judicious couple of years before settling in Cwmgwyrdd just on the far side of town.

Charlie had been a student in the same year as Rhiannon, though older than she through war service, and acquainted with her and her mates. He had heard as much about all this as most people not directly involved but had learnt no more since. He had not tried to find out and not been told; he had forgotten about the whole business until that morning. He wondered how well informed the other two here were: Malcolm well enough, as was shown in his every movement and inflection as he spoke, Garth probably not at all.

Malcolm finished his short recital. Evidently Peter, with Garth looking at him in expectation of something or other, could think of nothing to say. His glistening bald head moved from side to side in an agitated fashion.

Charlie gave him an easy one. 'Of course, you were never a great fan of Alun's, were you? As man or writer that I remember.'

Peter turned on him again, but appreciatively this time. 'Bloody Welshman,' he said with relish, doubtless referring to Alun.

'Oh, come on now, Peter,' said Garth, laughing steadily, being very good about not being indignant, 'we're all Welshmen here. Including you as far as I know.'

'More's the pity,' said Peter, draining his glass with a flourish.

On this the door burst open with a suddenness and violence that might well have killed Charlie half an hour earlier, its edge striking the back of his chair, though not hard. Into the sudden hush stepped a man and a woman, both young, both having on knee-boots and other wearables of synthetic material, both carrying crash-helmets. It was at once evident that the tumultuous door-opening had

36

been the result of thoughtlessness rather than any kind of hostility. Unaware both of the hush and of the four looks that went with it, from Peter's glare to Malcolm's mild curiosity, the couple strolled across the room and started looking at some of the DSRC mementos on the wall there and along the mantelpiece above the boarded-up fireplace. When they spoke their accents were not local, perhaps from Liverpool.

'Ladder as at 31st December 1949,' read out the young man and took a pull of what was probably lager. 'What kind of ladder would that be?' He spoke in simple puzzlement.

'Must be all the landlord's stuff,' said the girl. In her hand was an opaque greenish concoction with pieces of ice and fruit floating in it.

'Annual dinner . . .'

The girl studied the slightly mildewed photograph. 'Nowhere here is that.'

'Chairman . . . committee . . . You know, like some sort of club?'

'Served us all right, didn't they?'

The pair had begun to turn shyly towards the group of old men when Garth, having recognized without any sense of novelty that Peter and Charlie were too fat to be expected to make a move and Malcolm too windy, got up and shut the door as loudly as he could, which was not very loudly because it had already come close to shutting itself.

'Er, excuse me,' began the youth.

Garth stared at him without speaking.

'Er, is this some kind of club?'

'Not exactly a club, no,' said Garth, moving his head about and screwing up his face in a confidential way. 'It's more, well, we had been hoping to hold this private committee meeting in just a few minutes. Personal matters, you'll appreciate, er . . .'

'Oh . . . well . . . sorry . . .'

After an exchange of glances and no delay the two invaders set about leaving. The girl, who was rather tall and walked with a firm tread, looked briefly over at the seated three as she passed.

'And *shut* the *door*,' said Peter with elaborate movements of his mouth.

When the door had shut, almost soundlessly, Garth puffed out his breath, Charlie said, 'Well done, Garth, you're a great man,' and Peter gave a short roar like a lion keeping in voice.

Malcolm made no sound. He thought the girl's eye had caught his for an instant, not of course out of anything but habit or even politeness, and yet it set him thinking. How many years was it since he had noticed a girl? And what exactly had he seen in this one? – she was not all that attractive. She was young, yes indeed, not that he could have said what age, but not so much young either as fresh, new, scarcely out of the wrapping-paper with no time for anything to have got at her and started using her up. It was hard to believe that there had been a time when he had lived his whole life among people like that with occasional unimpressive distractions from an aunt or a teacher or a ticket-collector.

'That, that *breed* haven't necessarily been badly brought up, they're gross and boorish by nature.' It seemed that Peter thought the affray of a moment before had been far too lightly passed over.

'On the contrary,' said Malcolm, quite sharply for him. 'They blundered in rather crassly because they knew no better, but as soon as they grasped the situation their decent instincts took over and they were perfectly civil.'

'I'll go and invite them back in if you like,' said Charlie.

'It's my shout,' said Garth.

'No, mine,' said Peter.

But before he had got properly started on rising to his feet the door opened again, nearly as wide as before but smoothly and silently. There followed a frozen pause which a stranger might have found unsettling. Then a man came into the room and shut the door ceremoniously behind him, a man of the same sort of age as the company, a tall broad man, not fat, wearing an unusually thick natural-coloured cardigan with scuffed leather buttons. This was Tarquin Jones, known as Tarc, landlord of the Bible as long as any of the others could remember. On first sight of him standing behind the beer-pulls in the main bar, perhaps as far back as 1950, Malcolm had thought that he must have suffered a bereavement earlier that morning and had on the instant decided that he, Malcolm, was in some way responsible. But he had stood his ground and quite soon discovered that Tarc always had that expression on, at least in public. Now, grasping the backs of Charlie's and Peter's chairs, he leaned over the table and looked them all in the eye one after the other.

'So you managed to dispose of the intolerable intrusion,' he said in a grave tone, at once diffusing a cloud of the ambiguity that hung about so much of what he said.

'They went like lambs,' said Charlie. 'No trouble at all.'

Tarc nodded impatiently, already done with the matter. 'Last night,' he went on, lowering his voice, 'they were out there for an hour after I'd shut my house, revving up their bikes and the rock blaring out on their radios and yelling their heads off. They –'

'How extraordinary,' said Malcolm – 'as Charlie said they couldn't have been more tractable a moment ago. No hint of any . . .'

His voice died away as Tarc looked round the circle again, this time with stoical weariness. 'I was thinking in

39

fact,' he began, suddenly affecting a sunny forbearance, 'of a different group of young people altogether. Not the two who went in and out of here just now. No. Others. Who are given to behaving in the way I have tried to describe. As I was saying,' he went on, then said nothing for ten seconds or so before resuming in his original manner, 'They're not from round here, you know, most of 'em. Coming batting down the M4 from Cardiff or Bristol like fiends out of hell any time of the day or night, all with a chick behind there. I tell you, the other Sunday I was coming back from seeing my daughter in Penarth and a crowd of 'em caught up with me and started carving me up as I understand it's called, overtaking me and fanning out in front and then staying level three or four abreast and looking at me, staring at me for, I don't know, it seemed like minutes at a time and going at seventy. Seventy. And talking about me, shouting out to each other about me and pointing at me. I don't mind admitting to you,' he lowered his voice further, 'I was scared, honest I was. Scared.'

When he paused, none of his audience showed any sign of responding, then or at any future time. 'Because this isn't just high spirits or youthful exuberance – we're used to that. No no, what we're faced with is an orchestrated onslaught on our whole culture and way of life. And this concerns you gentlemen particularly. In your position it behoves you to take note and consider what is to be done. If the likes of you won't give a lead I don't know what is to become of us.'

'If you ask me,' said Malcolm, 'what could be at work there is an actual enmity towards the very structure of society.'

This observation seemed to take all the fight out of Tarc. He said in a bleating tone and with a slight quaver, 'I'm very glad to find you hold that view, Mr Cellan-Davies, because it's rather the one I was trying to put forward myself.' Then as he gathered up the empty glasses his manner began to rally a little and grew almost friendly for a moment. 'Er, warm enough in here, are you? Miserable old day out. Now remember all of you, you've only to say the word and I'll bring in the fire.' No one said it, so he withdrew, pausing at the door for his closing line. 'I do beg you to consider seriously the points I've put to you.'

'Dear, dear, there's a character,' said Garth, very much the sort of thing he always said after one of Tarc's visitations.

'I seemed to quieten him down all right,' said Malcolm modestly.

'Yes, you did, didn't you?' said Peter.

'He goes too far sometimes, old Tarc,' said Charlie. 'We know we have to take it and so does he, so he really shouldn't talk about orchestrated onslaughts and behoving, especially behoving. No, that was naughty.'

'I'm sorry, I don't understand what you mean,' said Malcolm.

'Well, teasing us. Defying us to tell him to come off it.'

'Are you saying it's all an act? I know he exaggerates and all that, but . . .'

Peter answered. 'Tarc doesn't know how much of an act it is himself, not any more. He's got so he couldn't tell you whether he means what he says or not. Far from the only one in these parts to have reached that condition.'

'Anyway,' said Garth, 'you and he do seem to see very much eye to eye on the modern world and the youth of today and the rest of it.'

Fortunately, before Peter could answer that one old Owen Thomas (no relation) turned up with a guest of his, a retired chartered accountant from Brecon, and soon after them came old Arnold Spurling and then old Tudor

41

Whittingham, who had beaten the British Empire amateur champion 9–3, 14–12, 9–7 at Wembley in 1953. Arnold had just won a few quid in one of the newspaper bingo competitions and insisted on drinks all round. Charlie started feeling quite good, and even Peter seemed able to put up with the presence of old Arnold and the others.

Owen Thomas went off to the bar for ham rolls and came back with all there was in the eats line, a plate of egg-and-cheese quiches prepared by Tarc's granddaughter, who was doing a course in culinary studies at the university. For different reasons Peter, Charlie and Malcolm turned them down. The three decided to leave after the next drink, or rather Peter, whose car was outside, decided that and the other two went along. They had that next drink, and then another quick one which Malcolm declined, and then they left. Garth lived within walking distance, so of course he was going to walk, perhaps as soon as he had finished explaining to Owen Thomas's guest about the importance of not brooding.

3

Peter's car was a Morris Marina of an archaic buff-orange colour relieved here and there by small archipelagos of rust. With nothing said, Charlie got in beside Peter and Malcolm got in the back. This was not easy for Malcolm with his long legs, because Peter had to keep his seat pushed back as far as possible in order to get his stomach behind the wheel. The other half of the back seat was taken up with wooden trays spilling earth and small stones and piled with potatoes, leeks, parsnips and perhaps turnips freshly out of the ground, or at any rate untouched since. Empty tissue cartons, very dirty cloths that had wiped the windows, dog-eared technical pamphlets, graphs and thick bundles of duplicated sheets with a forlornly superannuated look, publishers' circulars, an empty tube of children's sweets, a biscuit wrapper and several books and leaflets about dieting lay elsewhere. When Peter set the car in motion a small capless bottle that might once have held slimline tonic came trundling out from under his seat.

Malcolm peeled one of the diet leaflets off the floor at his side and looked through it. He wanted to be covered in some sense against the possibility that the subject of Rhiannon might come up again. Also diets interested him. His own eating and drinking practice was a conflation of several, often irreconcilable with each other. Thus the two halves of beer a day he reckoned he needed to help to keep him regular meant a cutback in calories elsewhere with the risk of a deficit in vital fibre. More generally, you never knew what one programme or another might come up with in the way of a new hankering-reducer or safe volume-limiter. And there was not such a hell of a lot to read anywhere these days.

Soon enough Malcolm was pretty sure that what he had picked up was no good except to get him through the five minutes now in progress. After forbidding all alcohol except a small glass of dry white wine every year or so, it ran through a remarkably full and imaginative list of everything anybody had ever enjoyed eating and forbade the lot, though surely with some risk of infraction. Anyway, your own eyes were enough to tell you that if old Peter, now listening to something Charlie was telling him about the price of a house in Beaufoy, had ever observed these constraints he had forgotten them again after a couple of hours. Then why did he bother to read or at least buy diet literature? To feel virtuous by laying out nothing more than money. To make promises to himself like a man looking at travel brochures of exotic places. No, more a man reading about polar explorers living off snow, moss and boot-leather. About Red Indian tortures.

Malcolm became quite dreamy. As in his boyhood he had deliberately used thoughts of school, of homework to obscure the prospect of a treat or a birthday before wallowing in delighted expectation, so now he let Peter's overweight problem be obliterated by memories of Rhiannon. The only trouble was that they were not as sharp in his mind as *Lettres de mon Moulin* and the South Africans playing at Gloucester. His clergyman uncle had taken him.

'Soft as lights, that fellow,' said Peter when Malcolm had been dropped at his front gate. 'Perfectly pleasant, I agree, but dead soft.'

'Something like that, yes,' said Charlie.

'I bet he fills in the month and year on all his cheque counterfoils.'

'Yeah, and writes out the number of pence in words.'

'And sends in box-tops to save three-fifty on a hand-crafted presentation decanter.'

'Oh really I think that's going a bit far. But I bet he watches documentaries on the telly.'

'In Welsh.' Peter spoke with genuine rancour.

'And I swear he swings his arms when he walks.'

'Do you know they have wrestling in Welsh now on that new channel? Same as in English oddly enough except the bugger counts *un – dau – tri* etcetera. Then the idiots can go round saying the viewing figures for Welsh-language programmes have gone up. To four thousand and eleven.'

'The commentary would have to be in Welsh too.'

'Doubtless, doubtless. Did you gather that young Malcolm had, let's say, an attachment to Rhiannon in the long-ago?'

'Something like that,' said Charlie again. 'He wasn't at all specific.'

'I thought he sounded a bit as though he had been attached. But I rather wonder when.'

'He gave a great lyrical spiel about her just before you came. Non-specific, as I said. That doesn't sound very nice, does it?'

'M'm. Non-specificity could cut either way. Meaning he never laid a finger on her but would like us to think he did. Or meaning he did but for some reason doesn't want us to think he did so he goes on as if he didn't. You've got to remember he's a Welshman too.'

'Christ, Peter, nobody would take you for one after that analysis. Anyway I don't think Malcolm's that sort of Welshman.'

'Oh, is there another sort? Actually you know I had a . . .' Peter's voice cut off so abruptly that it was hard to be sure he had said what he seemed to have said. He sat in a round-shouldered yet strained posture, arms out to their fullest extent to reach the wheel, legs and feet stretched too and still only just finding the pedals. After a moment Charlie got a quick half-glance from him where a steady look would have been more characteristic, and also feasible with the car drawing up at the Salt House lights. A growl of effort escaped him as he reached even further forward, squashing his paunch severely, and set the wipers going in the fine rain.

'Hard to be sure, of course, that any given bloke hasn't done a touch of finger-laying in a specific case,' said Charlie reflectively. 'Even young Malcolm. I wouldn't put it past –'

'You see, I was having an affair with her myself. You must have heard that, Charlie.'

'Yes.'

'And a bit more besides I shouldn't wonder. I didn't

come out of it looking particularly well, I know. I didn't behave particularly well, either.'

After a pause, Charlie said, 'I suppose we all –'

'Not as badly perhaps as some people probably imagine but still not well. Not at all well. So one way and another it was something of a bolt from the bloody blue just now, hearing about her turning up again. Obviously I'll do my best to keep out of her way.'

'Not very obviously after all these years, surely.'

'No, no, there's an awful lot of stuff . . . I'll tell you later. For the moment I'd just ask you to, you know, stand by. And there's more to it than steering clear of her. I mean there's him, you see.'

'Yes, there is him.'

'It's not the time now to go into that either. But I expect you can imagine how I feel. Part of it, at least.'

'I can. And I'm quite sure you can imagine quite a bit of how I feel,' said Charlie, making it clear with tone and look that he in his turn was making mentionable what had been known but unmentioned.

'Indeed.' Something not utterly unlike warmth entered Peter's manner. 'Does, er, does Sophie ever mention it or anything? I mean there was never very much in it, was there?'

'Not as far as I know, and Alun wasn't exactly the only one, but then you only need one Alun if I make myself plain. And it was supposed to be all over before I came along, or rather what there was of it was, but there again . . . Well, there was an afternoon while he was down here on one of his trips five or six years ago when the shop rang up for Sophie and she couldn't be found, and then I heard quite by chance that no one knew where he was at the time either. Probably nothing, I agree. And anyway there was nothing *else*, which is the main point. Because it's not *it* that matters so much, it's the bloody side-effects. Great man for side-effects, Alun. Of which a traumatically embarrassing poem would be a very mild example.'

'I see that. By Christ I see it. The time he broke down at that service for Brydan – at St Illtyd's?'

'Yeah, and the way he broke down. "*Gwae och*, I am unworthy to pronounce his praise" and the rest of it.'

'Welcome flash of realism,' said Peter.

'Oh, do you think so? According to me nobody could have been more suitable.'

'Well, yes, all right. When are they coming down, did you say?'

'Not yet. Couple of months. Could you drop me at the Glendower?'

'Sure. What shall I tell Sophie?' Peter's destination was the Norrises', where he would pick up his wife after the coffee-party.

'Just you've dropped me at the Glendower. It won't come as much of a shock.'

When they arrived Charlie asked Peter in for one, but Peter said he thought he had better push on, so Charlie went by himself into the Glendower, in full the Owen Glendower (no Owain Glyndŵr crap thank you very much) Tavern and Grill. Being part-owner of this, Charlie was by himself only for a very short time, in fact he found a couple of fellows he knew from County Hall in the bar, which thoughtfully offered seventeen different kinds of Scotch whisky, and in just a few minutes he was at the top of his form.

4

Two empty 1½-litre bottles of Soave Superiore (DOC) stood on the glass-topped table next to a silver tray bearing ten or eleven used coffee-cups, some of them half full of finished-with coffee. The air in Sophie Norris's spacious drawing-room was misty with cigarette-smoke and loud with several conversations. True to Welsh punctuality, most of the ladies there had arrived at or slightly before the off at eleven and so not missed any part of what was going. The coffee and attendant biscuits, having conferred a kind of legitimacy on the session, had been made short work of, swallowed down by some like bread and butter before cake, scamped or skipped completely by others, and the real business was uncorked and poured after about twenty minutes. Obviously it was drunk at different speeds thereafter, though you could have guessed that a couple of those in the room had been at the Soave, or perhaps the Frascati, earlier and elsewhere. After all, it was only wine.

Sophie herself was not one of the couple. Standing by the french window that gave a view of garden, golf links and, remotely, sea, she looked confident and comfortable, very much like the wife of a prosperous caterer recently semi-retired or more, and hardly at all like someone who in her time had been one of the surest things between Bridgend and Carmarthen town – quite a distinction. In tweed skirt and angora sweater her figure was still impressive, though her breasts no longer jutted out of her trunk like a pair of smallish thighs as they had once famously done. At the moment she and Gwen Cellan-Davies were talking about that day's star topic.

'Quite a good-looking man, I suppose you'd have to admit,' said Gwen fair-mindedly. 'Or he was, anyway.'

'Oh, not too bad if you like that rather flashy type.' Sophie spoke in the unreconstructed rather shrill tones of Harriston, well suited for expressionless utterances. 'Of course she's lovely.'

'Mind you, he's a terrible old sham.'

'Sorry?'

'At school with Brydan my eye. Oh, they were both at the Grammar right enough, but three years between them. He can't have known him. Well if he did, it means Brydan was taking an interest in boys three years younger, and I've heard a lot of things about him but that never. You ask Muriel. She'll tell you Peter's the same age as Alun exactly, they were in the same form, and he doesn't remember Brydan at all from then.'

'Yeah, well . . .'

'And evidently according to Peter that "Alun" business is a lark. "Alan" it always was at school, Peter said, in the English way. That was before he went in for being a Welshman professionally.'

Not many general topics appealed to Sophie, and the question of Wales or being Welsh stood high in her uninterests. 'Oh yes,' she said, quite dully enough to have checked anyone less tenacious than Gwen.

'When he came back after the war he'd been out in the great world and discovered the advantages of Welshness.'

'For Christ's sake tell me what they are, Gwen, and I can pass them on to my old man,' said Muriel Thomas in her breezy, booming voice as she moved closer. She held a freshly opened bottle of Soave, just a litre one this time, from which she refilled Gwen's glass. 'He seems to think it's about on a par with the brand of Cain.'

'I really meant just to appeal to the Saxons, Muriel, you

49

know, the way Brydan used to go on. But actually we were talking about Alun.'

'Oh God, were you? I'm afraid here's one Saxon who's managed to resist the appeal of both Brydan and Alun. I'll say no more because I am, after all, a guest in your country.'

'You're one of us, darling,' said Sophie.

This was certainly true in the sense that, for all her often-proclaimed Englishness, Muriel conformed closely to a prevalent Welsh physical type with her dark hair and eyes and slender build, a fact often remarked on, at least in Wales. If it occurred to her now she gave no sign. Holding back whatever had been on the tip of her tongue, she said, 'My purpose in grabbing you chaps was not to discuss the great Alun but to recruit a rescue expedition for poor Angharad's benefit. La belle Dorothy hath her in thrall.'

After a minute the trio began rather carefully to cross the room. The level of atmospheric pollution seemed if anything to have gone up slightly. Drinking rates among the company might have varied but there was a pretty uniform deep commitment to cigarettes, with the smoke from those actually being smoked well backed up by the three or four stubs left in ashtrays but not put out. Empty or forgotten packets and various bits of wrapping littered the rugs.

On the rug in front of the lighted gas-fire, a large and elegant appliance with fully simulated coals, sat Dorothy Morgan, who had been on Sophie's doorstep at ten to eleven. At her side stood a half-full 40-oz. flask of California Pinot Chardonnay and a brimming blue-glass ashtray with the distinction of having two cigarette-ends burning away in it at the same time. She was indeed talking strenuously though not loudly to Angharad Pumphrey, who often had to lean down from her leather armchair to catch the words.

Angharad was not deaf, or no worse than most of them; she was not drunk, not even drinking. What singled her out from those around her was her looks, which were those of a real old lady, though she was not the oldest in years. Part of it came from her clothes – no bright trouser-suits for her – and part her untouched or unretouched hair and the like, but there seemed nothing to be done about her collapsed mouth or the knobbly protrusions of jawbone on either side of her chin or the criss-crossed flabbiness round her eyes. There had been talk of a disfiguring illness at some time before she arrived in these parts from Capel Mererid and presumably after she married Garth, but nobody really knew or would tell.

Dorothy Morgan was saying, 'But it's not just that, their whole outlook is different, their whole view of life.' Her neat short hair-cut and unadorned black-framed spectacles gave her a misleading air of intellectual strictness. 'You can tell from the structure of their language. Do you know Russian at all? Well, it's full of conjugations and inflections. For instance . . .'

Meanwhile the arrivals were moving into position in businesslike style, Muriel on the arm of the chair, Gwen on a quilted needlework-box and Sophie squatting on the rug. As they did so they all said hello to Angharad and asked how she was and told her they were glad to see her and she said something to all of them back.

During the last part of this Dorothy rose to her knees and, in a slightly louder voice than before, said, 'I was telling Angharad about Russian and how extraordinarily more complicated a language it is than Welsh, and of course English, which means . . .' She spoke with an unvarying slight smile and her gaze fixed on some neutral point. '. . . not necessarily more sophisticated than we are, at least not all the time . . .' It was not known when she slept, because nobody had ever been there to see her departing for bed or, when staying in the same house, come down to breakfast and failed to find her already at the table with a cigarette and most likely a glass of wine. '. . . very primitive because they drop the verb "to be" whenever they can. Like Red Indians.' She was said to have been found once telling the man who was laying the carpets about eohippus.

Dorothy's heavy-duty mode took an appreciable time to come round from, so that when she paused for a second or two, as she did after the Red Indians, nobody had anything to say at first, until Sophie just scraped in on the last of the amber by asking to hear about the trip to Leningrad. Not again, surely? Yes, again, insisted Sophie, and very soon she was having the case for going by Aeroflot put to her with undiminished conviction.

Under this covering fire Muriel, Gwen and Angharad were able to withdraw in good order. Standard Dorothy procedure said that when she got into that sort of stride and someone had to sacrifice herself for the sake of the others, then whoever happened to be hostess stepped forward. The punishment seemed to even out pretty well except that on neutral ground, like Dorothy's own establishment, Sophie got landed oftener than her turn. The others would agree rather sheepishly among themselves that she somehow sounded as if she minded it less.

There was no trace at the drinks table of the almost-full litre of Soave Muriel had left on it some minutes earlier. An untouched magnum of Orvieto, however, stood within reach and she set efficiently about opening that, cigarette in mouth, eyes screwed up.

'We haven't seen you here for a long time, Angharad,' said Gwen.

'No, you haven't, and I wouldn't be here today if I

hadn't happened to have to take a clock in for repair at that place in Hatchery Road.' Angharad's voice was not old, so much not so that public-utilities men and other strangers still occasionally tried to flirt with her over the telephone. 'I bumped into Siân Smith when she was more or less on her way here.'

'Of course, it is quite a step from where you are.'

'Yes, and it's not much fun when I get here, either, if this is anything like a fair sample.'

'Sorry about old Dorothy. We're sort of used to her, you know. We could see you were stuck.'

'I hope I never have the chance of getting used to her. What makes that woman think I want to hear her paltry little observations on Russia or Russian or Russians? Or anything else on God's earth?'

No awareness, let alone appreciation, of having been unstuck showed itself in Angharad. On the contrary, her resentment of Dorothy's conduct seemed to grow when no one looked like offering to excuse it. Closely and with apparent curiosity she had watched Muriel expose and pull the cork of the Orvieto; now, all but incredulously, she followed every detail of its pouring, her own nearly empty glass held austerely to one side. People tended to forget about Angharad in the same sort of spirit as they forgot about her husband, whom, by the way, no living person had ever seen in her company, any more than anyone had ever seen the inside of their house. They wondered about the Pumphreys' domestic and marital life quite as much at these coffee-parties as at the Bible.

'Well, that's just how she is,' said Gwen, defending Dorothy rather late in the day and without much fervour. 'She's always been like it but she's got worse lately. Like everybody else.'

'I mean it's not as if I were a great friend of hers,' said

Angharad, accusingly now. 'I hardly know her. Hardly even spoken to her before.'

'You were there, that's enough,' said Muriel.

'What sort of a husband does a woman like that have?'

Muriel lit another cigarette and said, 'Very nice chap, old Percy Morgan. She doesn't do it to him. Not when we're about, anyway. They get on together like a house on fire.'

'He's a builder,' added Gwen.

'A *builder*.'

'Well, he builds things like town halls,' said Muriel.

After studying Muriel's next inhalation of smoke, Angharad returned to her point. 'But she wouldn't let me get a word in, not a single word. Not even to tell her how riveting she was being.'

'You always get one person like that at this sort of jollification,' said Gwen.

Angharad raised her bushy eyebrows. 'Oh, so that's what it is. Quite frankly, if it stopped short at one person like that I wouldn't mind so much,' she said, graciously looking over Gwen's shoulder as she spoke. 'I don't mind telling you it'll be quite a time before I come this way again. This sort of jollification, as you call it, quite defeats me. I'd better make my farewells. Where's . . . where's Sophie?'

The other two watched Angharad take brief, undemonstrative leave of her hostess and, without a glance at Dorothy or anybody else, limp heavily from the room.

'That's what I call mellowing with age,' said Muriel, topping up the glasses. 'Oh, I'm that thrilled she didn't mind telling us what she told us.'

'I thought only beautiful people could behave like that. Poor old thing, though. She's probably in pain.'

'I hope so. It didn't do us any good, sticking up for Dorothy.'

Gwen screwed up her face. 'Not a lot of that, though, was there, actually?'

'Now you mention it, no, there wasn't. It's not much of a defence of a burglar to say he's always been a burglar.'

'Perhaps we should have agreed with her about how terrible Dorothy is.'

'Then she'd have had it in for us for knowing her. There's no pleasing some people, as you've probably noticed yourself.'

A general stir began. Glasses were drained, but not always left empty because there seemed to be a feeling that no opened wine should be allowed to remain undrunk, perhaps out of some old Cymric superstition. Things might have gone differently, or just further in the same direction, if Sophie had broached the 3-litre box of Selected Balkan Riesling on top of the drinks cabinet, whose contents of gin, whisky and other strong liquor were of course perfectly safe from any or all of the party. Two, three women went to say good-bye to Sophie, who was so relieved at being able to speak again that she refused to let them go, at any rate until after she had answered the door-bell. Siân Smith fell down on her way out but soon got up again and made it into the hall. When Sophie reappeared she had Peter Thomas with her. The sight of him standing alone on the doorstep had been enough to let her know that he had dropped Charlie at the Glendower. Without consulting him, still less offering him a glass of wine, she crossed to the drinks cabinet.

Peter looked rather shaken. After a moment's hesitation he advanced into the room with a real reluctance that he tried, late on and not very convincingly, to hide in a comic pretence of reluctance. He and Muriel waved to each other and it was the same or similar with him and Gwen, him and Dorothy, him and a couple of others. Flapping his hand at the smoke-filled air, he said in a bantering tone, 'So this is what all you busy housewives get up to while your men-folk are slacking and boozing their heads off in the pub.'

It was not very good, though surely better than nothing, and he had done his best to sound pleasant, and he had sounded quite pleasant, at any rate for him, but nobody seemed to hear much and nobody came over, not even Dorothy, until Sophie brought him a gin and tonic, offering to fetch ice which he forbade. He and she chatted about something, very likely more than one thing, for however long it was before Muriel collected him and took him off. If his shaken look had departed it was in place again by this time.

Of all the guests only Dorothy remained. She would not move before another piece of standard procedure fetched Percy over from Pedwarsaint to shift her, probably, though not certainly, by the power of words. There was no standard procedure for that.

5

'Good party at the good old Bible, I trust,' said Muriel. 'Who was there?'

Peter told her.

'You wonder why on earth you go, especially when you've got there and find it's exactly like it always is, and then you realize that's why you went. I suppose once upon a time we did things for a change. Malcolm full of the news about the Weavers, was he?'

'Well yes, he was rather.'

'What was your reaction?'

'It came as no surprise. Alun's always threatened

to return to his Welsh roots, as perhaps you remember.'

'Perhaps I do, but that doesn't mean I want to remember.'

'Nor me. How was the do at Sophie's?'

'Much as usual, as I was saying. Quite enjoyable, that is, and many thanks.' With no perceptible pause and almost no change of tone, Muriel went on, 'Certainly not the assemblage of fools, bores and madwomen you made it crystal clear you took it for, losing no time in doing so let it be said. You emptied that drawing-room in sixty seconds flat. Congratulations. Super. Your best yet.'

Peter, behind the wheel as they drove towards Cwmgwyrdd, thought as many times before of a film he had seen about half a century earlier. In it, a sadistic sergeant broke the spirit of a soldier in a military prison by beating him up at systematically random intervals, from more than a day down to a quarter of an hour, so that the victim never knew when the next attack was coming, never felt safe. Life with Muriel, it seemed to Peter, had over the last seven or eight years turned into a decreasingly bearable version of that. There were times, it was true, and this was one of them, when you could be morally certain a drubbing was on the way, not from anything she said or did but because you had spotted something disagreeable to her, either in itself or in its associations, drifting to the surface over the past few minutes or so; that was enough for her. For some strange reason, though, this kind of early warning did little to soften the eventual impact. He actually felt the sweat break out now on his forehead.

'Could I ask you to hold it for a bit, until we're home? If you don't I might drive into something. I'm not threatening to, I just might.'

'You might well, I agree with you, any time, with your belly forcing you back into that dangerously distant and also incidentally ludicrous posture.' Muriel's style made it sound as if she had spent weeks thinking of nothing else. 'I don't think you can have appreciated quite how unattractive an object you are. I'm not *just* talking about physically though I certainly *am* talking about physically for a start. You emanate hopelessness and resentment and boredom and death. No wonder everybody shrank away from you.'

Again familiarly, this had an uncomfortable quasi-sense about it. If Peter had really wanted peace at this point, however limited, he might have done well to leave it there or to beg for mercy. Instead he found himself showing what defiance he could. 'I just happened to come in at the end. They'd started leaving before I arrived.'

'You sent them on their way unrejoicing. Which incidentally you're in process of doing to me. I'm not sure how much longer I can stand you.'

'The past is past. Nothing but a waste of time wishing it had been different.'

'Who's said anything about the past?'

'You have. Of course you have. Your great theme, isn't it?'

That one failed to go off. Muriel just talked on at a slightly enhanced rate about what supposed friends of his had said to her about him and harmless things like that. He concentrated as fixedly as he could on driving. If he could have been reasonably sure of killing them both outright he would have been inclined to swerve into the path of an oncoming bus or builder's lorry, but as it was he took them safely past the War Memorial, through Irish Town, across the River Iwerne and into what had once been the mining village of Cwmgwyrdd, now a semi-smart outer suburb. Every so often he tried to make himself believe something he knew to be true, that Muriel would not go on like this for ever and that after a few minutes she would go back to being rather mechanically affable until next time, but he stayed unbelieving.

They were home, getting out of the car in the built-on garage of their quite decent Thirties villa on the pricier seaward side. When Peter had locked up, Muriel gave him a glance of studied neutrality, the signal for some kind of change of direction. He was glad he had followed his instinct and left the vegetables (out of old Vaughan Mowbray's patch that morning) unmentioned in the car. To flaunt them now might have led to requests to come out and say what he had against the way he was normally fed, and further.

On the front doorstep she said to him, 'You know, I don't think that news about the Weavers is good news for anyone.'

After all these years they really understood each other very well. Her saying that in an ordinary tone meant that hostilities were suspended and more, that that subject was now free, cleared for bringing up at any later stage without penalty. Further yet, as might not have been instantly clear to anyone but him, it constituted an apology, or the nearest she was ever going to get to one.

These thoughts occupied him while he went and got a couple of cold fish-fingers out of the refrigerator for his lunch, so that he failed to consider whether he agreed with the content of what she had said or not. Muriel pulled on her wellies and tramped off into the garden. She never ate lunch.

Two – Rhiannon, Alun

1

A train, a particular train, the 15.15 out of Paddington on an afternoon some weeks after Peter Thomas had decided to leave the potatoes and leeks in his car, emerged from the Severn Tunnel into Wales. The area had once been called Monmouthshire but because of a decision taken in London was now called Gwent, after an ancient Welsh kingdom or whatever it was that might have formerly existed there or thereabouts. Anyway, it was Wales all right, as Rhiannon Weaver reckoned she could have told by the look of it through the carriage window. There was no obvious giveaway, like road-signs in two languages or closed-down factories, but something was there, an extra greenness in the grass, a softness in the light, something that was very like England and yet not England at all, more a matter of feeling than seeing but not just feeling, something run-down and sad but simpler and freer than England all the same. Ten minutes to Newport, another hour in the train after that and ten or fifteen minutes more by road.

This journey was the Weavers' final move and tonight would be their first night on Welsh soil as residents, though they were booked to stay with Gwen and Malcolm Cellan-Davies that first night. Rhiannon had rather expected to make the trip by car, and so among other things to be saved a fair amount of packing, but had soon realized that, for somebody wanting to be noticed arriving, trains had the great virtue that they turned up at a fixed place at a fixed time. In one way it would have been better to fly down, but scheduled flights only went as far as Rhoose, which was wrong anyway because of being the Cardiff airport.

She turned her head away from the window to find Alun in the next seat giving one of his special beams with the eyes half closed and mouth slightly lifted. It meant more or less that in spite of everything, which was saying something, he was devoted to her and that she knew, in spite of everything again, that there was no one like him. She would have had to agree with Gwen that he was quite a good-looking man, but more than quite – remarkably, at least considering the life he led. The skin had held up well, no more than pink, as if after a day watching cricket; the famous mane of hair, once and for a great many years a deep bronze, was now snow-white, at any rate much whiter than the streaky, lifeless grey it would have been if left to itself. Most of his friends were pretty sure that he improved on nature in this department as in others; not many of them would have guessed that Rhiannon put the whitener on for him while they giggled and had drinks.

Suddenly Alun jerked himself upright and started waving vigorously to the buffet-car steward who had come into sight at the far doorway. The man was smiling and nodding and coming for them at top speed, but Alun still waved. In the rear another, younger and subordinate, buffet-car steward approached less swiftly.

'Sorry for the delay, Mr Weaver.' The first steward looked and sounded really cut up as he unloaded a miniature of Whyte & McKay, a can of Idris ginger beer and trimmings. 'Always a crowd before Newport,' he added.

Then his manner changed momentarily to conditional consternation. 'You did say no ice, didn't you, Mr Weaver? Now you have got everything you want, have you? Mrs Weaver? Are you sure? Nothing to eat?' He looked swiftly over their shoulders and back again and went on, mouthing the words to show that they were not for all ears, 'Toasted sandwich, bacon or Danish Blue and ploughman's pickle? Are you quite sure now?'

Alun said he was, and reeled off a string of heartfelt appreciative expressions while he paid and moderately tipped.

Maintaining it had been a pleasure, Emrys said, 'Now here's a young man who as good as went down on his bended knees to me to be given the chance of meeting you. May I introduce Darren Davies. This is Mr Alun Weaver, OBE.'

The lesser steward was brought forward. He looked rather uneasy and not at all the type to go out of his way to meet an elderly Welshman famous for something unintelligible, but he managed a smile.

Alun sprang up and stuck out his hand. 'Actually, it's CBE. How do you do, Darren. What part of Wales do you come from?'

'Llangefni. Anglesey.'

'Yes, Darren's a North Walian,' said Emrys in the unshocked tone he might have used to announce that the lad was a soccer-player or a Roman Catholic.

'Anglesey's beautiful. I was up there two years ago. Aberffraw. Now Emrys I mustn't keep you any longer from your duties, it wouldn't be fair on other people.'

'Very well, Mr Weaver. But before I go I want to say just this. Everybody is delighted to learn that you and Mrs Weaver have determined to come and live among us here in South Wales. Proud too. Honoured.'

When Alun had said he was grateful and very touched and had shooed Emrys and Darren away and beaten down some of the stares from nearby passengers, not all of them reverential, nor all comprehending, he turned to Rhiannon and raised his eyebrows in a rueful, resigned way. 'You've got to do it,' he said as he had said many times before.

'Of course you have,' she said likewise.

'He'll be telling them in the pub tonight how he had that boring old fart Alun Weaver on his train.' He had said something like that before too but less often.

'Nonsense, he was thrilled, you could see.'

'Anyway a bloody sight more thrilled than he'd have been if I'd asked him to actually produce a bacon bloody sandwich.'

At Cambridge Street station it looked for nearly a minute as though there was not going to be anything that Alun had got to do, but then there appeared a squat man in a white raincoat with what Rhiannon considered was a very small piece of machinery in his hand.

'Alun Weaver?'

'Yes indeed – BBC?'

'Jack Mathias. No, Glamrad,' said the fellow hoarsely, referring to the local commercial radio station.

'Oh. Oh, very well.' Alun peered vainly about for a moment longer, then switched himself on. 'Good to see you, Mr Mathias, and thank you for coming. I hope you haven't had to wait too long. Now what can I do for you?'

Mathias seemed to be suggesting that he and Alun should conduct their business on a public bench on the station platform. They were under cover but drizzle came gusting in from the open and there was a good deal of noise of people and trains.

'Can't we go somewhere warmer?' asked Alun. 'And

quieter?' He tilted his head in an unnatural way to keep the wind from blowing his hair out of position.

'Sorry, we need the noise for the actuality.' Mathias was efficiently setting up his recorder on the bench beside him. 'The ambience. One, two, three, four, testing, testing.'

'Are you going to need my wife for any of this?'

'No,' said Mathias. The question evidently puzzled him.

'All right.' Dissatisfaction with the proceedings showed in Alun's face, but also acceptance. He said to Rhiannon, 'Go and have a cup of tea, love. No need for you to stand about here.'

She felt the same, but thought she would stay and just see or rather hear the start. Soon, so soon as to constitute a vague put-down, Mathias was ready. He had not yet looked either of them in the eye.

'Alun Weaver, Cambridge Street station, take one,' he said to nothing in particular. 'Tell me, what does it feel like to return to live in Wales after all these years away?'

'Many things grave and gay and multi-coloured but one above all: I'm coming home. That short rich resounding word means one simple single thing to a Welshman such as I, born and bred in this land of river and hill. And that thing, that miraculous thing is – Wales. Fifty years of exile couldn't fray that stout bond. Heart is where the home is, and the heart of a Welshman . . .'

The warm, lively voice was soon lost when Rhiannon started to walk towards the barrier carrying the overnight case that Emrys had fought so hard for Darren to be allowed to carry. She held herself very straight and still answered physically to most of Malcolm's description, though her grey eyes had never held the touch of blue he had said he saw in them.

On her two recent trips to these parts she had travelled by car and she had not seen the station for over ten years. So far, except for the signs, it looked more or less unchanged, and of course the outlook was just the same, the view of an expanse of hillside with those unmistakable terraces of small houses, some running along from left to right, some up and down, among patchy grassland with stretches and bits of cliff of bare rock, few trees and no bright colours anywhere. She had always thought it was incredibly typical, South Wales at one go, though not the kind of thing you put on a picture postcard, and looking at it now under thin rain she felt she had remembered it exactly as it was.

What they called the station concourse, the hall, was more or less unrecognizable: coffee-shop, travel bureau, passport-photograph booth and electronic-looking screen of arrivals and departures. Let into the wall below this she noticed a commemorative plaque, perhaps the one Alun had been so fed up at not being asked to unveil the previous year. After a nose round she went into the coffee-shop, where everything that was not colouring-book red, blue or yellow was black. There was a very poor selection of things to eat and drink and only one girl serving, who seemed to be waiting for something or somebody that was not Rhiannon and who, like that interviewer, never looked at you. When she had given up hope of whatever it was she wordlessly produced and handed over a cup of tea.

The tables and chairs each stood on a single immovable stump to prevent them being picked up and thrown about. In Rhiannon's experience Welshmen had never gone in for that type of behaviour, but probably that had changed too. The tea turned out to be as nasty as that served in the old torn-down refreshment room, but in a different way; hot, though. As she sipped it she wondered what Alun had been seriously expecting, what a radio man was a let-down from. The mayor, the MP, the chairman of the Welsh Arts

Council, a crowd of fans with autograph-books? Well? A TV team? He did a lot of TV and knew much more about it than she did, but . . .

Rhiannon had never settled in her own mind at any stage how important or well known Alun thought he was, or even really was except very roughly, but at times like this it crossed her mind that he might be making too much of that part of himself. That might go with being his kind of writer. And that was a bit of a puzzle too, how he was always saying he wanted to be regarded as a writer first of all and then always going on television and being interviewed.

He came in sight now, striding towards the glass door, stopping all at once as somebody recognized him, shaking hands, grinning, nodding enthusiastically and writing something – not in an autograph-book but never mind. That was a bit of luck. But when he reached her he had his discontented expression on, with frown and nose-twitches.

'That chap was a prick,' he said, staring at her. 'A *prick*. Do you know what he asked me? Whether I found my books still sold reasonably well. Can you beat it? And when I said Yes as crappily as I could – what else could I do? Well, then he said he meant in England as well as in Wales. I mean Christ, you'd think they'd have told him.' He stared at her a moment longer before letting his shoulders collapse and laughing through his nose, and she joined in. 'Let's get out of this place. Sorry, finish your tea. Are you sure?'

They went outside and stood where a sign used to say Taxi and now said Taxi/*Tacsi* for the benefit of Welsh people who had never seen a letter X before. It was starting to get dark and the lights were coming on, reflected in the wet pavements. Some of what she saw was no different or not much, but other things that she remembered well enough, from the old Mountjoy Arms Hotel with the green-and-tan frieze of classical figures to that mock-rustic

66

shop where you could get very good doughnuts, had vanished so thoroughly that it was impossible to say whereabouts they had stood. But the town was still the place where some of the special parts of her life had come and gone.

When thirty seconds had passed with still no taxi Alun started making tutting noises. 'I do think Malcolm might have met us,' he said. 'Lazy bugger.'

'I was there when you told him not to because the train might be late. Which it was, wasn't it?'

'Oh, were you and did I? Perhaps that's why he's not here. Let's say partly, anyway.'

After another minute, which was quite as long as any such minute with Alun about, a taxi arrived, in fact a London-model taxi, rare in this part of the world. Something about this displeased him. As they moved off he settled himself insistently on the jump-seat behind the driver and tried to talk to him through the open glass panel with a lot of shouting and calls for repetition. It was possible to guess that he had been expecting an ordinary saloon with a passenger-seat up front. Eventually he abandoned the struggle and came and sat beside Rhiannon.

'You can't have a proper conversation under those conditions,' he said.

'Of course you can't. What did you want one for?'

'Well, you know, I always like talking to drivers and people when I'm here. Very Welsh thing. It's a completely different relationship to what you get in England. Difficult to explain.'

'You needn't to me. I am Welsh too as it happens. Boyo.'

'Piss off,' he said, squeezing her hand.

2

Rhiannon and Gwen settled down in the kitchen after Alun and Malcolm had gone along to the Bible for a couple of beers before supper. The two women had been close friends at the university, members of a trio whose third party was Dorothy Morgan. Gwen had put a strong case for leaving Dorothy out of the evening's doings altogether, but Rhiannon had overruled her, mostly on the grounds that after all it was her inaugural, so to speak. Accordingly a false time of arrival had been circulated and the coast was reckoned to be clear for a good hour yet.

In Rhiannon's as well as Malcolm's eyes it was not an attractive kitchen, long and narrow with barely room for six people to sit down. At the moment you would have had trouble finding a vacant flat surface big enough to make a pot of tea on, the sink was full of pans not left to soak, just dumped there, and two or three of Malcolm's shirts hung from a cup-hook on the dresser. It took her back to Gwen's room in Brook Hall, the women's hostel – spick and span every Monday morning and in a frightening piggy mess by tea-time, all sandals, jam and lecture-notes, with plenty of sand underfoot in the summer term. There was always something that needed doing first, she used to say. Rather different now, you might have thought, but then it never worked like that.

With a small start Rhiannon noticed that the bottle of white wine on the table in front of her was not the same as the one they had started on quite a short time earlier. This had a green instead of a blue-and-white label and was also about half empty already. The excitement of getting here and of a sudden feeling, dim and out of nowhere but still real, that things had not stopped happening to her after all, that there were unknown possibilities lined up, had carried her away. Had she drunk two glasses? Three? Well, more than was sensible in the time. It would not do to start following in Dorothy's footsteps, if they were at all as Gwen had described a little while back and was now going on about again.

'Absolute hell. Sophie had to tell her there was no more wine and Charlie put on an act of trying to persuade her to have whisky. Of course if she had . . .'

If anyone was following in Dorothy's footsteps, thought Rhiannon to herself, it might be Gwen. A bottle's-worth of wine had gone down that throat since the start of the session and there was no one around to say how much had before that. The mini-story about Dorothy and the whisky had been touched on already that evening. It seemed quite a distance from the shandy-sipping Gwen of Brook Hall days. But the rest of her was unchanged: a little bit nosy, a little bit catty, but sensible, shrewd, down-to-earth, now as then the one to see through the shams and the wishful thinking. She was absolutely as before when, mixing hesitancy with cheek, she said, 'Haven't really had a chance to ask you this before, old thing, but, er, how do you feel about coming back to live round here?'

Rhiannon would have liked to hear Alun answering that. 'I've always thought I would in the end,' she said tamely. 'Nearly all the Welsh people I've talked to in London say the same thing.' And anyway here I bloody am, she felt like adding.

'But they don't actually come, most of them, do they? Too settled where they are, I dare say. Mind you, I always thought you and Alun were pretty firmly fixed there in Highgate. Especially you yourself, Rhi. You really cut yourself off from down here, didn't you, in the last few years anyway. Not like Alun. He's kept up with, oh, a lot of people here and there.'

'No, well I'm sorry, but you know, you keep leaving it and then all of a sudden you find it's too late, anyway without a lot of explanation.'

'Of course, and then your mother dying, you haven't got her to come down for. You'll soon pick up the threads again.'

There was a silence that was pretty clearly an interval before more of the same from Gwen's side. Rhiannon let it go on; she never minded silences. On this occasion she partly filled in with the thought that one of the reasons for not accompanying Alun on his Welsh trips, the one that had always seemed to come to mind first, was to give him a free hand in keeping up with certain people, people like that doctor's wife by Beaufoy and the woman with the extraordinary hairdo who had been second-in-command at the mental home. He had been a model husband for days, weeks afterwards when he got back. But Rhiannon was not going to tell Gwen any of that, nor that she hoped Alun would set about finding some people to keep up with out at Capel Mererid or further, once he was settled down here.

Gwen looked at her in an understanding, caring sort of way. 'But you did, *you* did really want to come? I mean you weren't talked into it however nicely?'

'No,' said Rhiannon, trying not to sound too flat or final.

'No qualms? I know you've got some painful memories of the old days.' Gwen had turned quite sad now, as though some of it had happened to her as well. 'Aren't you afraid at all of stirring them up?'

However much wine might or might not have gone down it seemed kind of early to get on to such matters, but they had been bound to arise some time. 'A bit. But it's all a long time ago, what went on then. That's if it's the thing with Peter you're talking about. Do you know, I never think of it.'

'Oh really. You can't forget it though, can you?'

'No, but you can stop feeling bad about it, I mean I have. No point.'

'No point, no, but women have an awful way of feeling things there's no point in them feeling.'

'I know what you mean all right. I suppose I've just been lucky.' Again, Rhiannon wanted to say something like there were times when one person could get away with murder as far as another person was concerned, and even after the times had changed completely, for good, that part stayed the same, but she had never told anybody that. She said, wanting to know though not necessarily from Gwen, 'How is Peter? Do you see him much?'

'Not a lot, no. Malcolm runs into him at the pub occasionally. He's fine as far as I can gather, for his age you know. Run to fat rather. And, well, I get the impression he's not very pleased with life.'

'I suppose he's retired now.'

'According to Malcolm he hasn't a good word to say for anyone or anything.'

'He's not the only one. Muriel's around, I suppose?'

At this name the two caught each other's eye and as if by pre-arrangement made remarkably similar frowning, blinking, whistling faces. On instinct they drew closer together in their chairs.

'Oh yes,' said Gwen. 'Yes, she's around. There's a strange one as they say.'

'Well, I hardly know her. I can't really say I know her.'

'I can never tell what she's thinking. There she is going on as nice as pie and I've no idea what's in her head at all. I realize I've no idea what's going through her mind.'

'She gives you that look, sort of measuring, summing you up. Actually I haven't seen her for God knows how long.'

'She may love us all but somehow I doubt it.'

'It's not exactly cold, is it, because in a way she's very friendly. It doesn't go with her voice.'

'I wonder how those two get on. They're funny together. Like two people at work who've got to hit it off while they're there but you can bet they never go near each other outside. Like in front of the servants.'

'What?' Rhiannon wondered if she was falling asleep. 'Does Malcolm hear anything, I mean from his mates?'

'Don't know. Sometimes I catch an awful look on Peter's face when he doesn't think anybody's watching. Afflicted. Stricken.'

'Oh, I know that stricken look from the old days. I used to tell him he was only . . .'

When no more followed, Gwen said, 'Christ, she doesn't half put it away, young Muriel. Not regularly, not every day, just occasionally, but then – wow! It doesn't show on her but whenever I happen to catch sight of her glass it's either full or empty. Not that she's anything special, mind. There's Dorothy . . .' Gwen paused, perhaps trying to remember whether she had told Rhiannon the one about the whisky. If so, the effort was successful, because she went on, '. . . and Charlie of course . . .'

'I haven't seen Charlie for –'

'No use expecting much sense out of him after about six o'clock at night. He's got this restaurant in Broad Street now. Co-owner of it with his brother. I don't know whether you remember Victor. Not my type at all. Absolutely not my cup of tea. He's . . . you know.'

'What, you mean . . .'

'You know,' said Gwen, nodding slowly. 'Well, we're

not supposed to mind them these days but I can't help it. I came to them late, sort of. For a long time I didn't know there was any such thing. And there wasn't really then, not in Wales. When I first heard about them they were in places like Paris and London. You know, Oscar Wilde. You can say a lot against the chapel but at least it kept them down. And I reckon everybody being poor helped. They couldn't dress up or anything.'

Rhiannon remembered Gwen talking in that style in her room in Brook Hall, about chaps among other things, saying what she probably really thought but being jokey too so as to stay in the clear about something. According to Dorothy, who had always been a great one for psychology, it showed a basic insecurity. Whatever it showed it was quite fun to listen to but it did tend to slow down the conversation, as now in fact. Gwen seemed to have dried up though she showed no sign of being insecure about that. 'This queer brother of Charlie's,' said Rhiannon.

'*Victor*, yes. He runs the restaurant with his, with a friend of his. Nothing for Charlie to do but chat to the customers and knock back the Scotch and tell himself he's working. Not conducive to health. Eventually he nods off at the table or in the bar and Victor sends him home in a taxi.'

'Not much of a life for Sophie.'

'Oh, I don't think she minds too much. She has got this shop – just a sort of boutique,' said Gwen in response to Rhiannon's quick look and hurried disappointingly on. 'The thing is, Charlie's got nothing else to do and he can afford it. It's quite a problem for retired people, I do see. All of a sudden the evening starts starting after breakfast. All those hours with nothing to stay sober for. Or nothing to naturally stay sober during, if you see what I . . . We used to laugh at Malcolm's dad, the way he used to mark up the wireless programmes in the *Radio Times* in different-coloured pencils. Never caught him listening to any of them but it was an hour taken care of. Drink didn't agree with him, poor old Taffy. Some of us have got a lot to be thankful for.'

Watching Gwen refill her glass and also send a minor stream down its outside, Rhiannon wondered what, if anything, she told herself she was doing. Did she just not know what she was really doing? As any wife of Alun's would have had to be, Rhiannon was almost as used to people getting drunk as she was to them having a drink, but she had learnt too that there was a stage beyond that. It was a little discouraging to find, a couple of hours after arriving to live among them, that everybody round the place seemed to be getting there regularly if they were not funny in some way. Or (Muriel) had a touch of both.

Gwen was turning serious and inquisitive all over again. She said, 'How did you actually react to the idea of settling down in these parts?' This had not got to be another bit of maundering; it was a trick of Gwen's to keep coming back to a point until her curiosity was either satisfied or else knocked firmly on the head – a very minor improvement on the maundering option if you asked Rhiannon.

'Thrilled,' she said rather loudly.

'You don't mind my asking? I suppose the two of you discussed it pretty thoroughly before you took the decision.'

'Not really, no. Over in a moment.'

'Oh yes. Which of you in fact got the idea first?'

'We found we'd both been thinking about it for some time.'

'But who was the first to mention it? Was it you? Just interested.'

'No, it was Alun. He came out with it one morning at breakfast.'

'And you fell in with it straight away.'

'Yes. I seemed to have my mind already made up. I don't really know why.'

'Oh. I expect you had a lot of friends in Highgate.'

Rhiannon nodded from the waist upwards. 'Yes, I was quite firmly fixed there. Look, old thing, if you're trying to get me to say Alun was the one who wanted to come and he managed to browbeat me into it then you're wasting your time. He was keener than I was to start with but I was keen enough. Not that that would have made any difference in the end to whether we came or not.'

'Have you always done what he wanted?'

'Yes, of course I have, in anything like that. He earns the money.'

'You let that man walk all over you, Rhi. I told you he would.'

'Did you? Well, this is one time he hasn't.'

At this Gwen seemed to give up. She scrumpled bits of cigarette-wrapping and stowed them in vacant parts of her ashtray and carefully blew some ash off the table-top. With a quirky smile she said, 'How is Alun?'

That sounded really nice for about half a second, like an easy exam question: anything you feel like saying on the subject will do. Rhiannon half wanted to answer with a run-down on Alun's medical check-up last month, featuring the part where the doctor had told him, rather coldly, apparently, that his liver as well as his heart and lungs was in excellent condition. But she felt she had to be a little more forthcoming than that. She saw that Gwen had switched to a smile with raised eyebrows. What a lot of expressions she knew.

'He's just the same as ever,' said Rhiannon. 'Always jolly

and lively except when I don't want him to be. That's the chief thing about him as far as I'm concerned.'

This went down less than well. Gwen got up quickly and toddled to the litter-bin behind Rhiannon. There, having let the empty bottle rustle and thump down inside, she was to be heard knocking out the ashtray on the edge of the bin. Silence followed while she presumably regrouped. When she spoke it was clear from the acoustics that her back was turned. Rhiannon shifted uneasily on her chair.

'You know, Malcolm was absolutely knocked sideways when your letter came. We'd heard talk but nothing definite. Knocked him completely sideways.'

'Not with horror, I hope.'

'Of course not with horror. With delight. With joy.' A loud smacking pop indicated what Gwen had been up to while out of sight. 'But something else as well, Rhi, you know that.'

Gwen came into view again with the new bottle and the emptied but still dirty ashtray and rather flung herself down in her seat at the table.

'You were his first love,' she said matter-of-factly.

'That's nice to hear. He's one of the sweetest men I've ever met.' Rhiannon meant what she said, and could not understand why she so much disliked speaking the words.

'He never talks about it,' said Gwen, looking at her watch. 'Never says what happened.'

'Gwen, really, there's nothing to talk about. *Nothing* happened.'

Rhiannon felt what was almost admiration for her friend and at the same time wanted to hit her a certain amount for the way she accepted the message without any nonsense about believing it or even somehow not believing it. She finished nodding her head and sat for a time fiddling with

76

her glass, which she had refilled, and moving her eyebrows about, as much as to say that here came the punch. At the instant she drew in her breath to deliver it the door-bell rang, a peremptory, office-type sound. When a moment later Rhiannon heard Dorothy's voice she sniggered to herself.

Then Dorothy came in, embraced Rhiannon at length, apologized for being early, asked to hear all her news and listened, or at least stayed quiet and watching, while she told some of it. This startling behaviour intrigued Rhiannon and obviously disconcerted Gwen, who twice at least seemed on the point of breaking in to protest that the whole thing was a put-up job, meant to bring her into disrepute, most unsporting and certain to wear itself out soon. On the last point at any rate she would have scored, for Dorothy sent her first glass of wine down in a little over ten minutes and her second in a little under, and not before Alun, Malcolm and Percy got back from the Bible, but well before the end of the evening, she started telling them all, and then telling just Gwen, about a tribe in probably New Guinea she had been reading about who built houses in trees that they never occupied and had perhaps at some distant era intended for the spirits of their ancestors to live in, but perhaps not, and other things like that. When the time came, however, she went off quite meekly, taking less than a quarter of an hour to move from just inside the front door to just far enough outside it. More than once in that time she had invited Gwen and Rhiannon to coffee at her house the following morning.

'Is she like that all the time now, did you gather?' asked Alun as he and Rhiannon were undressing in the little guest bedroom. 'Malcolm said something.'

'Quite a lot of it, evidently, but I think some of it tonight was the excitement of seeing us.'

'Seeing you, more like. She's never had much time for me.' He stood on one leg and shook the other with tremendous force to rid it of that part of his trousers. 'I can't think why not.'

Rhiannon got into bed and started on the considerable routine necessary to shape her pillow correctly. 'She was sober when she arrived.'

'Yeah, well when you're knocking it back like that all day every day you get a sort of float, or do I mean balance. You only need a bit of topping-up and you're off, gone. A plateau.'

'Poor little thing.'

'Poor little thing be buggered,' said Alun musically, also getting into bed. He turned the light out, lay down and put his arms round Rhiannon as he did every night, or rather every night he was there, with her. 'We're the poor little things having to take it. And poor old Percy's the poorest littlest thing of the lot.'

'I think he can handle her. No, I meant it means she must have some idea of what she's like. She stayed sober all day because she wanted to be in a good state to meet me, her old friend. Means she must know she normally gets into bad states. Mustn't she?'

'She may or may not know but she obviously doesn't bloody care or she wouldn't get into them.'

'I don't suppose she can help it much, it's a bit late for that.'

'If she can help it once she can help it again.' Alun worked his way through an intensive spell of sniffing, throat-clearing and grunting. When he had finished he said, 'Old Gwen hadn't been exactly short-changing herself either, had she?'

'No. Far from it. She didn't use to do that. She's a bit different all round, I thought.'

'Well, speaking from the old lofty pinnacle, I imagine decades of piss-artistry can't help leaving their mark on the character. Christ Almighty, what sort of lot have we got ourselves into? Well, should be fun. Of a kind, at least. One thing about you, sweetheart, you're never going to be any trouble that way. Or any other way. It's a marvellous thing. To know that.'

After a minute or two he pulled his arms back and turned away over on to his side of the bed. That was not what he did every night.

3

A few days later Cambria Television made arrangements to record an interview with Alun at the Weavers' rented house in Pedwarsaint, the suburbanized former fishing village in or near which they hoped to settle down. From the vanished quay the smacks had gone out in numbers for the oysters in the bend stretching over to Courcey Island on the east side, and sold their product from Bristol to Barnstaple until overfishing and industrial pollution wiped out the beds before the Great War. A marina stood there now, completed only the previous year, the resort of owners of medium-grade casinos or smallish chains of coin-op laundrettes from Birmingham and points north who came in at the weekends down the M5–M4 or, increasingly, by air taxi to the strip at Swanset on Courcey. And of course, where not so long ago it had been hake and chips, bottled cockles, pork pies and pints of Troeth bitter, these days it was cannelloni, paella, stifado, cans of Foster's, bottles of Rioja and – of course – large Courvoisiers and long panatellas, just like everywhere else.

Barring perhaps the oyster details for their elegiac

potential, none of this would have been worth a second thought to Alun, certainly not today. He was charged up by the television presence, more by the simple expectation of appearing in front of its cameras than by having pulled off any sort of coup in securing a spot, even the lead spot, on *The Week in Wales*. Necessary, though. Perhaps on reconsideration not insignificant after all. He had done England, got out of it what there was for him to get out of it; he could never have hoped to be omnipresent there. In Wales he could, or was going to have a bloody good try.

The house belonged to a remarkably opulent official in a local housing department, at present holidaying with his wife in the Caribbean, a man whose future acquaintance could not, given reasonable luck, be a bad thing. Nor could being filmed in his sumptuous drawing-room, as far as the *hoi polloi* went, at least. Any lefty sticklers who might find a bit too much silver, glass and teak on display there would be placated, when the future-plans question came, by talk of a swift removal to a modest place of one's own and a single half-amused glance about. At this stage he had not yet fully worked out minor finesses like that, but he was a great believer in thinking as far as possible round any subject beforehand.

Now he set out to ingratiate himself with the crew, but circumspectly, not in the style which had been good enough for Emrys on the train. He sensed that a little went a long way with this sort of youngster, especially a little of anything that could be described, however unjustly, as Welsh flannel, Taff bullshit, etc. Having done what he could in this out-of-the-way mode he turned his attention to the interviewer, a fair young man in a wine-coloured jacket who had nothing discoverably Welsh about him and who let it be known, with enviable speed and clarity, that this morning's task was no more than the sort of thing he was prepared to go through with while waiting briefly for a proper job a long way away. In other circumstances Alun would have sorted him out in five seconds flat, but as it was he concentrated on pretending not to have noticed and on not trying to make the young shit like him – that had to come naturally or not at all.

The interview went well enough. Alun soon saw the fellow had no particular approach, was in the manner of such fellows merely concerned to establish his superiority to the overall run of the play. So the angle to go for had to be knowing a lot, seeing a lot, caring a lot but only in unpredictable ways, or ways that could be passed off as unpredictable. It was not an occasion for pulling out the stops, but near the end, after magnanimously letting pass a touch of ignorance about the Attlee governments' policies for industry in South Wales, Alun took the chance of getting into his stride rather.

'It's all too easy for an exile come home to stay where he lands up, to cultivate his garden and never look over the hedge, to become something of a vegetable himself. That won't do for me, I'm afraid. I'll be going out, out in search of Wales, looking at things, looking at people. A small private voyage of discovery. I'm sure I'll find plenty of changes, for the worse, for the better, but there are some places where change can never reach . . .'

He went on to list, rather fancifully, perhaps, a few of that kind. In the normal way he forgot everything he had said in a broadcast as soon as it was finished, and good riddance – remembering might interfere with spontaneity next time. But now for once some of it stuck. Cultivating his garden he could dismiss right off, as anyone might who was as keen as he on what you could get up to indoors. In search of Wales, on the other hand, sounded distinctly good, might become *In Search of Wales* one day; it was a pity that old Brynford had done those programmes so recently. Meanwhile, the pursuit of a nebulous project of this sort would be just the thing for getting him out of untimely invitations and the like, and also covering any sudden disappearances he might feel impelled to make.

When Rhiannon came into the drawing-room after the TV lot had gone, she found him full of enthusiasm for his new scheme, full of ideas too: trips to Courcey Island, to Carmarthen, to Merthyr Dafydd, to Brecon; visits to metal works at Port Holder and Caerhays; rounds of the pubs in Harriston, in Cwmgwyrdd, in Bargeman's Row; a pilgrimage and a piss-up in Birdarthur, where Brydan had settled after his last trip to America. As he talked, she moved here and there round the room in an unsettling way.

'What are you doing?' he broke off to ask.

'Nothing. I'm listening. I was just making sure everything's all right.'

'What? How do you mean all right?'

'Just nothing's been broken or anything like that.'

'Don't fuss,' he said, but not sharply. 'You tip-toe round this place as if you're afraid to chip a bloody saucer. These blokes are very professional, you couldn't tell they'd been here if you didn't know.'

'All right, but I am afraid to chip a bloody saucer, and so should you be. People get attached to their things. Anyway, how did it go?'

'Uh? *Oh.*' He tossed his head, indicating that the presumably meant interview was nothing, no trouble, of no significance, already forgotten but satisfactory. 'I was thinking, I thought I might look in at the Glendower for lunch, you know, toe in the water kind of thing. See if it's any good. Why don't you . . .'

'There's this cleaner turning up, and then Rosemary's train gets in at 2.40,' said Rhiannon, naming their younger, unmarried daughter. Rosemary was taking a long weekend off from St John's College, Oxford, where she was reading law, to come and help her mother look at houses round about. 'Be a bit of a rush.'

'Oh God, four to one again. Still, it's only for a couple of days, I agree.'

'Come on, let's hear it.'

'I told you before and don't pretend you don't know perfectly bloody well in the first place. Any man in the company of two women is outnumbered four to one however amiable they may be. By definition.'

'So when it's just you and me I outnumber you two to one, is that right?'

'Affirmative. And it's not twice two when there are two of you. I mean if we had Frances on the party it would be nine to one. What they call a square law.'

'You will have your little joke, won't you, *was*? And I'll go along and glad to as long as we all know it's a joke. You outnumbered. That'll be the day.'

'Oh now now girl, easy by there, *cariad*,' he said, taking it off wicked of course but getting something out of it at the same time, or fancying so. 'No ruffled feathers now.' He put his arms round her.

'Relax, boyo,' she said.

The family car was Japanese and why not? – Alun would tacitly claim a special Welsh exemption from any lingering sense of duty to drive an 'English' model. It had been brought down from London earlier that week by a minor character from his publishers, minimal in fact and male too, thus rating no more than a gulped-down whisky before being packed off to the station. Today Alun took it into town and parked it in a building contractor's yard just behind Broad Street. A long-nosed man in a yellow helmet came out of a shed as if to order him away, but Alun's face

83

with the distinctive quiff was well enough known to be familiar even when not actually recognized, and a clap on the shoulder and a bellowed but unintelligible greeting did the rest.

The state of play in the grill at the Glendower, half full or more on a weekday lunchtime earlyish, suggested that the concern was doing well enough. It was a big part of Alun's stock-in-trade to seem to know things like what sort of people were sitting at the tables, but he would have tried not to be challenged on this lot. Part of it was that nobody dressed properly any more. Another part was that it was no longer just the young who were too young to be distinguished between. He cast his eye round the room. Tradesmen, he said firmly to himself. Housewives. When he had hung about for a minute or two without anyone coming near him or even looking up, he made for the door, noticing on the way that an attempt, pretty pathetic but not on that account less offensive to respectable sentiment, had been made to give the place a Nineties or Edwardian look with plush, iron, brass, wall-mirrors and long white aprons on the waiters. An ancient map of South Wales (c. 1980) hung between the windows.

Upstairs in what was called the cocktail bar there was more of the same: sepia photographs of archaic worthies on the mauve-papered walls and a barman in a striped waistcoat with brass buttons, and not only that. In fact he looked like the sort of girl who might be cast as Toby Belch in a women's-college production of *Twelfth Night*. An older man on the other side of the counter was talking seriously to him, a man with very neat wavy grey hair, a slim figure and uncommonly white whites to his eyes, and in other ways showing himself to be no exception to a rule of Alun's that men over fifty who took care of themselves were not to be trusted. This one was readily placeable as Victor

Norris and he turned and so introduced himself with impressive speed, going on with more of the same to order Alun a drink. Then he did a buttering-up job on Alun that was a good deal more efficient than might have been expected in a restaurant in a provincial town, even a Welsh one. When it seemed to be over Alun said, 'Expecting Charlie in, are you?'

Victor scratched the side of his neck, bending his hand back to do so further than some men might, and glanced at the grandfather clock that clunked near by. 'If he's coming he should be here any minute.'

'He told me he usually turns up midday.'

'Yes, he feels at home here. Which is nice for everyone.'

'I should have thought he felt at home in most places with a licence.'

'M'm.' Victor smiled with closed lips. 'Of course he is very outgoing. But behind that, oh dear, there's a very different kind of person. You wouldn't – you haven't seen that.'

'What haven't I seen?' asked Alun, who had found himself beginning to come round fast after the soft-soap session. 'I have known him for quite a few years, actually.'

'Oh, indeed you have, he often speaks of you. But that poor man my brother is vulnerable to all sorts of pressures and more than a lot of people he needs a settled, undisturbed kind of existence. I dare say you think that sounds silly but it's true.'

'Really.'

'Yes really.' At this point Victor took a silent message from somebody in the doorway, doubtless the friend one heard about, and in a flash his manner changed from faint menace all the way back to full warmth. 'No rest for the wicked. Super to have met you – Alun. Oh you are lunching? Do you like scallops?'

When Alun had said truthfully that he did, Victor held his hand out palm foremost, interdicting further speech, and strode rather mannishly away. Back at the bar Alun got another drink but had his money refused, and his respect for Victor went up another notch. Time was getting on, however. He looked round as he had downstairs: more tradesmen and housewives, a fairly unselfconscious sample. Just as he was starting to contemplate listlessly a solo lunch with perhaps bits of Victor thrown in, Charlie appeared. He was followed by someone who at first looked to Alun like an incredibly offensive but all too believable caricature of Peter Thomas aged about eighty-five and weighing half a ton. At a second glance he saw that it was Peter Thomas.

All three men seemed to turn rigid for an instant, then came back to life and motion. Alun raised his glass high, Charlie waved, Peter nodded. They converged. Alun shook Peter's hand not too hard, smiling not too broadly, trying to get it right. The difficulty was, he recognized, that he had grown so used to transmitting amiability, benevolence and all those for unreal that this confrontation rather stretched him. His will was of the best: he had a rooted and sincere aversion to any trouble not of his own making.

'Don't let's think how long it's been,' he said to Peter, genuinely enough. 'Now drinks.' While these were coming he went on, nodding at Peter's paunch, 'I don't know how you do it. I suppose it's just a matter of eating and drinking anything you like.'

'Yes, but it's the slimline tonic that turns the scale. Actually I have managed to reduce the rate of increase of the rate of increase.'

'Nice-looking place, this,' said Alun to Charlie, his glance panning to and fro. 'They won't let me pay here, I notice.'

'Oh, you've seen Victor.'

'*Yes*,' said Alun, enthusiastically this time. 'Impressive fellow, I thought. He knows his job all right. Very professional.'

Charlie seemed rather doubtful of that one, but then raised his glass. 'Here's to us all. Welcome to Wales, you poor bastard.'

The three looked one another seriously in the eye and drank with a flourish. Alun began to relax. He went on relaxing over the next drink, when they got on to politics and had a lovely time seeing who could say the most outrageous thing about the national Labour Party, the local Labour Party, the Labour-controlled county council, the trade unions, the education system, the penal system, the Health Service, the BBC, black people and youth. (Not homosexuals today.) They varied this with eulogies of President Reagan, Enoch Powell, the South African government, the Israeli hawks and whatever his name was who ran Singapore. They were very much still at it when they went down to lunch, or rather when Charlie, explaining that he was trying to keep himself down to just one meal in the evening, went and sat with the other two and prepared to drink while they had lunch. He had brought a fresh drink with him from the bar so as to ensure an even flow.

They had hardly settled in their seats before one of the long-aproned waiters went round unfolding napkins and spreading them across their destined laps. They were unexceptionably large and laundered and of linen, but they were also pale pink. Alun ostentatiously held his arms up well clear during the spreading. When it was over he put on an eager, didactic expression and said, 'This is called a napkin. Its purpose is to protect your clothing from the substantial gobbets of food that your table manners will cause to fall from your mouth or from some point on the way to your mouth, and to provide something other than your hand or sleeve with which to wipe your mouth. Explaining this to one of your understanding would take a long time and even then might not avail, so fucking well sit still and shut up.'

'Oh Christ,' said Peter immediately, his eyes on the menu. They had each been given one in the bar but none of them had looked at it. 'A bloody Welsh lunch and dinner. Well, roll on.' Looking round for someone to accuse he caught sight of Charlie. 'What's the idea?' he asked, apparently in sincere puzzlement.

'You have to do it in a way,' said Charlie. 'People are getting to expect it. We only do it on Fridays anyway, Fridays and St David's Day. And it isn't compulsory even then. Which is decent of us because it's pretty nasty, unless you happen to have a taste for chicken in honey.'

'You mean you actually get people eating that?' asked Alun.

'Not much, no. That's not really the point. Seeing it on the menu is what they like. Same with the signposts.'

'But you don't give an English translation here,' said Peter.

'Well, you see, that would rather spoil things for them. They like to feel they understand it, or could if they paid it a bit of attention. And they probably do understand some of it, like *pys* is peas and *tatws* is taters.'

'Christ,' said Peter again, with weary disgust this time.

'We're not going to war over this, I hope. It's all fairly harmless, isn't it?'

'No it isn't. There you're wrong. It's one part, a small part but still a part, of an immense Chinese wall of bullshit that's, I mean Offa's Dyke that's . . .'

'Threatening to engulf us,' supplied Charlie. 'I know. But I'm afraid I don't think putting a couple of dozen Welsh words on a menu lets the side down very far. Find a pass that's really worth holding and I'll join you there.'

'There never is one. That's the trouble.'

'We need more drinks,' said Alun. 'And I'd advise you to switch, Peter. I don't think that slimline tonic agrees with you.'

'Can I recommend the soup?' asked Charlie. 'I hope you've noticed it's called soup, not *cawl*. I might even have some myself. Potato and leek today, he does it quite well. Unless Peter thinks the leek is there for impure reasons.'

'All right, Charlie,' said Peter.

Just as they had ordered, Victor approached the table, using a much less emphatic gait than when making his exit from the bar. 'Do forgive me, but one of your fans, Alun, requests the honour of a brief word.'

'What kind of fan?'

'Well, I don't know what you'd call her, but if it was left to me I'd say she was a young person. There, over in the corner, just turning round now.'

From what Alun could see without his glasses, which was all he was going to see of her, the fan looked perhaps rather good as well as young. 'All right, but you will see she knows I'm having a little private lunch-party.'

'I'll make sure she understands that, Alun – leave it to me.'

'You more or less have to do it,' said Alun after a moment. He felt a little embarrassed.

'Don't worry,' said Charlie.

'I mean you can always get out of it if you don't mind looking like a shit but I'm afraid I'm a bit too cowardly to do that unless I have to.'

'We understand.'

Seen closer to, the fan looked quite seriously good, and late twenties. Alun found himself signalling to Victor, who with what could have been piss-taking alacrity sent a waiter scurrying forward with a fourth chair. The fan shook hands nicely with them all and accepted a glass of wine.

'And what can I do for you?' There was no point, Alun considered, in trying to hide his satisfaction at this turn of events.

'I'd like you to talk to my group.'

'Tell me about your group.'

It turned out to be a literary circle, thirty strong on a good night, though naturally there would be more for someone like him, twenty minutes' drive, and not worth asking about a fee. Yes, a reading would do if he preferred it.

'I'll consider it,' said Alun. 'Perhaps you'd like to drop me a line incorporating all that, care of the local BBC. Very kind of you to ask.'

'Nice to have met you.' Her voice was good too.

Charlie watched her go. 'Is that the lot?' he demanded.

'The lot? I might talk to her group if I'm feeling gracious. What are you getting at?'

'What? A bit off I call that quite frankly.'

'I don't know what you mean.'

'I mean, is that the worst you could do? You didn't even ask her for her bloody phone-number.' Charlie shook his head.

'Oh, I read you now. What I should have done was grab at her bosom. Of course.'

'Well that's how you're supposed to behave, isn't it?'

'You do me too much honour, Charlie. Age comes to us all.'

The fresh drinks arrived, whisky and gin to make up for the relative thinness of the wine. Soon afterwards the scallops arrived, and they were all right, eatable enough anyway for Alun to praise them extravagantly when Victor came to inquire. At this stage too Alun carried his point that he must be allowed to pay for the meal or would feel inhibited in his choice, and Victor gave in very gracefully and accepted a glass of the second bottle of Chablis *grand Cru*. For obvious reasons Alun made rather a thing of not knowing about wine, but any fool could have seen that this one looked and sounded good. At a suitable moment he revealed that he had done television that morning, hence, he said, his desire to get clean away afterwards and have a couple of drinks with a pal or two. He added that that was how he always felt after a do like that, even a little local one.

'You must have done a lot of it in London,' said Charlie.

'Yes I did, and why not? Some of the people up there, you know, bloody intellectuals, Hampstead types, they look down their noses at you if you go on the box more than once in a blue moon. Cheapening yourself. Well I'm not. I don't consider I'm cheapening myself by appearing on television. What else am I fit for? I'm just an old ham after all, so why shouldn't I perform where a few people can see me?'

'Oh, come along now, Alun, really,' said Charlie at once, and Peter said, 'No, you're not being fair to yourself.'

'You're very kind, both of you, but I've no illusions after all these years. Quite a successful ham, mind, but a ham none the less. An old fraud.' Here he paused for a space, as if wondering whether this time he had indeed been to some extent unfair to himself, then went buoyantly on, 'Anyway, forget it. Bugger it. Now who's for cheese? And it must follow as the night the day, a glass of port.'

Charlie said yes to that instantly, and it only took Peter a moment or two to do so. Alun asked for the cheeseboard, two large vintage ports and a glass of the house red, explaining that port had been playing him up a bit recently, and went off to the lavatory with more explanations about being an old man and envying you youngsters.

'We chimed in all right, did we?' asked Charlie. 'About the terrible injustice he was doing himself.'

'We did the best we could. Does he think we think he means that about him being a ham and a fraud? Him seeing himself in that light, that is.'

'I don't know. I doubt it. I shouldn't be surprised if he reckons that just saying that, whatever we make of it, is going to help his credibility in the future. Sort of, a fraud who's come out is more believable than a closet fraud.'

'Maybe. Anyway, he's buying us an excellent lunch. Well, buying me one.'

'There's always that. And it may go against the grain to admit it, but one's spirits do tend to lift a degree or so at the sight of him.'

'I know what you mean. Even I know.'

Alun came hurrying back as the drinks were being handed round by a wine-waiter who came out of the same sort of drawer as the barman and was got up in a fancy jacket with clusters of grapes depicted on the lapels. The cheese was there. Charlie took a small piece of Cheddar.

'What is the vintage port?' asked Alun.

'Port is a fortified wine from Portugal,' said the waiter, having perhaps misheard slightly, 'and vintage port is made from –'

'I didn't ask for a bloody lecture on vinification, you horrible little man.' Alun laughed a certain amount as he spoke. 'Tell me the shipper and the year and then go back to your hole and pull the lid over it.'

The lad seemed more or less unabashed at this. 'Graham 1975, sir,' he said in his Ruritanian accent, and withdrew.

'It's no use just relying on respect to get good service in a restaurant,' Alun explained, still grinning. 'There has to be fear too.'

'Perhaps it slipped your mind that I'm part-owner here,' said Charlie.

'Not at all, that's why I piped up. I could see it would have been difficult for you to say anything.'

'Excuse me a moment.' Charlie got up with deliberation and made off after the wine-waiter.

Alun watched him cross the room in an all-but-straight line, then turned purposefully to Peter and looked him in the eye. 'Gives me a chance to tell you this. What happened many years ago is over and done with as far as I'm concerned. For what that may be worth. I have no unfriendly feelings towards you at all. You'll want to hear about Rhiannon's feelings from her, and forgive me if I intrude, but as far as I know they're the same. I'll never say anything more on the matter.'

'That's generous of you, Alun.' Peter had dropped his gaze. 'Thank you.'

'One moderately interesting thing did emerge from that rubbishy TV chat this morning. It occurred to me while I was yammering away that it might be fun to take a few trips round the place.'

Here Charlie came back and sat down, again in commendable style. 'Keeping staff is a hell of a problem these days,' he said. His manner was conciliatory.

'I bet it is,' said Alun warmly, and went on in the same breath, 'I was just telling Peter I was thinking of going on a jaunt or two in the next few weeks, nothing fancy, a sort of scenic pub-crawl really. With, you know, some eventual literary creation held distantly in mind. Even a poem or two if the bloody old Muse can still walk.'

Charlie and Peter looked at each other. 'It's an idea,' admitted Charlie.

'Bit miserable, running about here and there on your own. Perhaps you two would like to come along sometimes if you're at a loose end. We might get hold of old Malcolm. Make a party of it.'

In those few seconds the expressions of the other two had solidified, Charlie's into cheerful mistrust, Peter's into surly mistrust. The mistrust was natural enough, but out of place on this occasion. Alun liked company, he liked an audience and he liked almost any kind of excursion and that was it. For the moment at least. When he protested some of this his hearers soon started to cave in, not so much out of belief as because each calculated that any attempt at hanky-panky could be better resisted nearer the point of unveiling, and after all it had been a pretty lavish lunch. And what else had they got in their diaries?

Charlie was the first to yield. Peter held out a little longer, declaring that he would have to see, maintaining that he was supposed to be taking things easy, but he was talked out of that in no time when it was explained to him that getting out and about a bit was just what he needed. All the camaraderie that had rather faded away over the wine-waiter was restored. Animatedly they suggested places to visit, discussed them, reminisced about them. Alun ordered two more large vintage ports and another glass of the house red, which he sipped at and seemed to lose interest in. After a few minutes he called for the bill, paid, tipped largely, and departed on his way – to take the car in and have its starter fixed, he said.

4

But when Alun reached his car and set about driving off, the engine fired in a couple of seconds, nor did he go near any garage or repair-shop before parking the machine at the side of the road in a smart residential area. There followed a brisk walk of a hundred yards to a short drive-way, at whose entrance he abruptly checked his stride. Standing quite motionless he gazed before him with a faraway look that a passer-by, especially a Welsh passer-by, might have taken for one of moral if not spiritual insight, such that he might instantly renounce whatever course of action he had laid down for himself. After a moment, something like a harsh bark broke from the lower half of his trunk, followed by a fluctuating whinny and a thud that sounded barely organic, let alone human. Silence, but for faint birdsong. Then, like a figure in a restarted film, he stepped keenly off again and was soon ringing the bell in a substantial brick porch.

Sophie Norris came to the door in a biscuit-coloured woollen dress and looking very fit. As soon as she had taken in the sight of Alun her routine half-smile vanished. 'You've got a bloody nerve you have, Alun Weaver,' she said in the old penetrating tones. 'I've a good mind to slam this in your face, cheeky bugger.'

'Ah, but you're not going to, are you, love? And why should you anyway? Just dropped in for a cup of tea. Nothing wrong in that, is there?'

Sighing breathily and clicking her tongue, she gave way. 'Ten minutes, mind. Ten minutes max. I've got to go down the shop. Think yourself bloody lucky I hadn't left already.'

'Sure. Charlie not about then?'

There Alun overplayed his hand a little. 'What do you take me for, Weaver, a fucking moron?' she said more indignantly than before, her eyes distended. 'Do you think I don't know you'd never dream of showing your nose here unless you were absolutely certain he wasn't around? You sod.'

'Come on, only joking. Yes, as a matter of fact I've just come from the Glendower. Peter was there too. The three of us had a spot of lunch. Quite good it was. All right if I sit down?'

She conceded this with an ill grace. 'Why didn't you say something the other night at the Morgans'? Or you could have just picked up the –'

'I didn't get the chance. No, no, that's not true. I probably could have. I didn't happen to think of it then.'

'And when did you happen to think of it, may I ask?'

'Well . . . this morning. Can't remember what time. One moment nothing could have been further from my mind and the next I was full of it.'

'And you reckon you can just turn up like this, out of the bloody blue?'

'You could always chuck me out. I'd go quietly. You know that.'

'Still the same old Alun, eh?'

'Pretty much, yeah.' He paused. 'Go for a drive, shall we?'

This apparently innocent invitation held overtones for them that resounded from thirty years or more back, when their drives had taken them to a convenient spot behind the mental home, in better weather to the woods on the far side of the golf links and occasionally to the Prince Madoc out at Capel Mererid, in whose snug they had more than once behaved in a fashion that had never quite ceased to perturb Alun in retrospect, even today.

'No need,' said Sophie in reply. Her manner was still faintly tinged with resentment. 'There won't be anyone along.'

'What makes you so sure?'

'I'm sure.'

'Yes, but what makes you so sure?'

'I'll tell you later.'

'No, tell me now.'

'All right,' she said. 'When Victor puts him in a taxi he always gives me a ring to let me know. Because once when he stayed very late he pitched up passed out on the stool thing in the passport-photo booth at Cambridge Street station. And it just so happened that old Tudor Whittingham was on his way back from London and spotted him and fetched him home in a taxi, another taxi. He couldn't even remember being put into the first taxi.'

Alun pondered. 'But Victor giving you a ring won't stop him pitching up passed out at the station or anywhere else, will it?'

'No, but it sort of hands over the responsibility, see. I can understand it.'

'Oh, and I can. What does Victor think? About how that arrangement might, er, have a bearing on your own plans for, er, whatever it might be.'

'I don't know. I don't know what any of them think.'

'Who does? Has it come in handy before?'

'If I ever tell you that it's bloody going to be later.'

'Has that arrangement with Victor come in handy before?' he asked later.

'Do you consider you have the slightest right to expect me to answer that?'

'Absolutely not and absolutely none. Presuming on an old friendship.'

'You are a bugger. Well, sort of, just from time to time. Not ridiculous. Not like when . . .'

'No, of course not. How much does he know?'

'Same as ever, the whole score and nothing at all.'

'I'd say you and he have a pretty good life together on the whole.'

'I don't know about together exactly, but yes, we do really. Most afternoons while he's in town I'm down the shop.'

'Yes, the serviceable shop. I remember well. What do you actually do there?'

'I look at a pattern-book occasionally, and friends come in, and I drink a lot of coffee. I do about as much as he does at the Glendower. All quite relaxed. He knew all about me when he married me, of course. Well, quite a lot about me.'

'You two haven't been married all that terrifically long, have you?'

'No, not what you'd call terrifically long, only twenty-two years.'

'Good God, is it that much?' said Alun absently. 'Well now, you've never had children, have you? I suppose that's . . .'

'Just as well and no one could have put it clearer, and quite right too. You've forgotten, you've only just remembered I've always never had children. I don't know, some men would have done their homework before they barged in for a quick snuggle, or at least a bit of bloody revision.' She was dodgy again for a moment. 'How's your life then?'

'Fine. Never changes.'

'Oh? In that case I suppose you'll be looking up a few old friends round the neighbourhood. Like a couple of dozen. Always been like that with you, hasn't it?'

'The Don Juan syndrome. Rather a high-flown name, I've always thought. You know what they say? Comes from a desire to degrade and humiliate women. Well, there may be something in it, but if there is you'd have expected me to be particularly hot on women who'd be better off all round for a spot of degradation and humiliation, go round the place bloody well begging for it, like Muriel and fishface Eirwen Spurling. And I tell you frankly they leave me cold.'

Sophie had not listened attentively to this. 'Beats me,' she said, 'why a bloke married to someone like that has to go messing around with all and sundry.'

'You mentioned homework, well homework or no homework I remember you saying that to me slightly more than twenty-two years ago, and I'll tell you again now what I told you then: like buggery it beats you, you understand it through and through. You know you're right – *has* to go messing around. No choice involved – necessity. Easier, wiser, kinder . . . to accept it. But to hell with the years. Forget 'em. No problem where you're concerned. Believe it or not, I can't really remember how you used to look. Whenever I try I keep seeing you as you are now. You're just not different enough. Isn't that amazing, isn't that . . . splendid, isn't . . . that . . . marvellous . . .'

Much too late to spoil it the telephone-bell rang on the landing.

'That might be Victor now,' said Sophie.

Left to himself, Alun glanced briefly and incuriously round the capacious bedroom. Large and small, the things in it looked as if getting through money had been a principle of selection, starting with moulded wallpaper apparently encrusted with gems. His mind was traversed by banal, inescapable thoughts about the passing of time. Quite a lot of time had indeed passed, but so far to surprisingly small effect. What he had said to Sophie just now about her appearance and so on was of course untrue, though it would have been much untruer, one had to admit, of most other people he had known that long. But in a general way, applied to experience, it had a bearing. All sorts of stuff, for instance what had been taking place a little earlier, seemed much as before, or at any rate not different enough to start making a song and dance about. This state of affairs might well not last for ever, but for the moment, certainly, the less it changed the more it was the same thing, and the most noticeable characteristic of the past, as seen by him, at least, was that there was so much more of it now than formerly, with bits that were longer ago than had once seemed possible. Alun went for a pee.

When he came back to the bedroom Sophie had returned and was dressing.

'How long have we got?'

'Fifteen minutes minimum,' she said without looking up.

'I've done it in two and a half in my time, and with cuff-links and shoelaces.'

'Not so much talk.'

Tying his tie, Alun saw in the dressing-table mirror what he had not properly seen direct and earlier, that across from the double bed where they had lain there stood a made-up single bed. 'Who sleeps there?' he asked.

'He does. It's where he usually is.'

'Usually is? You mean sometimes he comes and —'

'No, no, it's where he lands up. I kick out in the mornings, see, and he goes over there when it gets too much.'

'What a jolly sensible set-up.'

Something about its description puzzled Alun, but he had never been one to be afflicted with disinterested curiosity and he had long forgotten the matter when, with six minutes to spare, he and Sophie came to say good-bye in the hall. (Six minutes, eh? Not such a marvellous arrangement.)

'Lovely to see you,' she cried as if he had indeed just dropped in for a cup of tea, then changed register and said 'You are a bugger' again, but resignedly this time.

Rejecting a first thought or so he said, 'You're lovely. I'll be along again soon. But I'll ring first.'

A shitty irony hovered when the car refused to start at once, but then it did. He turned it round, something to get done on arrival in future, and slid off down the hill. Clear. Six minutes, eh? Like the old days. Sophie soon slipped from his mind, but as always at this stage he felt utterly free, not triumphant, just never freer, never so free as now. Softly, shaping the notes, he broke into a pleasing light tenor:

'Was it young Denise who spread disease through all the men in the room?

Oh no, it wasn't young Denise, it was Mrs Rosenbloom . . .'

He took the road above Beaufoy which brought the sea into sight at a distance and, across the bay, the umber and dark-green stretch of Courcey, with vague industrial shapes half misted over in the background. For the moment the sun was out, strong enough to turn the water into something a bit more rewarding than grey-brown. Flat-fronted terraced houses reached by steep flights of steps gave place to semi-detached brick villas put up between the wars, a cluster of 1950s two-storey pre-fabs and then, further along and from further back, the spaced-out stone-built residences of the coal-owners and ironmasters of prosperous times.

Hereabouts Alun eased up on the accelerator and caused his face to take on expressions of boredom, dissatisfaction, even disappointment, getting it ready for a going-over by his daughter Rosemary. There was a definite element of the creepy about the way that girl could get the wrong idea about her father's less significant activities and interests. Up to something was what he could reckon on being charged with having been, not a moment ago either, if at encounters like this he showed any more positive feeling than a fairly plucky resignation. The girl was even worse in this respect than her elder sister, now safely married, or rather safely out of the way most of the time on that account. He could not have explained why these challenges of theirs made him so uncomfortable.

In the drawing-room mother and daughter had staked out a little feminine enclave on the fireside rug and a low coffee-table beside it with coffee-cups, biscuit-tin, box of chocolates, box of tissues, handbags, manicure kit, wastepaper basket, local map and dozens of estate-agents' brochures and lists. If he could get through the first minute in one piece, Alun knew he was probably going to be all right. He crossed in safety the twenty feet of minefield from the doorway and embraced his daughter. As always it was a warm embrace.

'Good lunch?' asked Rhiannon when he had kissed her.

'Not really. Quite bearable. We'll go there some time.'

'You saw Charlie? Like some coffee?'

'No thanks. Yes, he was there. And Peter.'

'Oh, was he really?' said Rhiannon, with pleasure and interest in her voice. 'How was he looking?'

'Not very well I thought. He's put on a lot of weight. But he's, you know, recognizable.'

'Oh. Well, he never was much of a bean-pole, was he?'

Rosemary, a darker and more robust-looking version of Rhiannon, had stood waiting for this part to end. She had been told years previously that before meeting her father in the long-ago her mother had had some sort of attachment to a university lecturer called Peter Thomas. What more she might have heard or guessed was unknown and she showed no reaction now. Indicating one of the brochures, she said, 'There's a house in Kinver Hill with attractive Swedish-type sun-room and unusual walled garden Mum and I are looking at at five. You're just in time to run us along there.'

'So I am indeed. Tell me, how would you have managed if it hadn't been for me turning up?'

'Minicab, same as she's been managing all week while you've been driving yourself to the pub and wherever else has taken your fancy. Come on, how many houses have you actually seen?'

'Christ love, I don't know. Not many. As few as possible. Three was it? Not my kind of thing. There's nothing you can say that'll drive me off the position that that kind of thing's a women's kind of thing.' Alun was busy hiding his relief at not after all being asked to account for himself, despite the unpleasant tilt in his daughter's last speech.

'You mean we've got to do it so we might as well like it. Well, here's one you're not getting out of, boy *bach*. Two, in fact. That's right, the place in Mary Tweed Lane'll be viewable at six, wasn't it, Mum?' Rosemary turned through the leaflets. 'Extensive hall with recessed fireplace and carved Victorian overmantel. Mum tells me you've got some scheme lined up for visiting places of scenic and historical interest in the surrounding vicinity.' She put on a quacking local accent for the last dozen words, efficiently enough though she had never lived in Wales. 'We'll go into the places another time, but of course part of the deal is while you're in Bargeman's Row exploring folkways and getting drunk you can't be in Pedwarsaint and Holland looking over houses. Well, for the next couple of days, Dad, resign yourself to a lot of looking over houses. You're not going to get away with leaving it all to Mum while I'm here. Right? Are you with me?'

Alun nodded without speaking. They always took it out of you for doing anything on your own, without them, however innocent, like glancing at a newspaper. Now he came to think of it, he had seen quite early the avoidance of house-viewing as an extra benefit of going in search of

Wales. And by the way four to one was way off – four and a half it was, with Rhiannon, now furtively winking and peering at him, the half and Rosemary the four.

Well, roughly. Far from the least ill feeling the style of her harangue had shown affection of a sort, but the sort that mitigated the sense of her words not at all. She came and linked arms with him when at last they moved off, kissed him on the cheek and gave him a smile that exactly blended fondness and disapproval. It was the best he could reasonably have hoped for.

Three – Charlie

1

When Charlie Norris noticed that the smallest man in the submarine railway-carriage had a face made out of carpeting he decided it was time to be off. By throwing himself about and sucking in air fast and deep he got away and back to his bed in the dark. Intensely thirsty as usual he at once reached for one of the several glasses of water lined up on the low table beside him, but before he found it his hand was grabbed and worried by some creature with very long narrow jaws. It made croaking, creaking noises. He cried out, or thought he did, and pulled his body away like a swimmer surfacing, and then he was really back.

He could hear Sophie breathing quietly in the bed across the way and started to throw the covers of his own bed back before going on to scramble in beside her and nestle up to her. Then he worked out that he had done that twice in the last ten days or so and a third time now would be too much. She always woke up at his arrival however careful he was, whether he nestled up or not, and though she always said later that she dropped off again in a couple of minutes he doubted it. And after all, he had not found himself at the edge of one of those huge, brilliantly lit stretches of grassland with ruined pillars and water flowing uphill and changing its course as it went, nor had to deal with small things, small unrecognizable animals or machines behaving like animals. So for the moment he stayed there leaning on his elbow.

It was not really dark. He could even see part of Sophie's outline in the light of the hooded lamp next to him. Other gleams came from the passage doorway and its reflection in the tall mirror by the window. An early car receded towards the town. He was quite safe, also no less thirsty in the real world than in the unreal and standing in need of a pee. Not till he was back tucked up after supplying these wants did he look at his watch: 5.10. Not too bad. He felt as if about two-thirds of his head had recently been sliced off and his heart seemed to be beating somewhere inside his stomach, but otherwise he was fine, successfully monitoring his breathing over about the next hour until he fell into a kind of doze, not a very nice kind, admittedly.

It was light when he came out of that and he was not at all fine, nowhere near. As usual at this time, his morning self cursed his overnight self for having purposely left the Scotch in the drinks cabinet downstairs. Without that sort of help it was quite out of the question that he should ever get up. A mug of tea and a plastic flask containing more tea stood on the bedside table. He would in no sense be committing himself to getting up if it so turned out that he drank some. With this clear all round he got on his elbow and drank some, drank indeed the whole mug's worth in one because it was half cold, and dropped flat again. Before very long the liquid had carved out a new and more direct route to his bladder. He rolled over and fixed his eye on the stout timber that framed the quilted bed-head, counted a hundred, then, with a convulsive overarm bowling movement, got a hand to it, gripped it, counted another hundred and hauled with all his strength, thus pulling himself half upright.

In this position, still clutching the frame, he paused

again, said 'With many a weary sigh, and many a groan, up a high hill he heaves a huge round stone,' and plunged a foot to the floor. Of course it was understood that if he ever got to the bathroom he would dive straight back into bed the moment he got back in range. Having got back he went and laid his hands flat on the dressing-table either side of Sophie's chased-silver hand-mirror and looked out of the window, looking but not seeing. With a conviction undimmed by having survived countless previous run-offs he felt that everything he had was lost and everyone he knew was gone. Only because there was nothing else to do he stood there assembling the energy to move, to start dressing, rather in the spirit of a skier poised above a hazardous run. Ready? Right . . . *Go*. Up. Round. Off.

'I'm just popping over to Rhiannon's,' Sophie told him in the kitchen. 'They think they've found a house but she wants me and Gwen to go over it with her. One of the ones backing on to Holland woods. You know, where the Aubreys used to live. Er, Dilys'll be along at eleven and Mr Bridgeman's here, round the front he is now, so you'll be all right.' She referred to the daily woman and the ex-docker who tended the garden and cleaned an occasional window and suchlike. 'I'll be here from about half-four on. Hope your do is fun. Expect you when I see you, love,' she ended on a formulaic note, kissed the top of his head and went.

After ten minutes Charlie had made it all the way from the breakfast-room table to the refrigerator in the kitchen. Here he stood and drank a great deal of apple-juice and crunched a half-burnt, holed piece of toast Sophie had rejected; making his own toast – bread-bin, toaster, all that – was unthinkable. Along with it he swallowed a couple of spoonfuls of marmalade straight from the pot. The sight of a coffee-bag out in the open near an unused mug was not quite enough to make up his mind for him, but finding the electric kettle half full turned the scale. He saw the thing through and even got some sugar in, stirring with the marmalade-spoon. When a speck of saliva caught at the back of his throat he managed to lay the mug down before the father and mother of a coughing-fit sent him spinning about the room and landing up face to face with Mr Bridgeman, round the back now, eighteen inches away on the other side of the window-pane. Then the telephone rang as it always did at about that time of the morning.

'Charles, it's Victor. How are you today?'

'About the same as usual.'

'Oh, I'm sorry to hear it.' Sometimes Victor said that and sometimes he said he was glad it was no worse. 'Listen, Charlie, I'm fed up with Griffiths & Griffiths. Fed up to *by here*, my dear,' he said, turning a local vulgarism to his own purposes. 'Half of what they sent up yesterday was unusable. As you remember we talked of experimenting with Lower Glamorgan Products. May I proceed with that?'

'Go ahead.' Charlie had long since stopped wondering why his brother bothered to pursue the fiction of their joint responsibility for the affairs of the Glendower. The boredom of it was therapeutic, though.

'Good, thank you. The other thing is I've taken against the house white. Horrid little ninny of a wine. As regards a replacement I have one or two ideas to try on you. Will you be in later?'

'Actually I'm not quite sure today. There's the ceremony at St Dogmael's with a piss-up at the Prince of Wales after.'

'Don't remind me, I wouldn't have missed it for anything, the ceremony that is, chance to see Mr Posturing Ponce going all out. The trouble is young Chris. The poor boy's picked up some sort of bug and I've sent him to bed, no one to leave in charge. But listen Charlie, you round up three or four notables at that get-together if you can and bring them along here for lunch on the house. Only if you can. Ring before if possible. The coq au vin is going to be a positive dream. All right?'

'I'll have to study the ground but I'll try.'

'Oh good lad. You sound a little more cheerful now. Take care of yourself, Charles.'

The mug of coffee had not got any hotter but Charlie drank it anyway in the interests of rehydration. By and by he also drank a weakish whisky and water, having held off till then because he made a point of avoiding early drinking whenever he could. At eleven o'clock a minicab arrived to take him into town. While, yawning his head off, he climbed aboard he told himself, as he always did at this juncture, that he really must sell his old Renault, which sat in the garage unused for years except by Sophie when her own car was laid up. He would set about it tomorrow.

The journey took him past many places, but none of more interest than Lower Glamorgan County Hall, half a dozen times the size of the old Glamorgan County Hall in Cardiff, indeed a miniature new town in itself. Its inmates were said to enjoy the use of uncounted cocktail bars, tastefully lit dining-rooms, discos, jacuzzis, hairdressing salons, massage parlours and intensive-care units while not actually defrauding the populace, all this situated conveniently close to Jenkyn's Farm, otherwise the gaol. Notable too, and further in, were the docks where once Mr Bridgeman had earned a very respectable wage and enriched himself in other ways as well. Now, where once ships by the dozen had lain, bringing timber, ores, pig-iron, fetching coal, coke, spelter, there was just the harbour dredger, looking as if it had not yet been out that year, and a single dirty little freighter flying the blue, white and red of Yugoslavia.

Sophie's image as he had seen her an hour before, brisk and neat in her tightly belted light-blue mack, stayed in Charlie's mind. You only had to look at her to be assured that men with faces made out of carpeting played no part in her life; it took longer to establish that she made every allowance she could for anybody involved with such men. In those twenty-two years of marriage he had not perhaps got to know her very well, but almost his strongest feeling for her, stronger than envy, was respect, even admiration. Provided things were left to her there would never be any trouble, not even over Alun. If Charlie had not felt certain, as early as the moment of sitting down to lunch at the Glendower, where Alun proposed to go afterwards, the clean sheets on Sophie's bed midweek would have told him the score. But let it be. As always, he and Sophie had not exchanged so much as a glance about it. Let it be. Something like half-way through the twenty-two years he had in any case given up a large part of the right to a say in that area of Sophie's life.

St Dogmael's came up on the landward side, another of the town's deconsecrated churches. This one had been converted not into a pornographic cinema but, less inoffensively some might have thought, into an arts centre. The structure had been extensively restored in 1895, though parts of the clerestory were traceable to a fourteenth-century rebuilding by Henry de Courcy. These facts and many more were to be found in a pamphlet sold at the extensive bookstall and information office in the west porch. To one side of the porch entrance there had stood, longer than anyone could remember, a short, dingy stone pillar supporting a life-sized figure too badly battered and weathered to be recognizable even as a man, but always vaguely supposed to have portrayed the saint. Today the whole thing was covered with a great red cloth and seventy or eighty people, some hung with civic and other paraphernalia, were standing close by and producing a loud jabber of talk diversified with the sportive female shrieks prevalent in the locality.

Charlie had cut it fine. He stopped his car several yards short, paid the driver, a Chinese with an alarming Greenhill accent, and stole up to the edge of the crowd. A rather fat man of about fifty, with short white hair, a long doughy face and wide eyes, turned towards him.

'Good morning, sir,' he said loudly in a North American accent.

'Good morning,' said Charlie, and felt like running there and then. He had taken a turn for the better in the last half-hour, but it was nothing that could not be undone by any sudden bit of strain, such as this chap looked more than competent to provide.

'May I introduce myself? I am Llywelyn Caswallon Pugh.'

And at that accursed name the whole assembly fell silent. At least that was how it appeared to Charlie for a dazed moment, like something out of the Mabinogion. Then he realized that the hushing agent must have been one or another of the central group of notables and others that, he now saw, included Alun. Throughout what followed, photographers were to be seen and heard near this group and a man wielding what must have been a sort of portable television camera was there too.

A series of semi-intelligible pronouncements began by way of a microphone and one or two loudspeakers. As it proceeded the man Pugh, who now struck Charlie as distinctly deranged, kept sending him purposeful glances, promising him more to come, more to be communicated than just what he was called. Across the way, near the shape under the cloth, a smartly dressed youth who had to be the mayor introduced the, or perhaps merely a, minister of state at the Welsh Office. This man, who seemed scarcely older, spoke some formula and jerked at the end of an ornamental rope or cord that Charlie had not noticed before. With wonderful smoothness the red cloth parted and fell to reveal, standing on a plinth of what looked like olive-green marble, a shape in glossy yellow metal that was about the height of a human being without looking much more like one than the beaten-up chunk of stone that had stood there before.

There was a silence that probably came less from horror than sheer bafflement, then a sudden rush of applause. The presumed sculptor, a little fellow covered in hair like an artist in a cartoon, appeared and was the centre of attention for a few seconds. Another youngster, who said he represented the Welsh Arts Council, started talking about money. It came on to rain, though not enough to bother a Welsh crowd. On a second glance, the object on the plinth did look a certain amount like a man, but the style ruled out anything in the way of portraiture, and Charlie felt he was probably not the only one to wonder whether some handy abstraction – the spirit of Wales, say – had pushed out the advertised subject. Those close enough, however, could see Brydan's name on the plate along with just his dates, 1913–1960.

Alun's turn came. He played it low-key, avoiding a display of emotion so long after the event, sticking to facts, facts like Brydan being the greatest Welsh poet that had ever lived and also the greatest poet in the English language to have lived in the present century, together with minor but no less certain facts like his utter dedication to his art, though leaving out other ones like his utter dedication to

Jack Daniel's Tennessee whiskey and *Astounding Science Fiction*. Llywelyn Caswallon Pugh evidently thought he could afford to do without some of this. He stepped up the frequency of his glances at Charlie and slowly edged closer. He had a considerable power of instilling dread, in Charlie at least. When he spoke it was a little less loud than before.

'Excuse me, sir, but would that gentleman there be Mr Alun Weaver, CBE?'

'It would,' answered Charlie, panting slightly. 'That's him.'

'And would you yourself happen to be personally acquainted with him?'

'I would. I mean yes, I know him.'

'Might you be good enough to introduce me after this ceremony?'

He must be doing it on purpose, thought Charlie, and to no possible benign end. This really was the time to run, or at least walk briskly away – quicker, cleaner, kinder – but he was not up to breaking through the thin but solid cordon of bodies that now stood between him and freedom. So he babbled some form of assent and tried to shut himself off from Pugh and everyone else for as long as possible, dreamily looking back on those distant mornings of mere headache and nausea.

Alun was beginning to take a winding-up tone. As he spoke he moved his gaze slowly from one extremity of his audience to the other so that no one should feel left out. 'Too much has sometimes been made,' he said, 'of the undeniable fact that Brydan knew no Welsh, was altogether ignorant of the language. This was a matter of the purest chance, a matter of fashion only. Parents in the South Wales of the era before World War I saw fit to bring up their children to speak nothing but English. But nobody who knows his work and who knows Wales and the Welsh language can be in any doubt that that land and that language live in that work. He had no literal, word-for-word understanding, but at a deep, instinctive, primal level he understood. He felt and he sensed something beyond words . . .'

When Alun had finished, someone else pronounced a few phrases of thanks or thanksgiving or anyway termination. All present relaxed and looked about, but at first none moved. Charlie was trapped physically and by obligation of a sort, but also by his own curiosity: he was going to be around when this transatlantic Welshman came up against Alun or . . . Well no, not perish, but know the reason why. This resolve flagged rather when Pugh turned towards him again and drew in air to say more to him. He had been mad not to drop in at the Glendower on the way to a horror like this. Would he never learn?

'May I know your name, sir?'

Charlie gave it and found himself throwing in his occupation like a fool.

'I am an official of the Cymric Companionship of the USA,' said Pugh.

At this point something terrible happened to Charlie's brain. Pugh went on speaking in just the same way as before, with no change of pace or inflection, but Charlie could no longer distinguish any words, only noises. His eyes swam a little. He stepped backwards and trod heavily on someone's foot. Then he picked out a noise he recognized and nearly fell over the other way with relief. It had not been fair to expect an old soak whose Welsh vocabulary started and stopped with *yr* and *bach* and *myn* to recognize the rubbish when it came at him unheralded in an American accent. 'M'm,' he said with feeling. 'M'm.'

Pugh's wide stare widened further in a way that made

Charlie wonder what he had assented to, but that was soon over and more English came. 'A key objective of the Companionship is the forging and maintenance of ties with the mother country.'

A capful of rain blew refreshingly into Charlie's face and a seagull passed close enough overhead to make him flinch. 'Sounds a first-rate idea.'

'Uh-huh. In pursuance of which my purpose today is to solicit Mr Weaver to guest-visit with my home chapter of the Companionship at Bethgelert, Pennsylvania for a designated period. Consequentially my desire to make his acquaintance.'

Charlie appreciated this attempt at courteous explanation. He felt he understood the sense of it too; things were coming a little easier now. While he looked round for Alun he found he could imagine with ridiculous ease – he had perhaps even heard – him saying that all he needed was a free invitation over there, never mind to how God-forsaken a part, anything to give him a base, and he would be off and away. Well, the bloody old Welsh chancer's chance had come at last. But hey, those Stateside Taffs must hold an alarmingly high opinion of the said Welsh chancer. How could they have acquired it?

Alun, closely attended by three or four functionaries, had just begun to move in the direction of a line of official-looking cars, and in no time there was Charlie with Pugh at his side barring the way and doing the introducing.

'Mr Pugh has something to do with the . . .'

'Cymric Companionship of the USA. I'm honoured to meet you, sir. I wrote you care of your –'

'How nice to meet you, Mr Pugh. Where exactly are you from?'

'Bethgelert, Pennsylvania, which is situated –'

'Dear, dear, there are Welshmen all over the world,

aren't there? Saxons, give up hope of finding a pie under the sun that we harmless folk don't contrive to slide our sly fingers into. Carry my warmest cousinly greetings to the Celts of Bethgelert, Mr Pugh. Now . . .'

'Mr Pugh wants to invite you there,' called Charlie hurriedly.

The fluid, seamless way Alun converted his unthinking glance towards the waiting car into an urgent request for assistance, for somebody to accommodate his Mr Pugh, was something Charlie was quite sure he would never forget. Good too was Alun's look of measured eagerness to hear anything the fellow might say. Just ahead of them, somebody dissatisfied with some of the arrangements barred their way of departure for the moment.

'Bethgelert is situated in that part of the state containing a large Welsh element. In fact William Penn desired that the Commonwealth as a whole be designated New Wales, but the English government interdicted the proposition.'

Pugh laid special stress on the last few words, but if he had succeeded in whipping up separatist feeling in his hearers they gave no sign, though Alun's air of expectation perhaps waned slightly. But he seemed to cheer up again when Pugh started on his next offering.

'We in Bethgelert have been privileged to welcome many distinguished Welsh persons. We were honoured with a visit from Brydan in 1954. The occasion is memorialized by a plaque inscribed in Welsh and English in Neuadd Taliesin, our meeting-house. There also hangs there a portrait of Brydan in oil paints executed by Mrs Bronwen Richards Weintraub, a member of our council.'

'When were you thinking of –' began Alun, but Pugh raised a hand, just an inch or two from the wrist, and continued as before.

'Mrs Weintraub relied chiefly on photographs, but

visitors who knew Brydan in life pronounced it an excellent likeness.'

There was something final and definitive in the delivery and reception of that remark. Up front, the missing man or car had been found or despaired of and movement was resumed. Alun said thoughtfully, 'Tell me, Mr Pugh, where would I stay in Bethgelert?'

'Why, with me, Mr Weaver. A bachelor establishment, but comfortable enough I assure you. I'll enjoy showing you our neighbourhood.'

'I look forward to it.' Alun stood now by the rear door of his destined car. 'I think the spring of 1995 would be about right for my visit.'

'You must be –'

'No, better say the autumn. The fall. I am very busy just at the moment. Nice to have met you. Good day to you. Charlie, in round the other side.'

At the moment before he ducked his head under the car roof Charlie caught a last glimpse of Pugh, looking not totally unlike an inflated rubber figure out of whose base the stopper had been drawn an instant earlier. Charlie might have felt some pity if he had not been lost in admiration for Alun.

'Bloody marvellous bit of timing,' he told him when they were settled in the back seats.

'Yeah, nice bonus, but on a note like that I could have outfaced the bugger indefinitely. And by the way I reckon bugger is right, don't you? I'd whiffed it even before we got to the bachelor establishment, just in that second.'

'Probably, but I was a bit too overwhelmed with the rest of him to notice much.'

The car had still not moved. Alun squinted forward through his window.

'There he goes, poor dab. I should have recommended

him to that Gents by the fire station. Most likely not in business any more, though, like everything else.'

Out of pure devilment Charlie said, 'I suppose he did get the message all right, do you think?'

'What? How do you mean?'

'Well you were frightfully polite to him, you know. Took him very seriously.'

'Perhaps there was a touch of that.'

'I mean you don't want him coming through on the phone asking if he can discuss it with you. Find a way round your objections.'

'No, I don't, do I? My God.'

By now the car had started to crawl along beside the pavement. Again Alun peered through his window, then took a quick glance at the traffic ahead. He started to roll down the window with his left hand and arranged his right with the thumb and first two fingers extended and the other two clenched.

'That's English, what you've got there,' said Charlie quickly. 'Middle finger only for Americans.'

'Christ, you're right, thanks. Well . . . here we go.' Alun stuck his head and hand out of the opening and Charlie heard him bawl, 'Make it two thousand. The year two thousand. And fuck off.'

The car accelerated nimbly. By a blessed chance Charlie got another last sight of Pugh out of the back window, much reduced now from the comparative equanimity he had shown a minute before. What tale of this would he tell in Bethgelert?

'They do say fuck off in America, don't they?' asked Alun anxiously.

'I'm sure they understand it.'

'And it doesn't mean how's your father or anything?'

'Not that I know of, no.'

'I thought I'd better clinch it, you see. Sort of make assurance double sure.'

'Yes, I can't see him bothering you again.'

Alun laughed quietly for a short time, shaking his head in indulgent self-reproach. The driver, who had the collar of a tartan sports shirt turned down over that of his blue serge suit, spoke up.

'Trying to cadge a lift, was he, that bloke back there?'

'Roughly.'

'Funny-looking sort of bloke. He reminded me –'

'Yes, well we can forget about him now and concentrate on getting to the Prince of Wales as fast as we reasonably can.' Evidently Alun had no wish just then to pursue the special Welsh relationship with drivers of taxis as mentioned to Rhiannon. He lowered his voice and went on, 'Hey – timing really was important for that. A clear getaway afterwards. I got badly caught in Kilburn once telling a Bulgarian short-story writer, actually he *was* trying to cadge a lift, anyway telling him to fuck off for two or three minutes while the chap driving the open car I was sitting in turned round in the cul-de-sac I hadn't noticed we were at the end of. Amazing how quickly the bloom fades on fuck off, you know. Say it a couple of times running and you've got out of it nearly all of what you're going to get.'

'And there's not a lot you can go on to later,' said Charlie.

'Well exactly.'

'What really got you down about Pugh, made you dump him? One thing more than another. I mean apart from his interest in rugby. Of course he was unstoppably American, I do see.'

'He can't help that, love him. No, I could have taken that. Well, taken it more cheerfully than him being even more savagely Welsh. I've heard about those buggers in

Pennsylvania. You know what they are, do you? Bloody Quakers. You're doing well if they let you smoke there. And you know what they get up to? Speaking Welsh. Talking Welsh to each other on purpose.'

'Yes, he talked some to me.'

'Well, there you are then,' said Alun, glaring indignantly at Charlie. 'How can you deal with a bastard like that?'

'I wonder you didn't give him the thumbs-down as soon as you heard where he was from, at that rate.'

'Oh, I couldn't have done that. That would have looked rude. And anyway at that stage I couldn't be sure he wasn't going to, I don't know, say fuck or something and show he was a human being. I think a drink's what I'd like now.'

They went through the hall of the Prince of Wales, which by some reactionary whim had ordinary carpets on the floor and pictures of recognizable scenes on the walls, up in the photograph-infested lift and into the glittering meanness of what was no doubt called a banqueting-room with slender, softly gleaming pillars. But, fair play, it had a bar in it, plus a table serving wine only, which kept a few unserious drinkers out of the road. One advantage of Charlie's trade, now only to be called that in a manner of speaking but for many years an accurate description, was that he tended to know waitresses. Off this one he got, well ahead of his turn, a whisky and water that would have struck some other men as a nice lunchtime session's worth, and quite surprised himself by finding how much he had needed it. Clutching its successor, he made his way straight towards Alun, who had pleaded for moral support in alien territory. The Cellan-Davieses were also close by, in fact Malcolm was in the middle of asking Alun a question.

'Called what again? Llywelyn what Pugh?'

'I'm not clear, Charlie heard it.'

'It sounded like Caswallon.'

'Oh, Caswallon,' said Malcolm, with a tremendous hissing scrape on the double L. 'Better known as Cassivellaunus.'

'Now you're talking,' said Gwen, nodding busily.

'A British chieftain who fought the Romans in –'

'Look, baby, baby, cool it, okay?' said Alun. 'We've had enough history for one morning. William Penn and Cassivellaunus – next, the Patagonians, many of whom, my friends, are bilingual in Welsh and Spanish.'

'I think it's a pity you ditched Mr Pugh,' said Gwen. 'He and Malcolm sound as if they were made for each other. Can't you get him back?'

To Charlie's ear there was a bit extra there, but when he looked up it was to see someone of consequence joining the group. Nobody was to ask who he was and he knew all he needed to about who they were. In appearance, including hair-style and clothes, he was like a good average town councillor, from Yorkshire rather than South Wales, in a black-and-white film of twenty-five years before. Two lesser persons were with him.

'Well now,' he said in the kind of husky alto often put down to massive gin-drinking, 'what's the state of feeling about our new piece of sculpture?'

'Oh Christ,' said Alun as if before he could stop himself. 'Er . . . actually we haven't discussed it, have we? It's not what I'd call my field. Gwen, you're good on art.'

'That's sweet of you, Alun. Well, it hasn't got any holes in it. You can say that much for it.'

A short guessing-game followed and ended with the disclosure that the start-to-finish, all-in cost of having the sculpture there was £98,000.

'Makes you think, doesn't it?' said Alun. 'You could get a couple of torpedoes for that.'

'Oh, surely they're much more expensive,' said Malcolm. 'I was reading –'

'To hell with it – half a bloody torpedo, then. A quarter, I don't care.'

'It's the principle of the thing,' said Gwen.

'If you don't mind,' croaked the questioner, 'could we forget about torpedoes for the moment and get back to the sculpture? You, Mr . . . ,' he turned to Charlie, 'you haven't said anything yet.'

'No, well . . . I thought it wasn't at all figurative,' said Charlie rather complacently.

'Is that all? Has nobody anything more, er, more, er, more constructive to put forward?'

Nobody had.

'So nobody here shares my feeling that the Brydan monument is an exciting breakthrough for all of us in this town?'

Like everyone else, Charlie at once ruled out the possibility of any sort of irony being intended. There was general silence, with eyes on the floor, until Gwen said in a voice not intended to carry far, 'If you're going to call that, or anything like that, exciting, what do you call the late-night horror movie? When it's slightly above average?' She frowned and smiled as never before.

Alun nodded weightily. 'Very good point,' he said.

'My colleagues and I had hoped for a little bit of encouragement. Here we are going all out, fighting to bring the best in modern art to the people, to whom after all it belongs and not to any fancy élite, and people like you, educated people, don't want to know. You don't, do you? You're happier with your cosy, musty Victoriana. Safe I suppose it makes you feel. Anything challenging you give a wide berth to. Well, I take leave to doubt whether your reaction is typical. Good day to you.'

The man of position jerked his head at his aides to signal a move in a way that recalled a boss in a different kind of film, returning from a few paces off long enough to add, 'You're entitled to your opinions, it goes without saying, but they're clearly based on ignorance, whereas the artist in question was selected and instructed by a panel of experts. Kindly take due note of that.'

When he was clear, Alun said with great emphasis, his voice shaking slightly, 'It's all right when little turds and turdettes, especially the latter, go on about exciting break-throughs in advertisements and arts pages, well of course it isn't *all right* but we're used to it, we've got our defences against it. And it was all right when buggers like that were fighting to stop *Desire under the Elms* being put on at the Royal and going all out to get Joyce and Lawrence *and* *T. S. Eliot* off the shelves of the public library. You're too young to remember a bloody old fool and by the bye frightful shit called Bevan Hopkin who called the police in at a Renoir exhibition at the Trevor Knudsen – in 1953, not 1903. That's how he was supposed to behave. Imagine him in favour of anything challenging. Imagine him *knowing the word*. When Labour councillors in South Wales start blathering about taking modern art to the people everyone's in deep trouble. Come back, Bevan Hopkin, all, repeat all, is forgiven. Well, *Iesu Crist* and no mistake.'

'*Grist*,' said Gwen. '*Iesu Grist*. With the soft mutation.'

'Oh, bugger it. I'm going to give up. Had enough. Oh God here's another lot,' said Alun, turning to Charlie. 'We'd better be off soon.'

'I'm off now but I'll be back.'

Charlie just made it round the flank of the mayoral contingent and, picking up a fresh glass on the way, dodged into the lavatory. Here he waited for the two already present to leave, filled the glass at a basin, locked himself in a compartment and let go the ultimate coughing-fit that had been hanging about him for the last hour. Somebody else came in and used the urinal during it, groaning a lot as if in sympathy. He drank more water and took some deep breaths, feeling much weaker but clearer in the head, like a man in a book by John Buchan after an attack of fever. On departure he noticed that, as he put it later, the place reeked like an Alexandria knocking-shop.

He walked up the corridor, on carpet very luxurious to the eye but somehow disagreeable underfoot, until he reached a row of telephones separated from the outside only by small roofs shaped like Romanesque arches.

Victor answered his ring and sounded pleased. 'How are you, Charles? How reads the latest bulletin?'

'One of the more magical days. Look, er, I'm afraid I shan't be able to manage the lunch idea. There's a pub-crawl thing in Harriston I said I'd go on I'd completely forgotten. Sorry.'

'Charlie, I'm afraid I've no idea what you're talking about. A lunch . . . ?'

'You asked me to try to get some selected shits together and bring them –'

'Oh, that. Never mind, it was just a thought. Another time. How was Posturing Ponce?'

'Quite good, actually. Well, he was terrible at the unveiling thing, but came back stoutly later. There was a collector's-item Welsh-American queer there he brushed off in fine style.'

'Brushed him off? You mean he –'

'No, no. He invited Alun to go and stay with him in his bachelor quarters in Pennsylvania or Philadelphia or wherever it is.'

'I suppose there's no chance of him going? Because that really would be a turn-up for the book.' For a moment

Victor's voice went falsetto with laughter. 'PP in Pennsylvania with one of that lot.' That lot stayed in the third person in dealings between the brothers. 'Too much to ask. Well – enjoy your pub-crawl. You'll be in later, will you?'

'Probably, but for once I'm not too sure when.'

'Any time you like, Charles.'

When he got back to it the party seemed to have dwindled a good deal, or perhaps had merely spread out to the edges. At any rate the mayoral squad was on the point of leaving; the chap who had liked the sculpture was nowhere to be seen. An old man with a pink-and-white complexion – pink round the nose and eyes, white elsewhere – stood by the wall opening and shutting his jaws at a great rate. Large oval dishes of uncommonly horrible finger-snacks, a vivid green or orange in colour, lay here and there almost untouched, and quite right too, thought Charlie, also quite understandable now that everybody was either too fat or living off chaff and whey.

The drink, on the other hand, had been very popular, so much so that at the moment there was no Scotch available and no one to serve it anyway. Charlie placed himself at the corner of the bar where he could grab the waitress on her return. Two others with empty glasses had taken up the same station, a fellow in his sixties with a small face that seemed the smaller for the elaborately strutted and cantilevered pair of spectacles on it, and a younger, dark-complexioned man of melancholy, thoughtful appearance, not unlike Garth, a common Welsh type not often noted for either quality. Both looked up at Charlie's arrival and nodded to him in a subdued but friendly way, seeming to know him, and quite likely they did know him, had at least seen him more than once in the way of business, at a function of this sort, in a club, in a bar. Round here you had a pretty good idea of who everybody was, which helped on some kinds of contact without doing anything for others.

Accordingly the two pursued their conversation while going out of their way not to exclude Charlie from it. 'You'll find the same everywhere,' the older man was saying, 'not just in our chosen field. Did you see about that ambassador bloke who brought home too much wine?'

'No I didn't see that, I must have missed it,' said the dark man, glancing at Charlie, and Charlie nodded to show he had missed it too.

'Well, you couldn't have a more perfect illustration of the point under discussion. When you retired, you see, from your last ambassadorial post you got a duty-free allowance, known as your cellar, a certain amount of wine you were allowed to bring back to England as a privilege. The exact number of bottles was never fixed: it was left to your discretion, and everyone was happy. Until one fine day Sir This-and-that turns up with ten, twenty times what was reasonable. And that was it. As from the next day, no more allowance. No more cellar.'

'Ruined it for everyone. What appalling selfishness.'

'Indeed. I hope I needn't ram home the moral. In other areas the custom has grown up over the years of people in certain positions being deemed to be entitled to certain privileges. Of – and this is the point – a modest and limited order. And everyone is happy, until . . .'

'Until somebody goes beyond what is reasonable.'

'Exactly. Human greed,' said the older man, staring into vacancy through his spectacles. 'Human greed. Well,' he went on with humorous impatience, 'where's this bloody Scotch we've heard so much about?'

'What's the use of sitting in the dispensary when there's nothing for a sore throat?'

'A bit thick, I call it,' said Charlie.

'Ah – wait a minute. Remedy in sight. About time too. Grateful for small mercies. The relief of Mafeking. I knew you loved me, darling.' The three of them said all this and much more, until the glasses were refilled and the water, soda and ice had gone round. Everyone was very relaxed.

'Thankfully,' said the older man – 'thankfully the picture is not uniformly bleak. I'm thinking of one bright spot in particular. Aneirin Pignatelli.' This set the dark man nodding with his eyes closed. 'You know who I'm talking about, of course?'

'Well, naturally,' said Charlie, himself nodding. He was nearly sure he had heard the name somewhere.

'And I take it most people are sufficiently aware of what happened to him.'

Charlie went on nodding.

'He showed himself to be a man of the highest integrity. When he came out' – the pause here was not really necessary – 'he couldn't get into his front room for the flowers.'

At this stage Charlie did show puzzlement, slightly, briefly, unintentionally. In an instant the last speaker turned his small face aside. 'From all the people he hadn't brought down with him,' said the other with a hint of vexation.

Charlie hastened to say 'Yes yes' and make a silly-of-me gesture, but it was too late. The spell of something like intimacy was shattered. The interloper took himself off, though not before he had topped up his glass, with a couple of cold stares to speed him on his way.

Looking vaguely about, Charlie saw Alun and Gwen at the far end of the main room. As he came up behind Gwen he heard Alun say in his quick style, 'I try to get out of lecturing whenever I can these days. Would a reading do instead?'

'Oh, er, I should think so,' said Gwen, turning. 'I'll let you know.'

'But don't worry, I'll be there. Charlie, time to be away, old boy.'

'Why aren't you going to the mayor's lunch?' asked Charlie. 'There must be one, surely.'

'Oh, there's a lunch, but I've got a date with my mates, haven't I? Where's Malcolm got to? And even if I hadn't I couldn't face another mayoral do. Had enough officialdom for one day.'

'You've got to remember he's an artist,' said Gwen.

'And, doubtless more plausibly in the eyes of some, the lunch won't be reported, the ceremony will. I'll see you up at the Picton, Charlie – I've got to dash off somewhere first. One of those things that won't keep.'

2

To Charlie waiting at the exit, it seemed to take about as long for Malcolm to get his car out of the multi-storey over the road from Tesco as it would to get the country out of the Common Market. But, having little real alternative, he turned up in the end and drove the two of them through the outskirts on a good old rainy Welsh afternoon. They passed the ruins of the castle and not long afterwards the ruins of the copper-smeltery. Here and there were conical knolls covered with grass and even supporting bushes or young trees, the overgrown spoilheaps of long-vanished collieries. The road led upwards beside the waters of the Iwerne and the walls of the valley began to rise, with bigger hills fuzzily in view further off. Then, just as some sort of countryside seemed about to come into sight, human habitations reappeared, shops, offices, pubs too, all quite as grimy as when the air was thick with coal-dust.

'Here we are,' said Malcolm, steering round a corner. 'Or are we? I can't see any –'

'What's the trouble?' asked Charlie, ducking and peering.

'It just says Streets where the Picton sign used to be. Streets? What are they talking about?'

'Let's have a look.'

Malcolm parked outside a lilac-painted boutique on a site Charlie was nearly sure had once been occupied by a Marxist bookshop, only that would have been a bit too good to be true. Everywhere else was apparently selling either electronic equipment or large steakwiches and jacket potatoes with cheese-and-onion topping. A man's voice crying the *Evening Post* might have been from another world.

As they walked the needful not-very-many yards, huddled up against the thin rain, Malcolm spoke to Charlie, who for the second time in less than two hours had the experience of being addressed with one-hundred-per-cent unintelligibility by someone who had been making perfect sense a moment before.

'I'm sorry, Malcolm, I must be going round the bend, I couldn't follow a single word of that. Could you try again?'

'My fault,' said Malcolm, blushing a good deal. 'It was supposed to be your friend Cassivellaunus Pugh asking about General Picton. I mean I didn't hear him but I assume he had an American accent. I'm afraid I can't have done it very well.'

'Pembrokeshire man, wasn't he, Picton?' asked Charlie kindly.

'Yes, well part of Dyfed as it is now.'

'Fuck the lot of them,' said Charlie in a considered way.

'Who? Fuck who?'

'The London bastards who changed all the Welsh counties about. Even my kind of Welshman resents that. And then gave them all these crappy ancient names.'

'It was done in the interests of efficiency.' Malcolm was nothing if not fair-minded.

'That's where you're wrong. It was done in the interests of my bum.'

They plunged from the rain into the dark, echoing tunnel or underpassage that led to a side entrance, sometimes in the past scattered with boozers' muck, immaculate now and with its old cobblestones torn up and replaced by concrete. Indoors the continuing gloom was relieved by what looked like, and indeed proved on closer inspection to be, old-fashioned lamp-posts. More light, treated so as rather to resemble daylight, came from or through the glass ceiling. The walls were got up as shop-fronts, brick-pillared gateways, a park with railings, plastic shrubs and a white planking pavilion. The vast shape of Peter Thomas could be made out towards the back, sitting on a green-and-white-striped canvas chair near a stone-and-wrought-iron well-head. As the arrivals closed in on him the stuff they walked on changed from tiles to gravel.

'The affluent society,' said Peter. 'In the bad old days only very rich people could hope to enjoy surroundings like these. Now they're within the reach of all.'

Charlie went to the polygonal bar in the middle of the concourse and called for service.

'Be there now,' called a voice from out of sight, so not everything had changed.

When drinks had been dealt out Malcolm said, looking about him, 'Well, they've certainly transformed this place.'

'You can't even see where anything was,' said Charlie.

'Can you remember where the bar in the back room was? Where the door into it was?'

'I suppose everywhere's like it now except for a few backwaters like the Bible,' said Malcolm. His expression grew serious and withdrawn. 'It reminds me very strongly of somewhere I went a little while ago. Now where the hell was it?'

Peter had started to breathe heavily. 'Everywhere is not like it. I came up on the bus in a leisurely fashion and stopped on the way at the old Pendle Inn – remember? It's all metal now, would you believe it? Walls, floor, tables, chairs, bar, the whole thing. Bare metal. Matt, not shiny. Including the fast-food device. Naked metal. Except for a dozen or so television screens for the rock videos. I freely grant you may think the differences between that and this can't be considered substantial.'

This was a long speech for Peter, but Malcolm answered up readily enough. 'I expect it appeals to the young people. Same as here.' It was true that as far as could be made out through the murk most of the others present were under thirty or so. Some were under ten and ran about crashing into pieces of furniture.

An expression of ineffable loathing swept over Peter's face but he offered no remark.

'It's not meant to appeal to anyone,' said Charlie. 'That's not the idea. It comes to the brewer's turn to give his pubs a face-lift, and of course he hates forking out a couple of million quid on that, but he can just about face it if he grits his teeth and needn't ever think about it again. So he picks a noted designer and tells him to get on with it. A noted designer gets noted through having photographs of things he's designed published in Swedish magazines and stays noted through winning prizes from international commit-tees sitting in Brasilia. And that's that. The poor old . . .'

His voice faded out as Peter, who had been looking from him to Malcolm and back again with increasing speed, was evidently driven into speech. 'Where's Alun?' he demanded. 'I thought he was supposed to be coming with you.'

'He was,' said Charlie. 'He is. Coming, I mean. Later, though.'

As he spoke a telephone-bell sounded and a youngster with a fearsome slouch moved from behind the bar towards what was apparently a fully furnished old-style red GPO telephone-box standing on its concrete base near the centre of the area.

Peter said with some rancour, 'But it seems he was present, even active, at the ceremony to honour Brydan, which I gather from Malcolm unluckily went through without the gross humiliation of all parties.'

'Yes to all that, but something suddenly came up.'

'What sort of thing?'

'I don't know.'

The way Charlie said this made Peter glance at him sharply, then at Malcolm warily. But all three sat there in silence under an orange-and-white beach umbrella while they rather helplessly watched the crouching youth advance on them.

'One of you Mr Cellan-Davies?' he asked, pronouncing the first element of the name in a way no Welshman would have done.

Charlie hoped with some earnestness that Malcolm would not issue a correction, but it was all right: he responded after no more than his standard interval for uptake.

'Your friend says he's on his way.' A rearward jerk of the head went with this, to allay any doubts about its source.

For no reason that Charlie could define, the information failed to cheer them up, producing instead a condition almost of gloom, certainly one in which no further talk seemed possible for the foreseeable future. It was good old Malcolm who rose to the occasion with details of the event at St Dogmael's, as seen by him, and some account of Pugh for Peter's benefit while Charlie came comfortably near nodding off in his cabana chair.

Alun turned up really quite soon, striding vitally towards them over the tiles and gravel, grimacing apologies and deprecations of the décor, fetching fresh drinks. Though full of assorted prattle he had no information to offer about the preceding hour or so of his life. Charlie, now roused again to somewhere near full consciousness, found that the slowing-down of his intake and the general relaxation of recent minutes had combined to advance considerably his feeling that he might be drunk. He waited for Alun to finish going on about how today might or might not have been the first time for God knew how long since the four of them had been boozing together, and then said to him, 'I thought what you said at that do this morning was quite good.'

'Oh, well one just has to –'

'Except for that stuff about although Brydan couldn't actually understand Welsh he could nevertheless *understand* it.'

'For Christ's sake that's only what they –'

'I want to get this over to you while I remember and before I have too many drinks. When somebody tells you in Welsh that the cat sat on the mat you won't be able to make out what he's saying unless you know the Welsh for cat and sat and mat. Well, he can draw you a picture. Otherwise it's just gibberish.'

'Well, strictly no doubt –'

'The point is it's unnecessary. They'll be just as pleased

to hear how Brydan wrote English with the fire and the passion and the spirit of this, that and the bloody other only possible to a true or real or whatever-you-please Welshman, which if it means anything is debatable to say the least, but whatever it is it's only bullshit, not *nonsense*. Stick to bullshit and we're all in the clear.'

'How many of the people there could appreciate the distinction?'

'I don't know, but I can, and so can you.'

Alun sighed. 'You're right, Charlie. I didn't think. I was careless.'

'Look to it in future, good boy.'

'Hey, Alun.' Malcolm was leaning across and grinning rather. He went on in seriously incompetent but this time intelligible American, 'Would you say, Mr Weaver, that this here is a typical or characteristic Welsh pub?'

There came a noise that began rather like a fart of heroic proportions but soon proved to be made by the exhaustive ripping of the canvas seat of Peter's chair under his buttocks. Luckily he was too fat to fall the whole way through to the ground, remaining clasped round the hips by the metal frame of the chair, his drink intact in his hand. Before he or anyone else could move, a piece of rock music, with the compulsory slap on the third beat of every bar, started up all around them at enormous volume, giving the effect of an omission handsomely redressed.

'Out!' bawled Alun. 'Down drinks and out.'

Having downed his own drink he went over and held the torn chair in position while by fits and starts Peter heaved himself upright and was free. They hurried out after the other two. Nobody looked up at any of them.

'That was a near one,' said Charlie as they assembled at the mouth of the tunnel. The rain had of course grown heavier.

134

'Well.' Alun was glancing to and fro. 'Lunch. There we are, the very thing. Bengal Tiger Indian Bistro and Takeaway. Well, nearly the very thing. Hang on a minute, lads. Case the joint.'

He dashed across the road in full athletic style, marring the effect hardly at all by holding a newspaper over his head. The three left in the tunnel turned morosely to one another.

'Got to watch him, you know.'

'What's he lined up for us?'

'I'm not quite clear. There was something said about a trip to Courcey.'

'Bit late for that, isn't it? Most of the way back and out again.'

'Not half-past one yet.'

'Do I look all right?' This was Malcolm.

'Yes, you look fine,' said the other two. 'Why, don't you feel all right?'

'Yes, I feel fine. I just wondered if I look all right. Looked all right.'

'No, you look fine.'

'Christ, here he is already.'

Making washout signals as he came, Alun hurried back and joined them in the tunnel. 'Bloody awful. You can't even get – I'll hold it for now. We'd better be moving. I don't think we'll find anywhere bearable round here, so let's head for Courcey right away. There's all sorts of tourist spots there now. Where's your car, Malcolm?'

'Haven't you got yours?'

'Came by minicab. More fun if we all go together.'

It was certainly more crowded than it might have been, but really quite pleasant in the warm damp and the half dark. Charlie was comfortable enough in the back, with Peter's bulk next to his seeing to it that, although Malcolm's car was not particularly small, staying unbudged on corners was no problem. As number one, Alun had naturally secured the front passenger seat, and he was soon twisted most of the way round in it to push on with conversation.

'Nightmare place back there, you know. Like a seaside boarding house hung with fairy lights and log-cabin music playing. Completely empty, of course, in fact no sign anybody had been there ever. A nice-enough female appeared and what could I have, well, I could have a cooked dinner, that's beef dinner or lamb dinner with cheese after, or I could have chicken salad, but you gets the Indian chutney-stand with that if you wants it, and pickled onions. And cheese after.'

'As served in Chittagong,' said Charlie.

'Couldn't I have a curry? No, sorry, it's only English till the evening. The Indian, he don't come on till six. She didn't like telling me, poor little thing. I rather cantankerously pointed out that it said Indian-Continental cuisine outside, which she agreed was the case. And then . . . *then* . . . I asked her who owned the joint, and oh, she looked bloody uncomfortable. And what do you think? Arabs own it.'

There was a united cry of rage and disgust, given extra punch by the effect of the bump in the road that shook the car at that moment.

'I mean my God,' said Alun, glaring seriously. 'Arabs owning airlines, Arabs owning half London you can sort of . . . But Arabs owning the Bengal Tiger Bistro in a clapped-out industrial village on the edge of a mouldering, rotting former manufacturing centre and coal port in a God-forsaken province, it makes you, well I don't know what it does, it makes you sweat. Or something.'

'It's not only the province's fault,' said Malcolm. 'Perhaps not even chiefly.'

'Nobody said it was, boy, nobody said it was.'

Silence fell in the car. Malcolm drove it perhaps a trifle faster than his habit but safely enough, and they ran into little traffic. For some minutes Charlie dozed. When he woke up it was to hear Alun singing to himself in the front.

'Was it little Nell whose nasty smell diffused general gloom?

Oh no, it wasn't little Nell . . .'

Anyone in a position to compare Alun's style of rendering these phrases with his effort on leaving Sophie's might well have noticed a falling off, a downturn in force and conviction. Charlie hardly took them in. It seemed to be shaping into one of his good days. The rain had stopped, or just as likely they had moved out of it as they approached sea level, and there was watery sunlight. Courcey came up on a signpost. Everything was peaceful and safe.

Before people stopped bothering about such things at all, Courcey Island was widely considered to have received its name from the Norman family of de Courcy who had been lords of nearby Locharne. Various authorities had seen that name as actually a corruption of Corsey, from Welsh *cors*, 'bog, fen' and Old English *ey*, 'island', or possibly from an eponym *Kori* with *ey*, or again had derived it from English *causeway* or *causey* or from the Welsh borrowing of the latter, *cawsai* or *cawsi*. In the manner of authorities anywhere they had never reached agreement, though it remained true that a substantial causeway, last rebuilt in the 1880s, carried traffic the thousand yards or so between mainland and island on a fine broad road. It had only been about half as broad until 1965, in which year Courcey's three goods-and-passenger railway stations had been closed and the single track taken up.

Parts of this had once been known to Charlie, and more than those were no doubt still fresh in Malcolm's mind.

How he would have enjoyed imparting them to such as Pugh, and how lucky it was for everybody else that it was not happening. What might it not have done to Peter, fast asleep as he was and from time to time giving what sounded like a grunt of brutish consternation.

Once on the island and through Holmwood, the famous grove of ancient oaks once quite mistakenly thought to have druidic associations, Malcolm took the road to the left. East Courcey was always said to be the Welsh half of the island and its place-names suggested as much, including one or two anglicized ones like Treville, where they were making for. The western side had been English or largely English since Henry II planted settlers there in the 1160s. The former port of Birdarthur and nearly all the beaches of the island, overflowing with visitors in summer, lay on that coast. Along this one there ran for the most part a series of dark-coloured cliffs falling to narrow banks of pebbles or straight into the sea. In places they rose to a couple of hundred feet, their highest point being not far off the highest on Courcey. Hereabouts Malcolm stopped the car by agreement, and the occupants set about hauling themselves into the open, for a breath of air, they said, as well as a pee.

Charlie's first breath or sniff of air brought some redolence or other – salt, heather, pine-bark – that was gone before he could give it a name. He peed conscientiously into a grassy drain at the roadside. It was very quiet, or so he had just started to think when a small scarlet aeroplane picked out with yellow came buzzing over his shoulder in the direction of the Swanset strip. He fought his way up a short damp tussocky slope to the inconsiderable summit, which was marked by a fake Celtic cross of some antiquity, flecked with lichen, and a more recent tablet in a purplish material.

Although he had known right away the spot to make for he had no recollection of having stood here before. He had certainly forgotten how the land dropped gently off on almost every side, giving a view of the mainland through a clump of Scotch firs and in the opposite direction an unsteady blur, if that, where Devon and Cornwall must be, but hiding most of the island itself. There was just one clear outlook down a small twisting valley on to the top of a straggle of bushes and low trees, a band of grey rock and a sunlit stretch of turf so dense and green it made him think of the cloth on a snooker table. He found the whole thing a most agreeable sight. At one time he had thought that there must have been more in such sights than he could merely see, perhaps not in them at all, behind them or beyond them but somehow connected with them, and plenty of poems had seemed to tell him the same story. But although he had stayed on the alert for quite a long while to catch a glimpse of what could not be seen, nothing answering remotely to any of his guesses or inklings had ever looked like turning up. Still, if he happened to stroll about in the country or to come across one of the poems he often found the experience appealing, even today. He started back down the slope.

'Come on, for Christ's sake,' called Alun rather irritably. 'We haven't got all night.'

'Indeed we haven't,' said Charlie, the last back to the car, though not possibly by much. As advertised, the breath of air had cleared his head. 'Look, I was in some sort of torpor or stupor when I let you bring us down this way. You won't find anything in Treville – it's all packed up round there.'

'The pubs'll still be going.'

'And with luck they'll be as nice as the one we've just come from.'

'Let's get going anyhow. No, they won't be trendy there, it's not that sort of place.'

'What are you talking about?' said Charlie as they moved off. 'Everywhere's trendy now unless it's actually starving.'

'I know what he's getting at,' said Peter. 'He means they're more authentic. More Welsh, God help us.'

'More suitable for his television series. Shit, I believe you're right.'

'Where do you want me to go?' asked Malcolm.

'About half a mile along there's our last chance to turn off over to the west side. That must be a better bet, surely.'

'What do you expect to find open there at this time of year?' Alun sounded pained and resentful, as if at ingratitude.

'I don't know, you're the researcher,' said Charlie.

'Hey, I tell you what we could do,' said Alun in an immediately livelier tone that would have revived Charlie's suspicions had they had time to abate: 'we could drop in on old Billy Moger just a bit further on. He'd know all that.'

'I haven't seen him for years. Vanished from sight when he moved out, pretty well. Are you sure he's still living there?'

'Well, he was last week when I rang.'

'Was he now?' Some female connected with Moger drifted up in Charlie's memory, not wife, or if wife then second wife, more likely long-standing lady-friend, but anyway also to do with Alun in the long-ago. 'That's good to hear.'

'I was going through my old address-book.'

'I understand.' Laura something, that was the name.

'Shall I take this right turn or not?' asked Malcolm.

Charlie was fully expecting to be swept into the outskirts of Treville, but after no more than a few hundred yards the car pulled up in front of a bungalow built almost at the roadside. It would hardly have been anyone of Billy Moger's era who had required or accepted an original structure on the lines of a cottage in a whimsical book for children, but perhaps he or someone in between had ripped out the old-time twisty windows and goblin's front door and filled the apertures with steel and pine, and in the same spirit had put sensible housing-estate chimneys there instead of whatever funny-hat arrangements had cheered up the roof before.

'Nasty place he's got here,' said Charlie when Alun had gone to ring the bell.

'Who is this Moger?' asked Peter.

'For years he had that sports shop in Cambridge Street next to the off-licence. Jolly handy, that. Nice little chap. Played a bit for Glamorgan before the war. You remember him.'

'After, too,' said Malcolm. 'Left-arm over the wicket. Used to bring them back from the off.'

'Right, we're summoned,' said Charlie. 'That didn't take long.'

His squint at the garden at the side of the bungalow showed him a walled space landscaped like the small-mammal enclosure at some opulent zoo, including the dry bed of an artificial watercourse. But there were no animals in it and little in the way of vegetation either. On the threshold he was met by a strong but not obnoxious perfume, woody and spicy rather than sweet. He and the others got an outstandingly warm welcome from Laura, fully recognizable to him on sight, a small thin woman in a close-fitting black velvet suit, with piled blonde hair and a more than average allowance of jewellery round neck and wrists. Alun really performed the introductions.

Like a lot of people in Wales, though not only in Wales, Charlie had had a much more extensive education in horrible rooms and houses than in attractive or even so-so ones. So he was not much good on detail when, girded for the worst after what he had seen outside, he came across nothing of the interior loathsome to his practised eye, though others perhaps would have drawn the line at the well-stocked bar that filled one end of the living-room. He did notice flowers all over the place, numerous, varied, fresh, bloody marvellous in fact and, as another department of expertise told him, quite expensive in total, like other visible features. Yes, memory added now that at one period Billy had done very well, even too well for squeamish tastes, out of supplying sports equipment to local schools and other educational institutions, including the gaol. Well, that was how he had got his start.

Where was Billy? Laura rejoined them to say that he would be out in a minute. Charlie had missed her departure, having concentrated on the bar, where at her request Alun had started to deal out drinks. Separate from the others, Peter stood and glanced round with what seemed to Charlie an expectantly censorious air, on the watch for vulgarity, affectation, shoddiness, lingering over a suspect water-colour, moving disappointedly on. Malcolm evidently approved of what he saw, or what he had taken in, was enjoying the party. He still looked fine, though his normal gravity of demeanour had begun to show signs of coming apart, like the descended knot of his tie.

Alun set out to describe the supposed purpose of their call, but as soon as he mentioned eating in Treville or any such place Laura would hear no more.

Her eyes flashed fire as in the nick of time she put a stop to this dangerous, degenerate project. 'Quite out of the question,' she affirmed in her startling deep husky voice. 'I never heard such nonsense in my life. Thank God you mentioned it to me, that's all I can say.'

'We were only thinking of a snack,' said Malcolm.

'*Snack*,' said Laura, thereby banishing the topic. 'So let's be practical. Now – bearing time and trouble in mind the answer's obvious. Sandwiches for four is nothing to me, right?' Right, said Charlie to himself, and another fragment of recall checked in: Laura Makins, cold-lunch counter at the Three Feathers in Kinver Hill. 'No problem, gentlemen. Round again, Alun, and I'll see to it.'

'We can't let you do that,' said Malcolm, looking about for support.

'Don't you tell me what you can and can't let me do, young man.' For the first time she allowed humour to soften her pronouncements. 'I don't often get the chance to show off my talents. For making sandwiches, that is,' she explained, mischievously waving her beringed forefinger. 'Ah, here we are, darling – come along then.'

A small white-haired old man moved slowly but steadily over to the group, smiling and looking from face to face. He wore a burgundy-coloured silk dressing-gown with small white dots and a similarly patterned scarf high on one side of the neck, where it covered most of a reddened swelling. Alun and Laura between them told him who everybody was, and he shook hands and spoke in a thin voice. She handed him the weak whisky and water she had started preparing at first sight of him. He raised the glass and again glanced round the circle.

'I'm not off it, you see,' he said.

'Well, you've got this one here to keep you up to the mark, Billy,' said Alun. 'I bet she keeps it coming at you.'

'No, I'm not off it.'

'What do you think of the England bowling prospects this season?' asked Malcolm. 'Not much real quality there, is there?'

Billy chuckled and winked and nodded. 'Made an honest woman of her, I have.'

'About time too,' said Laura.

'I thought it was about time.'

She settled him now in a low leather chair with wooden arms and a Thai-silk back-cover in squares of red, green and buff. Close by was a small circular table on which stood a box of tissues, a box of mints, a silver pencil and a bowl of daffodils with their stalks cut short. The others moved round.

Laura said clearly but not loudly, 'Alun's only just come back to live down here. He was telling me he's seen a lot of changes.'

Alun described some of the changes, with accompaniment from Charlie and Malcolm. Pauses were inserted for possible contributions from Billy but he confined himself to a monosyllable or two, though as far as anyone there could judge he followed the drift of what was said. After a few minutes Laura shifted them all out to the kitchen, placing Billy at the far end of the long scrubbed table and Alun and Malcolm on either side of him. Alun was put on to opening and pouring wine. With speed and skill Laura prepared sandwiches – cheese and onion, tongue and pickle – for all except Billy, who very cheerfully ate baked beans and a couple of digestive biscuits and drank another weak whisky. The sandwiches were quite tasty and moist enough to arouse Charlie's professional respect and even to induce him to eat most of two of them. Soon they were all gone. Laura offered coffee and then at once disallowed it.

'You won't have time if you're to have a drink in Treville.'

'To hell with that,' said Alun. 'We'd all love some coffee – wouldn't we, boys?'

'Not now, darling. Some of us get a bit tired.'

'Oh. Right.'

They said good-bye to Billy there in the kitchen. When it came to Charlie's turn it struck him that at no time had he seen in him the Billy Moger he used to know. Laura went out to the car with them.

'Bless you for coming, all of you,' she said. 'Hope it wasn't too much of a shock.'

'Oh for Christ's sake,' said Alun.

'No really, it was sweet of you. He'll be cheered up for days now. He'll go over it a hundred times. Well, I'll go over it with him. You could, er . . . if you see any of his old mates you could tell them it's not too bad – you know. I think some of them stay away because they're afraid it's worse than it is. Good luck in Treville. I must say I don't fancy your chances anywhere there.'

By common consent they kept quiet well beyond the point where even the most preternatural powers of hearing, or the most sophisticated technology, could possibly have carried their words to Laura.

Charlie opened. 'So it's established that you didn't know what we were in for,' he said.

'I hope so.' Alun again turned to face rearwards, though less jauntily than before. 'Surely you could tell that straight away. Even I couldn't have carried off pretending I didn't if I did. No, she just said drop in when you're passing, we'd love to see you.'

'And what did you say?'

'I said we might make a trip this way today and if we did we might pop in for a drink. I didn't expect her to be expecting us.'

'I wondered about that,' said Malcolm. 'She could have had all that stuff just by her – tongue, cheese, onion. Not that it wasn't delicious and very good of her to do it.'

'Everything bar the bread,' said Charlie. 'Two large

loaves. She got that in on the off-chance. Not negligible, I agree. And it's quite possible she primps herself up like that every day.'

'Poor little bugger,' said Peter.

'Yes, no harm in sparing a thought for him.'

'Indeed, but I was thinking of his wife. How many times she must have told herself of course nobody would come. How disappointed she'd have been if nobody had. For half an hour out of twenty-four times God knows what. All right, she smartened the place up a bit for our benefit. In the remote contingency that we came, that is. Not daring to tell him why. But no mere smartening-up could have done that, what we saw. That's years of work, every day.'

'Are you feeling all right, Peter?' asked Charlie.

'Shut up, Charlie,' said Alun.

'Sorry. Well, there seems to be plenty to be said about her. Not a lot about old Billy.'

Nobody was ready to contest this view there and then.

'One consolation, though,' Charlie went on. 'We haven't got Garth with us to say what is appropriate to such an occasion.'

He got quite a good laugh out of that. Other thoughts he kept to himself, for instance that Laura had known her Alun in not saying anything to him on the telephone about her husband's condition. And likewise, if Alun had plotted everything and known everything in advance he could not have contrived a better position for himself: not only full conversance with the situation there but a huge fund of goodwill and a positive duty to return to the scene. Carte bloody blanche at zero cost. Billy must be dead keen for you to have an afternoon off once in a way, love. Oh well, there it was.

A few pieces of traffic turned up as they in fact reached the outskirts of Treville. As the car ducked down the last little hill before the village, the motto FREE WALES was briefly to be seen daubed on a brick wall in faded and dingy whitewash. An ironic cheer went up.

'Now would that be –' began Malcolm in his frightening American accent before Alun shushed him.

'Belt up, you stupid bugger. What's the matter with you? You hardly set eyes on that clown and everything you see reminds you of him. Forget him.'

'Remember what happened the last time you invoked him,' said Charlie.

'Dismiss Cadwallader *Twll-Din* Pugh from your mind.'

'Hey, I've thought of the thing to say to him about that slogan there. Show me a Welsh nationalist and I'll show you a cunt.'

'He wouldn't say thank you for showing him a cunt,' said Alun reasonably.

'That's my point, you bloody fool.'

'Oh Christ, it's the drink. Fuddling my mental processes.'

'It's certainly fuddling mine,' said Malcolm, wrenching at the wheel. 'Sorry.'

'And mine, thank God,' said Peter.

Despite everything said just now and earlier, expectation mounted as the time of arrival drew near. They passed traces of the railway station and of some of the eleven worked-out pits in the area, reached the shore and turned along it. Here until quite lately cockles and the edible seaweed laver-bread had been harvested. In the village itself rusty galvanized-iron roofs and shop-fronts that needed painting were noticeable. The first pub they went into had in it a half-size snooker-table, a TV set showing a children's programme with the sound turned down and only two people, the barmaid and her boy-friend, who while talking to her fed himself continuously from a dispenser apparently

147

called a Peanut Colonel. There was a move to withdraw at once, but Charlie remarked that there was no guarantee of getting a drink elsewhere. Nobody was sure about local licensing hours.

Twenty years before, Charlie had passed a whole day from rising to retiring without a drink. Rising in fact had very nearly not taken place at all: he had believed absolutely, would have told anyone who asked, that death was on him. In that frame of mind he had nevertheless found himself playing a hard game in the crowd that afternoon at Wales v. France in Cardiff. In the evening Sophie and he, then recently married, had been giving a party – too late to cancel. Orange-juice in hand, he had watched fascinated as one by one, with unbelievable speed and totality, his contemporaries had crumpled into drunkenness, their faces and voices disintegrating between one sip and the next. From rather nearer the fray he saw it happen to Malcolm now as they emptied their drinks by the coruscating fruit-machine, saw his eyes swell in time with some event inside him. He took a sudden half-pace forward.

Charlie stayed at Malcolm's right hand for the two-minute walk to the other waterside pub Alun had spotted earlier. The tide was out and a strong, not wholly pleasant smell came blowing off the saltings ahead of them, though there was nothing obvious for anybody to have done about that, nor about the rain that had come back into the air. As far as they could see there were only three or four parked cars about, unusually for any inhabited place in the kingdom. Someone, a middle-aged man, let himself in at a front door and disappeared, the only sign of life, apart from brand-new litter underfoot, at a time when the inhabitants might have been expected to be in full circulation. It seemed as quiet as it had been back there on the hill.

'What do they do here?' Malcolm asked quite distinctly as they crossed a side-road up which nothing moved, not even paper blown by the wind. 'Nowadays, I mean.'

'I don't know. Make lemonade or deodorant I dare say.'

'Some of them must commute to town.'

'No idea.'

'Mind you the unemployment figures for the area are as high as anywhere else in GB, along with Merseyside and parts of north-eastern England.'

'M'm.'

'Well, it's a terrible thing, Charlie, you know. A really . . . monstrous thing. I mean, imagine yourself stuck in a place like this with no prospects, no future, nothing going on. You can see for yourself. No . . . no prospects.'

'Ah.'

'I'd like to know, just out of curiosity, whether Maggie Thatcher's ever been out here, Charlie.'

'I shouldn't think so for a moment, not if she's got any sense. Certainly not since she closed down the first colliery in 1910, I think it was.'

More of this sort of thing soon brought them to the door or doors of the Ship Inn, which by appearance might easily as well have admitted them to a public lecture-theatre or bit of local government. But inside it was not at all like any of that, a typical old-style country pub with electric organ, round tables of pitted copper, triple-decker sandwiches and tremendously badly designed and written local announcements. And also a great many people. This was where they all were.

The considerable noise they were making lessened slightly at the entrance of the four visitors and some of those in view turned and had a look at them. This seemed natural enough at the sight of a group of obvious strangers in unconventional clothes like jackets and ties and including one or two – Peter, perhaps Charlie – worth a second glance anywhere. The hum of normality was about restored by the time they had moved to the further and less crowded end of the room and Charlie had waddled to the counter.

'Nothing for me,' said Malcolm when he was asked.

'Have a soft drink.'

'No I think I'll just go and sit down. You know.'

He sank into an armchair with tangerine loose covers that might have come out of a local auntie's front room, the generic source of most of the furnishings up this end, not least the parchment lampshades. In a moment he seemed to fall asleep. The other three nodded at each other, needing no words.

'That's nice,' said Alun. 'No question about him not driving now.'

'He's not the sort to try and insist,' said Charlie.

'No, but it's good to keep it civilized.'

Having unrestively waited rather longer than strict equity would have entailed, Charlie had his order taken by one of the fellows behind the bar, the one whose locks hung to his shoulders from either side of a bald pate. After unhurriedly assembling the required drinks he in due course uncourteously served them.

'Now we're all right for a bit,' said Charlie. 'More water? Well, how was Gwen?'

'Oh, Christ,' said Alun, and then, almost as differently as possible, 'Oh, Christ.' He stared malevolently at Charlie. 'You bugger.'

'Calm down, old bloke, it's all in the family, won't go any further. Not from me or Peter, that is. One of the reasons I've brought it up while I'm still stone cold sober is to warn you very seriously against letting the slightest suspicion enter Malcolm's head for a moment. He's –'

'Good Lord, what do you take me for?'

The grin lurking in this might not have irritated Charlie if it had not made him want to start grinning himself. 'Don't try and go devil-may-care on me. Listen: no sly quips or digs in the ribs or narrow shaves or delicious hints he couldn't possibly pick up and supposing he did what of it really, eh? He's not as, shall I say resilient as some of those we know.'

Alun betrayed little or none of the embarrassment he might have been expected to feel at this. 'No, of course, don't worry. It was her idea, not mine in the first place. She grabbed me in the Prince of Wales. As I was hoping you hadn't seen but knew you had.'

'But you went along with it. Yes, I saw. Anyway, how was it?'

With this Charlie glanced at Peter in the hope of spreading out the curiosity, making it a little more a matter of public concern, but he was looking here and there in his unfocused way, no bloody use at all.

'Oh, Christ,' said Alun, 'it was a . . . I just scraped home if you know what I mean. She was great fun in the old days but she's, well, she's gone off rather. Is that enough for you?'

'Just right, thanks. What sort of a state was she in when you left?'

'Bit on the subdued side.'

'M'm. I expect she'll liven up when she sees Malcolm, poor old bastard. You know, Alun, it might be a good thing all round if you took in the idea that we've rumbled you. We see through you, chum.'

'If you're talking about Laura . . .'

'No, I am not talking about Laura. The diaconate has given you a clean bill of moral health there. More than you deserve. I mean in general. Can't you sort of concentrate your attentions? Narrow them down a bit?'

'It's all this bloody temptation, you see. Growing in amplitude year by year. The percentage of women between my age-group and puberty, both ends inclusive, is unlikely to rise significantly higher.'

'The lower end doesn't seem to bother you unduly. You saw off that fan in the Glendower without any trouble. Any that I could see. And she was quite a – well, time was when I'd have been a horrible nuisance to her myself.'

'The lower end is largely hypothetical. Rather like the invisible cone that in theory extends upwards from the apex of your ordinary real God-fearing cone. The other way round in this case. More practically the young ones lack the essential security-conferring streak of gratitude to be found in the old ones. No problem resisting that temptation.'

Charlie gazed startled at his empty glass. 'Christ, what's gone wrong with this? Er, from the way you talked about it I didn't think Gwen sounded particularly grateful. I dare say you'll keep your mouth shut, but there's her too. Eh?'

'Yeah, I know.'

Vague Peter might be at times, preoccupied even, but shy on his shout never. He took Charlie's place at the counter and produced a pentagonal slice of plastic in which five one-pound coins were embedded: a children's toy, he would say, for children's money. Something between the used glasses and muscular dystrophy collecting box caught his eye and he bent to see better, fumbling for his spectacles. A moment later he gave a kind of snarling bellow, loud enough anyway to cause a nearby head or two to twist in his direction.

'Wouldn't you bloody know,' he said not much less loudly. 'ASH *yng* sodding *Nghymru. Diolch am* . . . What kind of madhouse . . .'

'Never mind, no one understands it,' said Charlie soothingly.

'Not content with trying to stop me smoking they have the bloody cheek to do it in buggering *Welsh*. It's enough to make you . . .'

He flung out a hand, probably just in contemptuous dismissal, but his fingertips brushed the folded card and sent it fluttering to the floor. Before he could have started to face bending down to ground level the man with the divided hairdo intervened.

'Would you kindly pick that up, please.' He spoke not in any Welsh way but in the thick, unvarying tones of generic middle-north England.

Peter grew flustered, sweat gathering on his upper lip, but still he made no move and it was Alun, as one doubtless used to finding himself the only male in the company capable of bending, who put the notice back on the bar.

'If you want to smoke you'll have to go down the other end.'

'I don't want to bloody smoke,' said Peter, 'that's not the point. I just . . .'

'And lay off the language if you don't mind.' The barman gave them an assessing stare one after the other. 'Welshmen,' he muttered finally and turned away.

On later inquiry it emerged that Malcolm had not in fact been roused up by the mild disturbance and come to see about it, but it looked very much like it at the time. His return to action certainly aroused more notice than his withdrawal had. When he reappeared he could not have been said to look fine any more, not too bad though, and his speech was all right too, at least as regards its utterance. But ten minutes' nap could have done nothing very reconstructive for him, and Charlie at once diagnosed a false dawn, being experienced in dawns of that kind if of no other.

Yet Malcolm started off quite well – he was excited,

admittedly, but for the moment in a contained way. 'I've remembered what I was trying to remember, it's all come back to me. That awful place in Harriston we were in, with the railings and the lamp-posts. I knew it reminded me of somewhere but I couldn't think where. Well, it was a pub in Chester we went to when we were staying with our son last year. Very similar. Same sort of idea.'

This was obviously no more than a minor shock to the others.

'Don't you see, I'm saying the place in Harriston was just the same as an *English* pub. That's what they're doing everywhere. Everywhere new here is the same as new things in England, whether it's the university or the restaurants or the supermarkets or what you buy there. What about this place we're in? Is there anything in here to tell you you're in Wales? At last they've found a way of destroying our country, not by poverty but by prosperity. I don't mind so much the decline and the decay, we've faced that before and we've always come through. No, what I abominate is the nauseous fruits of affluence. It's not the rubble I deplore, it's the vile crop that has sprung from it. It spells the end of . . .'

When he paused, less perhaps for breath than to concentrate on not falling over, Charlie said, 'Come and sit down and have a glass of dandelion-and-burdock.'

'I may be drunk but what I'm saying is very important.'

'There's no point in getting worked up about it,' said Peter.

'Oh there isn't, isn't there? It'll be all right with you, when everything's gone and we're left with a language that nobody speaks and Brydan and a few choirs, and Wales is a place on the map and nothing else? That'll be okay, will it?'

'No,' said Peter.

'Well then . . .'

'And if I'd talked in that strain you'd have told me I was bullshitting,' said Alun rather sourly.

'Well, you would have been, wouldn't you?' said Peter. 'You're not Malcolm.'

'Cheers.'

Afterwards Malcolm said he thought he had seen some people laughing at him. Again, he went on altogether as if he really had, granted some further temporary transformation of his character. 'You can laugh if you like,' he opened uncontroversially enough, not looking at anyone in particular. 'Pretty funny sight, a Welshman getting steamed up about Wales. Silly old bugger all in a tizzy about Wales going by the board. Specially funny of course to English people. Silly old Welsh bugger. But they'll be laughing on the other side of their faces before long. Because it's going to be their turn next. In fact it's already –'

That was all they gave him time for, not very much, not very offensive, not at all provocative, but it was enough for them to have fatally had a good look at him. Charlie had not taken in that anything much at all was happening till it was half over. Two or three or four men closed in on Malcolm, obscuring him from view. Voices were raised and some rapid movement seen. Malcolm went sideways over a table, an ordinary wooden one, and a glass or glasses dropped to the floor. The barman who had rebuked Peter threw up the flap of the counter with a crash and strolled forward advancing one shoulder at a time.

'Outside the lot of you,' he bawled. 'You too. Go on, you four. Out before I call the police.'

By now Charlie had reached Malcolm and found him bleeding from the nose. There was blood on his face and hand and jacket, not very much, but some.

'Let me clean him up, eh?'

'All right, but out straight after, see. The other two go now. That includes you, Fatso.'

There were no towels in the Gents, only a hot-air blower. Charlie did what he could with their handkerchiefs. The bleeding had almost stopped.

'I didn't say anything very terrible, did I?' asked Malcolm.

'Not that I heard.'

'So what was it all about?'

'They were rather a rough lot and they reckoned we were misbehaving on their patch.' Charlie decided against a satirical harangue on the demoralizing effects of unemployment and inadequate leisure facilities. 'And we knew you meant no harm but they didn't, or they could say they didn't.'

'A bit unfair, chucking us out like that. It was them, those local fellows.'

'Just as well perhaps.'

'Of course I see it was no use arguing. You know, Charlie, I think I must be a bit tight. Probably hurt more if I wasn't, there is that. No thanks, I can manage.'

'Fine bloody pub-crawl we've had, haven't we?'

'Sorry.'

'Not your fault. I suppose Alun made good use of the time. Some of it, anyway.'

Their way out took them through the bar where they had spent most of their short time on the premises.

'I could tell what sort they were the moment they came in.'

'Men that age, you'd think they'd have learnt how to behave by this time.'

Four – Peter

1

Peter's getting-up procedures were less taxing to the spirit than Charlie's or Malcolm's but they were no less rigid. They had stopped being what you hurried heedlessly through before you did anything of interest and had turned into a major event of his day, with him very much on his own, which was right for an oldster's day. Among such events it was by far the most strenuous performance. The section that really took it out of him was the actual donning of clothes, refined as this had been over the years, and its heaviest item was the opener, putting his socks on. At one time this had come after instead of before putting his underpants on, but he had noticed that that way round he kept tearing them with his toenails.

Those toenails had in themselves become a disproportion in his life. They tore the pants because they were sharp and jagged, and they had got like that because they had grown too long and broken off, and he had let them grow because these days cutting them was no joke at all. He could not do it in the house because there was no means of trapping the fragments and Muriel would be bound to come across a couple, especially with her bare feet, and that was obviously to be avoided. After experimenting with a camp-stool in the garage and falling off it a good deal he had settled on a garden seat under the rather fine flowering cherry. This restricted him to the warmer months, the wearing of an overcoat being of course ruled out by the degree of bending involved. But at least he could let the parings fly free, and fly they bloody well did, especially the ones that came crunching off his big toes, which were massive enough and moved fast enough to have brought down a sparrow on the wing, though so far this had not occurred.

The socks went on in the bathroom with the aid of a particular low table, height being critical. Heel on table, sock completely on as far as heel, toes on table, sock round heel and up. Quite recently he had at last found the kind of socks he wanted, short with no elastic round the top. They did his swollen ankles good, not by making them swell less but by not constricting them, and so leaving them looking less repulsive and frightening when he undressed at night. Pants on in the bedroom, heel and toe like the socks but at floor level, spot of talc round the scrotum, then trousers two mornings out of every three or so. On the third or so morning he would find chocolate, cream, jam or some combination of these from his bedtime snack smeared over the pair in use, and would have to return to the bathroom, specifically to its mirror for guidance in fixing the braces on the front of the fresh trousers, an area which needless to say had been well out of his direct view these many years.

There was nothing non-standard about the remainder of his dressing routine except perhaps for the use of the long shoehorn, a rare and much-prized facility he had once mislaid for a whole miserable week, filling the gap as best he might with a silver-plated Georgian serving-spoon from Muriel's kitchen, where it had naturally had to be returned after each application. He had worn the same pair of featureless slipper-types for years now, hoping to die or become bedridden before they fell to pieces and forced him to go to one of these do-the-whole-thing-yourself shoe-shops which he understood were all they had these days.

The part of the course that involved the bathroom hand-basin was less demanding only than the first. The foam went on to his face in two ticks, the sweeps of his razor were bold and swift and he hardly did more with his toothbrush than spread paste over his gums. But even so some bending and stretching and arm-raising was unavoidable, enough to see to it that by the time he was as ready to face the world as he would ever be he was breathing fairly hard and pouring with sweat, especially from his scalp. At one period he had tried to reduce this effect by leaving large parts of himself undried after his bath, but after several weeks of nonstop cold symptoms had surmised a connection and desisted. He went downstairs carrying the sleeveless pullover he would draw carefully over his head when he had cooled off.

Where was Muriel? – this particular morning as every other morning a question to get settled right at the start. Not in her bedroom: its door had stood open and she was an early bird anyway. Not out in the car: he would have heard it. In the garden? Likely enough at the moment, with no rain falling: as she often said, a great deal needed doing in the third of an acre with only Mr Mayhew, who had once worked in the manufacture of metal boxes, coming in to do some of the rough on Tuesdays and Thursdays. At times like this, Peter recalled the brief period when he had magnanimously volunteered now and then to lend a hand himself, and on every occasion had been told off to shift as it might have been five hundred gallon-sized flowerpots from one end of the estate to the other. It was almost as if Muriel would sooner have been able to complain of not being helped than be helped. Well, well, there was no fathoming some people.

Yes, there she was on her knees near the far hedge, getting a place ready to put something into the ground or even actually putting it in. He could not see which from the dining-room windows nor would he have cared at any distance, having disliked gardens ever since having been expected to amuse himself in one otherwise than by pulling up the plants. It was one of his earliest memories (he must have been about four) and his parents' garden had admittedly been much smaller than this, but the lesson had stuck, indeed he had been elaborating it off and on ever since. Gardens, he had long ago perceived, were all about power, from overawing you with their magnificence (sneering at your penury) to rebuking your indolence, mean-mindedness, barbarity, etc. Houses were pretty bad too and in the same way, but there was mitigation there, with so many people having to live in them.

The house he lived in himself, this house, had immeasurably more than that to be said about it. Nowadays there were only two people in it constantly, not more than half a dozen had ever come to stay at once and a maximum of twenty or so might turn up for a party, but almost that number could have found beds and a couple of hundred somewhere to sit. In the dining-room, for instance, the twenty mentioned would have had space to breakfast simultaneously while as many more waited their turn on chairs round the walls. These were smothered with pictures, every single one of which Peter thought was absolutely terrible. Either it was not a picture of anything on earth or else it was nothing like what it was supposed to be a picture of. Over the years he had got as used to them as he could, considering new ones were constantly appearing. Muriel would go up to London and the day after her return the two blokes made of purple plasticine would have been replaced by an arrangement of wavy lines and blobs. A new rug or coffee-table might well have turned up at the same time. And there was nothing he could do about any of it, for as many guessed and very nearly as many had been told, Muriel had money, and the house and most of what was in it were hers. He still wondered occasionally how much difference it would have made if things had been the other way round.

His breakfast stood on a tray at the end of the dining-table, prepared and put there by Mrs Havard, who came in every weekday morning. As always it was half a grapefruit, cereal, toast and coffee in thermos flask. He went to work on the grapefruit with the serrated knife, separating the wedges and swearing once or twice as he encountered awkward partitions between them. Digging them out to eat was no walkover either. Some clung tenaciously to their compartments after being to all appearance cut free, others came only half-way out, still joined on by a band of pith. He dealt with such cases by lifting the whole works into the air by the segment and waggling the main body of the fruit in circles until the bond parted and it crashed back on to or near its plate. How different from the accommodating spoonfuls of memory, emerging first go as perfect geometrical segments. The buggers were fighting back, he muttered to himself. Like everything else these days.

The struggle with the grapefruit, though troublesome, had not been really severe, and soon after it was settled he felt he had lost enough heat to make it all right for him to wear his pullover, which was draped over the back of the chair next to him. He muffed reaching for it and the thing slid eagerly to the floor. At the same time he caught a movement through the window and saw Muriel approaching the house. Hurriedly, he bent over in his chair, failed to make contact, got to his feet, crouched down, grabbed the pullover, put it on, sat down again, took three deep breaths. Then a pain, the pain, started up in the left side of his chest.

Try and time them, Dewi had said in a tone faintly suggesting that that would be as good a way as any of occupying himself. Peter uncovered his watch and kept his eyes fixed on it, hoping Muriel would not come into the room. Usually she did not at this stage, indeed he was given his breakfasts in here to be kept out of the way of something or other, but now and then she did, and when she did it was not always with the intention or effect of cheering him up. Describing the pain to Dewi he had mentioned a gripping, squeezing quality and Dewi had said that was characteristic, which was a great relief. He had said too that if things took a turn for the worse he was willing to consider prescribing some pills, adding in a similar spirit that while they would relieve the pain they would not improve his physical state in the smallest degree.

When the pain or series of pains began, a couple of years before, Dewi had asked him about possible sources of stress in his life. Stress? Yes, you know – tension, anxiety, irritation. He had said Muriel was not the easiest of women to get along with and Dewi had not quite managed not to grin, because of course from what the world saw he, Peter, was the difficult one. Well, difficult he might be, difficult he admitted, but not on Muriel's exalted level, surely to God. As to anxiety now, that was good. Fear was the true word for it, simple fear of her tongue, which nothing he had ever thought of would explain away, and specifically an ultimate fear that one day she would carry out her periodic threat to sell the house, which was inevitably in her name, and go back to Yorkshire on her own, leaving him to find a couple of rooms in Emanuel or somewhere.

He acknowledged that there was not much dignity about any of this, but again it was hard to see a remedy.

After four minutes and twelve seconds the pain left off. Even before opening his diary he knew it continued the downward trend since Christmas, if that counted for anything. Better ring Dewi later, though, he thought, trying to drive other thoughts away. Well, tomorrow, then.

He had brought himself to start on the cereal, which by his preference was of a resolutely unauthentic type, penurious in things like natural fibre, when he heard the telephone ring in the hall and stop after a few seconds and then Muriel's voice, a wordless mumble from where he sat. After only a few more seconds this too stopped and her heavy footfalls approached the door but stopped just short of it. Peter took a further couple of deep breaths. He had not told her about his chest pains and what Dewi had said about them, because for one thing he doubted whether the news would cut much ice with her, in fact . . . Another thought to leave unexamined.

But when she had evidently changed her mind for the second time and come into the room he almost smiled. At the sight of her it was hard to believe that this not very large figure with the jaunty manner, sort of hemispherical haircut and (at the moment) green plastic knee-pads for gardening could make anyone afraid, except perhaps of being mildly bored. Although they were meeting for the first time that day she did not come over, let alone come over to kiss him. They had not touched each other for nearly ten years.

'William,' she announced, meaning their son, their only child, who by no intention of either had turned up in 1955.

'Oh . . . right.' He gripped the arms of his chair.

'No no, don't bestir yourself,' said Muriel, raising a hand; 'the connection is terminated. Just a tip-off that he'll be collecting some lunch here and might see his way afterwards to shifting a clod or two if the monsoon hasn't broken by then.'

'Oh, great. But it's not Saturday. Or Sunday. How –'

'It's his day off. Estate agents stay open all the time but individual employees have days off. Which has a bearing on the matter in hand in that the said William Thomas is employed by an estate agent.'

Peter nodded wordlessly. The facts had just dropped out of his sight for an instant, but long enough for her to get in.

'I suppose it's easy for people who don't have days on to forget that other people have days off,' she said with an air of illumination. 'I take it you'll be putting your nose in at the Bible later?'

'Yes, I think so, but I'll be –'

'I think so too. He, young William that is, declared his intention of arriving about one so if you roll in pissed at three you won't see a lot of him.'

'Okay, fine.'

'I wonder if you'd mind calling in at that garden centre place off Hatchery Road and picking up some vegetation for me. It's all ordered and ready. Would you mind doing that?'

'No, that's easy.'

'Because do say if you would mind.' Muriel looked gravely at him.

'No, I don't mind a bit. No problem.'

She looked at him a while longer, then, apparently satisfied, flashed a smile (in the sense that it went on and off fast) and clumped out.

He exhaled slowly. There, that had been all right; the smile had been quite well worth having. It was all how she was feeling at any given moment, he told himself, with some conviction for once. She was not too bad really.

He finished his breakfast and went along to the sitting-room, where by now Mrs Havard had been and gone. As usual she had moved every object that could fairly be moved, from matchboxes to sofas, as evidence of her assiduity. When he had as usual shifted everything back where it belonged he settled down with a technical journal and put in a spell of pretending to keep up with his branch of chemical engineering until it was time to be going along to the Bible.

2

Most of those whose marriages have turned out less than well, say, might have been considered to have their ideas of how or why but not to know much about when. According to himself Peter was an exception. If challenged he could have named at least the month and year in which he and Muriel had been making love one night and roughly half-way through in his estimation, what would have been half-way through, rather, she had asked him how much longer he was going to be. He had got out of bed, collected his clothes, dressed in the bathroom and driven over to the Norrises'. He and Charlie had sat up most of the night with a bottle of Scotch while Charlie went on telling him he had not been criminally selfish all his married life and it was not his fault if Muriel disliked it or was indifferent to it. But he had perhaps not managed to take those ideas on board, not quite, then or since.

Anyway, since that night things had accountably never been the same between the Thomases. What it had become inexact to call their lovemaking dwindled in both frequency and duration. After a few years of this it had dawned on

Peter that, however strongly Muriel might have disliked it or however deeply indifferent to it she might have been, she expected him to go on going through the motions of providing it in token of still wanting it, and of course not so much it as her. A further decline set in, quite soon followed by the inception of the random verbal punch-ups, and that had been that, rubbed in by separate rooms, no hugs, no endearments. Even perfect love, he used to say to himself, was probably cast out by fear. With all this it was some consolation, though not much, to notice that not even the most colourful punch-ups had anything sexual in them, like references to lovers or what would have been jolliest of the lot, doubts cast on William's paternity, an enormous and surely significant omission.

Peter played back bits of this to himself while he made his way home from the Bible in the middle of a small spinney; he actually managed a new thought on the subject in general. Part of men's earlier average age at death than women's, perhaps a substantial part, might be traceable to wives driving husbands to coronaries single-handed by steadily winding them up with anxiety and rage. Put it to Dewi. But never mind Dewi for now. He focused on the Bible session just over: old Tudor Whittingham, old Owen Thomas, old Vaughan Mowbray and old Arnold Spurling, not to speak of old Garth Pumphrey, who had as good as chaired an impromptu Brains Trust on false teeth, giving unasked a full account of the events leading up to the final installation of his own current set – Peter's mouth tingled at the memory and he clapped a hand over it. But no Charlie, no Alun, no Malcolm. Boding ill, somehow, the last one.

William's smart Audi was thoughtfully parked so as not to block the way to the garage. The time was 1.23, specially selected so as not to do more than brush the fringe of lateness while still allowing mother and son some minutes alone together at the outset. He found them standing by the sitting-room window looking out at the garden and talking about something called mulch or mulching, or rather Muriel was talking about it and went on doing so till a little while after Peter had joined the party. She also remained arm in arm with William throughout, so that on the whole, any kind of Peter/William embrace seemed excluded. William had done what he could in the meantime with waves and cheerful grimaces.

In the end Peter touched his son on the shoulder. 'Hallo, Willie boy, how's it going?'

'Darling, you must have a drink,' Muriel insisted to William. 'Now what would you like?'

'Hallo Dad, fine thanks. Have you got a beer?'

'Sure. What about you, love?'

'Oh, er, anything for me. I don't care.'

'Oh, but you must have a preference. Gin and tonic? Vodka?'

'Is there any dry sherry?'

'I'm afraid not.' Peter never drank sherry himself and he could not remember the last time Muriel had asked for it.

'Oh, well don't bother then.'

'That's no way to talk,' said Peter in his best jocose style. 'Nothing's too much trouble around here. What about a spot of –'

'Is there any wine open?'

'No, but I can easily –'

'Oh, oh, never mind.'

'Come on, Mum, have a glass of wine,' said William.

'If you're going to take that tone,' said his mother, 'what is there for me to do but give in gracefully?'

And of course when Peter got back to the sitting-room

with the drinks they were no longer there, they had gone out into the garden. They could have gone out and in half a dozen times while he was looking for something to take down to the basement to open the new case of Muscadet with, and carrying on from there. When he reached them they were strolling, still or again arm in arm, down along the left-hand edge of the lawn with William on the inside, so that to be next to him he would either have to haul the pair of them a good yard to their right or walk on the flower-bed. Neither seemed advisable in the circumstances and he positioned himself instead on Muriel's other side. At the foot of the garden they did not make an about-turn but a right wheel, and stayed in the same relative positions till they were back in the house. It was much the same at lunch: Muriel at the corner of the table, William beside her, Peter at the end on a diagonal from him. They were just sitting down when the telephone rang in the hall and Peter went to answer it.

At his grunt a woman's voice said, 'Is that you, Peter?'

He nearly dropped the handset. He had no breath.

'Mr Peter Thomas?'

'Yes. It's me.'

'Rhiannon here, Peter. Just to ask, are you coming to our party tonight at the Golf Club? Your old haunt. I sent you an invitation.'

'I hadn't really thought. I'm sorry.'

'Do come. It's our house-warming, only the house still isn't properly ready yet so we're having it at the Golf Club. Six-thirty onwards. We'd love you and Muriel to come.'

'I'm afraid we can't. I'm sorry.'

'Can you really not come?'

He wanted to lie but could not, nor, he found, did he know how to say what he felt. 'I just don't think it would be a good idea.'

'Peter, listen. You can't keep out of my way for ever, love. It's incredible we haven't run into each other already by this time. And you think: it'll be much better not out of the blue and with lots of people there, won't it? I can't remember if you've met our daughter Rosemary. She's down from Oxford. Please come.'

'All right. I mean thank you, yes I will. I don't know about Muriel.'

'You turn up anyway then. See you later.'

Peter went on sitting for a moment longer on the pseudo-Chippendale chair by the telephone on to which he had dropped at the first sound of Rhiannon's voice. From there he could see the bottle of Famous Grouse on the kitchen dresser and hesitated. Then he dragged himself to his feet, hurried back to the dining-room and said before he could think better of it, interrupting Muriel to do so, 'That was Rhiannon Weaver inviting us to a party tonight at the Golf Club. Six-thirty.'

'What a merry thought,' said Muriel. 'Just my cup of tea. Two hundred assorted Welsh people standing up talking at the tops of their voices. Right up my street. You go.'

'Yes, I think I will.'

'I wouldn't want to spoil the reunion of two old flames.'

'Six-thirty at the Golf Club did you say, Dad? I've got to be off anyhow about then and it's right on my way, the Club. I suppose there will be females present. Not aged a hundred and fifty I mean.'

'Their daughter for one,' said Peter.

'Great. I can go instead of you, Mum. I can take Dad down and he can get a mini cab back. One more drunken-driving conviction evaded.'

'You must be pretty hard up for a bit of skirt if you think Holland Golf Club is likely country,' said Muriel.

'Pretty hard up for a bit of a lot of things is what you quite soon become out at Capel Mererid,' said William. 'Not boredom, though. No supply shortfalls there.'

Shortly before six-thirty Peter settled himself in the passenger-seat of the Audi. He felt what he had not felt for many years, the sensation of one about to sit an exam. William, serious, dark and already thinning at the temples, wearing a rather ugly tie his father had lent him, got behind the wheel. Peter was fond of him, at least liked him better than anybody else he knew, but was shy when alone with him because he found it hard to think of things to say to him that were not likely to bore him. This mattered much less than it would have done if he had been alone with him at all often or for long at a time. Anyway, he need not have worried on this occasion.

William set the car in motion. 'Seat-belt, Dad.'

'Sorry.'

'I can see you'd like to get out of it if you could. You know you're enormously fat, do you? Fatter than ever? No-joke fat? Well of course you do, you could hardly not. The booze I suppose mostly, is it? I'm not saying I blame you, mind.'

'That and the eats. Don't let what I ate for lunch fool you. I'm very good during the day, marvellous during the day, a lettuce-leaf here and half a sardine there, and then I'm sitting on my arse with the telly finished and I start stuffing myself. Cakes mostly. Profiteroles. Brandy-snaps. Anything with cream or jam or chocolate. Also cake, Genoa cake, Dundee cake with almonds. Seed cake with a glass of Malmsey. Like some Victorian female only this is one o'clock in the morning.'

'You can't be hungry, not then. Not really.'

'Well, it's partly giving up smoking. Four years now but then I still feel, you know, is this all there is for tonight?

So you start eating. But it's also partly, partly I don't know what to call it. Scared as much as anything I mean. I hope that doesn't sound too much like piling on the agony.' When William said nothing Peter went on. 'Well, there's quite a good selection of things to be scared of when you get to my age, as you may well be able to imagine.'

'And not only then,' said William. 'Yes, I was reading the other day where the fellow said, Welshman too by God, he said carbohydrates, which is what we're talking about, they're tranquillizing, just mildly. Well, that clears that up. But are you all right, Dad? You mustn't mind me saying this, but when I first saw you today I didn't think you were looking very well. Nothing wrong, is there? Silly not to tell me if there is.'

Peter told him straight away, sticking to physical facts, making not even the most indirect allusion to Muriel. When he had finished he felt a little better, but not much because of finding he was forced to listen to his own words as if he had been William, and they had sounded rather daunting like that. They drove in silence for a couple of minutes. Then William said, 'Mum still goes on those trips of hers to London, does she?'

'Oh yes, like mad. Every couple of months or so. In fact she's about due for one now.'

'Right, well when she goes, give me a ring and I'll pop down and we could have lunch or whatever you like. Just give me a ring. When Mum's in London.'

'Fine.'

'Or you could come up to me if you felt like it. Never been, have you? Not that there's much to see. There's this pad I share with one of the blokes at work. Miner's cottage it was, quite nice really, with a bit of garden at the back. And I'll tell you something about that garden. We've been there two years all but a few weeks and it hasn't had a fork in it the whole of that time. Don't you think that's interesting?'

Rhiannon was the first person Peter saw at the Golf Club when he went in by the side entrance from the car park and entered the large old-fashioned hall where non-members were entertained. She was standing in its opposite corner but seemed to have caught sight of him even before he saw her. At once she smiled with what looked like pure pleasure, pure affection, though how that could have been he had no idea, and hurried over towards him. He realized he had been afraid of not recognizing her after so many years, but when she came in range of his glasses (supposed to be for reading only but kept on most of the time out of inertia) he saw her face had not changed at all – well, a few lines, a fullness under the chin, nothing really, of course her hair was probably a bit touched up. The eyes were the same. Surely she was not going to kiss him but she was, she did.

'This is William,' he said almost without knowing it. 'My son.' He realized something else, that William had not said a word about her, or about Alun either, when he had had the chance. He must know, know something anyway.

'Hallo, William. Rosemary's round the place some-where.'

The voice was the same too, but he had noticed that already, on the telephone. He said something back and she asked about Muriel. The three talked for some minutes, had drinks, were joined by Rosemary. Peter took in very little: he was too busy looking furtively at Rhiannon and listening to her talking rather than following what she said. Now and then he tried and failed to explain to himself what he hoped to achieve (or perhaps avoid) while present. No sooner was the question sharpened for him by William steering Rosemary away than Alun came up and hailed him with his normal supernormal display of warmth. He was looking disagreeably fit, and well turned out: hair snowier than ever, new pearl-grey suit in some unfamiliar, doubtless fashionable cloth, pink carnation in buttonhole. The effect was in part that of an upper-second-rate actor, one of the sort you wondered about a bit too, which had to be accidental. But it was fair to say that the comic side of this was almost endearing, Peter considered, nearer to it at least than anything he was likely to come up with himself.

'You have the good fortune,' said Alun with all his vivacity, 'or as some would no doubt call it, the misfortune to find me in a state of euphoria. One based moreover not on artificial stimulants but on sober fact. Two facts. Today I received a commission for seven half-hour television programmes, title to be agreed but something about Wales, what else, all right Peter, and more important, incomparably more important, I wrote a poem, well, got to the end of the first draft. It's been a long time. I don't know whether it's any good but the point is writing it, getting it written, finding you can still do it. Marvellous bloody feeling. Like finding you can still, er . . .'

He fell silent abruptly and with seeming finality, blinking at the floor. After a number of seconds he flung up his head in triumph. 'Sing in the choir, sing in the choir. You thought you'd, er . . .' Another pause followed, but a much shorter one than before. 'Forgotten the harmony, forgotten how the part went, but you've still got it, it's still there. Very much the . . . Ah, here we are, there you are, you old devils, you.'

He turned with rekindled enthusiasm to Charlie and Sophie, to Garth, to Siân Smith and Dorothy Morgan, not abating it even for Dorothy; euphoria had been the word all right. When the cries and embraces of meeting were over Dorothy led Rhiannon away in the direction of a grim-faced female who looked like a retired bouncer in drag and shorty silver wig. Somebody's mother, Peter guessed; it had always to be remembered that there were still quite a lot of people about who had mothers.

Garth, quite natty in his usual tweeds, was eulogizing Alun's suit. 'Oh, lovely bit of garment you've got there, boy. Beautiful. Must have cost you a packet.' He reached out and turned a lapel over. 'Of course, I suppose having to look right for all your television appearances, this sort of thing comes off tax, does it?'

'I shouldn't be surprised. My accountant sees to all that. Anyway, what –'

'Do you know how long I've had this suit I'm wearing now?' Garth asked them all in a grim, challenging way. 'Thirty-seven years. You see, I've had a bit of sense, I've taken care of myself. Not like some, eh? Well, you're not as bad as these two, Alun, agreed, but you have let yourself go just a wee bit, come on, admit it now. Under here' – he tapped his chin – 'and here and –'

'I can't do anything about your terrible mind, Garth,' said Alun, grinning harder than before, 'I can't help your inability to notice anything that doesn't directly involve your pathetic self,' he continued, starting to shake with mirth, 'but when you start vaunting your supposed moral superiority, you bloody little cowshed mountebank,' and here he started laughing as he spoke, 'then at least I can tell you to shut your blathering trap before I slam your doubtless irreproachable dentures down your fucking throat.'

By now he and Garth had their arms round each other's shoulders, both of them bent in the middle and red in the face, roaring fit to bust, two old mates who had seen things so much in the same light for so long that they could be carried helplessly away together to a region of feeling no outsider could penetrate or understand. Charlie looked on with an unsettled smile, Peter without expression.

Alun was the first to come round. 'Well,' he said, breathing noisily and sniffing, 'that'll show the little bugger, what? Ah. Ah!' And he dashed off across the room to greet old Owen Thomas and his wife who had just come in the front entrance, near which there also stood a photographer.

'Oh dear, dear,' said Garth, 'there was a performance and no mistake. That boy's got a tongue to him, hasn't he? It's a treat to hear him use the language. God alive, I can't think when I last laughed like that.'

'How's Angharad?' asked Charlie.

'Oh, well enough, thank you, Charlie. Er, well enough.'

'I couldn't follow the bit about the cowshed,' said Peter when Garth had moved away.

'He's a vet, or was, at Capel Mererid. Sheep rather than cows, but you get the general gist. I thought everybody knew that. He doesn't give you a fair chance to forget it.'

'I knew. Well, after all, the mind's got to start going some time.'

'Not very nice, that just now, was it?' said Charlie. 'In fact not at all nice. It's odd, that was exactly what you've always wanted to say to him, you hoped somebody would one day and then when they do it's nothing like the treat you'd been banking on. Bloody . . . bloody little cowshed mountebank was it? M'm. There's trenchant, eh?'

'You think Garth got it?'

'No. If he told Angharad about it she would, but he probably hasn't told her anything for twenty years. No, if he'd got it, that would mean what he said to us about a treat and the rest of it would have had to be ironical and also played just right, and okay, perhaps you can never be absolutely sure a Welshman's not being ironical, not even that one, but playing something even approximately just right – Garth Pumphrey? No. What gets up my nose is Alun thinking he's got away with it. Like . . .'

'Or not caring if he has or not.'

'Correct. I don't think he'd have gone quite as far as that in the old days. Anyway, who cares? Let's get another drink.'

'Why not, it might be our last.'

'Cheers.'

3

Recalling his youthful self in this one respect, though not at all in any other, Peter spent some time trying without success to get Rhiannon on her own. Indeed even this much recall was faint: in those days he might well have brought matters to a head before very long by muttering a blunt directive to move elsewhere or, if it came to it, by seizing an arm and pulling fairly gently. Tonight he followed Rhiannon round tamely and, for the look of the thing, only some of the time. Dorothy Morgan appeared, stayed, went, reappeared, and while she was present and talking, in other words present, the best-case scenario, like Rhiannon and himself spontaneously taking to their heels, would have been no good because she would beyond question have come tearing after them. And when it was not Dorothy it was Percy and Dorothy, then Sophie and Siân again, then Alun briefly again, then old Tudor Whittingham and his wife and old Vaughan Mowbray's ladyfriend. Well, Peter kept telling himself, she was the hostess. When he saw Gwen approaching he gave up. She would have rumbled him in a moment and let him know about it in one taking-her-time look.

Glass in hand, hardly drunk at all, he stood or walked

here and there a few paces at a time. The heavy furniture, dark panelled walls, faded Turkey carpet in a style once seen all over the place but now disappeared everywhere else, or so he thought, persuaded him that nothing here had changed. The hefty flat-fronted gas-fire at the back of the room presumably concealed an open hearth, but if so it had been concealing it as far back as he could remember, whenever that might have been. He worked on it while he went out to the Gents. Though smartened up a little, this too seemed much the same, even to the fetching-up noises coming from one of the cubicles. Everybody had been in their twenties then; well, round about thirty. Now, from round about seventy, all those years of maturity or the prime of life or whatever you called it looked like an interval between two bouts of vomiting. Approximately. Not his genre, more Charlie's.

He went back into the hall trying to recall being in it when he had been round about thirty. It was likely, it was as good as certain that on at least one such occasion, drinking with a mate in the corner there, where you always went if it was unoccupied, or waiting for his father in the bar itself, he had thought of Rhiannon, felt excited about her, looked forward impatiently to seeing her. No doubt, but it had all gone, as finally as his childhood. His eagle two at the sixteenth in 1948 was still with him, though, and the champagne he had stood afterwards in the bar. How awful, he thought.

By this time he had reached the small dining-room that opened off the hall and was also open to non-members, though it was chiefly valued after sundown as a flaking-out facility for members. It was empty and in darkness now. He reached towards the light-switch, then left it and squeezed along the edge of the bare dinner-table to the window. Outside all colour had faded, but there was still a clear view of part of the course, including the pine-woods on one side and, furthest off, the nearly straight line of the cliff-top beyond which on bright days a shimmer was reflected from the sea. Whatever he might have made of this view in the past it looked only bare and desolate to him now, and he had hardly taken a good look at it before retracing his steps and turning the light on after all. His eyes moved half-attentively over the roll of members dead in the two wars: three Thomases in the second, one a cousin from Marlowe Neath, the others unknown to him. He realized he was waiting for Rhiannon to come and join him here. Well, if that sort of thing had ever happened in his life it was certainly not going to do so now. Time to be off.

The throng in the hall had thinned out a little but not much. He bumped into one or two people on his way through, partly because of drink no doubt, his or theirs, more that he had still not really learnt to allow for his increased bulk after the historic escalation of 1984, when he had eliminated all controls at a stroke, bar a few quaint medieval relics like slimline tonic. But he got to the opposite end without knocking anybody down and went to the telephone. Yes, a mini cab would be along in five to ten minutes, or so said a girl's voice that sounded almost demented with satisfaction at this prospect.

While he telephoned he had been aware of some disturbance, of raised voices, on the far side of the solid door that separated him from the party. On his return to it he saw that whatever had happened was just over. There was Rhiannon with her daughter watchful at her side, Alun explaining something with a good deal of head-shaking and hand-spreading, William in attendance too. Malcolm and Dorothy Morgan had their arms round Gwen, who seemed to be in tears, and were accompanying her, perhaps forcing her slightly, towards the side entrance of the Club. Everybody else in the room was making no bones about watching and starting to chatter excitedly.

Charlie turned to Peter and said, 'Quite a performance, eh? Pissed out of her mind, of course.'

'I was telephoning.'

'Your loss. It was all over in seconds but she got quite a lot in. Bloody this and fucking that, what would you, and selfish monster and windbag and hypocrite and broken-down Don Juan and phony Welshman. Nothing at all damaging.'

'The broken-down Don Juan part sounds a bit damaging in the circumstances.'

'Well not really, mixed in with all the other stuff. But the whole . . . I mean it was clear enough from the general tone and situation that there was or had been something going on. As it were.'

'Clear to Malcolm, would you say?'

'I don't know. That's his choice, isn't it? I warned him, didn't I, Alun that is, that bloody awful time we went down to Treville. You'd have thought he'd have picked up enough experience by this time.'

'He'll have forgotten it,' said Peter. 'A broken date, do you think?'

Charlie dismissed the question. 'That fucking old fool is going to do some real damage before he's finished. Hell-bent on it.'

'Good thing Gwen didn't actually, you know, say.'

'Yes, admirable self-restraint, what? Admirable buggery. She played it so she can say she didn't say anything any time she feels like it. It's called keeping your options open. Nay, stare not so. Peter, you don't mean you think when a woman loses control she loses control, do you?'

'It's not a settled view of mine, no.'

'Losing control is just another thing they do. Christ,

here's another one that doesn't seem to have noticed much what's going on round him. Hey, I'd have given a few bob to be over there a moment ago, Alun saying he hadn't done what no one had said he'd done. Anyway, I think he can be trusted to carry off that part all right. I think I'm a bit pissed, too. You off?'

'I thought I'd just have a word first.'

Charlie glanced over at the Weavers and back at Peter. 'Good luck.'

As Peter joined the group Alun left it, still shaking his head slightly in bewilderment. Face to face with William again, Peter was fully aware for the first time of what his son had said to him in the car and what it meant. The rush of understanding erased from his mind anything he might have been going to say. The girl Rosemary glanced at him sharply, not sure whether he was to be tolerated or not. Rhiannon gave him a little nod and no more, as if acknowledging him at a funeral. He waited. It was all he could think of doing.

'I was just saying, Dad,' said William, 'that crabbed youth has got to make allowances for the impetuous excesses of age,' – sterling stuff, thought Peter, and much better than anything he could have run up on his own account.

'Stupid old cow, you mean,' said Rosemary with plain indignation. 'I wouldn't mind so much if she didn't think she was being interesting.' She looked over her shoulder with no better-disposed an expression. By now Alun was nowhere to be seen.

'I noticed she'd been knocking it back quite a bit recently.' Rhiannon said this in her factual way, then turned brisk. 'Peter, love, I haven't talked to you at all. Let's go off somewhere and have a gas. Quick before Dorothy comes back.'

'I'm away in a minute, Dad,' called William. 'Be in touch now, right? I mean you with me.'

'Yes. Thanks, Willie.'

Rhiannon finished mouthing and signalling to her daughter from a couple of yards off and hurried Peter to the front door, wheeling nimbly round the mother-person he had classified earlier. It was obvious that the old creature was dying to grab her and stop her doing whatever she wanted to do, but she just failed to bring herself to bear in time. He had explained about the minicab and been assured that it would be safer to wait outside. Neither had a hat or coat. As they went down the front steps she took his arm. It was a fine night, overcast but dry and mild and gone altogether dark in the few minutes since he had stood at the dining-room window. There was plenty of light from the windows behind them, and the traffic was quite busy on the new multi-million-pound double-carriageway that curved round towards town.

'That was quick,' said Peter. 'Where are we going?'

'It wasn't awful leaving like that, was it? I had talked to everyone. It just seemed like such a good time to bugger off. I thought we could go and have a drink somewhere. Well, half a drink it had better be for me – I've had three glasses of wine already. Have you got a nice place you go when you want to be quiet?'

'I wish I had. Everywhere's so noisy these days.'

'I thought there's that place in Hatchery Road, the Italian joint, Mario's is it?'

'Oh, out to dinner, are we?'

'No, love, Alun's got this table at the Glendower later. I'll have to turn up to that, but we can have a gas before. You see, there's a little bar place at the back at whatever it's called where you haven't got to be going to eat. Er, Gwen knows them there. We'll talk about her and the rest of it another time. Actually it's not very nice really,' said Rhiannon, suddenly doubtful. 'I mean it's not very classy.

Sort of cheap and cheerful, if you see what I mean.'

Peter saw what she meant almost before they entered Mario's, clearly a former shop converted some short while before at no great outlay of cash or imagination. The front part held a few rows of flimsy tables for four laid with very clean red-and-white check cloths and napkins and a central line of bottled sauces and mustards. Long sticks of bread or biscuit in red-striped transparent plastic lay on every side-plate. A plump, heavily moustached waiter in a tartan jacket was serving, vocally and with great sweeps of his arm, plates of rather British-looking meat and veg to a quartet of silent youngsters. Their wary, first-date look made Peter feel a good hundred and fifty. He saw that Rhiannon was watching him to gauge his reactions, so he smiled and nodded brightly.

There hastened forward another plump man with a moustache and a notable jacket, one resembling an abbreviated dressing-gown. He too cut the air a good deal, proclaiming himself generally to be the proprietor, and of an Italian restaurant too. His greeting to Rhiannon fell short of kissing her hand but not by much. If he was not Italian himself by blood, which in this part of South Wales and in the catering trade he might quite well have been, he was the next best thing, even perhaps one better: a Welshman putting it on all-out. Peter got something different from him, the graver reception appropriate to a senator or international operatic tenor. 'Mario' or very possibly Mario led them through a curtain of hanging strips of shiny vari-coloured stuff into the back-of-the-shop part of the premises. Here, in a kind of boarding-house interior, a couple of groups of soberly dressed middle-aged people were drinking reddish or yellowish liquors out of glasses with a band of sugar round the rim or chock-a-block with straws and stirrers. Rhiannon and Peter sat up at a walnut table with barley-sugar legs and found it most handy for their drinks when they came, white wine for her, slimline tonic for him: he wished he had done without his last one or two at the club.

'Not too awful, do you think?' whispered Rhiannon.

'You'll have to speak up if you want me to hear you – deafer by the day. No, it's fine, I could enjoy a drink in a coal-shed as long as there was no music.'

In fact for the first time in his life he felt he could have done with some to take the edge off the silence. It had been all right in the car, but there they had had the driver not to say anything much in front of. After three seconds Peter felt he was never going to speak again. Then he brainily remembered that, except of course for Muriel, mothers liked talking about children and approved of fathers who did too, so he started on William, which allowed him to work in a lot of the necessary crap about houses, neighbourhoods and such. Rhiannon came back along the same lines with bits of Rosemary. Then they got on to the party and she said in a special offhand voice, 'I reckon William quite took to Rosemary, didn't you? Stayed close, anyway.'

'I was impressed by her myself,' said Peter. He meant it, in fact the sudden oblique reminder of the youthful Rhiannon had almost made him catch his breath, but he had to admit it came out sounding like hell. 'She struck me as, as . . .'

'I told you she's going to be a barrister? Arguing in a law-court. She's always had a way with words. Like Alun, I suppose.' She gave him a cautious, measuring look she probably thought he missed. 'William got a girl, has he?'

'I don't really know. I think not at the moment. He has, you know, had girls.'

'Oh, and Rosemary's had boys. Well, I say *had*, I just assume.'

'That's all I can do with William, assume. He's perfectly normal and perfectly fit and he goes about with girls. He's also thirty. And there we are.'

'Yes, and he's sure of himself in a good way. I think that's enough really. To be going on with, I mean. From your point of view.'

'I suppose so.' He went on without thinking much, 'I'm pretty sure my old man had a much better idea of what I used to get up to than I have about my son.'

'I wonder. If he had I doubt if he was any better off in consequence, your dad. But you can't help comparing, I catch myself doing it all the time. And things are much better now. Infinitely better than they used to be.'

'You and Rosemary, you're pretty close, I expect, aren't you?' asked Peter. Now he sounded sickly as well as fatuous. To improve matters he added, 'People say it's easier for mothers and daughters.'

'No great confidences, just a few little remarks she's dropped from time to time.'

'That make you think that . . . things have got better.'

'M'm. Yeah.'

That seemed to be that for the moment. Peter was not at all sure where this was leading but he could tell it was somewhere, if only from the look of slight tautness about the corners of Rhiannon's mouth that he had seen before. Then he noticed that she was goggling for his benefit at the nearest of their fellow-customers, who he was sure were too far off to hear them and not interested anyway. Oh Christ – Wales for ever, he thought: thirty years in London and further parts and when it came to *certain subjects* you still kept mum when strangers were present, or visible, so as to be on the safe side now, see. He smiled; after a moment of mild astonishment she did the same.

At this very juncture the Mario-figure came bustling up

and brilliantly announced to the party in question, 'Your table is ready whenever you like,' making about thirty syllables of it. Just as obligingly they started to move at once.

Rhiannon had evidently used those few moments to decide it was all right for her to go ahead. Not before the diners had well and truly departed, she began, 'What I meant about comparing, mostly anyway, what they don't seem to have now is all that awful routine you had to go through every time. I don't say they actually do any more of, you know, *it*, or less of it, or it's any better or worse when they get there but at least they're spared that. Sometimes when I look back, for a moment I can't credit it. It was like following an instruction manual – well, that's what it *was*, for goodness' sake. Stage one, arm round; stage two, kissing; stage three, more kissing; stage four, hand up top, outside; stage five, same thing, inside; stage six, really rude, not there yet but on the horizon. At one stage per date, max. It's like what some tribe in Africa used to get up to to make it rain before they learnt better. Only this used to go on for months often. And usually never get there. Same for everyone and no exceptions. Or am I exaggerating, do you think?'

'No,' said Peter, who in the last half-minute had found out he had not forgotten everything after all. 'Not in the least. And there were terrible sorts of tips on how to get round the rules.'

'Oh, and we had ours on how not to let them get round the rules. Phew. Could it have been a class thing?'

'I don't know.'

'No, unless it was just the aristocracy did different, because there were plenty of girls from the valleys in Brook Hall – you remember, and they were just the same. A bit nastier about it they were, I used to think, some of them. More cynical. I am exaggerating because it wasn't as clear-cut as that, couldn't have been. But there wasn't much that didn't more or less fit in with it in the end. I remember thinking once or twice at first it might all be Welsh, because of the chapel and everything, but I soon found out it was English as well. In a big way. So then I thought, well if I thought about it at all I thought it must be British. Couldn't be French. Didn't know about the Irish. The last thing was, do you remember those books by an American chap called Oh-something? Charlie was very keen on him. And the Sahara came into it somehow.'

'O'Hara. And the book you mean is *Appointment in Samarra*. I used to have them all at one time. John O'Hara. Good God.'

'That's the chap, but I'm not sure it was that book. Anyway, I started reading whichever it was and I nearly jumped out of my skin, it was exactly the same. That side of life, I mean. And they were meant to be ordinary average people, not millionaires or actresses but not hillbillies either. There was this guy and the dame he fancied, and first time out nothing, he may have kissed her goodnight, I can't remember. Then second time out you were expecting it to be here we go, but it wasn't at all, it was so far and no further the whole way. It was a good deal quicker than it would have been here, but then it's a book, isn't it? But it was the *same . . . thing*. In *America*.'

Peter still had little idea of what was expected of him, if anything. 'Could you call it the old Victorian ideas on their way out?' he suggested, trying not to feel like an exam-paper and failing soon enough. 'How did we ever agree to go along with it?'

She nodded absently and squared up her cigarette-packet and matchbox alongside one of the ornamental grooves that ran the breadth of the table-top. 'Not making yourself cheap, that's what it was all in aid of. Anyway that's what it was called.'

'A charade, in fact.'

'In a way, yes, but it was not-a-charade as well. That was the whole trouble. One moment you said it very, well, cynically and then a second later you'd find you'd said it completely seriously. *Cheap*. I expect the chaps called it something too, didn't they, that whole system?'

'Probably. I think they mostly took it as just part of existence, something you had to put up with, like getting up in the dark to get the bus to go to university. And it was a comfort to know that everybody else was in the same boat. Or you thought they were, which was just as good.'

'Oh, we had that too. Tell me something now, Peter: say a chap's girl had said all right straight away, would that have made him think she was making herself cheap?'

'Not unless he was a shit – he'd have been delighted. After he'd got over his surprise. But then I suppose if she started going round –'

'*That's* right. You can't make yourself cheap just with one person. Still, mustn't take it too seriously. As well as awful bits there were funny bits too, weren't there?' But apparently no funny bits came to mind for the moment. She lit a cigarette and when she went on it was at a reduced speed. 'So I'm glad that whatever Rosemary gets up to or might be going to get up to she's not going to not make herself cheap. It took too much out of people, that way of carrying on. Made them concentrate on the wrong things. And it was easy enough to go off the track without that. And what I saw was only half of it. The chaps' half must have been much worse.'

'We behaved much worse,' said Peter. 'On average.'

'A lot of it, some of it anyway wasn't your fault. I know you think you treated me tremendously badly, love, but you didn't, not really.' For the first time he got a look straight from those grey eyes and now he did catch his breath. 'It's more it sounds bad before you go into what actually happened, which was just we had an affair, not a very long one, though it would have been longer if I'd thought to do different, and you started to be attracted by someone else and we broke up. And it was after that, don't forget, I found I had a bun in the oven, and you took care of things, and *after* that . . . You were in love with someone else. I couldn't have expected you to walk out of it and come back to me, how could I at that stage?'

'I wish I had.'

'That's another matter. I'm sorry, I know we seem to have got on to this rather fast, but it could be ages before we're on our own again when I've had four glasses of plonk. And these days you never know how much time you've got. I wanted to tell you this before anyone starts dying. Just, it was lovely.'

He put out his hand across the table and she took it. 'Yes, it was.'

'So you'd better try and realize that some of the other bits aren't quite as bad as you thought.'

Not much later they were standing in the street outside the Glendower, he with his arm around her waist, she leaning her head on his shoulder. In the minicab, which waited near by now to take him on home, they had held hands all the way but barely spoken.

After about a minute she said, 'Would you like to come in for a drink?'

'No, I'd better be getting back. Unless it would make it easier?'

'No, don't worry about that. Look, I hope you don't think anything I've been saying was to do with anything that happened at the party. Or anything else.'

'No, no trouble there, love. I didn't take in everything about you during our thing together, not as much as I should have done, but I did get that far. So no, I don't think that.'

'Good. There's no reason why we shouldn't go out to dinner, you know.'

'I'll be in touch.'

'Rosemary goes back on Thursday. After that.'

She gave him a quick kiss on the mouth and went. He hung about a little longer, walking to and fro on the pavement with his head turned down and his hands clasped behind his back, not seeing what his eyes were trained on. Then he straightened up and went over to the car and got in the back.

'Cwmgwyrdd now, is it?' asked the driver, an oldster wearing what looked like his grandson's recent cast-offs. 'What part do you want?'

'I'll tell you when we get nearer.'

'Well, it makes a difference to how I go, see, with them shutting the old bridge over the –'

'Just take me there, will you, by any reasonable route.'

The man's head, white and unshorn, slewed intolerably round. 'Are you feeling all right, sir?'

'I'll live. Now kindly do as you're told.'

'*Duw, duw,* sorry I spoke. Not from round here, are you?'

'No, I'm from . . . from . . .'

'If you ask me, all the proper Welshmen are leaving Wales.'

'I say, are they really? Well, that's splendid news, by George. Over and out.'

But then when they drove up and the house was in darkness he remembered that Muriel was in Cowbridge, dining and staying the night with English friends she had told him he obviously had no time for, so he was free for over twelve hours.

Five – Rhiannon

1

The next morning Rhiannon and Rosemary sat at breakfast
in the new house; Alun had only a moment before driven off
for West Wales, there to see over a location for something or
other. Through most of the carpetless, curtainless ground
floor step-ladders stood, their summits linked by heavy old
planks, in the midst of opened drums of paint and other
applications, silently awaiting the return of the contracted
decorators from wherever they had been these last weeks.
It was possible to sit in part of the sitting-room, though it
helped if you were quite tired out before you started, and
to cook and eat in the kitchen. Here the poppies-on-white
cotton curtains were up but, for instance, a couple of boxes
of plates and saucers had yet to have their contents deployed
on the dresser shelves. Nelly, the new black Labrador
puppy, lay stretched out in her basket, idly chewing the
side of it from time to time in preference to her purple
plastic bone.

'Didn't I give you that mug?' asked Rosemary.

'When you were a tiny thing. It's really quite a nice piece
of china.'

The vessel referred to was of a rounded many-sided
shape that widened at the top, with gilt round the rim and
on the built-up handle, apple-blossom portrayed on the
sides and 'Mother' in florid cursive lettering. At the

moment it held some tea made from lemon-flavoured powder and a slice of real lemon floating on top. Also before Rhiannon were a plate that had an orange and a banana on it and a bowl of tinned pineapple pieces.

Rosemary ran her eye over these materials. 'Is that all your breakfast, just what I see in front of you? Wouldn't you like me to scramble you some eggs?'

'Of course I would, but they're terribly bad for you, eggs. Full of that stuff, you know, gives you heart-attacks. Fatty stuff.'

'And what you've got there is supposed to be good for you, is that right?'

'Yes. Oranges and bananas are full of potassium, which is very important for your liver.'

'Who says so?'

'Dorothy. She knows a lot about it. She's read all sorts of books on it. She sort of keeps up with it.'

'You mean as if it were something like nuclear physics. Nothing to stop her, I suppose. Surely there can't be much potassium left in that,' said Rosemary, nodding at the bowl of pineapple.

'It must be a bit all right, though. It's still fruit.'

'Well yes, I quite see how you must feel your liver needs all the help it can get after a night on the tiles like you've just been on.'

'I wasn't awful, was I?'

'I've never known you awful. Good time had by all, I hope.'

'Well, I had a nice chat with Peter. I think I told you, he's always felt bad about what happened years ago.'

'As well he might,' said Rosemary, but gently.

'No need to go into it all now. Anyway we cleared one or two things up between us.'

'Good, now mind you get a proper lunch. Something cooked, not snacks.'

'No, it'll be a proper lunch all right. You can always rely on old Malcolm to take care of a thing like that. Rather too much so, in fact.'

'How do you mean, Mum?'

'Oh nothing really. I say, talk about living it up. Drinks with one boy-friend last night and a lunch-party and tour with another one today. Dirty little stop-out.'

Unseen, Rosemary smiled for a moment at her mother with no great amusement, even with some sadness, but said only, 'Go over my duties while you're gone.'

'The main thing is that creature there, obviously. Take her out every two hours. And some men are ringing at eleven about an estimate for the roof.'

'I'll get them to ring again later. What time will you be back?'

'I don't know. Could you tell them –'

'Tomorrow morning, then.'

'The thing is, we've already accepted another lot's estimate which is lower, and these ones need to be told we don't want them. So could you tell them? You'd just be passing on a message.'

'Whereas if they found they were talking to the party who'd actually taken the decision not to have them they might fly into a rage. I see. Yes of course. Anything else?'

'Not really. It doesn't seem much to keep you in half the day.'

'Never mind, there's plenty round here that needs putting straight.'

And that puppy to impress, to make sure of being remembered by on future visits, and very sensible too, thought Rhiannon, but revised her thought at the quiet speed with which Rosemary left the room to answer the telephone.

A tabloid newspaper lay open on the breakfast-table, folded back at the horoscope feature, which was quite good fun to read, not that there was anything at all in it, in astrology, whatever Dorothy might say. It was the style of this feature, the clear lay-out and central position of the television programmes, the young-marrieds strip and the twice-weekly political column by old Jimmy Gethin that years ago had given the paper the edge over its rivals as far as Rhiannon was concerned. She still took it even though poor old Jimmy's liver had packed up once for all in the meantime, whether for lack of potassium nobody had said. In fact he had been Alun's pal more than hers, and she had never read his column unless its first paragraph happened to catch her eye by promising an attack on one or other of the couple of far-left politicians whose activities she fitfully noticed. That was about as far as her interest in politics went, and she was not much better when it came to literature: she only paid attention when Alun's concerns came up and, to be quite honest, not very closely even then.

At university, under Gwen's and Dorothy's guidance, she had done her best to put this right by reading or trying to read books on the two subjects and also on art, where some of the pictures had been nice, though not by any means all. But it had never taken, and at about the time she left there she had given up the attempt with relief and shame at the same time. The shame had lasted; it still troubled her to remember the time she had been taken out by a rather small chap doing German Honours, and at the end of the evening he had said wonderingly, 'But you're not interested in anything at all.' She had had no answer then or since; the things that did interest her were too small

193

and spread-over to add up to a subject you could sit an exam in. And that was that, but it would never do to feel all right about it, ever.

She heard Rosemary at the door, and guiltily stuffed back into the packet the cigarette she had started to take out. Pretending to be absorbed in the horoscopes she read that for Leo subjects (like herself) this would be a good day for clinching business deals provided they managed not to let rip with their famous roar.

'That was William. You know, William Thomas.'

'Oh yes,' said Rhiannon, trying to get the right amounts of interest and surprise in.

'It's his day off apparently, so I asked him if he'd like to come over. I hope that's all right.'

'Oh yes of course, good idea. That'll –' She stopped herself from going on '– give you something to do with yourself' and substituted '– be nice' rather feebly and only just in time.

'More tea?'

'No thank you dear. I think I'll go on up now.'

'Give me a yell when you want me.'

In the bathroom Rhiannon hung up her good roomy man's-fit towelling dressing-gown, originally a birthday present to Alun, but after a week or two he had gone back to his Paris one in chartreuse watered silk. Her slippers, knitted by Dorothy in red wool with a green R on each like the colours of the flag, were on the tight side, especially over the left instep, and it tended to be a relief to get them off. The nightdress rather played safe by being just white cotton with broderie-anglaise trimming.

On the glass shelf beside the basin there sat a fresh plastic bottle of natural-herb shampoo with a cardboard thing round its neck. Six such things, she saw on reaching for her glasses, would if sent in get you an absolutely free hanging basket for indoor plants and greenery, so she carefully removed this one and stowed it away in the cabinet. These days almost any special offer found her wide open. Going in for them was a bit like betting on the Derby: you could lose for instance, like that set of chef's kitchen-knives (eight pork-pie seals and cheque for £8.55 incl. p&p) that had stayed sharp for about twenty minutes.

She stepped into the shower, a glassed-in job featuring a massive control-dial calibrated and colour-coded like something on the bridge of a nuclear warship. Along with the central heating and parts of the kitchen it was understood to have been newly installed by the previous owner, a garage-proprietor who could not have had anything like his money's-worth out of it before driving his Volvo into a wall – dead of a coronary before he hit, they soothingly said. Rhiannon was still not really used to the shower and kept falling back on trial and error, though no longer seriously afraid of smothering herself with ice-water or saturated steam. The shampoo, which said it was mild enough for her to use it every day, went on, off, on again, staying on for the essential two minutes while she soaped herself, finally and thoroughly off before a burst of cold all over to tone up the skin.

As she stood on the self-drying mat she got going with the bath-towel while gauging the intensity of the sunlight coming through the frosted pane. Arriving at a decision she carefully pat-dried her legs and while they were still damp spread make-up from a tube evenly over them, thus among other things covering up any unattractive veins. A drop of Sure here and there, a dab of talcum top and bottom and then on with the dressing-gown and slippers and across the landing with a call down to Rosemary on the way.

Apart from a couple of bulging black sacks by the

window and a frock and suit or so the bedroom was in order, centring on Rhiannon's wonderful old Victorian marble-stand dressing-table with the heavy oval free-standing mirror and a tall jug, itself painted with rose-buds, holding roses from the garden. Here she combed out her hair, telling herself as always how lucky she had been in this department, thick as ever, easy to manage, even now only needing a little touching up. She was still at it when Rosemary came in.

'What's that on your legs, Mum?'

'Sheer Genius. I mean that's what it's called, I noticed particularly. Max Factor. I got it for my face but it turned out too dark. Honey Touch it says as well. I suppose that's a colour, is it?'

'All right, but what's it doing on your legs?'

'Well, it was that or stockings, and the weather's too nice for stockings, I thought.'

'You realize they don't match your hands?'

'Yes of course I do, but men don't think of things like that. Not as a rule.'

Rosemary gave up the matter. During its discussion she had been sorting out the drier and now she began to wield it on her mother's hair, no great test of skill or devotion but pursued steadily enough. As she worked away with blower and comb she glanced round the room, taking particular notice of the female garments on display, but before she could say anything the door was barged aside and Nelly the puppy came running unskilfully in. She seemed not so much thankful at having found the two women as indulgently gratified by the joy and relief her arrival must bring them. After a quick circuit for form's sake she went straight under the bed, starting to growl furiously somewhere in the alto register.

'I should have shut her in downstairs,' said Rosemary.

'She's all right. She's got to learn her way round the house.'

'Wouldn't it be better if she learnt that after she's trained?'

'Well, it's all part of the training, learning not to go when she's up here.'

Rosemary leaned over to see what the now emerged puppy was doing. 'You know she's got your slipper, do you?'

'That's all right,' said Rhiannon after checking that the Dorothy slippers were safely on her feet. 'She can have that one.'

'You can't just let her chew away at anything she happens to fancy. That's no way to train her.'

'It'll sort itself out.' Rhiannon considered telling her daughter that she might feel differently about such questions when she had had a couple of children of her own, but let it go. 'You can't watch them all the time. Right, that's fine, dear, thank you. I like it a little bit damp.'

'What, er, what outfit were you proposing to wear for this jaunt, Mum?'

'I thought the blue denim suit – yes, there.'

'M'm.' The accompanying nod was non-committal. 'What else?'

'There's a white cotton sports-shirt with long sleeves that come down out of the cuffs of the jacket. Then if it gets hot I can take the jacket off and roll the sleeves up. Only when he can't see my legs, of course.'

'Hey!' shouted Rosemary at Nelly, who in full view was carelessly lowering her hindquarters towards the carpet. 'Oogh! Urhh!' she added, scooping the puppy up and hurrying her out of the room.

'Don't forget to tell her –'

'I know, Mum, I know.'

Left alone, Rhiannon sat pushing her hair into place at the mirror. She wished very much she could look forward wholeheartedly to the coming excursion. The way Malcolm had sounded over the telephone when he invited her originally, and still more so his manner as he confirmed the arrangement at the Club the previous evening, had puzzled her, troubled her, nothing to do with his old awkwardness which had never been a problem. No, there was something, perhaps the way he had kept pausing as he talked, that had suggested to her that there might be going to be more to this half-day outing than met the eye. Still sitting, she crossed fingers on both hands.

The sound of her daughter's voice from below, duly raised in tones of unreserved triumph and admiration, got her moving again. By the time Rosemary came back to the bedroom she was in pants and bra at the dressing-table mirror putting on foundation.

'Just you think yourself lucky she didn't drop that lot up here is all I can say.'

'I will, I do. Thank you, dear.'

'Right, well now let's just take a look at this, this *suit* we've heard so much about, shall we? Tell me, you like it yourself, do you?'

'Well, I feel nice in it.'

'M'm.' Rosemary accepted the point. 'Any ideas about shoes at all?'

'I thought these,' – lace-ups in the same or much the same blue denim.

There was a bit of a hiccup over the shirt, with an alternative in frilled terracotta silk considered and briefly tried on, but in the end everything went through all right and, after a final squirt of Christmas-present cologne, Rhiannon trooped off downstairs carrying her linen-look sand-coloured shoulder-bag. She wore no jewellery, just her wedding ring.

In the kitchen again Rosemary made coffee and the contents of the bag were gone over in a comparatively relaxed spirit. Compact, spare handkerchief, purse with window showing essential telephone numbers on card, toothbrush – all passed in lenient silence. But then – 'What's *this* for God's sake?' asked Rosemary, sounding at the end of her tether.

'Plastic mac. Rolled up.'

'I'm not blind, you know. *Honestly*, Mum. *Christ*. Why haven't you got an umbrella?'

'I keep losing them. Leaving them in places.'

'There are ones that fold which you clearly haven't seen, and go in your bag and don't cost the earth.'

'Well, I haven't got one.'

'M'm. I suppose there's a hat to match, is there?'

'No, there's a hood attached to the collar that hangs over my eyes. I'll wear it all through lunch if you don't look out.'

Rosemary peered into the bag. 'Funny, I can't find any wellies here.'

'You wait, I'll fetch Dad's galoshes in a minute.'

'I'd better get you my umbrella.'

'No, I'll lose it. And there's no need to treat me as if I'm fourteen years old.'

'Oh yes there is, because that's all you are. When I was that age you were much older, but now you've gone back. You are fourteen years old. Aren't you?'

'M'm,' whined Rhiannon, cringing and trotting her feet on the floor.

The telephone rang. Rosemary was there first and asked who was calling. With a face of stone she passed her mother the handset. 'Gwen.'

'Hallo Gwen.'

'Rhiannon dear, this is old *Gwen*.' These words and the way they were spoken were enough to banish expectation that any sort of genuine apology or voicing of regret might be at hand. 'Thank you for a super party. I thoroughly enjoyed myself, in fact it rather seems a bit too thoroughly towards the end and got sort of carried away. Over the top I believe you're supposed to call it nowadays. I hope it wasn't too embarrassing for you.'

'That's all right.'

'I'm afraid I do tend to get ever so slightly cross with poor dear Alun from time to time over, well what the hell is it over, I suppose you'd have to call it *Wales* I'm sorry to say. The thing is that, you know, according to me there's a touch of the stage Welshman about him, he says so himself, fair play, but perhaps it's more than a touch – still, and he thinks I'm a dried-up schoolmarm. Well, there we are, and it's all right until I drink too fast because I'm having a good time and Alun says something to do with I don't know what and then I find I've –'

'That's all right, dear. All forgotten.'

'Well . . . It wasn't very seemly, I'm afraid. Turning nasty in my drink. Alun about?'

'No, he's away all day today.'

'I'll talk to him again. It really was a fantastic party. I'll ring you later.'

'Good-bye, love.'

'There's lucky you've got a fine day for your excursion now. Young Malcolm's on pins. Cheers.'

Rosemary, who after some hesitation had stayed in earshot, gave her mother what could not but be an inquiring look and got a kind of mock-doleful one back.

'She got cross about something Dad said about Wales.'

'Oh I *see*. Golly, what a terrific help. Must have cost her a bomb to come clean like that.'

'Well it is quite, a help I mean. One of us had to work out a way of us going on being friends.'

'Had to? She's not nice enough to be a friend of yours.'

'She's not so bad. When it's been long enough that sort of thing stops mattering.'

'You let her down too lightly.'

'It's much too late to start letting people like Gwen down heavily. Let's go outside. Malcolm's obviously on his way.'

Rhiannon picked up her shoulder-bag. As they moved Rosemary put an arm round her waist.

'Don't you mind about, well, any of it?'

'What are you talking about, of course I bloody well mind. But that's all I do, I stop myself doing any more than that. Like brooding or going back or joining things up, no point in it. As long as I don't *know*. And this isn't knowing.'

'Mum, I wish you'd let me –'

'Let's not say any more about it now.'

The garden in front of the house was not large but it had the bright green grass often to be found in this part of the world and a few flowers in half-overgrown beds, including an unexpected treat in the shape of a large clump of Canterbury bells. Nelly crashed into the side of it, then doubled back up the path effortlessly surmounting the obstacle presented by each three-inch-deep step. A good view stretched almost due south, over woods and shadowed lawns down over an unseen cliff to a wide stretch of sand shining wetly in the sun and, about as far out at the moment as it ever went hereabouts, the sea with half a dozen small boats sailing. Some cloud was drifting near the horizon but not much and none of it dark. There was nothing ugly or dull anywhere.

'You are looking forward to this do, aren't you, Mum?'

'Oh yes. Well . . . yes.'

'What's the not-so-good part?'

'Well, he's . . . He's a very sweet chap without a nasty or unkind thought in his head but he's a bit wrapped up in himself. He's liable to say things when he hasn't thought how they'll affect other people, just because he wants to say them. Just sort of blurts them out.'

'Such as he's never loved anybody but you in all his life?'

'Sort of thing, yeah.'

'Well if it's no worse I don't think you have much to worry about. Surely you can manage that. You must have had plenty of practice.'

'Oh, come on, dear.'

Rosemary looked at her mother for a moment before she spoke again. 'Of course, I suppose he might embarrass you about Gwen and so on.'

'No, he understands about not doing things like that, and besides he won't think anything happened.'

'How do you mean, Mum?'

'She'll have made him believe her version.'

'*Made* him?'

'Yes, nothing to it with him if she sticks to it, and she will.'

'Well, I dare say you'd know.'

Turning to address the dog, who watched her with an air of stark terror, Rhiannon said, 'You're not coming today. I'm sorry, but you're not.'

'Oh my God,' said Rosemary. 'You don't seriously imagine she can understand you, I hope.'

'It wouldn't do to be too sure of that. Probably not now, but she'll understand everything like that by the time she's grown up, and there's no knowing when they start. All part of the training.'

'Well, she's your dog . . . Is this him now?'

'I think . . . Yes.'

'Mum, if you're going to go out looking as nice as you do now I'm afraid you'll just have to grit your teeth and face up to him saying he loves you. Now . . .'

Mother and daughter proceeded to stand to. Without waiting for orders Rosemary went and dragged the puppy out from the laurel bush she had bolted under and held her in her arms. Rhiannon turned and put her hair right by her reflection in a sitting-room window, then neatly snapped off the half-open yellow rose she had had her eye on all along but had left on the plant as long as possible. Finally the two moved a little apart from each other so as not to look too lined-up and organized.

When he had got out of his very shiny bright-blue car and at a second attempt shut its driver's door, Malcolm revealed himself to be wearing a hacking jacket in dark red, green and fawn checks that were too large by an incredibly small amount, cavalry-twill trousers he must have been uncommonly fond of, a pale green I'm-going-out-for-the-day-with-my-old-girl-friend cravat or ascot and, thank goodness, a plain shirt and ordinary brown lace-up shoes. Seen closer to, he proved to have an ample shaving-cut on his cheek, about like a boil on the end of his nose to him and not worth a second glance to anybody else. He carried a florist's plastic-wrapped bouquet of a good forty-quid's-worth of red roses and pink carnations which he handed over to Rhiannon fast and at arm's length.

'Lovely to see you,' he muttered, obviously discarding on the spot an earlier draft, and called 'Hallo' with unmeant abruptness to Rosemary, whom he had met more than once before but never for long, and had not bargained on seeing now. Then he took in the puppy and loosened up a little. 'Ah, now here's a splendid fellow and no mistake.'

'Hallo, Malcolm,' said Rosemary, 'female fellow actually,' and went on with exemplary stuff about how he would not have said that if he had been on the spot just earlier, the awful chewing, etc. Rhiannon fixed the yellow rose in his button-hole and passed the bouquet to Rosemary, who had set Nelly down on the grass as now to be considered defused.

'Put them in that pretty Wedgwood jug – they'll look marvellous in there – and find somewhere in the cool for them.' Rhiannon was too shy herself to embark on a full-treatment head-on thank you. 'We'll decide on a proper place when I get back. That won't be before five at the earliest – I've got one or two things to see to in town first.' The last bit was said looking over her daughter's shoulder.

2

Immediately upon getting into the car beside Malcolm, Rhiannon noticed a peaked cap in nearly the same pattern as his jacket folded up on the shelf in front of him. All she could do about that was hope he had already tried this and thought better of it, rather than that he was keeping it by him to spring on her later. Anyway she sighed comfortably, or tried to. There was a faint pleasant smell hanging about and the whole interior told of hours of tidying and cleaning. In a way she hardly understood, it was like something she remembered from years ago: she had complimented Malcolm on his clear neat handwriting and he had thanked her and said, well, he reckoned however boring or no-good what he wrote might be, at least whoever it was would be spared the extra chore of deciphering it. Like a lecturer's duty to be audible, he had said.

The first few minutes passed easily enough with chat

about Rosemary, then Alun briefly, then Gwen no more briefly – Rhiannon's idea, that, to rub in that the subject was ordinary. The next few went even more easily with taking notice of the approaches to Courcey and after some delay the island itself. She had been along here quite recently with some of the crowd for a Sunday-lunchtime drink at the King Arthur just off the causeway, a brief or single drink as it had turned out, because the one huge bar had been full of fat young left-wing activists from a weekend school ordering things like blue curaçao with passion-fruit juice. But they were soon past there now and on to where she had not been for at least ten years, probably a good deal more.

To Rhiannon the greenery looked greener and also thicker than it had, the hill-tops perhaps not as high, but it was hard to notice when the whole place was so tremendously more crowded. Approaching Chaucer Bay down the west road they ran into traffic like a Saturday morning in town: cars, buses from Cardiff and – she was nearly sure – Hamburg, bikes and of course caravans, of which some hundreds were stationed in lines like those of a military cantonment across the whole width of the furze-covered slope that faced the bay.

'Sorry about this,' said Malcolm as they came to another halt. Far from sorry, he looked cheered up by the thought of how much worse matters would have to get before he had to decide or do anything.

'We've got plenty of time.' With a qualm she realized how much.

'I'm glad I allowed for it. But it is remarkable, eleven-thirty midweek and still in school term.'

Rhiannon mentioned the marvellous weather and said to herself that that was good old Malcolm for you: it would simply never have occurred to him to start going on about where did all the money come from was what some of us would have liked to know, and so this was what a recession meant, and the black economy and minimum-wage agreements and the closed shop and who ever cared a curse for the pensioners. Everybody else she could think of for the moment except Rosemary would have been well into that by now. And Alun unless there had been other people around too.

They moved on a few more yards and round a bend. Malcolm was keeping fussily closed up to the car in front, but she had plenty of room to see the shingly, littered way on to the beach through a gap in the cliff and the half-naked people hurrying along it, all loaded with food and drink containers, tents, boats, sports kits, games, anything and everything for children – plenty of them about, school term or no school term. When they drove past a minute later Rhiannon got a squint at the sort of village of plastic stalls and booths that had sprung up to screw the visitors in every available line, cosmetic, decorative, educational, you name it, some of them not so plastic, but surely . . . A beach-boutique on the beach? In South Wales? Now?

Then the lights changed and they started squeezing their way up the hill on the far side between the groups of young men straggling down from the car-park with no shirts on, satisfied with that being all right and not bothering about looking horrible, being it too for not bothering. From the top Rhiannon had a view of the whole of the long, wide expanse of sand scattered over with moving or still figures as she had never seen it before. Some had wandered along as far as Rundle Bay, which they would have to move back from when the tide came up or face a steep climb up to the road, all right in the day, she remembered, but not much fun after dark with a pushy chap trying to give you a hand.

'Seems a long time ago, doesn't it?'

For Malcolm, this bit of advanced thought-reading was uncanny. She gave him a special look of appreciation before saying, 'Yes, thank God.'

'What? I meant, you know, going on the beach and bathing and what-not the way everyone used to.'

'That's what I meant. Yes, everyone did use to, didn't they? Coming for a swim?' She speeded up before he could think he was being asked to come for a swim now. 'Coming out to Courcey with us, and you just went along without thinking. Like, well, like a lot of things then. I never really liked swimming.'

'As I remember you were pretty good at it.'

'Not bad, and of course it was lovely in the water once you'd survived going in, but awful being out. Hoping you looked wonderful with wet hair and feeling it standing out in the wind and starting to go like straw.'

'Surely, didn't girls wear caps in those days? Bathing caps I mean.'

'Only if you didn't mind your face going the size of a nut. It's amazing thinking of it now, I can hardly believe it. Sort of half sitting with your legs out to the side and smiling and trying to feel if half your bottom was out of your bathing-costume. And it wasn't just me either – Gwen was the same, Siân, Dorothy, everyone. We used to –'

'But you all seemed so absolutely marvellously . . .'

'Poised? You should have seen us. All that awful tanning. I remember a serious discussion in Brook Hall about how red in the face you could afford to let yourself get at a time. And what you did about the hair on your legs and arms. Choices to be weighed up there. Snags to all of them.'

'But I mean you did enjoy it,' said Malcolm anxiously.

'Parts of it.'

'Oh yes. You noticed things like your hair and what

horrible stuff sand is but you didn't really take it in. You were wondering how it was going and what would happen next and whether you could handle it. We weren't poised really, just trying not to give anything away. Of course, I don't suppose it was all plain sailing for the chaps,' she wound up thoughtfully.

'No.' He took a vigilant look at the now-empty road ahead. 'No, it certainly wasn't,' he added.

After waiting for a moment she started again. 'It wasn't only going on the beach, not being poised. It was a big one, the beach, but it didn't really touch dancing.' When she saw Malcolm smiling and blinking uncertainly she went on, 'You know, going to a dance. With a band and partners and quick-steps and all that. Sticking together was the thing. Dorothy used to get us on parade in Brook and make sure we'd all been to the lav before we started so there'd be no sneaking away later. Then you'd stand in a bunch waiting to be asked for a dance and wanting to bite your nails and hoping the bra-strap you should have pinned was still behind your dress-strap. I was, anyway. Didn't you worry about things like that?'

'Yes, I suppose I must have done.'

She thought to herself she might have another try later. So far she had obviously not been going the right way about getting him to say he had gone through the same little agonies as she and all the others had, which might have helped him to see that it worked the other way round as well, that she in her way had been as embarrassed and incompetent as he in his. The idea was to show him that she was not the curious creature, something between Snow White and a wild animal, that he had seemed to take her for, but an actual friend of his, and by now quite an old one. Well, there was still a lot of time.

'Those days, you know,' he said now, with a hint of

wisdom coming up. 'All I can say is I hope there were certain, shall I say mitigations.'

'Oh *yes* Malcolm, don't get the wrong idea. How awful, I was only –'

'Because this today, after all, we are, well, taking a stroll down *Memory Lane*.' He said this as if he thought he had just invented the expression, or at least was betting she had not come across it lately.

'That wasn't there before,' she said, so promptly that it took him a moment to see she meant something real, something in a field they were passing, a kind of cabin or pavilion with a factory-built look and talkative notices done in very aggressive lettering about things to eat in the basket or in the bag. There was a mass of tyre-tracks round it but nobody in range just then. Seen like that in the unexpected strong sunlight it seemed the sort of place you were meant to admire without wanting to go there, like a piece of new housing project in Mexico.

'How vile,' said Malcolm with feeling. 'New to me too, I think. Just spring up behind your back. Same everywhere you go these days.'

That last phrase kept coming up in Rhiannon's hearing, often along with another one about it being a waste of breath. It seemed to hit them all sooner or later, even someone like honest old Malcolm who never wondered where all the money was coming from. Once he got into this one the conversation would at least stay out of harm's way a bit longer. But nothing followed, and when he went on it was in a new, dreamy sort of tone, not much of a good sign with him.

'They say people change over the years,' he began, and seemed set to end too for a while before hurrying on, 'and indeed it does often happen. You remember a fellow called Miles Garrod? Used to act a lot. Quite good he was. He played Marlow in *She Stoops to Conquer* in the Arts Theatre.'

'Oh yes,' lied Rhiannon. When it was not going to make a difference she always did that except with Alun; it seemed fussy and cocky not to and you were going to get the rest of it anyway. This was a general policy of hers. People sometimes wondered gratefully how it was that she had never heard any stories before.

'Well, you wouldn't recognize him now, Rhi, that I guarantee. I bumped into him just a few months ago, at a wedding in Caerhays. Or rather I didn't bump into him, praise be, a fellow said there's old Miles Garrod, I said where, the fellow said there, and there he was, totally different. A different person. Not specially old-looking or unprepossessing. Just altogether different. A different individual.'

Having shown that one who was in charge he could have afforded to throw in something about what Miles Garrod was up to these days, but no. Returning to the dreamy tone and unmistakably starting paragraph 2, Malcolm said, 'But some people haven't changed, or only imperceptibly. You, Rhiannon Weaver, you haven't changed, not you. You're still the same person as the one I knew, well, let's call it *then*, shall we?'

'What nonsense, I've put on at least –'

'No, no, basically you're quite unchanged. The way you move, your glance, everything. The first sight of you that very first evening . . .'

She let him run on, but stayed alert for any wandering off into dodgy territory. Sudden blurtings of the type mentioned to Rosemary could not be guarded against, only watched for.

'. . . last glimpse of you eight years ago . . .'

A bit longer than that, but he had put it down very firmly, and what of it anyway. Not far now, surely.

'. . . never more than a few minutes at a time . . .'

Well, there again she seemed to remember proper evenings, even a weekend visit or two, in fact, certainly one thorough enough to have included a couple of chats with Gwen about the forthcoming arrival of what had turned out to be Rosemary's elder sister in 1959, but if he preferred to see it like this, well, fine with her.

'. . . I was seeing you for the first time since *then*. Ah, when I used to read about people feeling the years dropping away I thought it was just a phrase, just a fancy. But it's what *happened*.' He looked at her a little bit wildly but quite briefly out of the corner of his eye. 'And I'd known all along it would. Don't ask me how,' he told her, to be on the safe side.

STOGUMBER I PETERSTOW 2½ the signpost said, and Peterstow was where they were scheduled to have lunch. How many minutes did that mean? Five? One and a quarter? Rhiannon crossed the fingers of her left hand. It was awful to think the thought in this way, but hopeless not to: if things got no dicier than at present, then no problem. They had got as far as they had pretty fast, true, and unassisted by drink, but he might have been encouraged by not having had to meet her eye any of the time because of driving, and he had not actually *said* anything yet and it might all blow over.

The car came to the crest in the road a hundred feet or so above Stogumber village and from the sea on their right, limitless now, to the dense greenery on their left nothing showed that time had gone by.

'I don't just mean of course you're unchanged on the outside,' said Malcolm, dashing what could never have been more than a faint hope. 'Anybody with half an eye can see that.' He paused and drew in his breath. 'I mean on the inside too. But then I don't think anybody changes there much, do you? On the inside?'

She tried to consider it. 'No, I shouldn't think so probably.'

'Now I know I've changed a lot on the outside. A decrepit old bloke is what I've become. No complaints but that's how it is.' He wagged his head from side to side as he sat behind the wheel.

'I'm not having that,' she said indignantly. 'Decrepit is the absolute opposite of what you are. You're in jolly good nick and fit-looking and you've kept your hair and everything. You could pass for, for a much younger man.'

It had never been Malcolm's way even to try to hide things like pleasure at compliments, and here was one department in which he had certainly not changed. Another was making it very easy for the other person to tell when a compliment was called for and roughly how it should go, and then still enjoying it when it came. 'Oh, honestly, Rhi,' he said now a couple of times, continuing quite soon, 'anyway, I'm still pretty much the same on the inside.'

Dumbly-dumbly-dumbly-dum on the inside, she thought to herself, waiting to hear how, dumbly-dumbly-dumbly-dum on the outside, but crossing her fingers again. But then when it came it was fine, in the same style as before, covering rather more ground, not much though: incurable romantic – always tended to expect too much from life – rather envied practical man who just got on with things – triumph of hope over experience – incurable romantic – count your blessings – help us get through life – never really wanted to be one of the down-to-earth sort that just stuck to the job in hand – too old to change now, he maintained firmly. Matters took a slight turn for the worse after that with him saying how much he had been looking forward to today and how he still had his hopes for the future, but he stayed vague on that and quite soon stopped. The end of the beginning, with luck.

They were in and out of Stogumber itself in not much more time than it took to notice a jumble of flags, posters and stickers coloured lime-green, yellow, pinky-red and black and white. Then having turned up left along the further edge of the little valley they came to another sign-post, one of a new sort in dark green with a picture of a wigwam on it and thin white print which was quite easy to read from close to. This lot said Peterstow 0.8 km, and no doubt if you went the way it pointed you got there in the end.

Rhiannon had been hoping and expecting to recognize the village when they came to it, but she failed to do so. There was a raised stretch of grass with some lumps of grey-white stone here and there, and an old drinking-fountain sort of built into the side of the slope, the remains at least of such a thing with a place where a chained cup might once have been joined on. Next to it she made out four or five names carved on a tablet and realized she was looking at a local war memorial. Here and there were hefty cottages in a darker stone or in a dark brick behind low white gates, and on the far corner a larger building done with beams and tiles. A sign said it was the Powys Arms and also mentioned old-fashioned things like finest ales and ciders. Although there were other cars about, it was still possible to park near the front door.

Malcolm did that, pulling on the hand-brake with a rasping flourish. 'Well,' he said, turning to Rhiannon and smiling at her with his eyes crinkled up – 'here we are.' He was behaving as though he had given her a costly present which only he in his sensitivity could have chosen for her, and looked very sweet and sitting up and begging for a smart clip round the ear.

'Marvellous,' she said.

He got out of his seat and came round to open her door,

moving quite fast but not as fast as she did to forestall him. These days she never liked people 'helping' her out of or off things unless she could do a crone imitation with it, and not much even then. He arrived a second after she had got both feet to the ground, but in the nick of time to alert her against leaving behind the shoulder-bag she was just picking up. As they strolled towards the pub he put his hand round her elbow in case she started to fall over or tried to walk into a wall. She could just about recall him using this instant this-one's-mine-you-see indicator once or twice when he had taken her out in the old days. Actually this time it came in useful for stopping her from going ahead and heading into the pub just like that.

He glanced at her again and said, 'Hasn't changed a lot, has it?'

'Doesn't seem to have done.'

'Apart from the rebricking along under the roof there and taking the lean-to part into the main structure and paving over where the old well was. Not to mention the wall round the car-park. And wasn't there a hut in that corner?'

Rhiannon had no answer to that. She nodded her head slowly and mumbled to herself.

'And obviously the tables. Still, it is very much as it was. In essentials you might say.'

'M'm.'

'The rubbish-bins aren't very pretty but at least they're practical.'

After a last satisfied look around he made to steer her through the doorway, but again she was too quick for him, thinking that it – being too quick for a man – was not something she was often called upon to be any more. Inside, she looked round with a show of interest. Whether it was very much as it had been she had no idea, but anyway it was not crowded yet and not noisy. The only thing she noticed was the little brass rails or railings round the tops of some of the tables, to keep you on your toes when you – no, rubbish, she told herself, off a ship, ten to one, a point Malcolm might well be just going to clear up for her. He kept quiet on that, though, saying only that of course he had no idea whether the place was any good these days, a whopper if ever she had heard one.

The place, as regards food and drink, which he called victuals, was good enough, but with him there that counted as no more than a start. Of all the men she knew, he was right out in front the likeliest to be ignored at the bar, given a table the kitchen door banged into, brought his first course while later arrivals were drinking up their coffee, overcharged. However, he escaped without so much as a dab of butter on that cravat of his. By the end of lunch, sipping cautiously at a small glass of green Chartreuse, her treat drink, she felt quite relaxed. Parts of the action, like him finding a speck on a wineglass and waving it slowly to and fro to get it changed, or calling for a 'proper' pepper-mill and keeping on the lookout till it came, were telling-Rosemary material rather than good fun at the time, but the dialogue, or rather what he said, was unimprovable, boring almost to a fault. She forgot her misgivings as he took her through the histories of more people whose names meant nothing to her. They even got on to Wales, of all topics; well, friends in England had taken to going on a bit about England. When Malcolm said you got very unpopular for saying Wales was in a bad way, she thought at once of his nose and how he had had it bashed in the pub at Treville. It looked absolutely all right now, though of course no nearer his mouth than ever.

After finishing at last with Wales he said rightly that it was still early, called without too much urgency for more coffee and invited her to tell him about herself. So she told him a bit about Alun and the girls. She went carefully on them because of what Gwen had said, or rather not said when asked, about their own two boys now in their thirties. If Malcolm had something to get off his chest in that department he kept it to himself. Although he was paying her polite attention it became pretty clear after a few minutes that she was on some sort of wrong tack.

'Would you like another sticky drink?' he offered, as soon as she stopped speaking.

'No thanks dear.'

'Well, from what you've been saying you're very much content with your life as it is now.'

'Oh yes. Much more than I was with my life as it was then.'

'Oh really?'

'Considering I had as good a time as anyone it's funny how often I catch myself being bloody glad to think, well whatever happens I haven't got to do *that* any more,' she said, 'going on the beach or going dancing or going out, going out to dinner that is,' and one or two more along the same lines until she noticed he was not listening much, smiling away and nodding now and then, his eyes on her face but in a kind of spread-over way.

For a man not to be listening to what she said had always struck her as a sound scheme whichever way you looked at it, and nowadays its corresponding drawback was greatly reduced. Whereas in the past such a man would have had that much more chance of noticing a patch of surplus powder or a pimple pit, failing sight in age would probably have ruled that out, unless of course he unsportingly put his glasses on, which Malcolm had not done. But it struck her now that the ear-shutting thing was part of not wanting her to have changed into just one of his mates, preferring her to stay on out of his ken, so to speak, where he could go in for whimsy-whamsy about her. That, seeing that, rather cramped her style for the time being.

While he was asking one of the waitresses for the bill another of them was putting it in front of him. 'Not too bad, I thought,' he said after calculating the tip for a couple of minutes in his head, on paper, and then in his head again.

'Oh, very good. Proper food.' She had not managed the prepared-by-someone-else gravy dinner she had rather been counting on, had had to pass up the beef curry because of the rice, had steered clear of the lamb ragout on account of possibly lurking tomato seeds and had settled for the chicken pie, the meat moist enough but the pastry definitely waxy, pappy almost, needless to say fatty, but as against that she had eaten up all her lettuce and watercress and some of the green pepper, which with a good squeeze of lemon had hardly tasted of catarrh at all.

Alone in the very nice Ladies she tried to relax as far as she could and took a few deep breaths before getting down to work on her falsies. While she was doing so she straightened to her full height, shook back her hair and did her best in the way of putting on an important, haughty expression. The general effect might have struck Malcolm as bursting with poise, but the idea was to give herself a head start, an improved chance of facing down anyone who might presume to come barging in and find the sudden sight of an old girl with her teeth in her hand somehow remarkable, or embarrassing, or in any way out of the ordinary, unless in the experience of very common persons. As it turned out, no sweat: the miniature of Dentu-Hold was safely in her bag well before a harmless little thing, in jeans anyway as it turned out, sidled in and vanished into the WC. Rhiannon left in a flurry of self-assurance.

Outside, the sun had left the front of the building but the day was still bright and quite hot. Over near the car Malcolm was standing with his back almost turned, his head slightly on one side, just admiring the view by the look of him, and yet there was something calculated in his casualness that warned her of what was on the way. As she came up he edged into position by the passenger door. Yes, he was going to do it. At some figured-out moment he threw the door wide, stood extra upright with his chin in the air and did a tremendous juddering salute like a sergeant in an old movie. Feeling her cheeks turn hot she sketched a gracious Queen-Mum-type smile and lift of the hand and scurried into her seat. Performances like that were supposed to show how relaxed the two of you were together, but actually they brought out your awkwardness and almost your resentment of each other, or some of it. Well, at least Malcolm had not thought to bring that tweed cap into the act.

'So it seems I can safely assume you are not possessed by an overwhelming desire to immerse yourself in the ocean,' he said when they got moving.

'Yes indeed you can.'

'Nevertheless I take it you'd have no strong objection to a small sightseeing trip to a part of the coast of the island?'

'Oh no, lovely idea. Whereabouts?'

'That will emerge in due time.'

They drove back to the coast road and moved south again into the more countrified area that had mostly farms and woods and an occasional large house inside a park. After they had skirted the boundary wall of one of these with its fancifully bricked-up gateway, Rhiannon began to pick up small landmarks: an old-fashioned milestone showing the distance to Carmarthen, Cardiff and 'Brecknock', the momentary sight of a castle among whose ruins, it had been said, there grew a flower found nowhere else but in the Pyrenees, a National Trust plaque about something, the gable of perhaps a barn with the torn irregular triangle of bleached poster still stuck there as always and finally, unmistakably, the sudden steep turning that led down to Pwll Glân and, further along, to Britain's Cove. It was obviously Pwll Glân that Malcolm was making for, the only bay with a Welsh name of the score all round that coast, if not the finest then, all would have agreed, the most unusual, and known to Rhiannon from plenty of visits in the past.

For the first couple of hundred yards the slope was so extreme that right of way on that narrow twisting road went automatically to people driving up, and twice Malcolm had to pull into the side and stop. The second time, on a right-angle bend, brought Rhiannon a view of the half-mile or so of flat before the beach itself and then of most of the bay, the low curving arm to the south, the long almost-straight stretch of sand and, on the far side, the tree-covered headland where the church was. The road took them to the foot of the escarpment and through the marshes, formerly salt, freshwater now for many years and grown over with reeds of a peculiar and beautiful pale orange-yellow. At the end they turned along the top of the shore, where shabby greenish plants were scattered, and drove finally into the extensive car-park, unseen from above, unexpected almost until reached, but a matter of course after that, full of familiar things like people eating and drinking and making a lot of noise while they walked about.

Malcolm lost no time in leading the way out of it and down crosswise towards the sea, to an empty part where the sand was strewn with unattractive seaweed and broken by patches of bare rock. By chance it was also just about the part where, one far-off night, Rhiannon and Dorothy had tried to catch flounders in the shallows, or rather not to hinder too much the two, possibly three, young men who were supposed to know how and, for all Rhiannon could remember, had succeeded. There had been nobody about then. There was nobody about now, not at least up this end towards the headland, nowhere to bathe, nowhere to sit or lie or throw a ball, nowhere for the kids to run to and fro. Not saying much, but keeping a close eye on her, Malcolm took them across a stretch of quite rugged rock on to the path that led up to the moss-stained wall of the churchyard.

On the far side of the gateway here no sound could be heard from the shore, just waves. They were on a narrow granite promontory less than a hundred yards long, with the sweep of Pwll Glân bay on their left as they faced out to sea and another bay on their right too small to have a name, more of a creek really, heaped with stones of various sizes and always empty – well, in the past Rhiannon had seen a couple of fishermen there, serious ones in oilskins and thigh-boots standing into the sea, but it would have been safe to say that nobody went there now for any reason.

There was room on the promontory for not much more than the church itself, three or four lines of graves and dozens of mature trees, sycamores mostly, tall and flourishing even in the salt air and at this season deeply shading the ground underneath. Nobody came here either in a manner of speaking, but the two of them were here today, and somebody else had been here not long before to take a bit of care of the graves and make the place seem not quite desolate, though hardly a single stone remained in one piece or uneroded. But some names and dates could still be read easily enough, Welsh names, English names, none that she saw later than 1920. The church was very thoroughly shut up and impossible to see into from anywhere at ground level.

'It's still a church,' said Malcolm, having let the matter rest for quite a long time. 'That's to say it hasn't been deconsecrated.'

'But they can't still be using it.'

'The last service was held here in 1959. Longer ago than half the people on that beach can remember.' He smiled and went on confidingly, 'I looked it up. Perhaps they think there might be something left here some day.'

'Who? What sort of thing do you mean?'

'Well . . . I don't know,' he said in a gentle tone. 'At the moment it's too far for anybody to come, you see. Too far by car, that is. How many years would it be since it wasn't too far to come on foot, with that climb for most of them to face after? Eighty-four in congregation the nave held, according to what I read.'

'Do you believe in it yourself, Malcolm?'

'It's very hard to answer that. In a way I suppose I do. I certainly hate to see it all disappearing. I used to think things would go on round here as long as anywhere in the kingdom, but do you know I doubt if they have?'

'Well, there's nothing to be done about it, that's for sure.' Rhiannon tried to sound gentle too. 'One thing, it's too far for vandals to come too, by the look of it.'

'Yes. Small mercies. I like to come here occasionally. It helps me . . . no, it's impossible to say it without sounding pompous. Anyway, it's a wonderful spot. Peaceful. Solitary.'

'A bit lonely, though. Windy too.'

'I'm terribly sorry, Rhi, are you absolutely –'

'No, no, I'm fine.' She looked about. 'It certainly has an atmosphere.'

'You remember coming here before?' he asked eagerly.

'Oh yes, of course.'

She would have added 'lots of times' but he hurried on.

'What about that terrible concrete hut, I think it was concrete, just where the road stopped? That's gone too now, of course. Ha, one's quite glad to see the back of some of what they pull down. It was the only place to eat, though.'

'That's right, and the lady washed up so loudly you couldn't hear yourself speak, and kept the key of the lav in her apron.'

'Do you remember having lunch there?'

'Oh yes,' she said in the same spirit as a moment earlier. 'We took what we were given – sausages and chips and OK sauce.'

'M'm. There was a hopeless cat there too, that when you stroked it, it looked at you as though you were barmy.'

'I'd forgotten about that. You drank Mackeson stout, didn't you? It was your regular tipple in those days.'

'So it was. You never seem to see it now.'

'And the two of us went for a stroll after.'

She felt she probably should have spoken then but she could not think how to say it, just smiled and waited and crossed her fingers in her head. He stepped a pace back from her before he went on, still with insistence, 'When we got up here we found there'd been a storm a night or two before and there were leaves and bits of twigs and branches and stuff all over the place, and the sea was still very rough. And we went right up to the end there where it jutted out over the water – just there, remember? – quite dangerous it was, I suppose, but we do these things in our youth, actually I think most of it's fallen away now. And I said, I know I'll never mean as much to you as you mean to me, anywhere near, and I'm not complaining, I said, but I want to tell you nobody will ever mean as much to me as you do, and I want you to remember that, I said. And you said you would, and I think perhaps you have, haven't you, Rhiannon?'

If it had been too early a moment ago to contract out of his recalling of that day, it was obviously much too late now. Not sure that she could have spoken in any case, she nodded.

'Wonderful. Oh, that is lovely.' The tautness departed from his manner. 'Well, an awful lot of things seem worth while after that, I can tell you. Thank you for remembering me, with so much else in your life.'

He sent her a smile of simple affection and indicated they should move. As they began strolling down the slight incline towards the gate he put his arm chummily round her waist.

'Yes, I'd got my pal Doug Johnson to lend me his car for the day. It was the first time I'd taken it out and I was a bit nervous, I hope it didn't show.'

'I didn't notice anything,' she said.

'We stopped for petrol and the surly bloke wouldn't change a fiver, remember?'

'Oh yes of course.' With the heat off, Rhiannon would have agreed that she remembered General Tate's landing at Fishguard.

'And we'd hardly gone ten yards after when that terrific cloudburst started and I had to stop because the windscreen-wiper wasn't working properly.'

'That's right.'

'Ah, now I think I can almost fix the date. The Australians were playing at Cardiff and in their –'

He stopped walking and stared ahead of him. She knew something awful had happened. Her eyes skidded away to a horizontal stone gone almost black and read helplessly of Thomas Godfrey Pritchard who departed this life 17th June 1867 and was sorely missed. When she looked at Malcolm again he was still staring, but at her now.

'Doug Johnson was away in France the whole of that

summer,' he said, 'doing his teaching prac. He certainly wasn't around to lend his car to me or anyone else. So that must have been a different day altogether.'

'M'm.' She forced herself to go on looking at him.

'We must have taken the bus down. You couldn't have remembered it like that, the way you said you did.'

'No.'

'You don't remember any of it, do you? Not having lunch or walking up to St Mary's or what I said or anything.'

It was not to be got out of or away from. Coming on top of the little tensions of the day the unashamed intensity of his disappointment was too much for her. She hid her face, turned aside and started to cry.

He forgot his own feelings at once. 'What is it? What's the matter?'

'I'm so stupid, I'm so hopeless, no good to anybody, I just think of myself all the time, don't notice other people. It's not much to ask, remembering a lovely day out, but I can't even do that.' She had his arm round her now and was resting her forehead against his shoulder, though she still kept her hands over her eyes. 'Anybody who was any use would remember but I can't, but I wish I could, I wish I could.'

'Don't say such ridiculous things. You don't expect me to take them seriously, do you? It's sweet of you to worry about it just slipping your mind like that, but I didn't remember it very well myself, did I, confusing those two times? Anyway you remember coming down here? To Pwll Glân?'

'M'm.'

'And perhaps me bringing you? You know, sort of vaguely?'

'M'm.' Perhaps she did.

'Even this bit? Just . . .'

Suddenly it went impossible to say yes, even to this bit. 'Not . . .' She shook her head wretchedly. 'It's gone. Sorry.'

'I can't have you apologizing to me, my dear Rhiannon. Honestly, now.' He gazed over the top of her head in the general direction of the land. 'Well, put it this way, the fact you minded so much about not remembering, that's worth as much to me as if you had remembered, very nearly.'

That set things back a bit, but in the end it was only the clearing-up shower. She got to work with her tissues and comb and he wandered about making suitable points like the church being *probably* twelfth century and having effigies of a member of the de Courcy family and his lady in the south wall of the chancel and a battlement round the top of the tower, exactly what she wanted to hear just then, no sarcasm. When he saw she was ready he gave the bay a final going-over.

'It was all houses there once, before the sea came up,' he said. 'A whole village.'

Rhiannon thought she had heard that the sea had once been over the marshes and then gone back, but that must have been another time. 'I suppose they can tell.'

'At low tide twice a year when the water's calm you're supposed to be able to see down to what were streets. Houses even. I think another church.'

'Do you still do your poetry?'

'You remember that.' He smiled with pleasure. 'Indeed I do, yes. And I mean to go on. I'm lucky enough to have a few things to get off my chest still.'

Before he could get on to what they were she found herself saying, with a sense of instant inspiration that amazed her, 'There used to be a lovely rose-garden with brick walls and, you know, pergolas along the paths belonging to some grand house somewhere. You could look round it in the afternoon. I don't know whether you still can.'

'Let's see, would that be Mansel Hall? Over by Swanset?'

No prizes for not rushing in this time. 'I'm not absolutely . . .'

'No, I know where you mean – er, now, Bryn House, that's it. Bryn House, of course. Local stone with brick facing. Not far from here. Anyway, you'd like to go there, would you?'

'M'm. Didn't we go there once before, one summer, not a very nice day?' The not very nice day had stuck in her mind all right, not actually raining but chilly and dark.

'I think so,' he said, as he more or less had to. 'Yes, I'm sure we did. Come on, let's go and have a look. Might bring all sorts of stuff back, you never know.'

'It may have just gone, the garden, like a lot of things.'

'Let's go there anyway.'

He spoke dreamily again, as if he felt that he or they had started on some semi-fated course, and glanced at her in a way that suggested the lip of the frying-pan was still not too far off. Well, she would have to let him say what he liked now. She reached out and took and squeezed his hand as they walked down to the churchyard gate and took it again on the far side, in comfort or apology or what she hoped would pass as understanding, or perhaps like one person letting another know that whatever it was they were facing they would face it together. He squeezed back but kept quiet after all until they were on their way inland through the marshes, and then for once in his life he talked about nothing in particular.

Six – Malcolm, Muriel, Peter, Gwen, Alun, Rhiannon

1

'Bible and Crown Hotel, Tarquin Jones speaking.'

It was characteristic of Tarc to refer to his house in this way although, more likely because, the place was not and never had been a hotel in any bed-and-board sense, nor even called one by anybody until he came along. So much could be readily agreed but, as Charlie had once pointed out, or alleged, it was much less easy to say what characteristic of Tarc's it was characteristic of. And that was very Welsh, Garth had added without running into opposition.

At another time Malcolm would surely have been ready to consider such matters, especially the last, but not now. With strained clarity he gave his own name in full.

'Who?' – an unaspirated near-bellow with no fancy suggestion of actual failure to hear or recognize.

After an even clearer repetition Malcolm asked if Mr Alun Weaver was on the premises and met immediate total silence, relieved fairly soon by distant female squeals of pretended shock or surprise and what sounded like a referee's whistle indiscriminately blown. Malcolm waited. He took a couple of deep breaths and told himself he was not feeling at all on edge. After some minutes Alun came on the line with the kind of featureless utterance to be

227

expected from someone wary of unscheduled telephone-calls.

Once more Malcolm introduced himself, going on to ask, 'Many in tonight?'

'They've mostly gone now. I was more or less just off myself as a matter of fact. Don't often come here at this time, you know.'

His tone held a question which Malcolm answered by saying, 'Rhiannon, er, mentioned where you were.'

'Oh did she? Oh I see.' This time Alun spoke with all the artless acceptance of a man (perhaps Peter would have specified a Welshman) getting ready for a bit of fast foot-work.

'Look, Alun, I was wondering whether you might care to drop in for a nightcap on your way home. No great piss-up or anything, just *un bach*.'

There was a faint sound of indrawn breath over the wire. 'Oh, well, now it's kind of you, boy, but it's getting late and I think if you don't mind . . .'

'Actually I'm on my own tonight. Gwen's been in a funny sort of mood, I don't know what's got into her. Not like her to pop out on the spur of the moment. Well, I say popped, she told me don't wait up for her.' This was rounded off by a light laugh at feminine capriciousness.

'Well now, that being so, the case is altered beyond all recognition. Of course I'll be delighted to alleviate your solitude. Taking off in about five minutes.'

The simple prospect of company made Malcolm feel better for a moment. He picked up his glass of whisky and water, not a habitual feature of his evenings, and carried it into the sitting-room. This was so full of unmasculine stuff, like loose covers and plates not meant for eating off, and so narrow in proportion to its quite moderate length that some visitors had taken it for Gwen's own little nook where she might have held tea-parties, very exclusive ones, but in fact there was nowhere else to go or be outside the kitchen but Malcolm's study, and even he never went there except for some serious reason.

Tonight a small masculine intrusion was noticeable in this sitting-room, not in the obvious form of the gramophone or record-player itself, which was of course common in gender, but of actual records fetched earlier from their white-painted deal cabinet in the study. The machine, called a Playbox, black with timid Chinesey edging in a sort of gold, now faded, had been pretty advanced for the mid 1960s. The records were from the same period or before, deleted reissues of micro-groove 'realizations' of even more firmly forgotten 78s made in the 1940s in a style said to have been current two or three decades longer ago still. Most of the performers were grouped under names like Doc Pettit and his Original Storyville Jass Band, though individuals called Hunchback Mose and Clubfoot Red LeRoy were also to be seen, accompanied here and there by an unknown harmonica or unlisted jew's-harp.

Malcolm had been meaning to play some of these to himself as a means of recapturing more of the past, going on, so to speak, from where he had left off with Rhiannon earlier that day. He had put the project aside when Gwen said her piece and flounced out of the house; now, it seemed possible again. Only possible: first he must visit the bathroom, or rather the WC, and check how matters stood in that department. They had not been too favourably disposed that morning, and once or twice he had had to fight quite hard not to let the thought of them overshadow the outing. His left ball had played up a bit as well, but he was learning to live with that.

He set down his drink and went upstairs and lo and behold it was all right. As he was finishing up he thought to himself that on this point at least he was two people really, a bloody old woman and worryguts and a marvellous ice-cold reasoning mechanism, and neither of them ever listened to the other. Actually a *real* split personality, one fellow completely separate from the other, would have had a lot to be said for it: every so often each of them could get away from himself a hundred per cent, guaranteed.

In the sitting-room again he at once switched the Playbox on and took out of its cover a recording attributed to Papa Boileau and his New Orleans Feetwarmers. They looked back at him from the sleeve photograph, a line of old men in dark suits and collars and ties, six, seven faces about as black as could be, sad and utterly private, no imaginable relation to those Malcolm was used to seeing on his television screen. He arranged the disc on the central spindle and in due time it plumped down on to the already rotating turntable where the pick-up arm, moving in a series of doddery jerks and overshoots, came and found its outermost groove. Through a roaring fuzz of needle-damage the sounds of 'Cakewalkin' Babies' emerged. Malcolm turned up the volume.

The stylus was worn and the playing-surface too, but this bothered him not at all, any more than he cared that the recording was poorish even for its era, the clarinet slightly flat, the cornet shaky in the upper register; he was gripped by the music from its first bars. As always he listened intently, trying to hear every note of every instrument, leaving himself when it came to it no time to reflect on the past or anything else. Too excited to sit down, he stood in front of the Playbox and shifted his weight from one foot to the other in time with the music. At appropriate stages he took a turn on an invisible banjo, beating out a steady equal four, did all any man could in the circumstances with a run of trombone smears and punctually signalled a couple of crashes on the Turkish cymbal. Precisely at the end of the number, which came without warning to the uninitiated, he went rigid and breathless, coming to life again at the start of 'Struttin' with some Barbecue'.

By now he was thoroughly sent, as he would have put it in the old days. He had heard that a barbecue had to do with cooking out of doors, but had always assumed that this here was a different use or even a different word, perhaps a corruption, and that 'some barbecue' meant a fine fancy woman and no mistake. Seeing such a one pass by, people would say in wonder and admiration, 'Now that's what I *call* a barbecue!' Malcolm had never strutted or, assuming to strut was to dance, danced in any fashion with such a woman, nor was he really pretending to now, just going off on a heel-and-toe shuffle round the small circuit of the room.

Breaking his stride when the doorbell pealed made him stagger. Until he saw that yes, he had pulled the curtains, he was afraid he might have been observed from outside – some treat for the neighbours, an oldster capering about on his own like a mad thing. He straightened his jacket, wiped his eyes, squared his shoulders and went out to the hall. Voices could be heard from the far side of the door.

When he opened it, two persons at once entered with all possible certainty of being expected. One of them was Garth Pumphrey, the other a taller, perhaps younger man Malcolm half took at first to be a stranger. This second visitor had a full head of white hair, very neatly cut and combed, and a tanned skin. The combination gave him something of a look of a photographic negative, or perhaps just of an old cricketer; in any case his wide brown calm eyes made the negative idea worth forgetting. He turned his head when he caught the music from the sitting-room.

'Hold the door a minute, Malcolm,' said Garth – 'Peter's on his way now.'

'Oh, right.'

'You remember Percy, don't you, Malcolm?'

Of course he did immediately: Percy Morgan, builder, husband to Dorothy, to be seen from time to time dragging her out to the car after the end of a party, encountered less often, not for about a year indeed, up at the Bible. Garth's occasional usefulness with this sort of reminder was to be set to his credit, against his rather more frequent and famous senility-imputing introductions of Charlie to Alun, Alun to Malcolm, Malcolm to Tarc Jones, etc.

After a short interval marked by awkward standing-about in the hall Peter toiled up the garden path, groaning and muttering as he came, and the party moved into the sitting-room. The Feetwarmers sounded very loud in here – they had started on 'Wild Man Blues' by now – and Malcolm reduced them somewhat before offering drinks, wondering as he did so how far his just-over-half-bottle of Johnnie Walker would go among four – five, rather, which raised a point.

'Alun's coming, is he?' he asked Peter.

'Is he, I've no idea. I say, do you mind turning down that noise?'

'I thought you used to like that old New Orleans stuff – Jelly Roll Morton, George –'

'If I ever did I don't now. If you don't mind.'

Percy Morgan looked up from turning over some of the records when Malcolm approached.

'Have you any Basie or Ellington? Or conceivably Gil Evans? Thanks.' The thanks were for an offered glass of whisky and water. 'I can see it's no use asking for Coltrane or Kirk or anybody like that.'

'Not a damn bit of use, boy,' said Malcolm with slight

hostile relish. 'And my Basies stop in 1939 and my Ellingtons about 1934. And no, no Gil Evans – I seem to recall a baritone man of that or a similar name playing with somebody like Don Redman, though you obviously don't mean him.'

He reached out to lower the volume as requested, but Percy Morgan held up a demurring hand and indicated that he should attend closely to the music. A clarinet solo was in progress. 'You wouldn't call that melodic invention, would you, seriously?' asked Percy at the end of the chorus.

'No. I wouldn't call it anything in particular. Except perhaps bloody marvellous.'

'He was just running up and down the arpeggio of the common chord with a few passing-notes thrown in.' Not a vestige of complaint or dissatisfaction coloured Percy's tone. He seemed perfectly resigned, seeing it as quite out of the question that the performance could ever have been different.

'Was he now.' This time Malcolm did manage to turn down the sound. 'No doubt he was, I don't deny it.'

'Oh, don't turn it down, Malcolm,' said Garth in real protest. 'I love these old Dixieland hits, they really swing, don't they?' He mimed a bit of simplified drumming, hissing rhythmically through his teeth. 'Which lot is this?' Malcolm passed him the sleeve. 'Oh yes. Papa . . . Oh yes. Have you got any, any Glenn Miller discs?'

'I'm afraid not.'

'Any Artie Shaws?'

'No.'

Malcolm was as close as he usually came to being angry at the way his quiet drink and unburdening chat with an old friend had been turned, without anywhere near as much as a by-your-leave, into a jazz discussion group. Not that he would in the least have minded the right sort of attention being paid to his records: a respectful, if possible attentive, silence broken only by a personnel inquiry or so and one or two – not over-frequent – appreciative cries of 'Yeah!' He realized he had been half hoping for this sort of outcome ever since the three had arrived and longer than that in the case of Alun. Yes, and where the hell was Alun?

He was on the doorstep a couple of minutes later with Charlie at his side, crying out in loosely intelligible greeting and apology, pressing on his host an unopened bottle of Black Label – like old times, except then it would have been a flagon of John Upjohn Jones nut-brown.

'I hope you don't mind me bringing these boys along,' said Alun. 'Only Tarc was calling stop-tap and they all seemed to feel like another.'

'I see. No, that's all right. Of course.'

Charlie crossed the threshold with real dignity. 'Or even him sending them on ahead. Known as the advance-guard or covering-party tactic.'

'I'm sorry,' said Malcolm, 'I don't –'

'Ah, the old righteous sound!' cried Alun, hurrying over to the Playbox. 'Surely I know this one, don't I? Wasn't there a Louis version with, with Johnny Dodds? On the back of, was it "Skip the Gutter"?'

'It was "Ory's Creole Trombone" actually.'

'*That's* right – on the old Parlophone 78, correct?'

'Correct,' said Malcolm, beginning to smile.

Alun set about vivaciously looking through the pile of records. Percy Morgan glanced briefly and without hope at the rubric of every third or fourth one he came to. Malcolm went off for more glasses. Charlie turned to Peter and nodded to him in a pleased way, as though the two had not met for some weeks.

'Cheer up,' said Charlie. 'Cheer up and enjoy the music.'

'I'm afraid the effort of cheering up sufficiently to enjoy this music would be beyond me.'

'What's wrong with this music more than any other?'

'Not much, I suppose. When I look back, you know, music's like chess or foreign coins or what, folk tales. Something that only interested me when practically everything else interested me as well.'

'I wouldn't have gone to the Bible in the first place if the Glendower hadn't been shut.'

'While they fit the new stove. You said.'

'Where are these bloody drinks?' Charlie gave a searching look round. 'And where's bloody Garth? I thought he was meant to be here.'

'He was and is. As you came in he was going up the stairs, in all probability on his way to the lavatory.'

'Hey, there's one very good thing about Garth,' said Charlie, including in this announcement Percy, who had finally given up on the records, and repeating it for Malcolm's benefit as he approached with the promised drinks. 'Mark me closely. Whenever you see, er . . . What?' He frowned and looked from face to face. 'Oh, whenever you see *Garth* you get the most wonderful feeling of security. You can relax. You know, m'm? – you *know* you're not going to suddenly run into Angharad. No chance of it. You can relax. Eh? And a very much more minor benefit of seeing *Angharad* . . . is knowing you're not going to suddenly run into *Garth*. Well.'

Peter had looked away sharply at this, but the other two at least showed they understood the reference, namely to the frequent observation or supposed fact that the Pumphreys never both appeared at once. It gave rise to regular good-natured speculation about the homicidal-maniac uncle or two-headed son who needed attention of some sort at all times. Anyway Charlie was on well-trodden ground.

'You know I was thinking about that pair the other day,' he went on. 'Now: if they were in a detective story there'd only be one of them. See what I mean? Only be one of them really. One of them would have knocked off the other years ago and now whichever one it was would be going round posing as the other. As well, I mean. Just some of the time. They're about the same height, aren't they?'

'Why only some of the time?' asked Malcolm, glancing at Percy, who shook his snowy head very slowly from side to side.

'What? Well, Christ, because the rest of the time he'd be going round being himself, wouldn't he? Or herself if it was Angharad, of course.'

'I don't seem to have given Alun a drink,' said Malcolm, and moved off.

Alun had that moment slid a record out of its sleeve and was peering at the label in a vigilant way but, without his glasses, surely in vain. 'Ah, *diolch yn fawr*, dear boy. I can't make out, I can't make out whether this is a remake or the original –'

'Could I just have a quick word?'

'Sir, a whole history.' He sighed briefly. 'I mean take as long as you like.'

'Thanks, Alun. I wanted to ask you . . . Well, something Gwen said gave me a really nasty shock.'

2

'Well, I treat the whole thing as a joke,' Muriel was saying. 'Which I can just about manage to do most of the time if I keep my teeth well and truly gritted. Take it easy, lass,

I tell myself when the adrenalin starts to flow – you've seen it all before and you've come through without a scratch. Well anyway you've come through. Say it slowly and calmly: you're in Wales, land of song, land of smiles, and land of deceit. Taffy was a Welshman, Taffy was a thief all right, and by Christ boyo Taffy has been keeping up the old traditions indeed in a bloody big way oh yes now look you.' The last couple of dozen words were delivered in an accent that sounded as much like a West African one as anything else, Ghanaian, possibly, or Ibo. 'I thought counting the spoons was just an expression till I came to live down here. Nothing more than a colourful catch-phrase.'

Dimly recognizing this as the end of a section, and even more dimly aware of having heard something rather like it before, Dorothy Morgan looked up. She had lost the initiative a minute or two earlier. Astonishingly, she had found herself out of immediate things to say about New Zealand, the adopted home of one of the Morgan sons, a whole country gloriously unknown to anyone she was ever likely to run into round here and in many other parts, serving her as a magic wand or spell for reducing great assemblies to silence. Now, she missed her chance of coming in with alternative unanswerable stuff on what Percy had said to the County Clerk, or what she remembered of a magazine article about DNA she had recently happened to read. It was not of course that she was actually listening to what Muriel was saying, just that the continuous sound of another voice distracted her, put her off even the unexacting task of knocking one of her starters into shape.

What Dorothy had looked up from was the stylish Scandinavian table, made of different sorts of wood, in Sophie's apparatus-packed kitchen. It, the table, was strewn with the debris accumulated in twelve hours of drinking wine, smoking cigarettes and not eating all manner of biscuits, sandwiches, portions of cheese, little plastic zeppelins of pâté. Muriel and Dorothy were the only two still present and active: Siân Smith was thought to be asleep somewhere upstairs and Sophie herself, never a keen partaker, had gone off to her sitting-room TV quite a while before, though at the moment she was in the hall on the telephone trying for the second or third time to get hold of the much-needed Percy.

'I think I may have told you about a long-service warrior I ran into in Monmouth,' said Muriel now, sounding in no doubt whatever on the point. 'Twenty years up-country in the thick of it, doing something to do with reservoirs and pipes among the Welsh hill-tribes. Normally, of course, at home that's to say, Yorkshire people don't think a lot to Derbyshire folk, but it's different when you're abroad. Anyway he and I got on all right, and he was very knowl-edgeable about, you know, what makes Johnny Welshman tick. Quite fascinating. One day, he didn't explain how but I imagine it involved showing tolerance for local rituals and such, one day he found himself among those present when the village man of God preached a sermon in Welsh. Which no doubt would have meant plenty to you . . .'

Here Muriel made an audacious pause, confident that she could gauge Dorothy's coming-round time to a nicety, and resumed on the dot, '. . . but, as far as he was con-cerned, the fellow might just as well have been rabbiting on in Apache. But one thing he did notice, did my chum. The fellow, the Welsh fellow, kept using a word that sounded like the English word truth. As in veracity, honesty and such. There'd be a flood of bongo-bongo chatter, and then, suddenly, truth, and then more monkey language. Apparently, when he asked afterwards, appar-ently it was, it had been, the English word he'd used. Why not use a Welsh word, he asked him. Well, he said,' and Muriel's accent shifted again to the Gulf of Guinea, 'there isn't a Welsh word with the same connotations and the *force* of the English word. And if that isn't funny enough for you, he said, there is a Welsh word *truth*, same word, spelt the same anyhow, and it means falsehood. Mumbo-jumbo. As you well know. Talk about coming out in the open. I've often meant to check that in a Welsh–English dictionary. After all there must be such things. Just a matter of knowing where to look.'

Sophie had come into the room in time to hear the last part of this. The sight of her went down remarkably well with Muriel, who liked holding the floor as much as anyone living but preferred a more normal audience, one that could safely be allowed a turn now and again. It would have been good if Dorothy had been listening too, especially to the yarn just recounted, but then she had heard it, had had sound-waves bearing it strike her ear-drum, a couple of dozen times before, so there was a chance of its entering her mind by some route or other, perhaps by-passing the conscious part of it. As it was, talking to Dorothy, or rather in her presence, was a bit too close for comfort to being that type in the story who found himself shut up in a prison cell somewhere nasty with a mad murderous Arab for company, not a lot in the way of company because you very soon found that the only way of keeping him quiet was by staring him in the eye: take too long about blinking, let alone nod off, and you were for it. Muriel lit a cigarette in one continuous operation rather than as when addressing Dorothy – piecemeal, like somebody driving a car at the same time.

'Any luck with Percy?'

'Still no reply – it's not like him. I had Gwen on just before, phoning from that Eyetie joint in Hatchery Road.'

'Oh, Mario's, I know. What had she got to say for herself?'

'Fed up she was, according to her,' said Sophie, who had actually been prepared to pass on this information unprompted. 'Malcolm given her a big row.'

'No, really? That doesn't sound the gallant Malcolm's style at all. I can't imagine him giving any size of row to a cocklestall proprietor.'

After a short pause, Sophie said, 'Well, you know. She asked if she could come up, so –'

'And how did you respond?'

'I thought why not, more the merrier.' Sophie glanced at Dorothy. 'Right?'

'Oh, every time. I couldn't agree more.'

'Maybe she'll have something to tell us about the great day trip.' Malcolm's excursion with Rhiannon had been speculated about earlier.

'Very possibly. I must say our Rhiannon has been *going it a bit* recently. She can hardly have recovered from her piss-up with my old man.'

This time Sophie paused a little longer. 'I always think, the way you feel about the Welsh, Muriel, it must be fantastic, you and Peter seeing absolutely eye to eye on a thing like that.'

'I must go,' said Muriel. 'Well actually not as much as you might think. It's perfectly possible to go a long way with somebody on some point or other and then suddenly find you and the other chap are literally rolling over and over on the bloody *floor* about it. Easiest thing in the world.' She picked up a nearly full bottle of Corvo Bianco with a slight clunk against an unopened tin of laver-bread (from Devon), got a no-thanks from Sophie and poured unstintingly for herself. 'But of course it doesn't go very deep with me. More a matter of being a little bit naughty among

240

friends.' This, driven home at need with a where's-your-sense-of-humour gibe, was her standard retort to any Welsh person who might take exception to being categorized as a liar, cheat, dullard, bully, hypocrite, sneak, snob, lay-about, toady, violator of siblings and anything else that might strike her fancy. 'Yes, I'm a long way from getting my official invitation to join the Peter Thomas Anti-Welsh Brotherhood, and not only on grounds of sex, which I dare say the chairman's prepared to waive these days. No, it'll take a –'

'Oh, and there's another way you don't qualify, Muriel,' said Sophie with a bright smile. 'Only Welsh people can join. Born Welsh. Peter must have told you, surely. I remember him going into it one time after Christmas dinner at Dorothy's. Very particular he was on the point. Two non-Welsh grandparents was too many, he said.'

After the sound of her name had triggered her dinosaurian reflexes, Dorothy lifted her head for the second time in ten minutes. The talk between Sophie and Muriel, animated to begin with, had lost its impetus and that too might have percolated through her nervous system. Behind the black-framed lenses her eyes steadied and focused. With majestic deliberation she drew in her breath. The other two struggled wildly to think of something to get in ahead with, but it was like trying to start a motor-bike in the path of a charging elephant.

'Of course you know in New Zealand they celebrate Christmas just the same as here,' she said, showing a notable sense of continuity. 'Roast turkey and plum pudding and mince pies in the middle of the antipodean winter.' She pronounced the penultimate word correctly and clearly, as she did every other, as she invariably did while she could speak at all. 'I mean summer. Imagine roast turkey and stuffing and hot mince pies in July.

Howard and Angela have got some friends in Wanangui, that's in what they call North Island . . .'

'I think I'll try Percy again,' said Sophie.

3

'I'd just like an explanation,' said Malcolm. 'Just the merest hint of an explanation. That's all.'

'You're the feeblest creature God ever put breath into,' said Alun. 'Why any woman should have spent thirty-three minutes married to you, let alone thirty-three years, defies comprehension. You've no idea in the world of what pleases a woman: in other words' – he seemed to be choosing these with care – 'you're not only hopeless as an organizer of life in general, you're a crashingly boring companion into the bargain and needless to say, er, perennially deficient in the bedroom. Correct?'

'That about sums me up. Oh, I'm also cut off.'

'Cut off?'

'Cut off from real people in my own little pathetic fantasy world of dilettante Welshness, medievalism and poetry.' Malcolm drained his glass.

'*Poetry*? You ought to be ashamed of yourself, a great big hulking fellow like you. What are your other shortcomings?'

'That's all I can remember for the moment. And as I say I'd love to know the explanation. There'd been no row before, no upset, nothing. It's most odd. Anachronistic in fact. She hasn't spoken to me in that strain for God knows how long.'

'M'm.' Alun pursed his lips and blinked at the wall, as if reflecting upon one or two mere theoretical conceivabilities, preparing to eliminate them for form's sake. He said, 'She didn't happen to, er, mention anybody else, I suppose, *refer* to anybody who in any way might have . . . ?'

'Not a soul. I'd have remembered if she had.'

'Yes.' Now an expression of considerable relief appeared for an instant on Alun's face before he added quickly, 'That's a, that must be a considerable relief to you. Well, quite a relief.'

Malcolm nodded and sighed. His neck was aching and he wriggled his shoulders around to ease it. 'But of course what's bothering me, what I'm trying to work out is the connection between this and the way she flew off the handle at you. Which I may say I'm very sorry ever happened.'

'The . . . ?'

'Last night in the Golf Club,' said Malcolm, himself starting to blink slightly.

'Oh. Oh yes. Yes. Yes, I wondered when we'd get round to that. Yes, quite a little hatful of words, wasn't it? What did she say to you about it?'

'Well, I had to drag it out of her. But I wasn't going to let it pass.'

'Quite right, it doesn't do. Never. Anyway . . .'

'Well, she was tired, she'd had a few, she was a bit under the weather, and the rest of it was, quite frankly, Alun, I mean I'm being quite frank now, she was furious with you, no not furious, annoyed. Irritated. Some linguistic point which I must confess I didn't really –'

'Oh, I know. She grew up in Capel Mererid speaking Welsh and I didn't. I know. To be frank with you in return, Malcolm *bach*, she thinks I'm a fraud, and worse than being a fraud I peddle Wales to the Saxons, so of course I irritate her. No no, don't . . . We won't argue about it, it's not the topic under discussion. Talking of which . . .' Alun leant forward and said emphatically, but in a lowered voice, 'Don't take what she said at its face value, not any of it. There's something more basic at work there, and yes, you're right, it's connected with what she said to you this evening. Now, the whisky's in the front room.' He spoke to the purpose, in that he and Malcolm had retired to the kitchen for this part of their talk. 'Can I freshen that? Come on, it'll do you good.'

'Do you really think it will? All right, just a small one. Thank you.'

After getting up, Alun laid his hand gently on Malcolm's arm. 'It's all right, boy. I'll explain it to you now. It's not easy but it's all right.'

Malcolm sat on alone. He realized he must be drunk even if only slightly, a state unfamiliar to him for over thirty years, in fact about as long as he had been married to Gwen, until Alun had come back into his life. He felt confused but not dejectedly so, half reassured about Gwen, keeping Rhiannon at the back of his mind for later, not making any connections between the one woman and the other or what each might signify for him. Decent of Alun to come along and listen and, the chances seemed good, sort out what there was to be sorted out. And yet somewhere he felt an apprehension that faded away whenever he started trying to account for it and came creeping back again as soon as he stopped.

Since moving out to the kitchen he had intermittently heard a mumble of voices from the sitting-room, the music first faint then inaudible, once or twice Garth's laughter. Now Alun's voice was raised in some flight or other and more general laughter followed. No, he was not cracking a joke at his, Malcolm's expense – nonsense, paranoid even to think of it. And here he came straight away, not lingering, bustling responsibly back with the two drinks. All his movements were as lively as they had ever been.

Stern-faced, intent on seeing the thing through, he pulled

his chair up to the table, which incidentally Malcolm had cleared earlier of most of the odds and ends of supper and earlier meals and nibbles Gwen had left there. He sat up specially straight in his own chair.

'Right,' said Alun in a military bark. 'Right. I'll give it to you in one word. Jealousy. Plain old-fashioned jealousy. Also envy, which isn't by any means the same thing, but no better. I was reading where someone made that point recently – envy's worse for a marriage than jealousy. Welsh writer too. Can't think who for now. Anyway. Something nice, something a little bit romantic has come your way, to wit, Rhiannon. Nothing like that has come her way, poor old Gwen's,' he said, staring quite hard at Malcolm. 'You have a nostalgic day out, you come back in triumph, she punishes you. Simple as that. Don't think hardly of her. Happens all the time wherever there are women. Like a reflex.'

'But I wasn't in triumph, I thought of that, I'm not a complete fool, I guarded against that. I said it was quite fun, food nothing much, bit chilly and so on and so on.'

Foreseeably, Alun had started shaking his head before the last was half over. 'Listen, you come back after that sort of jaunt anything short of minus your head and you come back in triumph, got it? That's how they all . . . oh Christ.'

'But you're saying she was just trying to hurt me.'

'Check.'

'But I wasn't trying to hurt her.'

A fervent groan suggested the hopelessness of any kind of answer to that one.

'But she . . .'

'She'll have forgotten she said it by tomorrow morning.'

'But I won't.'

'Yes you will, not by the morning but eventually, and

the sooner the better. Repeat after me – no, you needn't literally but pay attention. She didn't mean what she said. She used words instead of howling and screaming. She was upset – rightly or wrongly doesn't matter. And you swallow it. That's an order.'

'Well, you'd know, I suppose.' Malcolm sighed again. 'All right, I'll do my best. Anyway, how's it meant to fit in with what she said to you?'

'M'm . . .' Alun had whisky in his mouth, in front of his teeth actually, and he held up a finger while he put it out of the way. 'More of the same, only pointing in the other direction. I mean seeing Rhiannon, probably seeing her talking to you, that did it. Gwen wanted to bash her but she couldn't bash her direct because they're old buddies and all that, so she got at her via me, not that she didn't get at me *con* bloody *amore*, what? No problem. Jealousy . . . and envy. More sort of direct envy in this case because it was one female's of another of roughly the same age and circumstances. Plain as the nose on your pikestaff. Happens every day.'

Garth's laughter was heard again faintly, or fairly faintly. Malcolm said, 'It sounds pretty devious to me.'

'Devious my eye. When you've –'

'Sorry, I think that should be tortuous.'

'All right, tortuous my eye then. Once you've – Christ – relinquished the perverse, pig-headed expectation that women should mean what they say and say what they mean except when they're actually lying, this sort of thing gets to be all in the day's work. Tortuous, or devious, *my* . . . *eye*. Couldn't be more obvious and straightforward.' Alun's voice softened. 'I know Gwen's different in all sorts of ways, but she's the same in some other ways and this is one of those. Agreed?'

'Yes,' said Malcolm after almost no hesitation. 'Of course

you're right. It'll just take a bit of getting used to. Well. Thanks, Alun.'

'All part of the service, boy. Now don't mention it to her again, right? Go on as if it had never happened. And be nice to her – but your own experience and common sense'll guide you there. And hey,' he went on as they rose from the table, 'what did you get up to with Rhiannon on Courcey, you old monster? The bloody girl was treading on air when she got back.'

'Oh no,' said Malcolm, turning his face away.

'*Yes*, honest. Looked about twenty years younger. Now just you watch it, Jack, okay? Sardis and Bethesda have their eye on you, see. Christ,' said Alun with regard to the time. 'Just before I go, it's marvellous to hear some of that old stuff again. Let's have an evening of it on our own without all these philistines and Ornette Coleman fans like Peter. But I was going to say, there was one of that lot used to appeal to me particularly, a trumpeter with a French name, would it be Matt, Nat . . .'

'Natty Dominique, a great man. Yes, I've got quite a few tracks with him on. Fancy you remembering him.'

'Perhaps we could hear just a couple before I take off. Didn't he do a lot with George Lewis?'

'I think Dodds more.'

These last exchanges took place as the two were filing from kitchen to sitting-room, so naturally enough Malcolm missed Alun's transitory but enormous looks of release from tension, thanksgiving to tutelary powers, lubricious glee, etc. They found the Playbox inactive, though its ruby on-light still glowed, and Garth telling the others what he had done or seen on some occasion in the past. From the way he shut up at the sight of them it could be deduced that he had not only been talking for the sake of talking but for once knew it too. Peter sat with pursed-up non-specific displeasure. Charlie faced the blank screen of the television set, if not hoping it might spontaneously jump into life any second then merely happening to have his head pointed in that direction. Percy, half settled on the table where the gramophone was, half propped against it, indicated without word or movement that he was not with the others, in no way ill disposed, just belonging to a different party close by, though about ready for his flight to be called. Nobody seemed to be drinking. After bringing them this far, vitality had given out.

'I thought we might have a last record,' said Alun. 'And perhaps a small one for the road.'

'You have one,' said Percy. 'Of either or both. Thank you for your hospitality, Malcolm. Now I think some of us could afford to be on our way, don't you? Peter, you've got transport . . .'

Garth drew himself up with a fierce exhalation of breath. 'I'm going to walk,' he said. 'Get some fresh air into my lungs.'

'Yes, well there's only Charlie to worry about and I'll take him home. I've got to go there anyway to pick up Dot.'

'You mean from our place?' asked Charlie, twisting round energetically in his seat. 'How do you know she's there?'

'Dorothy went to Sophie this morning for coffee and drinks.'

'I mean how do you know she's still there? Have you rung Sophie?'

'She went to Sophie for coffee and drinks,' said Percy, speaking slightly louder but without in any way changing his placid, matter-of-fact tone.

'But you haven't rung Sophie.' It seemed that Charlie wanted this or something similar put into the file.

'Shut up, Charlie,' said Alun.

'Look now, the sooner we're away,' explained Percy, 'the sooner we can get our heads down.'

They were away very soon after that, all of them, including Alun, who might perhaps have been expected to seize on this capital chance of hearing his couple of tracks undisturbed, but he went off with the others muttering something about having to make an early start in the morning. So, nearly but not quite sure that Alun had come up with the right answer to the Gwen problem, and with his head swimming just slightly, Malcolm poured himself a glass of almost colourless whisky and water and played himself a last record, not all agog and on his feet now but sunk in his uncomfortable little chair.

The choice was what had once been a previously unissued alternate master of 'Goober Dance' (featuring Natty Dominique, cornet). He kept the volume good and low for fear of provoking the retaliation, then or another time, of the reggae-loving butcher's assistant who lived on that side. When 'Goober Dance' finished Malcolm thought he might as well hear another couple of tracks, and fell asleep trying to think of Rhiannon but instead wishing Gwen would come home.

4

'I asked this friend of Angela's what it was,' said Dorothy, 'and she told me it was a Maori dish – you know, the people who went there in boats first of all. Very civilized people. They have all their own things. For instance . . .'

Seated at the far end of Sophie's kitchen-table, her husband looked at his watch. 'Two minutes, darling,' he called.

'What happens in two minutes?' asked Peter next to him. 'I'm afire with curiosity.' Well, he was quite interested, and to tell the truth he felt awkward sitting there and saying nothing. He had not had to explain that his presence was part of a routine, the rest of which embraced going wherever he had last heard of Muriel in case she needed a lift home or elsewhere, this without prejudice to her right to leave at any time by taxi without informing him. Having to do that, and so perhaps saving him an hour's profitless drive, made her feel tied down. Tonight he was lucky, in the sense that she was still where she had gone earlier that day, though not visibly so at the moment.

'You'll see, if you're still around then,' said Percy, helpfully answering his question.

'It's more than likely. Finishing a chat with Gwen might take all night.'

'What? Oh, is that what Muriel's doing?'

'Isn't that what you gathered?'

'I didn't gather anything, Peter, I was busy here, as I still am, but it won't be for much longer. Yes, compared with some I consider myself a pretty lucky fellow, having such an easy-to-cope-with wife.'

Peter could think of nothing to say to that. He had been running into Percy for years and years without ever having had to notice anything in particular about him, and had left it a couple of seconds too late now to scan his face and posture for intimations of irony. Of course the fellow was a Welshman. While he was still considering the point without urgency the door slowly opened and Charlie came slowly in, staying near the threshold for a nimble exit if required.

'I think I'm going to bed,' he announced.

'Okay,' said Peter when no one else spoke.

Sophie, next to Dorothy and now as so often her official

250

auditor, looked round. She said through or over some information about the financing of the New Zealander health service, 'Siân's in the little room.'

'What's she doing there?' asked Charlie in the slightly contentious style he had fallen into at Malcolm's.

'Well, sleeping's what she went there for.'

'Can't she do that at home?'

'She's got nothing to go home for any more. You know.'

'As long as nothing needs doing about her.'

'Just leave her,' said Sophie.

This exchange had caused Dorothy's discourse to falter severely, but the flow was soon re-established. With a gallantly assumed smile Sophie turned back to her. Charlie wandered half-way down the room.

'Alun in cracking form,' he said.

Percy looked at him brightly and in silence. Peter grunted.

'Rising to the occasion. Just the sort of thing that brings out the best in him, convincing a chap like old Malcolm that any misgivings he may happen to have about his . . . personal life are quite without foundation. Tones him up. Mind you, I'd love to know what they actually said to each other, wouldn't you?'

'I think you're jumping to conclusions,' said Peter, his eyes flickering towards Percy.

'Maybe. A summons to the telephone followed by what about paying a call on old Malcolm, that notorious night-owl and reveller. M'm. I predict a catastrophe.'

During these last words of Charlie's, Percy had again looked at his watch and now moved at a moderate pace to a position immediately behind and above his wife.

'They've even kept their own cuisine,' said Dorothy. 'A friend of Angela's cooked a Maori dish for us one evening. It had raw –'

Still unhurriedly, Percy leaned forward, put his hands under her arms and hauled sharply upwards, using great but seemingly not excessive force. Dorothy shot to her feet as smartly as a nail responding to a claw-hammer.

'Here we go, darling,' said Percy, pulling and pushing while Sophie at first stood by, then followed their joint progress. After a short interval Peter and Charlie heard him in the hall saying, 'Piece of cake.' Then the front door shut.

'Quite impressive in its way,' said Charlie.

'I hadn't seen it before.'

'Quite impressive. Sometimes she moves under her own steam without waiting to be counted out. No doubt depending on how she feels.'

'Yes, I suppose it must boil down to that in the end.'

'I think I'm going to bed,' said Charlie to Sophie, who had come back into the room.

'You do that, love. Are you all right?'

'Absolutely fine. Yes, really.'

'I won't be too long. Siân's up there.'

'I'll be fine.' Charlie kissed his wife on the cheek and turned back for a moment to Peter with a distant sparkle. 'Be seeing you. Bit pissed now.'

He had hardly gone, and Peter had hardly had time to start wondering how to handle whatever it was he had to handle, before Muriel entered the kitchen, closely followed by Gwen, whom Peter had barely set eyes on since arriving. Both carried empty glasses and the way each moved brought out for the moment a striking physical resemblance: rather short in the leg and moving slowly and softly, shoulders bowed but head well up and forward, rather pointed nose questing for the wine-bottle. None of those immediately on view had any wine in it. Without verbal or other comment Sophie produced a full one, a litre flask of Emerald Riesling, from a carton next to her sentry-box-sized refrigerator. Sharing the work, Muriel twisted the *in-situ* cork off the corkscrew in no-nonsense fashion, her head enveloped in cigarette-smoke. Gwen attacked the foil round the neck of the new bottle with a fruit-knife. Neither spoke until liquor was pouring.

'Exit our Dorothy,' said Muriel. 'Not before time let it be added.'

'The sound of the front door shutting was music in our ears,' said Gwen.

Muriel settled herself in her previous place. 'Young Percy didn't exactly fall over himself coming to the bloody rescue, did he?'

'He probably felt like an hour off,' said Peter, who was still rather impressed with Percy's smooth, resolute action and, even more, envious of his air of seclusion in some adamantine sphere of his own. 'That seems very reasonable to me.'

The three women looked at him in silence, Sophie only for an instant while she made for the door, Gwen, seated, rather longer. Muriel's look came over the top of her glass and lasted till she had put it down on the table. Then she said, 'Well, Pete lad, now's your chance for a small break yourself. My friend Gwen and I are just about to settle down for a nice cosy little sisterly chat which I don't honestly see you contributing much to, so you could take off right away, couldn't you? No point in sticking around, eh?' She smiled, or drew back the corners of her mouth and raised her eyebrows.

He had been expecting to be asked to hang on while his wife had one more drink and then to have to hang on while she had one more after that. Under this arrangement he would have been open later on to a charge of having spoilt the drink(s) in question by a display of impatience – this no matter how hard and continuously he might have beamed at everyone in sight – with another in reserve about having dragged her away while she was enjoying herself. She was not an inveterate boozer but when she was on it there was a routine for that too. He was accordingly ill prepared for being ordered out of Sophie's house.

'Oh . . . that's all right,' he said. 'I can easily –'

'No, no, I wouldn't keep you up, old boy.' Muriel gave a waggish laugh. 'You look as if you could do with an early night. Granted it's not that early, but every little helps.'

After another tepid protest or two he was driven from the room. Gwen gave him a farewell twiddle of the fingers and stylized simper that made him feel quite sorry for Malcolm, but only in passing. In the hall cloakroom he reflected, as frequently before, that if the Thomases had a second car, which they or rather she could readily have afforded, then all this would never have arisen. *All* this? A drop out of the ocean. And of course there would still be times like tonight, with her too pissed, or about to become too pissed, to drive. Well, at times like that, when she actually needed him, she could ring him or . . . What was he talking about? Let herself in for feeling tied down and pass up a gilt-edged chance of buggering him about at the same time? He must be joking. He must also have got this far almost as frequently before.

Outside in the hall itself he nearly ran into Sophie wearing a turquoise-blue scarf over her head, which was just unexpected enough to make him say, 'Off somewhere, are you?' Now he remembered, he had heard the telephone tinkle a minute or two before.

'Yeah. Why?' Her normal intonation had never needed much sharpening in order to sound snappish.

'Charlie'll be all right, I suppose?'

'Why wouldn't he be?'

254

'Well . . .' Peter shifted his head about in a way intended to remind her that as an old friend he rather naturally knew something of her husband's nervous troubles.

'Should be safe enough, shouldn't he, with three people in the house?'

'Oh yes. Yes of course.'

'If you're worried you can stay around yourself.'

This time he moved his head in a different way, thinking perhaps she had been pulling his leg.

'I like a bit of time off too, you know, now and then.'

Before he could give his answer to that, if any, Sophie went back into the kitchen.

5

Gwen and Muriel looked up at the sound of the outside door shutting a second time.

'Peter in a funny mood,' said Sophie.

'You know I don't think drink agrees with him,' said Muriel. 'Never has.'

'Decent of the old boy,' said Gwen, 'to stick up for Percy like that. And shows a great breadth of sympathy too.'

'You'd think he'd realize there's others needs a break,' said Sophie, and went briskly on, 'I'm just off round to Rhiannon's for half an hour. Now you won't be rushing away yet awhile, will you? Stuff in the fridge if you want it,' she said further, though there was enough stuff on the table to keep both the other two chewing hard for a couple of hours. 'Stay if you like, mind, there's another bed in the –'

Muriel interrupted to say she would get a minicab and Gwen interrupted her to say she would drive her, and the two fought over it briefly until Sophie had actually left, though they each managed to get in their thanks for the party and their sendings of love to Rhiannon. After assuring herself that they were indeed alone Gwen turned to Muriel with an intent frown.

'What we were saying – a tin of a good brand with a spoonful of yogurt stirred in . . .'

'And a spot of chopped parsley . . .'

'. . . and they start asking you just which vegetables you've used, isn't there endive in this, can't I taste celeriac. And wanting to know *how* you did it, surely you melted them in butter and so on. I just tell them, the old way, m'm, it's the only proper way.'

Muriel laughed with more elation than might have been expected at a simple discussion of kitchen methods. 'Right, there's not much they can say to that. And of course when it comes to chicken or Scotch broth or whatever, well, what is it, it's cubes and booze, that's what it is, cubes and booze. A tin of oxtail soup and a cube and a tablespoon of whisky and that's it. Not only easier, incomparably easier. *Better*,' she said challengingly. 'Better all along the line.'

'When I look back,' said Gwen, resting her chin on a hand that also had a lighted cigarette in it and squinting towards a recent wine-stain on the tablecloth, 'and think of all that carry-on with the wretched stock-pot, never let it leave the stove, in with every scrap of the joint and you'd have thought a chicken carcass was worth ten times the chicken itself and . . . Do you know, Muriel, would you believe it, time was when I'd go along to the butcher and get bones for the dog, no dog, straight into the bloody pot with the beef-gristle. And for what? What possessed us?'

This time Muriel's response was affectionate as well as appreciative, or at least it sounded like it. In the usual run of things she and Gwen got on no better than all right even when she was not finding Gwen sly nor Gwen finding her loud or strange or both, but midnight could bring some display of amity. Part of this must have come from mere co-survival at the drinks table, as both had reflected before now. But not all; not this time, at least.

Gwen waited for a moment, then said more or less at random, 'After all, it's not as if anybody in the world's going to notice, let alone appreciate even the most obvious . . .'

'Don't make me laugh.'

'I mean they don't even *know*.'

'Of course they don't *know*, love. You can only know if you want to know, and they don't want to know. They have other claims on their valuable attention, as I imagine you must have noticed before.'

'I can't bear the way they –'

'What, them bestir themselves to notice how life's lived in their own home, what makes the bloody world go round? Not them. Why should they? They've won.'

By this stage there was little doubt that those now under discussion were not the same as those who asked Gwen just which vegetables she had used. Nevertheless whatever the two women most wanted to talk about had pretty clearly not yet been broached. Give it time, as they used to say in South Wales when an unlooked-for silence descended on the company. Gwen was the one who let it come, that being what you did if you were the one with the luck when everybody present had given it time.

'Of course she still is very striking, I quite see that, I wouldn't call her beautiful, I never thought she was beautiful, but she is very striking.' She left the name out not through any Cymric instinct of non-committal but because her thoughts were undeviatingly fixed on Rhiannon, as in fact they had been for some minutes past.

Perhaps Muriel's were too: she joined in promptly

enough. 'Oh, agreed, with the benefit of a small fortune laid out on facials and massages and health farms and I don't know what all. Plus never having to do a hand's turn in the home.'

'Oh fair enough, but you don't get skin like that out of a tube. And that carriage, you're born with it or you're not. But as for –'

'Not so much as heave a plate on to the bloody rack.'

'It's when it comes to the what would you call it, the social side that I start, um, veering away from the consensus a bit. The conversational –'

'Airs and graces at her age.'

'I mean she's fine on the chit-chat level, nobody better for a good chinwag, oh, I'll give her that, it's just all rather run-of-the-mill. You know, humdrum. Of course, I'm not asking for a discussion of Wittgenstein over the coffee and gingernuts, nothing like that, but it's all very agreeable and chummy and then at the end you ask yourself what has she actually *said*. Nobody's demanding a coruscating shower of wit . . .'

This speech had given Muriel time to do some catching-up. 'Always found her a bit of a bore, quite frankly.'

'Well, I don't think I'd . . .'

'Look, wasn't she . . . didn't you . . . weren't you . . .'

'Wasn't I what, pet?'

'You know, at the . . . place along the road, the . . . *you* know, the poly is it?'

'The university,' said Gwen a little stuffily.

'Yeah, that's right, well weren't you there together about a hundred years ago, you and her?'

'As a matter of fact we were, yes, way back as you say.' Gwen tried to remember what sort of place Muriel had been at. Surely if it had been another university or any other proper seat of learning then Muriel would have impressed it upon her many times over. So it must have been a teachers' training college or some other lowly institution where they had envy dinned into them. She realized she felt pretty vague on the whole topic. 'If the matter is of the smallest interest.'

'Sorry, I was just wondering what sort of showing she made as a student, you know, from the academic point of view.'

'*Oh.*' In the interval, not long but extended by a couple of soft interpolated belches from Muriel, it had returned to Gwen's mind that the place in question had been a school of art named after one of the industrial towns in the North of England and presumably responsible, to some degree anyway, for Muriel's taste in pictures as seen in her house. This made Gwen feel comfortable enough to go on, 'Well, actually now you come to mention it, er, it is quite interesting. She went to all her lectures, well that's sensible if you're not too sure of your own capacity to shine, as it were, and did all her essays, good girl, and would probably have ended up with a pass degree which was all she was going for, if she hadn't . . .'

'Right. What was she, what was she studying?'

'She was reading –' said Gwen with some weight on the word, then carried on all offhand, '– biology main with botany subsidiary or the other way round, I can't remember. Some English in her first year I think.'

'Not a very distinguished career do I gather?'

'She was a conscientious student but she didn't seem to take any interest in her subjects the rest of the time. Did her work and that was that, then off out. No shortage of offers as you can imagine. She, er, she never took much part in the swapping of ideas, midnight discussion side of university life.'

Muriel made a backhand gesture putting off consideration of that side of life indefinitely. 'Popular enough with her teachers I dare say.'

'Well: if you mean by that there was any –'

'No no, nothing improper, I'm not suggesting that at all. A girl doesn't have to go anywhere near that far to make herself agreeable to her pastors and masters. Winning ways'll do it.'

'Well,' said Gwen again, and stopped. She wanted quite strongly to oppose what was being insinuated without much idea of why, except that the vertical furrows along Muriel's top lip struck her all of a sudden as most unattractive. They had shown up extra clear in the last half-minute, which was just about when Gwen had found she was no longer being borne along by the thrill of disloyalty. She had talked and drunk herself off the heights of her revolt, though that was not at all the same thing as saying she wanted to go home. And it was miles and miles away from saying she was beginning to grow reconciled to what had taken place, what had almost failed to take place, between herself and Alun. It had been *all her fault* – for not having learnt her lesson years before, for being drunk too early in the day to be allowed for, for chancing her arm with a contemptible sod like that. In the past she had never quite made up her mind whether Alun was on balance to be despised or to be regarded as some sort of engaging rogue. Well, if nothing else, the events of the early afternoon of the day in question, that of the unveiling at St Dogmael's, had settled that one for good and all. But no point in going over it again now, if ever.

Evidently it had been the right moment for Muriel too to take a break. Sitting hunched over the table, she was making patterns with a matchstick in the loose ash that half filled the roomy blue-glass ashtray in front of her and hissing quietly through her teeth, perhaps in search of a new topic, if so in vain, as soon appeared.

'It doesn't make any odds whether you're bright or stupid or anywhere in between,' she said. 'They don't care what you think, what you say, or what you're like at all.'

'They don't even notice.' Gwen reckoned she ought to be able to hold her own here.

'You thought so at first, mind you. At least I know I did. Tell us what you think, love – no go on, I really want to hear. And then when you did tell 'em, well it was quite a long time before I started noticing the glaze in their eyes. They were being good about you talking. You can say what you please because it doesn't matter what you say. It's like, I was reading about one of these Russian satellite places, was it Hungary, anyway wherever it was, what you say's neither here nor there just so long as you don't set about bloody *doing* anything, it might have been Poland. And then they wonder when you start screaming and chucking things at them. Hey, that's like, dead funny isn't it, I never thought of it like that before, but it's like when somebody like a dissident or a minority finds they can't get anywhere through the legal channels so they go round blowing up power-stations. Of course I don't hold with people actually literally doing that, but by Christ I promise you I know how they feel.'

'And then they're never angry back. *You* get angry but *they* don't on purpose, so as to show how silly and childish you are and how mature and marvellous they are. Objective too.'

'It's all right for them to be fed up first, don't forget, like when you're late or they're late. You might be cross when they're late when what they've been up to *matters*, see? When you've not batted an eyelid.'

'And they go off to the club as if they don't love it.' Gwen had started to enjoy herself. 'As if we *don't know*.'

'Why we bother to talk to them passes my comprehension.'

'Ever. I often wonder.'

'They're all shits,' said Muriel. 'And the ones who pretend not to be are the worst of the lot.'

'I suppose so. Sometimes I think we're a bit hard on them.'

'Serve the buggers right, I say.'

It was very quiet in Sophie's kitchen. Even in the 1980s South Wales still kept industrial hours: early to work if any, early home, early in the pub, early to bed. The tendency gave sitting up an extra relish. Muriel poured wine with a mention of one for the road, and Gwen accepted some with a cautionary hand lifted, as at every previous pouring. Then, as if struck by sudden inspiration, Muriel snatched up a cigarette and lit it.

'This may not be a very edifying way of carrying on,' she said judicially and with a demonstrative jerk of the hand, 'but it's a long sight more fun than anything my poor old female parent had a chance of getting up to in her declining years. No cars or parties or telly then. In those days you had your chair and your stick and your cat and that was it.'

'Oh come off it, Muriel,' said Gwen, sharply enough to make Muriel twitch a little. 'I met your mother a couple of times, and one of the times I remember she was waiting for somebody to come and pick her up and drive her somewhere to play bridge. And I'm not at all sure she hadn't got a gin and tonic in her hand while she waited. Stick and cat indeed.'

Apart from the twitch, soon suppressed, Muriel showed not the smallest discomfort or sign of regrouping at this contradiction. 'All right, she was lucky. Thousands weren't. I'm thinking of the days pre-war now, you understand. A different world in all sorts of ways. Altogether different attitudes.' Muriel was talking faster and with more concentration than before, like somebody determined to get through a number of remarks already in mind, more than one perhaps long in mind. 'About marriage for instance. Now we're supposed to think that that generation never discussed anything like that. Well that's probably right enough and they didn't *discuss* it, go into the bloody business in every mortal detail – but you see you can discuss a thing till you're black in the face and end up knowing less about it than when you started. Understanding it less, less well. My mother,' said Muriel forcefully and quickening up further – 'my mother used to talk about the unpleasant side of marriage. No she didn't, she didn't talk about it, she referred to it, that was how she referred to it when she did. Now just you try and imagine the kind of roasting you'd get if you called it that these days. From everybody. But I wonder how many women would disagree with you in their heart of hearts.'

When Muriel did let up, plainly not out of any shortage of material, Gwen looked encouraging and prepared to pay close attention. Whatever was to follow she would pass on to Rhiannon at the first opportunity, not only on intrinsic grounds but also to offset earlier treacheries. Besides, any informed account of relations between Muriel and Peter, long suspected of being bad enough to be interesting, would win no small kudos among the other wives.

Even at prevailing speeds of thought Gwen was quite ready when Muriel went on, in no less of a rush than before and just where she had left off, 'Because they never had time to get used to it, to adjust. It's supposed to come naturally and I expect it does for a very great many, it must do, but not for all. But it's no use saying anything because they don't notice, and then when they do notice they think it's just a female acting up or asserting herself or getting back at them for something else in the way everybody knows they do. So then it's either a huge set-to or hoping it'll be better next time, and funnily enough it always seems to turn out the same way, isn't that striking? And *then* . . . it gets to be too late, very natural that, just like when you're talking to someone and you don't know their name, and you hang on because you're hoping they're going to say it or you'll remember, and then before you know where you are it's too late to ask them. Well, when you've got that far it's no time at all to when it's really too late.

'Some people seem to manage quite okay to keep up with their old buddies after not seeing them for twenty years. Siân was telling me she's still in touch with a mate of hers who went to Toronto I couldn't tell you when but a hell of a long time ago.'

Gwen still said nothing. Very reluctantly, and feeling fed up as well, she saw that she would not after all be able to tell Rhiannon what Muriel had let out, could at most drop a hint or two along with a plea of amnesia. That amnesia might easily turn out to be genuine enough, and even the hint or two might stretch her morning self too far. It could be that Muriel had been half rationally counting on something like that, trying out an unusual form of self-revelation, one that popped back into the box over-night. Certainly her last couple of sentences had been just the sort of thing you expected to hear on coming round from a fit of extreme apathy in the small hours. No harm in passing that on.

'Would you very kindly telephone for a minicab on my behalf?' said Muriel after a minute of complete silence. She spoke with rather better control than before from much further out. 'The number can be found in my handbag which is somewhere.'

More of the same, thought Gwen, picking up the handbag from within reach. But she made up her mind to be less bothered in future when Muriel seemed to her strange or loud, if she could remember the reason, of course.

6

'Was it baby Babs whose hideous crabs distressed Father Muldoon?

Oh no, it wasn't baby Babs, it was Mrs Rosenbloom . . .' Alun sang quietly not out of any ordinary precaution, for he was alone at the wheel of his car, but to avoid giving way to anything in the nature of vulgar triumph. On leaving Malcolm's in a mood of heavily qualified satisfaction he had happened to find himself passing, or as good as passing, the house of an old friend. Until the party at the Golf Club they had not met for something like twenty years, met even then hardly long enough for him to tell her she was obviously in terrific fettle and how sorry he had been to hear about Griff. In his day Griff had been a successful and venturesome doctor, unstinting with the early pep pills, master of a sizeable red-brick villa on the Beaufoy road. Alun had just had time to ask where she was living now – same place actually, good old Griff, trust him to see her right. Alun had notified himself, more or less as he turned into that road, that if a light happened to be showing there at this hour then he would pull in for a moment and give a toot, or perhaps better a quick ring, just on the off-chance. And there had been a light and the chance had come up.

To take a fresh step in that general direction so soon

after nearly coming a cropper over a previous one, while not yet out of that danger in fact, might have seemed foolhardy to some. It certainly did to Alun, or had until the moment he was invited in for a couple of minutes. After that, and especially now he was driving away, it felt more like having successfully gone up in his own light aeroplane immediately after a bit of a spill. That of course made it no less foolhardy in the undertaking. No, well there it was.

At the age of twenty-six or so, having noticed that he was obviously not a particle more grown-up or less reckless than he had been at thirteen, he had been greatly relieved to come across a newspaper article by some fashionable psychologist saying that adolescence among human males could be a drawn-out process, lasting in some respects and cases until the age of twenty-five or even thirty. This assurance had given him intermittent hope and comfort of a sort until about ten years later, when it had come back to him in a moment of what had been, even for him, an outstanding act of goatish irresponsibility. Thereafter he had clung to the consolation that there was nothing he could do about it.

The house in Holland when he approached it had a light on in the sitting-room, a departure from his expectation that brought mild vexation cross-hatched with foreboding. The vexation went along the lines of here he was, having taken all this trouble to leave people to themselves, give them plenty of time to get themselves off to bed, faced now with God-knew-what hold-up before he could get himself off there after a hard day. The foreboding was less straight-forward.

For Rhiannon to be still up and on her own much after eleven, never mind getting on for one o'clock in the morning, was unheard-of, imaginable only in bombshell

266

situations, good news it might be, bad much more likely. Short of that, she would most probably have Rosemary with her, back from her evening out (or somewhere) with William Thomas, who seemed to have been around since first light or thereabouts. It was no trouble at all for Alun to picture the bloody girl looking up alertly this very moment at the sound of his engine, getting into position next to her mother as president of a two-woman court of inquiry into his recent activities and overall behaviour. Or it would be Rosemary on her own, no more alluring an option. Whereas other possibilities hardly bore thinking about: Gwen with an expanded edition of her grievances? Malcolm with a more accurate one of his? The police he ruled out unless a mistake had been made. An incident in Harriston in 1950 involving a woman probationary sergeant and a patrol van might well have seriously displeased them at the time, but at this date could surely be passed over as grounds for a midnight descent on a non-black.

These speculations and others went through Alun's head while he was still driving up to the house. When he got closer he saw there was a car parked outside it, one he was nearly sure he had seen not far away not long before. That was the best he could do: he knew well enough that car recognition was an important proficiency for one who led his sort of life after hours, but he had been neglecting it, was still dangerously unschooled in local detail. Moving on foot to the front door he let his neck go rubbery and his eyes uninquiring, getting ready to lurch into action as a drunk. Then he sort of remembered it was Rhiannon he would be hoping to fool and went ordinary again, in so far as he now could. After it was too late he started trying to think of a topic to take the initiative with.

When he walked springily into the sitting-room he was faced with Rhiannon in towelling dressing-gown over nightie and Sophie in day clothes; no Rosemary. Neither of the two present smiled very positively or spoke. Without thought, intent only on action, he moved over and kissed each of them in turn, then, as his brain began ticking over once more, he stepped back and gave Sophie a sequence of cheerful interrogative nods.

She responded at once. 'I had Dorothy, I was saying to Rhiannon, and then I had Muriel, she's probably still there. Really one of her nights. Bad as I've ever known her, she was. Cruel. You don't see her like it, you know, Rhi. Gwen dropped in and I left Muriel putting her through it. Just nipped out,' she ended, with a girls-together half-wink at her chum.

'I don't blame you,' said Alun warmly. Good old Soaph, he thought with more genuine warmth – never any need to worry there from the word go. Not really bright as you usually thought of it, but bright as a button when it came to anything that bore on the old ins and outs: the throwaway mention of Gwen was a typical touch. With a quick switch he added, 'Rosemary gone to bed, has she?'

'Just this moment,' said Rhiannon. 'I wonder you didn't bump into William as you drove up.'

'Oh, he just dropped her off like that, did he?'

'Well, yes.'

'I see.'

At no point could Alun have said what he meant by his last question. But whatever it might have been intended to convey – surprise, resignation, outrage, boredom, disappointment, fatherly concern, heartfelt co-masculine approval – he of all people had no business to be asking it in front of these two, or perhaps anywhere on earth. This dawned on him a bit at a time while he stood there taking in the information. Then he suddenly said, 'You know if by any chance this ridiculous weather carries on, we could probably do worse than go down to Birdarthur for a couple of days. Old Dai the Books still keeps up his place on the cliff there. Sophie, you've stayed in that cottage, haven't you?'

'Oh, I'm included in this, am I?'

'Why not, there's two decent bedrooms and Charlie can leave Victor at the tiller for a spell. Not next week because I'm filming then. Dai's only ever there at weekends, he was telling me. I didn't manage to get him at the shop today . . .'

It would have been miraculous if he had, not having gone within a league of the place, tried it by telephone or even admitted Dai the Books to his thoughts more than a few seconds before pronouncing the name, though the facts were as stated. Anyway, with his talents for persuasion, which had less to do with direct pressure than with making something sound fun for long enough, he soon had Sophie's assent to the Birdarthur project with Charlie's thereby taken for granted. Rhiannon's had been taken for granted from the start.

'Well, I'm off,' said Alun finally. 'Don't break the party up on my account, now.'

'You needn't think you're going to get away like that, *was*,' said Rhiannon.

Into Thy hands, O Lord, thought Alun to himself. Although he often said where he was going, or might have been going, he never said where he had been, nor did Rhiannon ever ask until . . . unless . . .

'You take that creature out, outside, and then settle her down in her basket in the kitchen. And mind you wait and make sure before you let her back in.'

Enfeebled by the exertions of her day, Nelly had responded to Alun's arrival with no more than a couple of paltry thumps of her tail and a lunatic gleam out of the very corners of her eyes. Now, hearing herself referred to, she made a slovenly attempt to sit up and did a thorough squeaking yawn that would have been quite impressive in an animal of any size. He took her away as bidden, but in a style that emphasized his decency in doing so, his detachment from the whole concern. It was not that he disliked the puppy, rather the contrary: he just could not afford to let it be thought that he could be roped in any old time to minister to her needs. Why, next thing he knew he would be rushing back from Griff's or somewhere to give the bloody hound her tea!

7

When the door had shut behind Alun there were two releases of breath of which neither quite amounted to a sigh of relief. Sophie lowered herself to the floor, twisted her head about till it rested comfortably against the arm of the chair behind her and said she must be going. Rhiannon suggested more coffee, adding that it would only take a minute, and rearranged her legs under her on the sofa. They sat in a more or less habitable corner of the room with bare boards and half-decorated walls hardly out of reach.

Sophie had probably missed the coffee proposal altogether. 'You ought to get out more, you know, Rhi,' she said.

'Oh no. It's so lovely not having to after years of not wanting to and having to.'

'It'd be easier if you learnt to drive.'

'Not you too,' said Rhiannon, bouncing upright. 'I can drive as well as anybody if I haven't actually forgotten how. I drove a dry-cleaner's van for eighteen months in London when we were hard up. It's not I can't drive, it's I don't drive. There being no car except the one with Alun in it. Can't afford a second car, he says, at least he'd say if I brought it up again ever. He does all the shopping I can't do round the corner and if I want to go anywhere there's a minicab. Much cheaper than running another car ourselves. And no parking problem. He'd say that too. You try him.'

'Funny, he's never been one to pinch the pennies. I mean . . .' Sophie looked about her, but there was little evidence of lavishness except perhaps the only picture so far on display, a large Cydd Tomas over the fireplace, dated 1981 under the artist's signature and yet attractive enough – it very likely showed Dragon's Head from the sea – to be almost worth its place on that ground alone.

'Sure, no trouble there,' said Rhiannon, 'but it's nothing to do with that, the point is with him having the car nobody ever knows where he is, and me not having a car, everybody knows where I am, only that's not nearly so interesting. Take tonight, now.'

'M'm. Any idea where he'd been?'

'Not the faintest, have you?'

'I only hope it was somebody sensible.'

'Oh, me too.' Rhiannon paused before going on. 'How was Gwen really?'

'Oh. Coming round, I reckon. Still a bit shirty but going to be okay as long as he doesn't make any waves for a bit.'

'If only he had the sense to keep it in the family, sort of.'

'I know,' said Sophie, 'I couldn't agree with you more. Especially now he's down here. It's not like London down here.'

'Absolutely. It's silly of him in another way too. It lands up there are things we can't talk about, him and me. I

271

don't mean important things, I mean unimportant things, but they're still quite important when you add them together. Who was there and how they seemed and what was said . . . At least it makes it harder.'

'M'm. Is he all right, Rhi, do you think?'

'All right?' repeated Rhiannon in alarm. 'How do you mean?'

'No, nothing, he just seems to have got a bit wild. You'd think he'd know by now not to take up with Gwen all of a sudden like that and then expect to get away with treating her like . . .'

'Take up with Gwen *again* all of a sudden like that, but it doesn't really make any –'

'Oh, I didn't realize they were –'

'Oh yes. Funny, I never thought he was very keen. In fact I wonder a bit who took up with who, either time. Of course it was more all right for her then, not being exactly the only pebble on the beach. She had other things in her life then.'

'Like Malcolm,' said Sophie.

'Yeah.'

That was all for the moment. Sophie sat with her arms round her knees, shapely sleek dark head towards the thick shaggy rug as if she was following a train of thought, not a thing she often gave any sign of doing. Rhiannon lit a cigarette, holding the flame as usual a couple of millimetres inwards from the tip. She had wondered a little at the time what had brought Sophie along to her so late, nearly too late to find her up. Something to do with Alun, it had soon emerged; saying she hoped he was settling down all right after the move from London, not saying what she could well have been thinking now, that she also hoped his recent goings-on did not mean she had lost her special bit of hold on him, however lumpy that bit might have looked to the outside world. For various reasons Rhiannon too hoped as much, but felt that here in Wales that was not the sort of thing you could really say. So with no particular intention she asked how Charlie was, rather less inquisitively than when she had asked after Gwen.

'That bugger knocks it back like a fool,' said Sophie without looking up.

'Yes, I thought . . .'

'I never realized how much he drank till the night he came home sober. A revelation, it was.'

'Not even nice at the time, I don't suppose.'

'What had happened that day I'll never know. Anyway it was a hell of a night after that. He made me sit up with him till he was asleep which wasn't till after two, and then it couldn't have been much after four he was cootched tight up to me, stiff as a board and breathing in and out, in and out as if he was doing it for a bet. And he wouldn't say what it was, what the matter was. I went on and on asking him but he wouldn't say. Next day he was paralytic by six, Victor said.'

'If he's going to make you sit up and all that, he really ought to say.'

'He's never said, except being alone makes it worse and the dark isn't good. I've given up trying to get him to try and say what it is. All he's ever said is it's nothing to do with anything and it doesn't mean anything. I'm fed up. He ought to say *something*. I mean about *something*. It gets depressing when a bloke never says anything. There's not as much difference as you might think between him pissed as a lizard and him passed out. Not when he's with me there's not. I quite like him, old Charlie, or I used to, and I miss him, sort of.'

Rhiannon took her time about finishing her cigarette. 'Sounds as if the two of you could do with a nice break.

You will come to Birdarthur, won't you? You and I can have a proper gas. Alun'd like you to be there too. He's always complaining he never seems to see enough of you.'

Now Sophie did look up. 'Oh, he doesn't, no, does he really?'

'*Yes*, always going on about where's Sophie these days.'

'Oh no, really?'

'Won't do him any harm either to get away for a bit. Now there's a bloke who says something if you like. If only the silly little thing would learn to leave it at that.'

Seven – Alun

1

Soon after eight o'clock on a Tuesday morning Alun lifted the hatch at the rear of what he occasionally called the family car, or even our family car, though not in Rhiannon's hearing. The two were off to Birdarthur shortly. It had been agreed that Charlie and Sophie should follow them out the next day in time for lunch, with all four set to return late on the Friday. Alun's move to let the Cellan-Davieses know of the impending trip had consisted in full of ringing their number once the previous noon, a foredoomed venture seeing that Gwen was expected at Siân Smith's for coffee, etc., and Malcolm strongly presumed to have left for the Bible, but it counted as not having been able to get hold of them. Peter had been told he really must come down, pick any time to suit himself, just turn up, and after a word or two about a bloody Welshman's invitation had conceded he might try. First categorically disowning any responsibility for anybody or anything, Tarc Jones had consented to write down the number of the people called Gomer who lived two along from the telephone-free abode of Dai the Books.

Alun had not so much lifted the hatch of his car as flung it boyishly upwards, which was something he would have done with no more and no less vivacity if he had thought he was being observed, and in that event whether by jobless school-leaver or high-ranking TV executive. First into the cargo-space went, in quick time, a carton of drinkables: twelve-year-old Scotch, classy spring water to put in it, gin, tonics, a rare bottle of Linie-Aquavit from Oslo, a much commoner bottle of Bailey's Irish Cream, ostensibly for Rhiannon, in fact no more than chiefly for her, one each of Asti Spumante and Golden Sweet Malaga absolutely solely for her, four large cold Special Brews in wet newspaper for him, and a spot of coffee liqueur and other muck he could not quite face simply throwing out of the house. Next he stowed a box of hand-picked groceries, featuring soused herring fillets, allegedly smoked oysters, German lumpfish roe and other dainties thought to be proper to accompany the aquavit. He laid on top of this a flat paper bag containing a new pullover in yellow cashmere and two sports shirts still in their packaging.

Trips, up to and including ones directed at funerals, had always heartened Alun, livened him up in prospect, and not just because you never knew what you might run into even in Blaenau Ffestiniog. It was admittedly getting a touch late with him for breaking new ground, however cruelly he might ravage the old. In addition, this coming trip was not a fit occasion for any of that, and besides there was nothing under Birdarthur in the for-his-eyes-only address book. A big part of the thrill could probably be put down to nothing more than anticipating a journey by car, by no means an everyday experience in the South Wales of the 1930s and later, as he had been known to remind his London friends. But with all that said he got through the first part of the loading in fine breezy style, as also the second and duller part involving actual luggage and bedclothes and pillows assembled by Rhiannon after managing to get hold of Dai at the shop. The third part slowed him down.

This part began with a typewriter, not the one from his study upstairs, the noble Japanese office-pattern needless-to-say electric job, but the lowly Italian portable, an acoustic model, as he would express it when he had the energy. Another carton followed it, not nearly such a nice one as the one full of drink, containing books and papers. The books included the *Concise Oxford*, a collapsing Roget's *Thesaurus*, *Y Geiriadur Mawr* – The Big [Welsh – English/English–Welsh] Dictionary to him, a compilation notable for its *golygydd ymgynghorol* – the Rev Tydfil Meredith's *Courcey and Its Churches*, Sefton-Williams on Celtic mythology and the Brydan Complete Poems. Out of simulated personal need as well as feigned piety he took the last-mentioned volume with him everywhere he went within reason, pointless at best this trip perhaps with only Charlie and Sophie and possibly Peter to bowl over, but there it was. The papers in the carton consisted of typing paper and forty-six pages of a novel of whose existence only Rhiannon knew, together with a few notes.

Doing some more work on this novel was an unstated reason for going to Birdarthur, already present somewhere in his mind before he blurted out the suggestion a couple of weeks before. He had knocked off the dreaded forty-six in six days in the spring, when a little bastard in BBC radio had tardily cancelled the definitive talk on the Welsh nonconformist conscience he had engaged to prepare and record, and he had not looked at them since. Now, under the self-imposed pressure of a measured length of time in semi-confinement with no excuse for shirking, he was to apply himself to the hideous task of adding to them. As they stood, or with some minor surgery, they were supposed to be, he had striven to make them, his devout hope was that they were, the opening section of the only really serious piece of prose he had written since his schooldays. In more sanguine moods he softened this to his most serious, etc. But anyway a great deal, including the prospects for the whole undertaking, hung on whatever he would make of those forty-six in two or three hours' time.

No wonder then that his demeanour was staid as he settled the creative container into place. And yet he felt an obscure excitement, nothing to do with any literary burgeoning except very remotely, just an internal squaring-up to a tiny bit of a leap in the dark. 'I was ever a fighter,' he muttered defiantly, continuing in a milder tone, 'or perhaps more accurately ever a medium-range light bomber designed for night operations and low-level reconnaissance. Thank you.' He reckoned he had it about as near right by now as he was ever going to get it.

After that it was a cakewalk to shuttle the bloody puppy round to the char's daughter's, cancel the papers and fetch the ordinary suitcases and the rest of the gear out to the car. Last to go in were the heavy waterproofs and gumboots indispensable to the visitor to rural Wales at any season. The weather for the moment in fact was clear without being bright, though scattered showers were unadventurously forecast. Rhiannon turned up for the off at blokes' time as usual, wearing a dress with some sort of pattern, also shoes, or so Alun assumed. Likewise as usual on any journey she reached over and squeezed his hand when the wheels started turning.

On Courcey the roads were practically empty, flushed of visitors by a lightning revolution in taste or nuclear accident. Even the streets of Birdarthur itself were unobstructed, with no obvious tourists to be seen. Brydan Books, dimly viewed by Dai as a pillar of greed and also as unethical competition, held no customers for the moment, nor was any Continental bus stuck on the acute-angled turn up to St Cattwg's church, in whose shadow the poet slept. There was some activity in the approaches to the Brydan Arms, though that had been just as true at mid morning when the place was still called the White Rose. With the end of its function as a port and the closure of the metal works and the silica quarry, Birdarthur had shown marks of unemployment, but none were visible now that the town had been designated or turned into an enterprise zone and the unemployment had gone away somewhere else.

Alun took them round the corner by the Brydan Burger Bar and into the road – unmade for centuries, metalled now to suit visiting traffic – that ran above the foreshore and the larger and deeper part of the bay. The tide was full, near the turn, the sea flat calm and ginger-beer grey touched with green and yellow. The sight of the sun going down here had been a special favourite of Brydan's, people were always saying, and indeed he had been well placed physically to witness it from his cottage near the start of the row facing the water, though how often he had been up to taking it in, even when technically conscious, was another question. After extensive refitment to mend the devastations of his tenure, the building had been converted into a museum and gift shop, especially gift shop, and the one next door a little later into a coffee shop and refreshment bar that, excusably in the circumstances, sold no strong drink. From the secured outer door of this a lone elderly female in a parachute jacket, of necessity an American, was turning away in bafflement just as the Weavers passed.

They passed along to the end of the line of cottages where there was a rough triangle of waste ground spread with refuse old and new. A cinder-path led on from here, signposted Brydan's Walk, though again local opinion doubted whether you would ever have got boyo to set foot on it, there being no pub or free-pound-note bloody counter at the other end. By prearrangement Alun sent Rhiannon on foot down the walk while he turned the car round and backed it after her for eighty yards or so, until the path was too narrow for him to go on. So he stopped there and more or less watched her unload all the stuff through the hatchway. Then he drove back to the triangle and parked arse-first up a muddy and precipitous lane and hurried to rejoin her.

'There must be an easier way of doing this,' he said, catching her up actively with the case of booze clasped in his arms, 'but I can't seem to think of one.'

'Oh, I can. You climbing over and out of the back and taking the whole lot out and carrying it to the cottage and putting it all away.'

'Strange the way things come back to one. Before we left I could hardly have told you which direction Dai's place was, and now we're here I haven't even had to hesitate.'

'Whereas I remembered this bit perfectly. Very strange.'

'Put those down and I'll come back for them, go on. Oh, all right, suffer then. What's for lunch?'

'Pork pie and baked beans.'

'Did you bring the mustard?'

'Yes, and Spanish onion and sweet pickle.'

'Little genius.'

They had reached Dai's place, not the prettiest or best-situated on this side of Birdarthur but by no means the dampest or the smelliest, a two-up-two-down affair with a sliver taken off one of the two up to form a narrow bathroom-lavatory, so narrow that only someone with thighs rather on the short side could have expected to use it in full comfort. Rhiannon went to and fro opening all the windows.

'No trouble round here guessing who was brought up in a bloody town,' said Alun. 'Say the word and I'll knock a hole in the kitchen wall for you.'

'You can take these out to the bin,' said Rhiannon, passing him a trayful of elderly foodstuffs. 'How long has anyone not been here?'

'Hey, some of these are all right, aren't they? What about this pot of –'

'You eat what you fancy.'

When he had checked in with the Gomers and established that no dollar-laden commissions had materialized in the last couple of hours, Alun cleared a space for his typewriter at one end of a smallish table by the front-room window. Doing this entailed shifting a number of uncommonly horrible china dogs and other creatures. Their surfaces were blurred, with a buggered-about look as though someone, perhaps under Muriel Thomas's influence, had caused a flame-thrower to play upon them at some stage of manufacture. Their colours were off too. He bundled them away in a cupboard, thinking it was a bit hard to have come all the way out to south-west Courcey and walk into a bunch of boldly innovative china dogs at the end of it.

To put off the evil hour he ran his eye over Dai the Books's books and soon saw there would be nothing worth even short-listing for removal. The works of Brydan, on the other hand, were present in all sorts of editions, rendering his own copy of the poems an even more superfluous piece of luggage than before. Like everybody else in middle South Wales over the age of thirty, not to speak of many further off, Dai had his Brydan connections. On the wall there was a framed blow-up of the famous almost pitch-dark photograph of the two of them he kept in his shop. He used to say he had had Brydan in there to lend him a hand once or twice in the school holidays – liked to think he had done a bit to help the lad out. In fact Brydan's main association had come rather later, when he used to drop in on his way to the station to steal a few pieces of new stock for subsequent resale, or rather sale, in that second-hand joint off Fleet Street. Alun shook his head at the memory. A great writer, he sometimes thought to himself and had often said in non-Welsh company, but in too many ways a sadly shabby human being.

Almost in the act of turning away from the shelves he caught sight of a strip of jacket he recognized, that enwrapping *The Blooms of Brydan*, a selection by Alun Weaver. Some alchemy, compounded of a nervy literary agent, a gullible publisher, a matter of coincidence with the date of Brydan's death and a historic review in *Time* magazine, had turned the produce of three weeks' work into a quite decent and lasting annuity: 5,000 last year in hardback in the USA alone and *Brydan's Wales* still very much alive. Whenever reminded of this Alun was tempted to think of himself as quite good at making money in his line, better than at pushing himself forward, not enough of a power man for that, too much of a sensual Celt. And in recent weeks he had been wondering rather about how he was doing, how he was making out as the organ-voice of Wales in Wales. Perhaps after all he had been more audible in England, where competing strains were fewer and less clamorous. He had never quite got over the paucity of his welcome home at Cambridge Street station. So be it: here squarely in front of him was a chance to do something about that all round.

He was sitting at the table looking out of the window at the seashore when Rhiannon came in wearing – well, he was nearly sure she had changed her clothes.

'Sorry, are you –'

'No, just wool-gathering. Can't think how that's got

itself a bad name, can you? Pricey stuff, wool. Getting it for free, too.'

'I thought I'd just take a look round the town. I haven't set eyes on it for donkey's years.'

'Fine, see you later, love.'

'What did you make of Ingrid?'

'Ingrid?'

'Ingrid Jenkins or whatever she's called. You know, Norma's daughter.'

'Who's – of course, the char, the char's daughter. To be sure. Well.'

'M'm, what did you make of her?'

'I don't know, I don't know that I made anything of her. Seemed perfectly pleasant, I only saw her for a moment. Why, what should I have made of her?'

'Oh, nothing. Did she seem the sort to look after Nelly properly, did you think?'

'Christ, Nelly's the puppy, right? Yes, fine. Well, I mean the whole place looked respectable enough. Clean. Things like that. I mean . . .'

'Oh, good.' Rhiannon's manner changed. 'I couldn't have brought her here, could I?'

Alun thought he saw now where this conversation was designed to lead. 'No, no,' he said, frowning at the idea. 'No, out of the question.'

'You can't leave them on their own for a minute when they're that age. I'd have had to be taking her out the whole time or else stay indoors with her here. Or make you.'

'Cheers. No, of course. You couldn't have brought her along and have any kind of proper break yourself. Out of the question.'

'M'm. Are you going to look at that stuff of yours?'

'Just glance at it, you know.' He always kept her roughly

283

abreast of what he was up to in the writing part of his life. About broadcasting, with the sudden excursions here and there it might require, he was sometimes less informative.

'Good luck, dear. Be about an hour.'

She was gone. Yes, what she had wanted was moral support for farming out the pooch. Normal and understandable. He made to pick up the horrendous buff envelope in front of him, then paused with a groan. There had been something crappy about what had gone before that. What the bugger had it been? Something to do with Ingrid. He had barely glanced at the girl – well, female, pushing forty he had supposed, smallish, pale; nothing else. So obviously there could be no question of . . .

He gave a muffled cry, then, remembering he was alone in the house, unmuffled it. His glance dropped to the floor at his side, to the carton of books there, to the scuffed green cover of the paperback *Thesaurus*. Absurdity, he subvocalized: stuff and nonsense, fiddle-de-dee, bosh, bunk, rats. *Ffwlbri*. Tell it to the Marines. *Credat Judaeus Apella*. If Rhiannon had been stirring the pond to catch him betraying an interest in this Ingrid, if she really thought he might have in mind getting off with the charwoman's daughter, then she was barmy. Unless that kind of suspicion, suspicion of stuff at that level, though unfounded in this case, was not unreasonable in general, was no longer unreasonable, in which case he was the barmy one. Was that the way it was going to take him – not willingness or ability but judgement, nous?

Several unalluring trains of thought presented themselves at this juncture. He found himself in pursuit of the one about anybody of any sense knowing when he was well off with Rhiannon. But he had not got any sense, or enough sense, or . . . But he had got this far a thousand times without ever having got any further. He hoped his

284

unpreparedness for the Ingrid question had let his innocence show through, because if not there was nothing he
could say about it; it was much too late for any of that,
ever. Almost eagerly he picked up the envelope.

Before he had got as far as pulling the contents out his
demeanour changed to a frenzied casualness. Head on one
side, eyebrows raised and eyes almost shut, mouth turned
down at the corners, he condescendingly turned back the
flap, exposed the top half of the first sheet and allowed
himself to let his glance wander over the typewritten lines
there before he actually fell asleep as he sat. What he read
woke him up with a start and set him doing what he had
very, very nearly done a minute before: leap out of his chair
and go glug-bloody-glug with the Scotch, not forgetting to
top up his glass before returning whence he had come.
There he slumped and stared out at the bay and tried to
reason with himself.

Of course the first couple of sentences had reminded him
of the opening passages of dozens of stories and novels by
Welshmen, especially those written in the first half of the
century. That was the whole point, to stress continuity,
to set one's face against anything that could be called
modernism and to show that the old subject, life in the
local villages, in the peculiar South-Wales amalgam of town
and country, had never gone away, in fact had a new
ironical significance in these days of decline. Worth doing,
agreed, but had he done it, any of it? Well, he might
have. Like Socrates now, who when his time came (he
remembered reading) had quite willingly and cheerfully
drunk off the hemlock, he laid the typescript down on the
table just like that and began at the beginning.

After five minutes or so he began to relax his rigid
bomb-disposal posture. From time to time as he went on
he winced sharply and made a correction, screwed up his

face in pain or goggled in disbelief, but several times gave a provisional nod and even laughed once or twice without mirth. At the end of an hour Rhiannon came back and found him at the typewriter with four lines and a bit along the top of the paper. When he looked up she spoke.

'How did it go?'

He scowled ferociously at her and held his hands in the air with the fingers crossed. 'It may be remotely conceivable,' he stage-whispered with precise delivery, 'that not every single syllable is absolutely beyond all hope of redemption.'

'Oh, good.'

'No no no, not good, nothing more than a bare possibility. It needs a lot doing to it. But I thought I'd better press on while I felt like it, rather than go back and start tinkering. No, keep your distance, girl,' he said as she seemed about to close in and deal him a congratulatory hug. 'Later, if ever.'

'All right, though, isn't it?' She went on standing near the foot of the stairs. 'There's just . . .'

'What?' he asked ill naturedly.

She made a crying face. 'Dorothy rang while you were taking Nelly to Ingrid's . . . and she asked us over for tonight . . . and I couldn't not tell her why we couldn't go . . . and then she asked if she and Percy could drive down tomorrow evening . . . and I couldn't tell her they mustn't . . . sorry . . .'

Having filled all the gaps in Rhiannon's speech with strong language or wordless howls, Alun waited till it was a theatrical certainty that there was no more to come and said, 'Is there more to come? Siân or Garth or old Owen Thomas or bloody fishface Eirwen Spurling or . . . Because if there is . . .'

'I couldn't help it, honest.'

286

'No, of course you couldn't, dull,' he said, embracing her. 'You'd need a tank division with close air support to fend off the bag in question. No, we'll manage. Think yourself lucky the work of words went all right this morning, mind. Now drink – gin and tonic coming up. Go on, *myn*, you're on holiday.'

He finished his paragraph in the few minutes it took her to put the lunch out in the kitchen. When they had eaten and, quite freely in his case, drunk, Rhiannon declared she would never have thought getting shut of the puppy would be so much like getting shut of the girls years ago and disappeared for a rest. Alun found on Dai's shelves a book of short stories about Cardiganshire life in the 1930s by a Welshman whose name he barely recognized – right up his street, especially at this stage – and an old Alistair McAlpine paperback about a raid on a Gestapo HQ in Holland, now a feature film, it said, and by the time he fell asleep in Dai's beaten-up armchair by the midget fireplace the colonel (Richard Burton) and the wing-commander (Trevor Howard) were already synchronizing their watches for the drop. On awakening he fell asleep again with no trouble at all, but on reawakening took Rhiannon a cup of tea. Then he wrote a dozen lines of dialogue while she pottered about overhead, and then they went out for a stroll.

The land and sea were quite boringly normal to look at, mousey grey at any sort of distance, but there were some yellow and slate-blue patches of sky that might once have meant something to the locals. They went along Brydan's Walk to the far end where it petered out among scruffy bushes and long pale grass, down a cliff path to the beach and back along the foreshore. A part of this was in the process of being flattened for something to be built on it. Half a dozen birds were wandering about near the water's edge, herons or oystercatchers; Brydan would have known which, or would have said. A few sailing dinghies heaved sluggishly in the harbour. At its corner they took a shallow flight of steps up to the main level and walked up the High Street with the name Birdarthur to be seen on shops, offices, posters, postcards wherever they looked. At the beginning of the narrow part, opposite what had been a bakery on their last visit, stood the pub, almost unchanged since longer than that except that it looked somehow newer. The sign, White's Hotel, was brilliant gold on navy-blue.

The inside looked much newer still and was not at all unchanged, so little so that Alun could have sworn he had never been in there in his life, but he was used to that by now and took comfort from the forbearance of the music, generic sleepy-lagoon muck full of swirls and tinkles. On a window-sill next to a fat potted plant there rested an object without a name in his vocabulary, a kind of video-screen on which streams of sparkling coloured light flowed through clouds and bands of steadier illumination. In some equally undefined but still horrible way a connection with the music seemed to be suggested. He would make a note of the phenomenon for putting into the *In Search of Wales* file, but first he sat Rhiannon down in a kind of medieval pew against the opposite wall and went to the bar. Here the order of white wine produced a glass of white wine instead of the stare of gloomy triumph that could once have been counted on in these parts, and he was asked which whisky he preferred instead of settling for what was planked in front of him, as fond memory would have it.

Rejoining Rhiannon he found an old man had settled himself on a padded stool facing her and was going on as if he was a great friend of them both by all means short of speech. Seen from in front he looked a really very old man, fit to give Alun himself a good four to five years, the precise model of the kind of sturdy, self-reliant Welshman who had tilled the neighbouring acres and fished the waters since time immemorial, and also one of the kinds of bloody *lossin* and berk he would dearly have liked to hit in the eye straight off with a jet of soda-water in the days before syphons went out. On his white head the fellow wore a white hat, though it was not obvious what this signified or how it had arisen.

Seating himself next to Rhiannon in the pew, Alun conversed with her for a few moments about the place and the people until he was sure that this was no previously undeclared uncle of hers. Then, telling himself he was buggered if he was going to be diverted, he brought out his ring-spine notebook and started on a pen-picture of the sparkling-light facility as intended.

If the white-hatted sod had missed anything that had taken place in front of him in the last couple of minutes it could not have been by much. He said now, in a bass voice that sounded to Alun like a close imitation of a dance-hall proprietor he used to know, 'Yes, well, you're a writer, aren't you?'

'Yes,' said Alun when Rhiannon had banged him in the ribs.

'Yes. Here after Brydan, are you?'

'What? Well no, not exactly.'

'A lot of them comes after Brydan. Brydan was a famous poet used to live here in Birdarthur. He used to come into this pub quite frequent, with Americans. He used to call it White's Club. Because it was like a club, he said. He was a Welshman, Brydan, but he wrote in English, see.'

'Yes, I know.' Alun's life was coming to consist more and more exclusively of being told at dictation speed what he knew.

'Brydan was a Welshman himself, but he wrote . . . his poetry . . . in the English language.'

'Indeed he did, in fact –'

'But he was a Welshman through and through. Don't you go thinking you can understand Brydan,' boomed the old sod, rocking back and forth slightly on his stool and smiling, but making it three parts plain he meant Alun rather than the world in general, 'that's *understand* Brydan, eh? – not being Welsh yourself.'

'For your information I am Welsh myself. I was born and brought up not twenty miles from here.'

'No, no, I say *not* being Welsh yourself you can't understand Brydan. It's Welsh people can, right? Appreciate. Appreciate is better. Yes, appreciate. Fully appreciate.'

'But . . .' Alun could think of nothing to say. His awareness that Rhiannon was sending him furtive hushing looks did nothing to loosen his tongue. Actually of course he could think of an enormous number of things to say, though none at all that would not make him seem to have lost some argument or other. 'But . . .'

'A writer, you say. For a paper, is it?'

'No. Yes. Sometimes.'

The sod seemed to think this a full and satisfactory answer, or at least one worth thinking over before moving on. He had got as far as stretching out a finger in Alun's direction when a young man with very short, almost colourless hair hurried in from the street and came over. As well as having pale hair he had a large face and was slightly moist about the nose and eyes. Looking at Alun and Rhiannon he lifted his head sidelong in consternation or apology.

'You're late, Grandad,' he said loudly. 'Tea'll be on the table now. On your way, Winston Churchill.' Without lowering his voice much he added, 'I hope he hasn't been too much of a pest.'

Alun could only think of saying, at the cost of some

damage to his sense of justice, that he had had a most pleasant chat.

'No kidding?' The youngster looked more closely at him and his large face broke into a smile. 'Hey, I know you. Seen you on television, haven't I? What is it, the Welsh something, the Welsh side of things? Tell me now, that, what's he called, Bleddyn Edwards, is he a great mate of yours?'

'No, I don't think I've even –'

'Well, I'm no expert but it's perfectly obvious to me – he's not up to the job – you are. All the difference in the world,' said the young sod with an authority his alleged ancestor would have had to acknowledge. 'No comparison.'

'That's very nice of you.'

'Get away, marvellous to have met you. Good luck, and thanks for putting up with old buggerlugs here.'

'Well, that was all right,' said Alun as he and Rhiannon came out of the pub a little while later. 'Not like life at all.'

She squeezed his arm against her. 'Good boy for not going for that old fart.'

What with one thing and another he felt quite pleased with life for the rest of the evening. Pre-eminent among the things there featured prominently and foreseeably the provisional clearance, or seven out of ten, he had awarded the existing portion of *Coming Home* – the sterling anti-trendy title for the complete work he had somehow captured over the last hours. The elevated mood lasted long enough to prompt him to make love to Rhiannon when in due course they got into the surprisingly cosy little bed.

They stayed lying there for a few minutes with the light on uttering contented mild animal sounds as they had done at such times for thirty-four years. Something about the bedside lamp was setting up a bit of a hoarse sort of screaming noise, but it was quiet enough in general to hear the waves breaking on the beach, not all that far away because by now the tide had come in again nearly to the full.

'Lovely day it's been,' said Alun. 'I'd forgotten how nice it was here.'

'Jolly good about your work.'

He shushed her and made disclaiming faces but with less conviction than earlier. 'They haven't managed to bugger the place up totally yet.'

'You must be tremendously relieved, or a bit relieved rather. It must be all right to say that.'

'What? Oh yes, I'll have another look at it in the morning.'

'Do you good to stay in one place and put your feet up for a couple of days.'

'Yeah, well . . .'

'I thought you were looking a tiny bit peaky, you know, just one per cent. There's nothing worrying you, is there?'

'No.' He was not going to let on about bloody Gwen, not now, not with no exterior limit on the discussion. He would have to see if he could pick a spot like three minutes before the arrival of a television team. 'No, not a thing. Bar wondering how long they'll go on making Scotch the way that suits me.'

'. . . Good,' she said without much sense of relaxation.

After more silence, he said, 'What time are they due tomorrow?'

'Twelvish. Evidently Charlie doesn't want to start drinking too early.'

'Oh I see. Well I'd better get some shut-eye if I'm to do any good before they turn up.'

The thought of television had set going something he had left unexamined in the meantime: the identity of

Bleddyn Edwards, said by the young sod in the pub to be inferior to him, Alun, but still mentionable in the same breath. The name was not unfamiliar, the face and everything else stayed out of view. What a pissy poser to be stuck with at this time of night. He fell asleep before he had got anywhere with it.

2

Alun went out early the next morning and got newspapers. On his return he stood facing the bay in pale sunlight, took some deep breaths and thought to himself, if a waft of industrial pollution had ever been perceptible here there was no question of any now. When other thoughts, to do with time and age and all that, started to occur to him he rather consciously went indoors to breakfast, a scheduled fatty's flare-up presenting two boiled eggs turned out on to fried bread and fried potatoes as well as bacon and tomatoes. While he ate it he worked animatedly at the *Times* crossword. 'You *fiend*,' he said, writing in a solution. 'Oh, you . . . you *swine*.'

At the typewriter afterwards he got through another half-page of dialogue, very rough, almost token. It had turned out hard for him to concentrate: he felt fit, the sun was shining on the water and Sophie and Charlie were on their way. Several times he glanced up from his table, fancying he heard or saw them. When they finally appeared he ran out on to the path with whoops of welcome, snatched their suitcases from them, chivvied them indoors. Some who knew him used to say that Alun never came nearer convincing you he meant it than when he was being glad to see you.

Like other enthusiastic hosts he had definite ideas about

how the party was to be organized. Coffee and drinks went round in the front room while the Norrises' offerings – a fresh sewin picked up in Hatchery Road that morning, a 57% Islay malt whisky – were brought out and admired. The women were not hindered from going off on their own, for the moment only as far as the kitchen. Alun refilled Charlie's glass and said, 'I want you to do something special for me if you would.'

'I'll have you know I'm a respectable girl and never touch kinky stuff.'

'No, it's . . .' Alun had rehearsed this part but he still had to squeeze it out. 'The thing is, I've started a sort of novel, it's supposed to be a serious novel, a proper one, you know, with no ham or balls or flannel about it, look you to goodness boy *bach*, but it's hard for me to tell. So if you could just sort of glance through the first pages of the thing, not bothering about merit or the plenteous lack of it, but just seeing if . . .'

'If I can give it a free-from-bullshit certificate.'

'Exactly.'

'Well . . .' Charlie's glance was uneasy. His familiar battered look seemed intensified without actual bruising or laceration, as though he had been perseveringly beaten with padded cudgels. 'Unless I give you my honest –'

'I'm not asking for a bloody bunch of roses – of course you must speak as you find. Please, Charlie. Go on, you old bugger, you're the only one.'

'As long as you . . . All right. Where is it?'

'Here, but don't look at it now. In a few minutes I'll herd the females into the village, where booths and bazaars of hideous aspect and degraded purpose display wares of varied and arresting squalor. But – they are useless, and they are for sale. What merit more demands the female heart? I'll go up to White's and see you in about half an hour or three-quarters. If you run out of water there's plenty in the tap.'

Wearing among other things the new cashmere pullover Alun did much of what he had promised, but before making for White's he looked in at Brydan Books. He told himself that it could do no harm and that he had never much cared for sitting about in pubs on his tod. But as soon as he was fairly inside the shop he was recognized and plurally shaken hands with. Customers were introduced and all asked for his autograph, a copy of his old *Celtic Attitudes* miraculously appeared and received his uninhibited inscription, and an elderly lady in a Brydan Books, Birdarthur, Wales apron who had no other obvious connection with the trade was brought from the back of the premises simply in order to have sight of him. He left bearing a newish book on the Rebecca riots that nobody would take his money for and telling himself now that the whole concern was a lot of bloody nonsense.

The bar at White's Hotel was filling up, but he achieved the same seat as the previous evening. He looked round quite eagerly but in vain for the white-hatted sod, whom in his present mood he would have thoroughly enjoyed seeing off, doing so with a minimum of exertion, further-more, like a whatever-it-was Black Belt. Just as he was starting to wonder whether it had been such a good idea to shut Charlie away like that with a bottle of whisky, in he came. His face seemed to have smoothed out slightly in the past hour or less, no doubt through assisted abatement of hangover. Nothing was to be read from his expression.

'Well, fire away,' said Alun briskly when they were settled with their drinks. 'Let's have it.'

'You did ask for my honest opinion . . .'

Alun's glance fell. 'Which you have now made clear enough. How much did you manage to struggle through?'

'I read twenty pages carefully, then skipped to the end.' Charlie spoke with a hesitancy unusual in him. 'I must emphasize that this is just my personal –'

'Spare me that if you will.'

'Sorry. Well now. I can see here and there what you're trying to do, and I think it's worth doing, and . . . you've probably made the best attempt at it you can, but . . . I'm not sure if it can be done at all, very likely it can't in the 1980s I don't know. But you haven't done it, that's to say you weren't doing it in what I read.'

'What about the bullshit?'

'The whole tone of voice, the whole attitude is one that compels bullshit. If I say it's too much like Brydan I mean not just Brydan himself but a whole way of writing, and I suppose thinking, that concentrates on the writer and draws attention to the chap, towards him and away from the subject. Which I suppose needn't be Wales in a way except that it always *is*, and somehow or other it's impossible to be honest in it. Now I'm sure you've tried your hardest not to put in anything you didn't mean or you thought was playing to the gallery, but it all gets swallowed up and turns into the same thing.'

Alun was still looking down. 'Nothing to be salvaged?'

'Nothing I saw. I'm sorry.'

'You're saying I've got to the stage where I can't tell what's bullshit from what isn't bullshit any longer.'

'No. I don't think I am. I'm saying if you want to talk seriously about that place of yours and the people in it you'll have to approach the thing in a completely different way, as if you've never read a book in your life – well no, not that exactly, but . . .'

Before Charlie had spoken a word Alun felt as if he might have been going to faint, only never having fainted before he found it hard to tell. The feeling had passed after a few seconds, since when he had had a good half of his attention on keeping his head from wobbling about, another sensation new to him. He had also been distracted by suddenly remembering who Bleddyn Edwards was, namely a man who came on at the end of the six o'clock news on Taff TV and spent a couple of minutes trying to be comical about piquant Welsh happenings of the preceding twenty-four hours. Another man did this turn-and-turn-about with him at a slightly lower level of wit and sensitivity, a man called something like Howard Howell about thirty years younger than Alun Weaver and of less refined appearance but, all too plainly, confusible with him just the same. Cheers *yn fawr*. With quite enough competing for his notice he saw with brief amazement that Charlie had not yet touched his drink. Quietly, trying as hard as he could to make it sound right, Alun said, 'Well, it looks as though I'll have to junk what I've done and have a totally fresh stab at the whole affair. Simple as that. I do agree, one can get horribly inbred in Wales without realizing it.'

Now Charlie did drink. 'Sorry, Alun,' he said again.

'Oh, come on, what are you talking about, you've just saved me several months at least of wasted work. Do you think I'd rather have been given the green light for a load of crap? In case you're wondering, the answer's no. Well, now we've got that out of the way we can get down to the serious business of the occasion. Knock that back and have another.'

'I'll make room for it first if you don't mind.'

Left alone in the pew, Alun relaxed and prepared to let his head do its worst, but it had cleared up now. Other things had not, though, not quite, and he sat there telling himself to stop swallowing like a fool and to breathe normally and to come out and admit he had had a sneaking suspicion all along that the stuff was bloody useless, so it ought to be a relief in a way to be told so in no uncertain terms.

Soon Charlie came back carrying two large whiskies. 'Well, the bog hasn't changed,' he said. 'Even to your pee hanging about instead of running away properly. Did I hear something about Percy and Dorothy coming down?'

Alun knew just what to say to that, but when he came to say it he found he could not get the words out, nor any others that he tried. He opened and shut his lips and blinked at Charlie.

'Are you feeling all right?'

Laying his hand flat across his upper chest Alun nodded vigorously and did some more swallowing. He kept trying to push words out with his breath. His head was perfectly stable as an object and clear inside, but he was beginning to feel a little frightened. Then, with an effort no different from the previous ones, he found himself saying, 'Yes, Charlie, to answer your question, Percy and Dorothy are indeed coming down, some time in the late afternoon or early evening if my information is to be relied upon. Hey. Bloody hell. What was that? Phew. Quite enough and to spare, thank you.'

'Can I get you anything?'

'It's here,' said Alun, grabbing his drink and taking a swift pull. The sights and sounds of the pub, really full now and noisy with pitched-up talk and laughter, rose about him as if for the first time. 'Well, whatever it was we don't want any more of it, right? – however popular a Weaver-suppressor might prove in certain quarters of Lower Glamorgan and beyond.'

'You've gone a bit pale. Or you had.'

'No wonder, with the rare and deadly *dorothea omniloquens ferox* poised to descend on our peaceful and happy community. Now there's one who could do with a few fits of silence visited upon them if you like. Can you remember, who was it who said about Macaulay's conversation . . .'

Charlie still had a look of concern and compunction and Alun worked on driving it away. By the time he had done so he had restored his own spirits too to the extent that, provided he kept the thought at arm's length, he could believe he was going to have a whole proper new crack at *Coming Home* after the holiday – keep the title and also the typescript, which was bound to have some material in it that could be rescued with a bit of imagination, or nerve. He continued satisfactory through the pub session, another couple back at the cottage, and lunch off the pickled fish with plenty of gherkin and chopped onion, the whole firmly washed down with aquavit and Special Brew and tamped in place with Irish Cream. By a step of doubtful legitimacy the men thinned their glasses of the heavy liqueur with Scotch.

After that there was a natural break. The women went off for a walk, Rhiannon grumbling that she ought to have brought the puppy after all. Charlie threw himself by instalments up the stairs and was heard all over the building, and perhaps further, dropping on to the bed in the back room. Alun took to the armchair as on the previous afternoon and dreamt Mrs Thatcher had told him that without him her life would be a mere shell, an empty husk, before jerking awake to find the image of a bearded man mouthing at him (the sound having been turned down) and frenziedly drawing cartoons on the postcard-sized screen of the little Sony they had brought down with them.

Hardly a minute later the women were back from their walk, pink-cheeked, brisk of step, determined at any price to get the tea. He sat on and listened to them shouting and laughing to each other in the kitchen and the minor thumps and crashes they made as they shut cupboard doors or set up crockery. At one point Sophie burst out of the kitchen and ran up the noisy wooden stairs, calling over her shoulder to Rhiannon as she went. Her glance passed over Alun as if they were unacquainted guests at a hotel. The same happened in reverse when she charged down again with a packet of biscuits in her hand. He knew it was not done to annoy, to set up an offensive contrast with male lethargy: it was just an illustration, more vivid than some, of the old truth that women were drunk half the time without benefit of alcohol. (Children over the age of about two were of course drunk all the time when not asleep.) Queers aside, men above twenty-five or so were never drunk however pissed they might be. Rather the contrary, he said to himself, hearing now some widely separated footfalls above his head.

When Charlie appeared he stared mutely at Alun in mingled appeal and reproach, as if covered with blood after a plucky lone fight against oppressors. So far from being in any such state he looked rather well, whatever that might mean applied to him. Comparatively, again, he had so far been restrained in his intake, not urging the rounds along in the pub, sitting behind an empty glass for long periods like ten minutes on end. If he went on like this he could just find himself still on his feet quite far into the night. Alun felt it might be done for his benefit and was touched.

Tea was brought in, with anchovy toast and Welsh cakes featured but not Sophie's biscuits, which she and Rhiannon had presumably wolfed in the kitchen. The meal was eaten, finished, cleared away and then nightmarishly reanimated when Dorothy arrived with Percy and brought out scones from a paper bag, strawberry jam, Devonshire cream and chocolate éclairs. After greeting all four in POW-reunion style she could likewise be seen to be well in arrears of her usual state at five on a weekday afternoon. This meant that she would also likewise stay around longer than usual, but on the other hand she would presumably take longer to become unbearable, and might always fall down dead before that stage was reached.

Not many people unacquainted with Wales or the Welsh would have found it the easiest thing in the world to reconcile Dorothy as she would be later with Dorothy as she behaved now, when the tea-things were removed for the second time and a bottle of white Rioja was brought from the kitchen. Far from clear at first, it seemed, about what was in the wind, she watched with a slight frown while Rhiannon took out the cork and poured three glasses. After some thought she picked up the bottle in a gingerly, furtive way and, head craned forward, read the label from beginning to end through her black-bounded spectacles. Then, carefully following the movements of the other two women, she lifted her glass, drank, and looked interested and rather tickled: so this was wine.

Alun watched all this in some professional distaste. He knew he overdid that side of life a bit himself, but in his case it was just high spirits, buggering about, derived from an only child's self-entertainment, whereas old Dot was seriously trying to create an effect. Well, hardly that, perhaps, at her time of life, in front of this mob; though the present carry-on would have had to be descended from the beginning of her career of piss-artistry, when she could still pretend she got sloshed out of not knowing about alcohol. Sort of a ritualized version.

'Let's go and pay our respects at Brydan's tomb,' said Sophie.

'It was more of a grave when I last saw it,' said Charlie. 'Of course they may have shifted him to a mausoleum since then. Or a cromlech, on account of him being Celtic and all.'

'Grave is fine with me,' said Alun.

Percy turned to Dorothy. 'Would you like to go, darling?'

'Lovely idea. It must be twenty years since I was last there. When I've finished this.'

'I think they shut the churchyard at six,' said Rhiannon.

The way she said it dispelled any lingering doubts about the unspontaneity of Sophie's suggestion. Alun would have loved to know whether the idea had come from her or Rhiannon in the first place – quite liked to, anyway. Whichever it was, Dorothy was hooked, about to be irresistibly sundered from the wine-bottle not only for the period of the respect-paying but later too. There were the shops that would be staying open late or late enough, shops no doubt marked down earlier as ones she could not in conscience pass by. (The chaps would be safely in the pub for that part.) With luck and further good generalship she might not be recoupled with the bottle for getting on for two hours. But after that . . .

As the company rose to leave there was talk of how they might as well be getting along if they were going, only a few minutes' walk and such while a couple of sets of facial signals were exchanged. Charlie wanted to know if Alun had anything to do with this obnoxious plan and Alun tried to indicate not. At his side, Percy watched Dorothy stoutly knocking back her drink in one so as not to keep the stage waiting. Sophie and Rhiannon left theirs. Rhiannon's glance at Alun admitted complicity and also managed to plead that it would have been no good trying to keep the wine away from Dorothy in the first place. Granted, and indeed he could just imagine her wonderment at happening upon the bottle in the refrigerator or, if things had gone that far, the gauche impetuosity with which she would have pressed upon her hostess the funny wine-bottle-shaped gift parcel she had nearly forgotten having shoved into her luggage at the last minute.

Defying local odds, the summer sun shone brightly up the gentle slope of the churchyard, which at this time of the year proved to stay open till seven, a pleasant spot with carefully tended brilliant green turf between the graves. That of Brydan lay towards the end of a row of newish ones in the south-east corner. It was no different in arrangement from any of its neighbours: a stone, a grassy mound enclosed in a stone border, some fresh flowers in glass vases. The inscription was severely factual except for a single appropriate line from the writings. The nearby ground had been only a little marked by intruding feet, as if word had gone about that there was not much to be seen up in the churchyard.

The party stood apart from one another in silence, almost as if trying to show respect. Only Dorothy looked recognizably like someone standing by a grave in a film. At least Alun hoped so, feeling Charlie's eyes on him as he bowed his head and tried dutifully to think of Brydan, whom he had run into on several occasions and once spent most of an evening with. He had several times compared the poet's character to an onion: you successively peeled away layers of it, with frightful shit and quite decent old bloke alternating, until you got to the heart. The trouble was he could not at this stage remember, and certainly not decide off the cuff, which of the two you ended up with. There was something of the same difficulty with the works: talented charlatanry, or deeply flawed works of genius? Or perhaps they were just beside the point.

Imperiously giving a lead, Dorothy swung away and led off down towards the gate with Rhiannon and Sophie in attendance. To one side stood the low mound called Brydan's Knoll, formerly and less tastefully called Brydan's

303

twmp or tump, though never much called any such thing outside print. The poet was half-heartedly feigned to have spent untold hours squatting on it and gazing over the town and the bay, well worth while perhaps if there had been nowhere else to see them from. Some support for the feigning was given by a passage in one of the late poems, and now the erstwhile *twmp* was sure of its place in the indexes of learned works as well as in guide-books.

Percy gave the spot a friendly wag of the hand. 'Rather agreeable up here, isn't it?'

'Somebody's fought the good fight,' said Alun, and went on quickly, 'not letting them turn the whole thing into a tourist attraction. Full marks to that man.'

'Oh yes of course, I remember now, you were at school with Brydan, weren't you?'

'Well, there must be a thousand people who could –'

'Ah, but the personal link is there. It must give you a feeling of special intimacy when you read the poems. Adding, I mean, to your sense of kinship, being a poet yourself. Something to be profoundly grateful for. Aren't you aware, perhaps keenly aware, of a peculiar insight into the man's mind? Into his soul?'

'I don't know, I suppose so,' said Alun, resolutely not looking at Charlie on Percy's other side and far from being inclined to look at Percy.

'Oh, for God's sake, Alun, don't speak self-deprecatingly about a thing like that.' Percy intensified the mournful solemnity of his tone and expression, which managed to save him from being picked up and thrown over the lofty privet hedge they were passing just then. 'It's a miraculous privilege. Not your own doing.'

'No, I do see.'

'Because let's face it, you are Brydan's artistic heir. Not in any obvious, reminiscent way, but . . . Surely at least you're conscious of being part of the same stock, sprung from the same root?'

'Well, there's obviously something inescapable in the blood of every Welshman that unites him . . .' Alun tried not to panic as he heard his voice relentlessly modulating into the old practised tones. He let it die away.

Percy did not press him. 'Well, these things will be as they will be,' he said, steadfastly accepting the duty to move on now with the round of mundane affairs. 'See you in the pub later, then? Right.'

'Dry-ballocked bugger, that,' said Alun as he and Charlie watched Percy's tall white-haired figure hurrying down the hill to catch up with the women. 'I mean I assume he was taking the piss?'

'No idea.'

'For Christ's sake, Charlie, he must have been. Miraculous bloody privilege. He did it well, I grant you.'

'What about it? I've never seen enough of him to say, but there are plenty of people about who talk like that for real, or semi-real, as you may have observed. And not only in Wales, either.'

'What? It's probably something to do with being married to Dorothy. That must bring out any dormant piss-taking proclivity, don't you think?'

'I don't know.'

'And why's he so brown? I know he's a builder, but surely that doesn't have to mean he's on the site all the hours God sends. And it can't be Morocco because he'd have had to take Dorothy with him, and if she'd been there we'd have heard by now. Sun-lamp. But why?' Alun finished in chapel style, 'In God's name, my friends, why?'

Charlie shook his head without replying. The group of four ahead of them had reached a shopping street, with

Percy walking on the inside. That was so he could block Dorothy off if she tried to go into an off-licence. It was to forestall that that he had joined the group a minute earlier. If she made a dash across the road his superior physique and condition would, from so near, enable him to overhaul her. Something deterred Alun from putting this rationale to Charlie, who presently spoke up.

'Mind you, the last bit of what he said was a bit too close for comfort, intentionally or not.'

'Oh, but –'

'I don't know what you think of Brydan's stuff these days, and I dare say you don't yourself, and I'm sure you'd deny indignantly or even sadly that you were his successor, but it's his influence that makes that stuff of yours you showed me so awful. Well, I don't say you're not capable of making it awful without assistance from anyone, but you see what I mean.'

Now Alun said nothing.

'I didn't put it strongly enough in the pub, but if you want *Closing Time* or *Coming Home* or whatever it's called to be any good at all, you must scour Brydan right out of it, so that not a single word reminds me of him even vaguely. Whatever you think of him, you must write as if you hated and despised him without reserve. You said you wanted my honest opinion, well, now you've got all of it.'

Alun said nothing to that either, but by then he and Charlie had come up with the others, who had halted on the pavement to gaze, none more intently than Percy, at a stationer's window. Actually it was that of a stationer in the extended sense, with not only writing materials and accessories visible there and in the shop behind but also framed photographs of local sights (including guess-who's cottage), mantelpiece ornaments including manufactured *objets trouvés*, mugs, ashtrays, scarves and tea-cloths with generally Welsh or specifically Birdarthur matter printed on them.

'Well, what of it?' asked Alun when everyone else seemed speechless at the sight. 'Somebody want to buy something?'

'We thought perhaps you might,' said Dorothy, smiling artlessly at him.

'Me? What, what the hell would I be buying at a little shithouse of a place like this?'

'Oh, all sorts of things.' She switched slightly to a humouring tone. 'What about a nice tea-towel to help you with all that washing-up you do?'

At a better time Alun would probably have recognized these remarks as attempts, tiresome no doubt but far from malicious, to egg him on, to bowl the local funny man an easy one, and he would probably have responded. But now he was silenced yet again, seeing Percy with an expectant look, Rhiannon's mind on a hot bath and putting her feet up, Sophie no more than ticking over, and Charlie of course there too. He made to walk on, but his way was barred.

'Or perhaps some typing paper. I noticed you'd been tip-tapping away.'

This found him his voice all right. 'You need a drink,' he very nearly snarled at Dorothy, adding just in time, 'we all do. Now for Christ's sake let's get moving. Come on, *move*.' Then he turned on Percy. 'And if you were thinking of asking me if I feel like dropping in at the cottage to commune with the shade of my poetical progenitor, my advice to you would be to relinquish the venture.'

There was some laughter at this, not much, but again just enough. Alun took a stealthy but far from nominal punch in the small of the back from Rhiannon for getting cross. Outside White's, Percy said he thought he would look round with the girls for a bit before joining the session.

'Having seen Dorothy safely on her homeward way,'

said Alun after carrying the first two drinks over. 'Towards Dai's I mean.'

'Where there's enough booze to float a battleship,' said Charlie. 'A light cruiser anyway.'

'It wasn't my idea, you know, that cultural expedition.'

'Well, it's over now and no bones broken.'

'It did cross my mind that I might have been getting a spot of stick here and there for having turned the party out of doors.'

Charlie looked at him. 'Don't be ridiculous,' he said.

3

Most of the evening was all right as far as it went. When eating came to be discussed it was felt but not said that Dorothy might consider she ought to hold back a bit in a public place, while what was said was that of course Rhiannon must not be allowed to cook, so no sewin tonight. Either half-sensing the unsaid part or out of simple awkwardness, Dorothy argued for a takeaway. Alun objected that the food was certain to be vile anyway, but if you ate it on the spot at least you could insult them for it, not much of a point perhaps, sufficient though to carry that assembly. Off they sped in the twilight past the Brydan Burger Bar and up the hill, the six of them hardly filling Percy's Swedish limousine, which smelt unexpected but all right, rather like a cough-medicine factory.

When it was just too late the restaurant they chose turned out to have some sort of formal dinner going on in it, with toasts and speeches. Dorothy was subdued, talking barely half the time and making Alun reflect that they might have been too hard on her in the past and could afford to have her expire painlessly after all. The meal itself proved to be of no more than common-or-garden vileness, below the threshold of insult-incitement. Both Alun and Charlie were noted for grabbing the bill on these occasions, but tonight Percy got there first. The party spent almost the entire journey back arguing about what the place had been called. Or some of them did; others – Rhiannon first, then Sophie and Charlie – fell asleep or relapsed into silence. Percy said nothing much either, driving at ferocious speed but with great concentration. And nobody seemed to feel like going on after Alun had asserted that Welsh cooking was nothing more or less than bad English cooking, or possibly just English cooking.

It might have been anything from New Zealander income-tax allowances to the future tense in colloquial Russian that Dorothy got going on in the pub; nobody could remember afterwards, nor cared to try. Whatever it was, she made up for lost time and went critical within a few minutes. Percy got her to her feet and Sophie gave him a hand. Together they urged her towards the door, a troublesome business among the crowded and slow-reacting peasantry.

'Quite comforting, really,' said Charlie. 'Makes me feel no end posh.'

'I'd better go along too or Sophie'll never get away,' said Alun. 'Should be fun to watch too.'

'Do you really think so?'

'I find the whole thing absolutely fascinating. Somebody who –'

'No accounting for taste, is there?'

'See you in a few minutes.'

Alun had taken it for granted that Dorothy was to be loaded with what speed was possible into the limousine and whisked back to town. So clearly had Percy, but it was not to be. First she insisted on fetching the cardigan she had left in the cottage. Dragged off that, she refused to leave without wishing her hostess good night, and short of disablement there was no obvious way to drag her off *that*. So the end of it was she led the other three back to Dai the Books's, beating off assistance the couple of times she stumbled on the uneven, unlit ground of Brydan's Walk. The moon was hidden behind the high ground on the landward side.

There was a light in the front room but no occupant, and no light upstairs. As asserted many times in the last few minutes, Rhiannon had gone to bed. Oddly in view of her previous firmness of purpose, Dorothy rather passed this over. With a preoccupied look she went out to the kitchen, came back with a bottle of Banat Riesling, looked slowly but briefly about for the corkscrew and went out again.

'You can get off back to the pub now, you two,' said Percy. 'I can handle the next stage. You really shouldn't have bothered to come this far.'

'Are you sure you can manage?'

'Oh yes, after another glass or two she should go torpid quite fast. Piece of cake.'

'Well, I'm going to have a quick one,' said Alun. There was not much chance of any real money's-worth but he would hang on a moment in case. 'That pub Scotch, it's all very well when you're not used to anything better.'

'Suit yourself.'

Percy, head bowed, had been edging along the book-shelves. Now he gave a satisfied grunt, straightened up and moved away carrying a paperback called, Alun saw, *Kiss the Blood Off My Hands*. This he opened and began to read attentively while he established himself in the battered armchair with more contented noises. When Dorothy re-appeared and handed him bottle and corkscrew in meek silence, he successfully eased apart the binding of his book and spread it flat on the arm of the chair so that he could continue to read during his operation on the bottle. In due course Dorothy sat down on a stray dining-chair next to the table and got stuck into a glass of wine. Her silence had attained a serene, meditative quality.

After a sample of this, Sophie turned to Alun. 'I think we ought to be getting along to Charlie – you know.'

'Yes, yes, let's be off.' He was quite keen to leave now there was no mileage in staying. 'Er – are you sure you'll be all right?'

'Yes, thank you, Alun,' said Percy, turning a page and looking up. 'Nice evening. See you soon.' Then, after just the right hammy interval, he half-called, 'Oh, Alun.'

'Yes?' said Alun without parting his jaws.

'Don't, er, don't forget what I said about Brydan now. And your heritage.'

'I won't, never fear.'

'See you stick to it, boy. Good night both.'

As soon as he and Sophie had taken five paces outside Alun said, not loudly but violently, 'That man is a *shit*. And a fucking *fool*. A *shit*, a *shit*, a *shit*.'

'What? What's the matter with him? What did he say?'

'Well, you heard him . . . It was what he said earlier. Anyway, never mind. He's just a *shit*.'

'What did he say earlier?'

'Oh for Christ's sake forget it, I can't start on all that now,' said Alun, angrily increasing his pace.

'What did he say about Brydan?'

'Never *mind*. It's not worth going into.'

She pulled him to a halt. 'It's not worth going into anything, is it, not with me,' she said at top speed and sounding pretty angry herself. 'You think I'm a fucking moron, don't you, Weaver? Always have done. Can't even be bloody bothered to pretend. Just another stop on your bloody milk-round. Another satisfied bloody customer. Well, thanks a million, mate.'

'Keep your voice –'

'And I thought you thought I was special. That's bloody foolish if you like.'

'You know very well I –'

'When you can't even put yourself out to give me the bloody time of day.'

Dodginess, a display of temperament from old Soaph was of course nothing new, nor its headlong onset. What was new was the last bit or the bit before and the tears under it. After no great struggle he got his arms round her.

'You silly little bag,' he said gently.

One thing led to another, or went some way there. Near where they stood there was a very serviceable little grassy hollow between Brydan's Walk and the edge of the cliff. He remembered it well, remembered it as if it had been yesterday without any memory at all of whether or not he had any time acquainted Sophie with the place. Leading her to it now and then coming across it by chance would need care, though for the moment that was looking ahead rather.

'What about a spot of num-num?'

'Don't talk so soft.'

'There's been not a drop of rain for weeks.'

'*No.*'

Matters had reached an interesting pass when the two heard a loud thump or crash in the middle distance, not so much loud when it reached them as obviously loud at source, clearly audible anyway above the sound of the waves quietly breaking on the beach below them. The disturbance had come from somewhere in the row of cottages, perhaps seventy or eighty yards from where they stood in shadow. As they looked in that direction, a light came on upstairs in one of them: Dai's, no question. After a quick glance at Sophie, Alun set off towards it.

'We ought to be getting along to –'

'Leave it for now,' he said urgently. 'Come on – Christ knows what's happened there.'

She hesitated a moment but followed him. They arrived back at the cottage not so very many minutes after leaving it. What had happened there was essentially simple and needed no thought to be found likely too: Dorothy had come out of the lavatory and fallen down the stairs, giving the noise added resonance by overturning a chair next to the front door with two empty suitcases on it. Far from being visibly hurt or in any way reduced by the experience, she seemed invigorated, toned up, though ready to agree she needed a drink.

When it was clear that all was well and nothing needed doing, Sophie said to Alun, 'We really must go back now to Charlie. He'll be wondering what the hell's kept us.'

Alun looked at his watch. 'You know, now I come to think of it, by the time we get there it's hardly going to be worth it. Fifteen minutes, if that.'

'What time do they shut round here?' asked Percy, who had not also asked how Alun and Sophie had come to be in earshot of the great fall. 'Country hours are different, aren't they? Earlier.'

'Well, he'll be on his way back then.'

'He doesn't like the dark,' said Sophie. 'And it's very dark, that last bit.'

'If he gets into a tizzy he could ring up, couldn't he?' Alun had an air of cheerful puzzlement. 'I can't see what's so –'

'He can't ring here, only the neighbour,' put in Rhiannon. In her towelling dressing-gown and knitted

313

slippers, she had been present all along. 'He wouldn't have that number.'

'It's only a few yards, for Christ's sake, and there are bound to be people –'

Dorothy had heard everything too, and had evidently taken some of it in. 'I'll stroll back with you,' she said, topping up her glass and draining it. 'I could do with a breath of fresh air. It gets quite stuffy in here, doesn't it, in the hot weather.'

'What about this neighbour?' asked Percy, after a longing glance at his book. 'If he really is a neighbour I could go there and ring the pub.'

Rhiannon explained and he went out after Dorothy and Sophie.

'I don't care for that fellow at all,' said Alun. 'Nasty piece of work, if you want my opinion. Malicious. Well, we had to get her out of the pub, you see, and then she wouldn't go in the car, kept saying she wanted to say good night to you, so we had to bring her along here. Then Sophie and I were just on our way to the pub when we heard the bang and saw your light go on, so we rushed back.'

It sounded absolutely terrible, and he wondered in passing whether everything he had ever said when he had anything at all to hide had sounded like that. Remarking affably that he supposed another one might well not kill him, he poured himself an unwanted drink. He saw that Rhiannon, on the chair lately occupied by Dorothy, was fiddling in a preoccupied way with a small irrelevant object like a shampoo sachet.

'What made you change your mind?' she asked.

'What about?'

'Going back for Charlie.'

'Oh, I just hadn't noticed the time before. Everything was a bit confused. Just popping up for a pee.'

While he was up there he thought about the things he could not say, all manner of them, most of them true, most of them already known but still unsayable. There had been a case for simulating concern for Charlie and going along with Sophie and Dorothy, but that would have looked to Rhiannon like evading her. Oh bugger, he thought wearily, and a stupendous yawn almost clove his skull in two. He wiped his eyes on lavatory paper and went down.

Although he knew well enough that inside those walls Rhiannon could hardly have blown her nose, let alone gone anywhere, without being heard all over the place, he was none the less disagreeably surprised to find her still sitting there. Then he thought of something and took himself to the chair he had sat on to do his typing.

'Amazing Dorothy managed to follow that conversation when you think how much she'd had. In the restaurant alone she must have –'

'Well, she'd have heard before about Charlie's troubles about being afraid of the dark and all that. Like most of his old friends must have done, including you.'

'Why including me particularly?'

'Because you're the only one that doesn't seem to care. Look at Percy off to telephone like that, no questions asked, and he hardly knows him compared with you.'

'I honestly can't see what all the fuss is about. Good God, if he's scared of the dark it's bright street lighting all the way to where the cars are, and after that, well even then it's not *dark*, and it's what, two hundred yards. Less.'

'Quite far enough if you're afraid. Remember how it was when you were a kid.'

'What? He's supposed to be a grown man. My observation tells me old Charlie makes a bloody good thing out of being scared of this and that. Gets himself picked up and shifted to and fro and generally feather-bedded wherever he happens to bloody be.'

'He may do that too, I hadn't thought of it.' Rhiannon put the sachet in the waist pocket of her dressing-gown. 'Did you show him that stuff of yours?'

'Yes, he thought it needed pretty hefty revision, which was much what I thought, you remember.'

'Yes,' she said. 'Good. I'm going to make a cup of tea.'

'Marvellous, I'd love some.'

Alun grabbed his whisky, telling himself he needed it after all, and started to relax, but he had not had time to do much of that before he heard the sound of voices approaching outside. For a moment he thought they were those of strangers, but he soon recognized Sophie's, then Dorothy's, in a tone he had never heard either use before. There was a third voice, a high-pitched whining or wailing that varied in intensity. When Alun realized it must be Charlie's voice he could hear he sat up straight and felt quite frightened. Rhiannon hurried in from the kitchen, opened the front door and stood on the step. Alun got to his feet and waited.

Charlie had turned a curious colour, that of a red-faced man gone very pale. His eyes were tightly screwed up and he was pressing hard with both hands on a grubby handkerchief that covered his mouth, in spite of which the wailing noise was quite loud at its loudest. Saying comforting things to him, Sophie and Dorothy got him into the armchair, and Rhiannon knelt down beside him and stroked his bald head. When he seemed comparatively settled, Sophie dashed upstairs and came down with a box of pills and gave him one. Alun stood about and tried to look generally ready for anything within reason. Dorothy, whose words of comfort far outdid the others' in range and inventiveness, was obviously having a whale of a time distinguishing herself in fields like responsibility, compassion, etc. So he said to himself. He also tried to consider fully the question of how much of this she would remember in the morning. But it was hard work driving off the thought that whatever Charlie might be going through, and however it had come about in detail, he, Alun, was to blame.

Now and then Charlie took the handkerchief away from his mouth and got out a word or two in a brief squeal before stuffing it back again. Several times he said he was sorry, twice perhaps that he had thought he was all right or could make it, and once, 'Get Victor.' That came just as Percy reappeared to announce no success with his call to the pub. He had hardly had time to take in the scene before Sophie bundled him off again whence he had come with instructions to telephone the Glendower.

Nothing surprising or of consequence happened after that for half an hour or so. Percy soon returned and said Victor was on his way. Charlie had two or three calmer and quieter spells but relapsed after each. Dorothy, sitting on the floor next to him, fell asleep or into a stupor, head down. Sophie told the others that when found he had been crouching by the corner of a wall at the edge of the part where the cars were, apparently unable to move. Rhiannon handed out cups of tea, not looking at Alun when she came round to him or at any other time. He just went on standing about.

Finally Victor arrived. He was wearing a dark jacket and trousers and a ribbed black shirt with a polo neck and his face, closely shaven, was quite expressionless. Looking neither to left nor right he walked straight across the room and held Charlie tight in his arms for a minute or so. Then he straightened up and ordered everyone else but Sophie from the room, taking a leather or plastic case about the size of a spectacle-case out of his pocket as he did so and starting to open it.

In the kitchen, where the ejected party found themselves with notable speed, Percy suggested to Dorothy that they would only be in the way if they hung about now and should slip out by the back door. When she had taken in the proposal and vetoed it, he readily produced *Kiss the Blood Off My Hands* and settled down with it directly under the ceiling light. Now Rhiannon did look at Alun, only once and for a moment and telling him only what he knew already, but it was enough to make him suddenly interrupt his breathing. He knew there was nothing he could ever say or do that would change her mind. She had gone straight on with piling the cups in the sink and now went quietly outside, leaving the door half open behind her, perhaps to invite him to follow, more likely just because she had always been rather inclined to leave doors open. Alun decided it would be best to follow her. There was still nothing useful he could say but sooner or later he would have to say something.

There was no breeze, and the air seemed to him to be of exactly the same temperature as that in the kitchen. The moon had come round a corner of the hill and lit up those parts of the neighbouring ground that were not shadowed by small trees and straggling bushes, more or less everywhere Rhiannon might have been expected to be. He took a few indecisive steps up the garden path between huge clusters of weeds and rank grasses, half-way to a low fence beyond which the slope began to rise too steeply to be taken on without some serious reason. Nothing moved anywhere. He was trudging down the narrow strip at the side of the cottage when a larger wave than usual broke audibly down on the beach, and at the same time he noticed that Charlie's voice could no longer be heard, at least through the wall and then the front door. Alun stepped on to where he could see up and down Brydan's Walk: still nobody. After more hesitation he quietly lifted the latch and went in.

Victor and Sophie were talking in low tones, but they broke off now and looked up at him expectantly. Between them Charlie sat sprawled and apparently asleep.

'Is it all right to come in?' asked Alun.

Neither spoke in reply, but Victor nodded.

'He seems quite peaceful now, doesn't he?' Alun went nearer Charlie but still not very near. 'What have you – what have you done for him?'

'Largactil it's called,' said Victor in his clear tones and staring rather at Alun with his clear eyes. 'A powerful tranquillizer. Injected intramuscularly.'

'Really.'

'Yes really. Yes, you can learn how in two minutes. Charlie and I arranged that I should keep the stuff by me. He was afraid if he had it he'd start trying to inject himself when he was pissed. Very sensible of him.'

Alun had just enough wit not to ask why Sophie had not been deputed to keep the stuff by her. 'What was the matter with him?'

'He's not mad, if that's what you were wondering. An attack of depersonalization. Panic brought on by being cut off from the possibility of immediate help and then self-renewing, as it were. Very frightening, I imagine. Well, we haven't got to imagine, have we?'

'Will he be all right now?'

At this point Victor suddenly stood up. 'Yes. Thank you. Is there anything else you'd like to know?'

'I feel responsible.'

'Yes,' said Victor warmly. 'M'm. You had heard about Charlie's dislike of being alone after dark and so forth.'

'Are you asking me? Not in detail, no.' Poofter, thought Alun shakily to himself. Ginger-beer. Brown-hatter. 'I mean I hadn't heard in detail.' Taxi-driver.

'But a bit, from what . . .' Victor's jerk of the head did no more than allude to Sophie. Nothing in his glance touched on her connection with Alun.

Finding himself expected to go on, Alun said, 'Yes, I'd heard enough. Enough to have a good idea I might fuck him up by leaving him to come back here on his own in the dark. I wanted to do that because I was angry with him for saying that something I'd written was no good, just copied from Brydan. Who does he think he is, I thought. I wanted to pay him out for . . .'

He stopped because neither of the others gave any sign of paying attention.

Victor turned his head and said with exaggerated suavity, 'Oh, yes, well, of course, absolutely, I do very much appreciate that. Now I suggest we get things moving.'

The first thing he or anyone else got moving was Dorothy and Percy, cordially and shortly thanked for their help and sent on their way, an unaccustomed mode of departure for them as some might have thought. Then Victor told Sophie she was to drive the Norris car while he travelled in the back with Charlie – who all this while had sat perfectly quiescent in the armchair – and would later arrange for the collection of his own car. Finally, at the front door, with Rhiannon now present, he said, rather less smoothly than earlier, 'Mr Weaver – we met, if you remember, at the restaurant owned by my brother and myself. I'm afraid I wasn't able to give you a very nice meal on that occasion, and I had been so much hoping to give you a better one. Well, I'm afraid various problems like supply and staff, and as you may have heard our new stove has had teething troubles – all that has rather got in the way. In fact I shouldn't advise you to venture into the place at all until further notice. We just can't offer you what you're used to in London. I'm sure you understand. *Nos da.*'

'It's the worst thing I've ever done,' said Alun a minute later. 'No need to tell me it doesn't make any difference but I'd like you to believe I realize it.'

'Oh, I don't know about that,' said Rhiannon. 'Do you mind sleeping in the spare room now it's free? That bed in the front's rather narrow and I want to get a good night's rest.'

After another minute he walked over to the table where his typewriter and papers still were, idiotically trying to do so in no particular way at all, took *Coming Home* out of its envelope and held it up to be torn in half, thumbs tip to tip, elbows lifted. Then he thought it could look good to make a present of a couple of pages of it to the next little non-paying bastard to write in for a contribution to a student magazine or an item to be auctioned for charity or something – anyway, you never knew. Having spared his own work he could see no overriding case for going ahead with his next project, the destruction of the Dai/Brydan photograph, which after all would not have been the original. Nor did he as intended finally push his copy of the Complete Poems in among the books on the shelves where he would never have to see it again. He would quite likely need it for reference the very next time he wrote a piece or prepared a talk or whatever you bloody well like that involved the master. He could always stop doing that, of course. But of course he never could.

Eight – Charlie

'It boils down to this as far as I'm concerned,' said Garth. 'Pink gin. Thank you, Arnold. – Oh yes: is a man for Wales or is he not? Simple as that.'

'With all respect, Garth, I'm afraid it isn't as simple as that,' said Malcolm. 'A man can be for Wales in such a way as subtly to denigrate the country, and that's what I'm sorry to say and rather surprised to have to say I thought Alun was doing. He –'

'Excuse me interrupting,' said a thickset man with a heavy moustache and the Turkish or even Assyrian facial appearance to be seen in some Welshmen, in fact a quantity surveyor from Newcastle Emlyn and old Arnold Spurling's guest. 'Didn't you use to be the English teacher at St Elizabeth Grammar? Years ago?'

'No,' said Malcolm rather curtly, as if he had been taken for a schoolmaster once too often. 'Not at any time.'

'Sorry if I've made a mistake,' said the guest, not sounding or looking at all satisfied that he had.

Malcolm went on with a touch of gameness, 'To write a newspaper article about the Eisteddfod in a humorous and entertaining style is one thing. To portray those taking part as figures of fun is quite another. In my submission.'

'I accept that,' said Garth. 'Certainly.'

'When did this . . . article appear?' inquired the guest.

'A couple of weeks back, possibly more. It was one of a –'

'But, I mean surely the Eisteddfod is an occasion for old friends to meet and exchange news and gossip.' The guest's lustrous dark eyes moved round the circle, canvassing support for this obvious view of the matter. 'I haven't been to one now for I don't know how long, but I used to attend quite regular, and in those days I was *constantly* running into people I hadn't seen at least since the previous year. *All the time.* Or were you thinking of the *Inter*national Eisteddfod?'

'*No*,' said Malcolm more curtly. At the same time he seemed bewildered.

'Tony Bainbridge,' said the guest straight away and shoved out his hand as he sat. 'I don't think you caught the name before.'

Malcolm gave his own name without impetuosity, especially at the second time of asking.

'Ah,' said Tony Bainbridge, narrowing his eyes now. 'M'm.'

He stopped short of actually arresting Malcolm, which Charlie, on the other side of Garth, had been half preparing for. One of Malcolm's troubles, and many others' too, was that he expected not only to follow conversations himself but that those around him should do the same, without any allowance for their being bored, mad, deaf, thick, or drunk without having been seen by him personally to set about becoming so. There he was now, as Charlie watched, looking furtively at Tony Bainbridge's glass, considering, looking at his own, wondering. And this after sixty-odd years in Wales, or just on the planet.

Before the silence had stretched too far Arnold Spurling reappeared with six drinks on a tray. The sixth went to Peter, who had said nothing since arriving, though he had snorted a couple of times when the Eisteddfod came into the conversation. The Bible had not been open all that long but, with the low cloud and heavy rain outside, the twilight seemed to be closing in already. Never mind that by the calendar it was still summer, the local weather had always had its own ideas on that.

Charlie had not found much to say for himself either. Today was only the second time he had left home unaccompanied since returning from Birdarthur a fortnight previously. For over half of that period, home had meant the Glendower, a sofa-bed in the flat there and the close proximity of Victor. What had happened on the evening in question was far from clear and without any detail in Charlie's memory, but he was quite decided that Sophie had not been there when he needed her. He also remembered, however, having taken a bad gamble on his own account, having thought he could manage without her, and he bore her no resentment. Nevertheless, rebuilding his confidence in her would take time. He wondered now and then how much time.

'I heard,' said Garth, lowering his voice but not quite talking behind his hand – 'I heard you'd had a little spot of trouble down at Birdarthur.'

'Just a bit of a dizzy spell. Nothing to worry about, Dewi said.' Dewi had said several times over that Charlie's case was not uncommon and that actually he had nothing to be afraid of after all. 'Got to take things easy for a bit.' This was to explain his restricted movements.

'Has he given you anything for it?'

What you would have to have the matter with you before Dewi would consider it necessary to give you something for it was a good question; not he but an unnamed friend of Victor's had been the true supplier, once upon a time, of the Largactil and syringe. It was a far cry from the days of Griff, who was said to have had half the infant population of Lower Glamorgan groggy with opium as a matter of course in furtherance of soothing their chests in a hard winter. But then Griff had belonged to the vanished breed who saw it as part of their job to make their patients feel better.

Garth interrupted this rather Peter-like train of thought by asking, 'Had he anything to suggest about your weight problem?'

'Dewi, you mean? No, not a word. I was reading a –'

'Still, I imagine you'll be making arrangements off your own bat, as it were.'

'What?'

'Thing like that, dizzy spell or whatever you call it, that's a warning. Nature's warning. Reminding you you won't be able to go on in your old ways for ever. Did you know that being just *half a stone* over weight measurably reduces your life-expectancy? Seven pounds. Seven pounds avoirdupois. My metabolism . . . my good luck . . . your metabolism . . . your bad luck . . . poor Roger Andrews . . . fat . . . sugar . . . salt . . .'

Others had been known to find Garth's homilies bothersome, even offensive; never Charlie. Just a part, an insignificant part of the great fabric. Life was first boredom, then more boredom, as long as it was going your way, at least. Charlie made these and other representations to himself while Garth quacked indefatigably on. In a comfortable half-listening state he let the whisky do its work on him and ran over in his mind the bomb-proof security of his next few hours: more drinks here; safe conduct to the Glendower in the charge of Peter, who knew the story; Victor eventually driving him home; Victor assuring him that Sophie would not leave him alone in the house. At the moment Peter too seemed content to let matters proceed while they showed no clear signs of worsening. Beyond Garth, who had now veered into autobiography, the other three pursued some Welsh topic.

So it trickled along until Alun arrived. He too had somehow failed to come up to scratch that evening in Birdarthur as Charlie recalled, or more as Victor had once or twice implied to him – well no one with a titter of wit had ever relied on him for more than the way to the Gents.

Having passed over the stranger, Alun's glance returned and stayed. Charlie saw with placid horror that Tony Bainbridge was smiling with his lips pushed up so that his moustache was squashed between them and his nose. His eyes were half closed again too.

'Hallo, Alun,' he said with awful quiet confidence, chin raised.

After a count of three Alun went into an equally awful but very watchable sequence of slow-motion Grand Guignol, from incredulity that came to border on naked fear through dawning recognition to joyful God-praising acceptance with double handshake. 'Who the fuck are you?' he asked at this stage, but it was clear to all present that he quite likely did remember and given a moment might even have come up with the name. 'What is it, thirty years?'

'Oh, not that. Fifteen more like.'

'Oh. Tell me, where are you based now?'

Tony Bainbridge told him that and more besides, receiving information in return. The others sat in silence, cautiously shifting position in their chairs as if a sound-recording was in progress.

'Now you had, what, two girls you had, wasn't it?'

'Spot on.' Alun gave a respectful nod. 'One married, one at Oxford.'

'Oxford. There. Well, that's what time does, no question. It goes by.'

'I'm afraid I can't –'

'So you've got a girl at Oxford. I haven't. I haven't got anybody. What are you drinking, Alun?'

'No, my shout.'

At this point the door opened and Tarc Jones advanced into the saloon lounge. He wore the heavy cardigan that, for all anyone knew, he never took off, and carried an unfolded sheet of paper printed in green, evidently an official form of some sort. This he planked down on the table some of them were sitting round, in front of Peter as it happened. There was silence while he stared accusingly from face to face.

'So this – this is the kind of slough into which our democracy has declined,' he said with much bitterness and gigantic quotation-marks where needed. 'Have any of you any idea of what has just reached me through Her Majesty's mails?'

Evidently none of them had. Garth did a slow wink at Tony Bainbridge to let him know that he was not really expected to be able to throw any light on the question.

'The Lower Glamorgan Water Authority,' went on Tarc without mending his pace at all, 'desires to be informed within twenty-eight days, date as postmark, how many rooms in this establishment possess water facilities, of what nature these are in each case and their main uses and the approximate volume in gallons per day of water so utilized. For external appliances see back. Approximate. There I detect and welcome a ray of sanity and a spark of common human consideration. They might well have required measurement to three places of decimals. No. No. They drew back from that. Approximately is good enough. To the nearest gill is deemed to suffice.'

His listeners, even Alun, seemed completely demoralized by this show. Nothing was attempted or said while Tarc glanced this way and that and crouched forward over the table.

'Power,' he said in a whisper that was like a puma snarling. 'That's what it's all about. Some little jack-in-office is having the time of his life, drawing up forms and chucking them round the parish and generally trying to put the fear of God into the rest of us. How am I to deal with it, I ask you? What am I to do?'

Now Alun twisted round in his seat to look at him. 'What are you to do? If you really don't know what to do then God help you. But I'll tell you what you don't do, so at least you'll know that much for next time, all right? You don't go on as if they've told you they're coming round to take you to a gas-chamber and you don't hold the floor for half an hour with a bloody music-hall monologue when you could just be boring us stiff about the price of booze like anybody else. That's what you don't do, see.'

As well as visibly infuriating Tarc this caught him off balance. With a jerky movement he snatched up his paper from the table and started asking Alun how he dared, what he meant by it, who he thought he was talking to and similar questions. He, Tarc, sounded uninterested in the answers and also, compared with previous form, altogether under-directed. But he came back strongly towards the end. While he spoke and during what followed he doggedly, almost obsessively scooped away with a middle finger at the resistant deposit in the corner of one eye.

'I don't have to take that shit from anyone,' he said with returning assurance. 'Least of all from a second-rate bloody ersatz Brydan.'

Afterwards Charlie always wondered in what measure Tarc understood and intended this remark. The grin of anticipation with which Alun heard him out remained in place.

328

'Just to take you up on who I think I'm talking to. Not just a miserable idiot but the kind of idiot who's ruining Wales.' Charlie had heard Alun pronounce two or three different kinds of men to be that kind of idiot. 'Turning it into a charade, an act, a place full of leeks and laver-bread and chapels and wonderful old characters who speak their own highly idiosyncratic and often curiously erudite kind of language. Tourists sometimes –'

'He's having you on, Tarc,' said Garth. 'Pay no attention. Fellow's idea of a joke.'

Tarc ignored him. 'Out,' he said, extending arm and forefinger horizontally to demonstrate his meaning. 'Out, the bloody lot of you. Off you go now. Go on. Now.'

'Take it easy, Tarc, for Christ's sake. I don't know what's got into him. Have a drink.'

'The bloody lot of you. Starting with you, Squire Weaver. And this also applies furthermore and notwith-standing to you, Professor pissy pernickety thick as two planks Cellan-Davies. And you, little Garth, on your way, brother. And this pair of bloody soaks by here.' This seemed most unfairly to mean Peter and Charlie. 'And you, Spurling and whatever your name is. No, sorry, I withdraw that, no fault of yours, sir, but you'll oblige me by leaving too. If you'll be so good.'

Garth made one last effort. 'Can't we just –'

'*Out.* If you're not gone in two minutes I'll send my lads in and then you'll know all about it. And you can take this squash-club pathetic bullshit with you. Every bloody scrap of it – I'll burn anything you leave, I promise you. I've been dying to get rid of you buggers for years and now's my chance. On second thoughts one of you can come back in the morning and pick up the junk then. That's if you think it's worth the bother. Now get moving, the lot of you. Two minutes, mind.'

Under his louring eye they filed out and assembled ridiculously in the passage that led to the front door, embellished as it was with speckled greenery and dismal old photographs and littered with the remains of packages that might have held footwear or clothing. Here tongues broke loose.

'That was a disgraceful piece of behaviour,' said Malcolm. 'On your part, Alun. Quite indefensible. You're supposed to know better.'

'I'm sorry, I just can't stand that kind of posturing,' said Alun.

'Whereas other kinds you've no rooted objection to,' said Peter. 'Anyway, thanks for destroying our pub for us.'

'I'll have a word with Tarc tomorrow,' said Garth.

'We're off,' said Arnold Spurling with decision, and he and Tony Bainbridge left at once and were not soon to be found in those parts again. At the same time a great general roar of laughter sounded from the bar and Charlie saw Doris the barmaid at the hatch peering at them through her upswept glasses.

'It's shocking that an educated man should descend to downright verbal brawling,' said Malcolm.

'I said I was sorry.'

'Oh, that's all right then,' said Peter.

'Tell you what,' said Garth: 'it's early yet to pack it in and we could all do with a drink and what shall I say, a pause for consideration. Why not come up to my place? It's only just round the corner. Angharad's away seeing her mother,' he added. 'Ninety-one, she is.'

There was a pause there and then, for consideration of Angharad, perhaps, or her mother. Eventually Alun said with a touch of defiance, 'Yes. Why not? I certainly fancy a drop. Thank you, Garth.'

'What about you, Peter?' asked Charlie. 'Unless you feel you . . .'

'No. Let's go along. Why not indeed.'

'I ought to be getting back,' said Malcolm.

'Oh for heaven's sake,' said Garth. 'Never even seen the inside of the Pumphrey domain, have you?'

'Go on, move, you old pests,' bawled Tarc's voice from up the passage, booming and resounding in a frightening way. 'Outside, the pack of you, you're making me nervous.'

Without a rearward glance they hurried out into the rainy, windy gloom where what light there was came mostly from shops and houses and reflections in the roadway. Charlie had a close impression of heavy bodies piling into cars, the lights of the cars coming on suddenly, loud grunts and door-slamming and the whinnying of starters. Now was a time for the years to roll back. But no, they stayed where they were. Beside him, Peter gave a whistling sigh and pushed the car into gear.

'You all right, Charlie?'

'Full of fun.'

'Well bugger me.'

'Absolutely.'

They said no more for the moment. Charlie's mind drifted off to one side. The ancient sanctuary of the Old Gods, he thought. No: when the primeval fastness of the Ancients is, is menaced by unknown powers, its guardian, the giant Tarc (bass) comes before them with a moving plea for counsel (*'Ach, was muss ich?'*). In response, the most illustrious of the Ancients, Alun (baritone), haughtily rebukes Tarc for his presumption (*'Vergessen nun Sie'*). A stormy exchange between the two, which the fool Garth (counter-tenor) tries vainly to quieten, introduces an elegiac portrayal of desolation and defeat. In a climactic . . . In a ritualistic monologue of great power and beauty (*'Heraus*

Sie alles sofortig'), Tarc invokes his immemorial right to banish the Ancients from their refuge, ordains and salutes their passing one by one and compels the removal of their age-old trophies. The Act closes with an Ancients' chorus of . . .

'Wake up. We're there. I think.'

The Pumphrey house, which Charlie could not remember ever having seen before, was unlit within. There were slippery wet leaves on the flags of the garden path and he nearly stumbled over the trailing stem of a rose-bush or something similar. The two clambered up half a dozen rounded stone steps to a Victorian Perpendicular porch with stained glass to be faintly seen. Charlie stamped his feet rhythmically on the tiled floor.

'Is this right?' he asked. 'If it is, where's Garth?'

'I think he took a lift with Malcolm. Even he isn't going to walk it in this, I mean Garth.'

'Oh well, there we are then. Be here till midnight. Well no, er, eh? Unless Garth doesn't know the way either. Brilliant of you knowing. I suppose this *is* right, is it? It certainly feels right, it's giving me the shivers before I've even crossed the bloody threshold. Like a house of the dead.'

Peter pulled his raincoat more closely round him. 'Here they are. And Alun. Do you think he's mad, by the way?'

'No, just fed up because . . . I'll talk to you later.'

At once upon entering, Garth turned on the lights, first startlingly overhead in the porch, then two in the hall. Both of these seemed of low wattage, not doing much to cheer up the heavy parental or even grandparental furniture or help to identify the wide-mounted engravings that covered large parts of the walls. Charlie noticed a cylindrical stand full of superannuated umbrellas and walking-sticks. When everyone was indoors Garth switched off the porch light, switched on a staircase light to indicate the lavatory on the landing, switched it off again and led them into a room at the back of the house.

It was cold in here, in a settled way that suggested it had not been warm for some time. Garth activated a small mobile electric fire, from which a smell of scorching dust soon began to issue and loud clangs were heard from time to time as the metal warmed up. Some large armchairs and a sofa were theoretically available, but none looked very inviting. The party clustered round the sideboard of some unpolished black wood on whose top a number of bottles and glasses were arranged.

This display had attracted Charlie's attention on entering and almost immediately thereafter his disquiet as well: all the liquor-bottles, which included, he saw, ones containing port and sherry as well as gin, Scotch, brandy and vodka, had optic measures like those used in pubs fitted to their necks. Then he brightened up again at the thought that Angharad would not have been the first or the last wife to try to limit her husband's drinking, heavy-handed as this particular scheme might appear. No cash-register was on view and when his turn came Garth served him a double whisky and passed on without delay. Water came out of a half-empty plastic bottle beaded on the inside with air-bubbles of unknown antiquity.

'Welcome to my humble abode,' said Garth as soon as they all had drinks. When nobody said what a nice place they thought he had or anything else, he went on, 'Rather sad to think it took a dust-up at the Bible to get the gang of you along here. I don't think we need be too despairing about that, by the way. I'll pop round in the morning and see how the land lies.'

Whether or not his words had any cheering effect, resentment of Alun's conduct seemed to have cooled or petered out in apathetic acceptance; anyway, no more was expressed. After a few minutes Charlie glanced at Peter and led the way towards a grand piano which showed every mark of having been *in situ* since about the time of the death of Brahms. Photographs of various sizes stood along its lid or hung from the wall behind it.

'God, what a shower,' said Charlie, moving on from the likeness of one staring bearded fellow in a high-collared jacket to another. 'They can't be Garth's or Angharad's parents or uncles et cetera – too far back.'

'In their comparative youth perhaps. That would be quite far back.'

'Oh, but not . . . Look at this old bitch here. Are those ostrich feathers, would you say? What would that make it? Not even the Boer War, more like the Zulu wars in when, the 1880s?'

'Well . . .'

'You know, I don't think this lot are anything to do with the Pumphreys. I think they must have come with the house, like the carpets and the curtains. And the furniture too by the look of it. There's something . . . Don't you get a funny feeling in here?'

'How do you mean, Charlie?'

'I can't see any sign of anybody actually living here. No bits of possessions. Of course it could be this room's just kept for visitors. Not such a ridiculously antediluvian idea in these parts, after all. But it's more like a time I remember when a bloke from round here called Lionel Williams, perhaps you came across him, anyway he took me home once in Kinver Hill for a nightcap after the pub, and it was quite a bit like this. Very much like this. It turned out, I'd naturally assumed it was, you know, the marital domicile, but it turned out his wife had divorced him, oh, fifteen years before and he'd gone on living in the house as a lodger, her house it was. And it was very much like this, the atmosphere. Imagine that. You don't suppose it could have happened here by any chance, do you, Garth living here as, er, as Angharad's lodger?'

'No I don't,' said Peter rather sharply. 'That's absurd.'

'What? Well, of course it is. Not meant to be a tremendously serious suggestion. But it was very odd at Lionel's that time, you know. The atmosphere.'

Drink in hand, Charlie moved from the piano-top to the dozen or so photographs on the wall. Over by the sideboard Alun had coaxed a rather reluctant smile from Malcolm and got a falsetto squawk of laughter out of Garth. Willingness to amuse Garth was to Charlie a sign of great humility. Or perhaps above-average vanity. Nevertheless he was glad of Alun's presence and of the others' too. There was no such thing as a good room to be shut up alone in, though the one at Birdarthur where he had read Alun's typescript had been not too bad, tolerable enough to have given him false confidence in himself. This one here could never do that. He pulled himself up and passed over an elongated coloured print of a desert sunset or dawn, complete with camels, palms and pyramid, that he would have laid a thousand quid he had seen a clone of in seaside lodgings in Porthcawl fifty years before. What he came to next made him stop and stare.

'By Christ, what's this? Hey, I could have done her a bit of no good in days gone by. Proper little bugger too, you can see with that mouth. Nobody made that one do what she didn't want to do. Ever. Who the hell would that be?'

He noticed now that Peter had sat down on a nearby sofa and was looking at the floor. 'That would be Angharad. I never thought . . . It never occurred to me . . .'

'What?'

'Angharad as she was before her illness.'

Charlie lowered himself beside Peter and put his drink on a small polygonal table of Oriental suggestion. The leather or synthetic material of the cushion-cover at once struck cold, even damp, to the backs of his thighs. 'What?'

'Serves me right for coming here. It doesn't do her justice, what you see there. Not to what she was when I first saw her. It was her I left Rhiannon for, not Muriel – Muriel was later. I didn't want to give Rhiannon up . . .'

Peter's face had grown dark red and he was pressing his hand against his chest. He breathed in and out noisily a couple of times, as if he was going to cry.

'Can I get you something?' asked Charlie.

'If you could just sit back, that's right, so they can't see me.' Quite briskly Peter took out a small tubular bottle and from it a white pill. 'Could you just sit with me, it'll go off in a little while.'

Not swallowing the pill, keeping it under his tongue, Peter held himself rigid in his seat with his eyes shut. Now and then he winced sharply, once so sharply and with such a screwing-up of his face that Charlie thought he was going to die the next moment. Charlie also stayed still, with his hand ready in case Peter should want to hold it, and listened for any pause in the others' talk or any stir of interest, though he had no ideas about what to do in that event. The electric fire hummed away. It was not really so long before Peter's colour improved and he began to breathe more normally. After another minute he opened his eyes, smiled a little without parting his lips, as he always did now to keep his teeth out of sight, and sipped his drink. This was whisky and water, lately his preferred tipple in place of the old gin (which he had said he thought made him depressed) and slimline (bound to retain some baneful calories however rigorously pruned).

'Well, that's it for this time round. Where was I?'

'What? Well, you were on about Angharad. Are you sure you want to –'

'Yes, I'm all right. Thanks for sitting there, Charlie. Yes. Angharad said – please let me tell you this – she insisted I had to give Rhiannon up completely if I wanted ever to see her again. She was the insisting type, as you astutely perceived from that photograph. Well, a girl like that, you can understand it in a way, and understand it even better if you allow for the bloke being a selfish shit who's rather thrilled to be the object of it. Then not so very long afterwards Angharad was doing some more insisting, but what she was insisting on this time was that I shouldn't see her any more. Some other fellow had . . . well . . .'

When he broke off and gazed at his empty glass, Charlie said, 'Can I get you another?'

'No. Don't go, Charlie. Can I finish yours? Just for this minute.'

'You're not to regard it as a precedent, mind.'

'Thanks. Then, of course, I should have gone back to Rhiannon, or tried to. But I couldn't face her. A bit hard to understand now, perhaps. And there was cowardly stuff about my job which is much easier to understand, I'm sorry to say. It's all so obvious really, but I'd met Muriel by then. She was a friend of Angharad's, if you can credit such a thing.

'All this was well before Angharad got ill. Cancer of the womb it was, or that was what it boiled down to in the end. Quite rare at twenty-nine. They took out the whole works, gave her a total pelvic clearance I believe it was called. Plays hell with the hormonal system and the rest of it, or it can. I didn't see anything of her for four or five years, and when she did turn up she looked within shouting distance of how she looks now.

'So there we are. They didn't know a hell of a lot about these things in those days. I don't say they know much more about them now, but then they thought that kind of thing was brought about by excessive sexual indulgence, as they would have phrased it. Or anyway helped on by it. Well, even then I could see it would have been altogether too funny for words if I'd done all the damage myself, but I could have done my bit, along with one or two others. Yes. No doubt that's something you dismiss from your mind if you've got any sense, and also if you happen not to have grown up with a lot of bloody Methodists and Calvinists and Calvinistic Methodists.

'Anyway, thanks for listening, Charlie. At least I suppose a lot of it you hadn't heard before.'

'Some of it, yes. Everybody was wondering but there were things nobody knew.'

'People always say you can't keep a secret in Wales, but there's no problem if it's nasty enough. They know all too well what they're like, what talkers they are. And hypocrisy's good too. Comes into its own, you might say.'

'But Muriel knew.'

Peter actually laughed. 'Oh yes. When I look back, me marrying her is about the hardest thing to believe of all. Next to her marrying me. She was keen, of course. She wasn't quite a virgin but near enough not to count. She may even have thought she honestly didn't mind coming third to Angharad and Rhiannon. If so the scales fell from her eyes with . . .'

'Prodigious precipitation.'

'And comprehensiveness. And irreversibility. And everything else. Well, it's done me good to get that off my chest.' Peter was breathing naturally now and just with this mention of his chest he finally removed his hand from it. 'How long I can expect it to last is another matter. Oh,

God, there I go – moan, moan, moan. It is a time for the recharging of glasses.'

As they got up thankfully from the sofa Charlie asked, 'How much of the story does Rhiannon know?'

'All of it, I should think. Well, not everything I've told you. I haven't discussed it with her since.'

'No, I can see how you wouldn't.'

Charlie tried to set it all in order in his mind. He told himself he could not be expected to manage the whole thing straight away. There was quite enough for an old josser to take in in one evening. Whatever the time might be he was beginning to feel like moving on – after another here he would suggest to Peter that they should drift along to the Glendower for a bite and a swallow. The fire had failed to warm the room appreciably and a headachy reek of damp had emerged, with a touch of stale flower-water thrown in. But if Garth was not living in the house then where was he living? Or could he really be a lodger after all?

Peter and Charlie came up to hear Garth saying, 'Well, whose shout is it, then?'

As if by pre-arrangement first Alun and Malcolm, then Charlie and Peter looked at each other. It fell to Malcolm, as sometimes in the past, to say what everyone else was thinking and not saying.

'Sorry, Garth, I'm not with you. How do you mean, shout? We're not in the pub now.'

'No, boy, of course not, of course not,' said Garth, laying his hand reassuringly on Malcolm's arm. 'Just with the prices things are these days we simply can't afford unrestricted hospitality. Of course we'd like to, but we can't. So?' He sent round an interrogative glance.

'All right, if it's shouts we're on to, I'll shout first.' Alun still looked very much astonished.

'Good for you. Double Scotch, is it?' Garth tipped the bottle twice while the rest of the company paid close attention. 'Right. Help yourself to water or soda.'

'You don't mean to say they're free? Oh, goody bloody goody, what?'

Garth nodded without speaking, his eyes on a pocket calculator that had appeared on the sideboard before him.

'Mind you don't forget to add on the cost of the first round.'

At this Garth moved the calculator aside, though not far. 'I regard that as distinctly uncalled for, Alun,' he said in a sorrowful tone. 'If not downright gratuitous. Those first drinks were not a *round* in any sense of the word. They were my freely offered hospitality. Good God, man, do you take me for some kind of Scrooge?'

Instantly Alun choked on his large first sip of whisky and water. Coughing with marked violence he shakily clunked his glass back on the sideboard, strolled a pace or two and went down sprawling with most of his top half across one of the sofas and his legs spread out on the thin carpet. This seemed even for him an unusually thorough imitation of a man collapsing with rage or revulsion. So at least Charlie considered. Since he was the nearest he stooped down over the sofa. Peter followed him.

Alun was breathing loudly and deeply through his mouth in the guttural equivalent of a snore. His eyes were wide open and to all appearance focusing, though not on Charlie or Peter, nor on Garth when he too bent over him. In a low voice but quite distinctly he said a couple of meaningless words and his mouth moved. Then his eyelids drooped and he stopped doing anything at all.

'I think that's it,' said Garth.

'What?' Charlie felt utterly bewildered.

'I think he's dead,' said Garth, continuing none the less

to loosen Alun's tie and unbutton the neck of his shirt. 'Yes, I'm afraid he's gone.'

After a few moments Peter asked where the telephone was and on being directed went out into the hall, closely followed by Malcolm. Charlie helped Garth get Alun into a more or less natural position lying on the sofa. By now he seemed quite unmistakably dead.

After less than a minute Peter came back into the room. 'On their way,' he said. 'Malcolm's trying to find Rhiannon. Well now. Well indeed.' He stood uncertainly by the door.

'Have a drink.' Garth sat and continued to sit on the arm of the sofa beside Alun. 'And Charlie. On the house. There's an irony for you if you like. Go on, help yourselves.'

'What was it? Any ideas on what it was?' Charlie looked over at Alun's body from where he had instinctively moved to, the furthest possible corner of the sideboard. 'Was. Christ.'

'Heart. Or stroke. Perhaps not heart because he didn't seem to be in any particular pain as far as I could see. Of course it was only those few seconds. But they don't usually go off just like that, not with heart, not as a rule.'

Charlie missed Alun's being able to say, I suppose you mean sheep and bloody bullocks don't. Not as a rule. His glass was empty and he poured himself a treble, or another treble.

'Do you know if he'd had any funny turns recently?' asked Garth. 'Or headaches or . . .'

There had been something a couple of weeks back, but Charlie could not call it to mind. He shook his head. Malcolm came in and said he had not been able to find Rhiannon or learn where she was. If the others agreed he proposed to travel down to the hospital in the ambulance and go on trying to reach her from there. Before they could even think of any other option the ambulance arrived. Its crew declined to pronounce Alun dead but they would not say he was alive either. With almost too much speed they had him on to a stretcher, out of the house and away. Malcolm had said good night briefly and hurried after them.

'To think not ten minutes ago he was standing there as alive as you and me,' said Garth. 'A breath of fresh air is quenched for ever.'

Charlie responded. He wanted very much to get Peter away and to leave himself, but as things were they could hardly go stalking out just yet. Peter, he guessed, felt this too. So they hung on, keeping to the same spot by the sideboard as before.

'Good little drinker he was,' said Garth. 'You can say that without fear of contradiction. Good little pourer too.'

'He what?'

'He kept pouring. Drinks. He was always one who was calling for more drinks. Very characteristic almost his last words were ordering up more drinks. He'd have liked that.'

Whereas absolutely his last words were pissing on you for asking for money for drinks in, according to you, your own house, which he'd probably have liked even more, thought Charlie. Then he relented a little: Garth had just refilled the glasses without question. But, again, it would have taken some strength of character to ask who was going to cough up now Alun had defaulted. 'Do you think whatever it was could have been brought on by that row with Tarc?'

'No.' Garth fingered his chin. 'No, I don't. No, that sort of thing only happens in films. No, he had it coming. In fact that's the one great comfort of the whole sad tale. There wasn't a damn thing he or anyone else could have done about it. Not a thing.'

'Oh, fabulous,' said Peter, breaking a long silence. 'Well, that certainly softens the blow and no mistake. Blessing in disguise, really, looked at in that light.' He paused to allow the mantle of solemnity to become resettled, no doubt hoping to be excused from making any definitive pronouncement in farewell. 'We'll be off, then,' he said weightily. 'If that's all right with you. Thank you for the drinks.'

Garth gave a sonorous sigh and clasped both Peter's hands in his own. With sudden awful clarity Charlie foresaw he was going to call upon them to salute the passing of a great Welshman. But before another word was said there was a low sound from outside the room, hardly a sound, more like a tremor. Whatever it was Garth turned his head, dropped Peter's hands and compared his watch with the wall-clock, an instrument unnoticed until now, disquieting in appearance but only to a minor degree, about right for the billiard-room or butler's pantry in Castle Dracula. The three waited as if for an explosion until the door opened and Angharad was to be seen.

What with one thing and another Charlie found it really hard not to give a shudder or a groan of dread and despair at the sight of her. She wore unnameable dark garments high at the neck and long in the cuff, topped by a waterproof of some sort which she very slowly unbuttoned, took off and draped over one arm as events proceeded. Her general aspect reminded Charlie, after a moment's utter blankness, of the photographs he had been looking at not long before, perhaps even an individual one. By the look of her eyes and mouth she had aged perceptibly since last seen. At no time did she send the least glance in his or Peter's direction.

'You're back early, love,' said Garth, smiling at her.

Angharad said crisply in her out-of-keeping voice, that

of a woman half her age or less, 'There was no point in hanging about – it was quite obvious she didn't know me. If you remember, it's been coming on for some time. I told her clearly and repeatedly who I was, kept saying my name, going on I was her daughter, and she heard me but she didn't take it in. No idea in the world. So I came away. That woman, Mrs Jeffreys is it, she was seeing to her perfectly well, and I wanted to watch that Great-Gardens-of-England programme, which you really do need colour for and she's only got black and white. Not that I could have concentrated on it properly anyway.' She too looked at the time and added, 'I did telephone, but the line was engaged.'

'Yes, well . . .'

'So we're having a party, are we?'

'Not exactly.' No relish or any other tinge of ill will could be heard in Garth's tone. 'Alun Weaver fell down dead just about where you're standing now, it would have been, well when you rang you'd have run into Peter dialling 999. And . . . there we are.'

'Ah.' She acknowledged the objection and continued, 'More like a wake, then.'

'Sort of.'

Charlie wished Malcolm had been present to list some of the ways in which what had just been taking place could not fairly be said to have constituted a wake. He watched Angharad while, the removal of her outer piece of clothing now accomplished, she stood between him and the door pulling her cuffs down over the backs of her mottled hands and casting her eye over the sideboard top, perhaps in quest of the cash Garth should have taken off his patrons. Finally she gave this up and turned towards him again. 'Well,' she said with an upward, munching movement of her jaws, 'I'll be getting on,' and made to leave the room.

'I'll be going for my usual,' said Garth with a kind of wink at her in his inflection.

Five-mile jog? Aberystwyth BA (Hons)? Chicken and chips? Without staying to consider, Charlie got Peter out through the hall and on to the porch as soon as the coast was clear. The rain had packed up and there was a great tapping and plopping as what had already fallen dripped off the trees and the eaves of the houses. With the sky mostly clear now there was if anything more light than when they had arrived.

'Charlie,' said Peter as they stood at the top of the steps. 'I simply –'

'Yes, I know. Listen: I'm too drunk to drive and you're too, er, drunk to drive. As you may or may not have noticed there's a pub on the top corner where we turned off. However gruesome its appointments it must sell drink and possess a telephone. While you're working on a very large whisky I'll mobilize Victor. Then sandwiches and our own bottle in the flat at the Glendower and your car fetched. How about that, Major?'

'Oh . . . fine. I mean coming on top of . . .'

'Of course. Tell me later. Left at the gate, then eighty yards or so along to the corner. Not more.'

Nine – Peter

1

'That was William,' said Peter. 'Not dressed yet. He says we're to go on and he'll see us at the church.'

'Hardly a bolt from the blue.' Muriel was moving a hat about on her head in front of her dressing-table. 'I can't remember having this out of the cupboard since the day the lad took his degree.' She turned lingeringly away from her reflection. 'Well, what do you think, then?'

Peter thought in general that most people seeing the two of them as a married couple would wonder what cruel fate had landed such a comparatively presentable female, still slim and well taken care of as to skin and hair, with such a bloated, beaten-up old slob. More to the purpose, he thought that the subtle fore-and-aft groove or corrugation in the crown of the hat gave it a slightly sat-on look. But that was not called for either. He concentrated his attention. 'Fine,' he said, widening his eyes and giving a succession of little nods. 'Fine.'

'Or there's this one. I'm not sure I've ever even had it on till now since the bloody shop.'

It was like a sturdy cake-frill in pale pink with a re-inforced gauze or netting top. He nodded at it more slowly and judicially, finding no words.

'Which do you think is better?'

After a moment of the usual attempted clairvoyance he

reminded himself sharply that the day might have come when, in defiance of all history, she was asking him what he thought because she wanted to know. Still no help. Trying not to smirk at his own cunning, he said, 'I suppose some of the women will be wearing hats, will they? I thought even for weddings it had more or less faded away. Of course I'm not much of a –'

'Oh, it's a dead duck in England, wearing hats. Never see them in London.'

'Well then . . .'

'Ah, but we're not in England.'

'I'm sure it would be perfectly all right. Nobody would object.'

'Well, I don't want to offend the native wives by flouting ancestral taboos.'

He had thought that line quite funny on its first appearance about the time of Suez. 'I don't think you need worry.'

Rather to his regret she took off the cake-frill piece and laid it on the dressing-table. 'How do I look without it? Go on.'

'All right,' he said soberly. 'You look all right.' Yes, she had been going to do that all along.

'Good. That's settled that. Well, we'd better be getting . . .'

'Oh, we've got a bit of time yet.'

'There's a case for being in position when you're expected to be.'

To hear this sentiment on Muriel's lips marginally astonished Peter, but he said nothing more than, 'Okay, well I'll go and bring the car round. You come down when you're ready.'

As he almost ran down the stairs he affirmed internally that he must put top priority on pulling himself together. If he went on in that kind of strain, going off at tangents, giving brilliant imitations of a man who really wanted his wife to look her best and things like that, he would soon come to grief. From the moment early in the year when William had announced his intention to marry Rosemary Weaver, Peter had been given a new lease of life. Every time he thought of it he felt as if he had been reading a communiqué announcing a catastrophic defeat of the shits.

In the hall now, moving with exemplary speed for one of his weight and condition, he climbed up on the pseudo-Chippendale chair by the telephone and swung about just in time to fart with a kind of gulping sound into an enormous green and mauve face, rendered in a mixture of paint and filth, that hung from the side of the stairway. On descending, much elated, he spotted the necessary bottle of Famous Grouse in its place on the dresser in the kitchen. Spotting it was all that was needed. Without bothering about surely on this day of all days, etc., he took just one small quick nip and then just one more small quick nip. Irrelevantly, he remembered Charlie once informing him that ghillies or crofters or some such persons in the Scottish Highlands would drink regularly, as a matter of routine, a tumbler of whisky before setting out on the day's round, so at least Charlie had said as he put down a similar quantity to see him through their twenty-minute car-journey to a lawyers' piss-up in Welsh St Hilarys.

It was a fine bright morning in early March of the sort much more often recalled in these parts than actually met with, the air calm and mild along the whole of the coastal plain and inshore waters. On days like this gardeners recently in London, but not gardeners alone, would say how much further forward everything in Wales seemed to be: daffodils, rhododendrons, azaleas, even the sticky-buds on the chestnuts were two or three weeks ahead of what you saw in the London parks and squares. Low in the sky still, the sun made long shadows, casting a light no stronger than that on a summer's evening, clear but not vivid, with a softness that would be gone by May. Cwmgwyrdd gleamed gently in the sunshine, and Peter, who had noticed the good weather, felt for a few moments that it was not such a hopelessly bad place to live as he let himself into the garage.

'Am I all right?' he asked Muriel when she came down into the hall.

'Quite suitable for the occasion.'

'I was thinking really of stains, you know, custard, chocolate, that kind of thing. There's not much else I can do anything about at this stage.'

'No, all clear. Tie could be tighter.'

Tightening it, he looked her over summarily and said, 'Much better without the hat, no doubt about it.'

They got into the car and drove towards town. He considered their exchange in the hall and some bits, at any rate, of the one in the bedroom just before. They had talked like that a good deal in past weeks, with studious normality, like an English couple in a socialist country, fearful of being eavesdropped upon, conspiring to be dull together. But there was a lot underneath that. When she asked him about the hats she had not looked at him, not really, not properly, any more than he had looked at her when he answered. His enjoyment of parts of the charade was real enough but had something hysterical in it. Time to play safe now.

'They couldn't have wished for a better day,' said Muriel.

'No rain forecast before tomorrow.'

'I think it's warm enough to sit out.'

'We'll have to see how it goes.'

And this little piggy cried wee, wee, wee all the way home. A run-through, thought Peter suddenly. A series of rehearsals for being parents-in-law, the very image or images of a decent, comfortable and above all ordinary old couple rather unexpectedly turned back into part of a family some time after anything of that sort had perceptibly lapsed. And of course merely to put on an in-law style when it seemed called for would be very slipshod and insecure; something more fundamental was required. To adapt the concept of the couple in Eastern Europe, this was the period of pre-drop training. On his mind's television screen Peter could see an MI6 man, one of the fashionable aloof but hot-eyed sort, saying he would have them thinking, feeling, dreaming like Darby and Joan before they were through. And yes, the new style of talk, which was really only new in quantity, in proportion, had begun to be noticeable just about when or after William had told them he and Rosemary were going to get married.

'Well, now the day's here at last the whole thing seems to have happened rather suddenly,' said Muriel.

'Yes, I suppose it does in a way.'

'And isn't it extraordinary, we've hardly discussed it at all.'

'No, there wasn't a hell of a lot to discuss, really, was there?'

'And now it's too late, whatever conclusion we might come to.'

For Peter, that exactly defined a signal superiority of this day over its predecessors. He said nevertheless, and not in pursuance of any intention of playing safe, 'Oh, I wouldn't be too sure of that. You'll agree we're still in Wales.'

'What are you talking about?'

'There were some people called Ungoed-Thomas over in Caerhays, related to a cousin of my father's I think. Anyway, there was a daughter there called Gladys, a couple of years older than me. Now Gladys had got hold of an American, can't think how she managed that in Caerhays in those days, but she had – this would have been 1937 or so. Well, it got to the point where Gladys was going to marry her American, and indeed it was all fixed up, ready to go. Haven't told you this story before, have I? No, so the night before the wedding a call comes from Gladys and my parents nip on the train for Caerhays – you could do that in those days. I wish I'd gone too. Would they use their influence to stop Gladys's mam stopping the wedding.'

'And did they?'

'Yes. Marvellous, those two being on the progressive –'

'What could she have done anyway, the old girl? How could she have stopped it?'

'I agree she couldn't have stopped it indefinitely, even in Caerhays in 1937, but she could have caused a large upset instead of just a small one. What was interesting was her reason for being against the American. He was an American.'

'I heard you.'

'No, I mean that was the reason. Why the old girl was against him, according to her anyway. Not that it isn't a pretty serious charge in general, but in fact this one was hilariously proper. Name of Foster, Ralph Foster. Funny how you remember things that are nothing to do with you. Professor of physics at Yale University he was. God knows what he'd find to do in Caerhays in 1987, let alone 1937. He was so proper he fell down dead of excitement at a baseball game not many years later, but Gladys was well settled in the States by then.'

After saying she heard him, Muriel had begun wriggling her torso over the back of her seat, arm extended from the shoulder towards a blue-and-white box of tissues on the rear shelf. Having captured it she pushed herself forwards again by degrees, almost rolling over laterally when the car took a fair-sized curve, and twisted round into her original position just as he finished with the baseball game. 'I'm listening,' she said.

'That's it.'

'What?' She pulled down the shade over the top part of the windscreen in front of her and stared at her reflection in the oblong of mirror there while she picked repeatedly at the tissues. 'What, what's interesting about that?'

'Well. Scene from Welsh life. I thought you liked them. Caption, in Wales you never know.'

'You mean if I could think of something like that I'd try to put a stop to William marrying what's-her-name, Rosemary, if there was just something I could come up with. Otherwise what's the point?'

'Oh, no. No, no. Of course you're as pleased as I am. Still, she was born in London, and I've noticed you've been getting really quite noticeably Welsh in your old age. I was staggered, quite frankly, when you said just now it was a good thing to be seen in your place on time. You couldn't hope for anything more Welsh than that, not off the cuff. Chapel you'd think we was going to.'

Beside him Muriel suddenly opened her mouth as wide as possible consistent with keeping her lips stretched over her teeth, perhaps in unspoken comment but more likely so as to get those parts of her face lined up for the application of the tissue she had now managed to wrest from its box. She still said nothing.

'Oh, er, what line would you have taken if we had discussed the marriage before today?'

'Nothing very much,' she said, going on peering, 'and after all there's no sense arguing about it now.'

Well no, no more than five minutes ago, and he had not really expected to hear how much she felt like killing him at the idea of a son of hers and her only child marrying the daughter of a woman her own husband would rather have married, and that just for a start. But he realized that asking the question had been the latest spurt of the dangerous euphoria that had again possessed him. Take it *easy*, for God's sake. *Watch* it.

After doing something undetectable to her mouth she put the tissue away and said, 'You've got quite saucy these last months. You know, cheeky.' She spoke in a tone of measured approbation more suitable to telling him he had shown signs of becoming well read or kind to animals.

And interfering with the body after death more than cursorily to pay him out for being pleased at something that displeased her. 'Yes, I probably have been a bit full of beans seeing William looking so happy.'

'It's not just that. It started before that. It was in full swing by Christmas.'

'Was it really? I can't think of anything to explain it,' he said without trying to at all.

If Muriel could think of something she kept it bottled up. They drove in silence over the old bridge, repaired now, past the roofless smelt-houses, through St Advent, past Victoria Station, up the Strand, past the Trevor Knudsen Fine Arts Museum, Marks & Spencer, the Glendower, the Royal Foundation of Wales, the cricket and rugby ground and the university and round by the hospital towards Holland.

'Peter,' said Muriel when they were a couple of minutes from the church: 'I'm selling the house.'

'What?'

'This time I mean it. Now William's settled, that's my last reason or excuse gone for hanging on any longer round here. Yes, it's back to Middlesbrough for me, and if you care to come along too there'll be a bed for you at the end of the road. Now it could so be, sooner than shift to sunny Yorkshire or Cleveland or whatever it's called these days you'd prefer to go it alone here, under your own steam as it were. Well, I dare say that can be arranged. Entirely up to you.'

So much for the parade of cosy domesticity. Muriel had spoken with all her usual matter-of-factness, even perhaps a little more. It occurred to Peter that the presence of William and his best man as first arranged would have made no real difference; she would have seen to it that he got the lot, or enough, some time or other before entering the church. This was now just round the corner and the early guests were on their way to it. He caught sight of old Owen Thomas and his family getting out of their car.

'There's no more to say,' she began again. 'These people may be good, they may be bad, and I'll not say I'm not fond of one or two of them, but they're not *my* people, and I mean to do something about that while I've still time. So I'm checking out. The house goes on the market first thing Monday morning. And that's that. Okay? Understood? No appeals, no conditions, no stays of execution, no compromises, no practical alternatives. Final. Now I may be completely wrong again and you've been bursting to get shut of the place since whenever, but if I'm not wrong I'll give you one piece of advice. Start getting used to the idea right away. If I were you I'd go left here and park in the Holland Court car-park.'

'Go and . . .'

'Nobody uses it much this time of day.'

So it turned out, but Muriel had barely had time to take up groom's-mother station at Peter's side before they were fairly among old Tudor Whittingham and his wife and son and daughter and son-in-law and two grandchildren and married sister and niece whom he hoped it was all right for him to have brought along only they were staying with them. There was more, much more, all the way to the church and on the broad asphalted walk surrounding it. Some, like Percy and Dorothy, Malcolm and Gwen, old Vaughan Mowbray and his arthritic lady-friend, a few dimly remembered figures from university, industry, Golf Club, various youngsters identifiably or presumably connected with William, came and went; others, like Garth, Siân Smith, Arnold and toffee-nose Eirwen Spurling and two quite independent funereally-dressed couples, unknown, silent and demoralizing, came and stayed around. No family of either parent were to be seen. Muriel's of course were all in England, and evidently staying there; Peter had two brothers living, but these days he hardly knew as much as where.

Grimly, with an air of putting down any nonsense about celebration, an attendant removed the two of them and escorted them inside – at the last moment Peter spotted Rhiannon coming in at the churchyard gate and waved, but was not sure if she saw. The small delay provoked the man into an impatient jerk of the head, a bit of a risk in view of the glossy pudding-basin wig he wore on it. His general bearing suggested that he thought he had come to a funeral. If he did he was not deviating all that far from the spirit of a good slice of the congregation, who stared pessimistically at the groom's parents as they passed, on full alert for hiccup or tell-tale stumble. They reached the front pew without offence, though, shuffling in beside Charlie and Sophie.

As far as he could remember, Peter had never been in here before. Enough sun came through the unstained parts of the stained glass to make the place look bright and very clean, like new, in fact. The light-coloured woodwork seemed familiar, personal to him in some way, and presently he realized that it reminded him of the kind of furniture, said to have been Scandinavian in inspiration, that had been fashionable when he and Muriel got married.

Having reached him by a side route, thoughts of that time and what had followed it, up to and including today, proved impossible to drive off. They were not so much thoughts as a confusion of memories and feelings. The memories were powerful but misty and spread over, with Angharad and Rhiannon in them as well as Muriel and a mass of all-but-forgotten faces and places he could not have named. Of his feelings the two foremost ones were remorse and self-pity. Well as he knew them both, he had never learnt how to deal with them, and he stood and sat in his place now vainly trying to see past them to his son's marriage ceremony, which he had been looking forward to a dozen times a day since first hearing it was to come about, and which he had determined to take in and value minute by minute. Instead, what was happening in front of him took the short cut and went straight into the past to blend in with everything else. As usual in these last years.

He went through most of the service in a state similar in important respects to boredom. At the same time, screened off as he was from the centre of the picture he still managed to catch on to details at the edges. So he heard the congregation singing – no choir, naturally, because somebody was on holiday or had just thought of something better to do – and found it puny, thickened by men singing the air, some of them an octave low half the time, the whole performance to be defended only as far as it showed any English present how wrong they would have been to expect anything out of the ordinary from singing Welshmen in the flesh as opposed to on television. Or so he might have said if he could have been bothered. Charlie stood out quite a bit from the mess, in tune and probably accurate with the bass in the hymns and making a good shot in the psalm – much more testing. Peter found he could remember him years ago sneaking off to practices with some secular choir in Harriston or Emanuel, promising to be back by half-nine at latest to sink propitiatory pints.

He noticed that the ceremony was performed by two or more clerics and that they wore embroidered vestments of some white material, not cotton. Parts of the service were chanted. Peter had started to welcome these touches of High as likely to affront some parts of the congregation when he saw that a subordinate figure he had mistaken for an effeminate boy was actually a female, a young woman, not a bad-looking one either. Oh *Christ*. He had come to think that almost the whole point of Wales these days was that you were going to be spared that kind of thing, for the time being at least. He was overcome by a great weariness, a longing to be done with everything, but in a couple of moments that too passed. Then right at the end, when William and his bride were supposedly being blessed, he found Muriel's hand groping for his and made out a tear-track on her averted cheek. He put this down as all part of the performance, but it was impossible not to grasp her hand, and to be on the safe side he at once ran up a well-disposed look in case she should turn her head, though this soon turned out not to be needed.

2

The organ sounded out with Mendelssohn: there in the loft was one man (or of course woman now, bugger it) who had not taken the day off. As he passed down the aisle William glanced towards his parents. Without seeming to do anything at all with any part of his face he conveyed unmistakably to Peter a cheerfully hangdog confession of surrender but of surrender none the less; Peter wondered suddenly what he thought his mother thought of his marriage and his wife. Rhiannon gave a smile, too friendly to be called impersonal and yet still not personal. It was time to move. Those still in their pews stared at Peter as before, with no hint of having been appeased by what had taken place in the meantime.

'Well, I reckon we done the young couple very tasteful,' said Charlie. 'I don't know about you, I wouldn't presume to presume, but I could do with a drink.'

These words, or the manner in which they were spoken, made Peter look at him for a moment. He said, 'Yes, me too.'

Charlie grinned briefly. 'Bad as that, eh? It's these bloody new sleeping-pills of Dewi's. Finest thing out, he says, no systemic effects, you know, like actually getting the system off to sleep. Well, we'll get it off tonight all right. Look, if you want to slip away later we could have a couple down at the Glendower. I'll be there in any case. Just one stipulation. Don't bring Garth. On this happy day . . . this day of typically Welsh family feeling and good fellowship . . . our thoughts naturally turn . . . to stringing up Garth Pumphrey, FRCVS, outside the Bible. Jesus, there he is.'

'Somebody's got to say all those things.'

'Oh no they haven't. Well wait a minute, perhaps they have. There's an awful lot of filling-in to be done in life, isn't there?'

'Anyway he has one great virtue, young Garth, as you pointed out some time ago. When he's around you know for a certainty you're not going to run into Angharad.'

'When did I say that? I hope at least I said it lightly. I'm sorry, Peter.'

358

'Nonsense, you were quite right. You spoke better than you knew. And never more applicable than today.'

'I suppose so.' Charlie looked seriously at his feet as they halted in the porch. 'She'd have been nothing but a . . .' He started on another word and stopped.

'Skeleton at the feast, yes. Oh dear. Once again, very well put. You know, it's a funny thing . . .'

'What is? I think I can –'

'Just, ever since that evening at Garth's I've had the –'

'I'll see you down at the house. But . . .'

They were being borne onwards and outwards into the sunshine among hurrying or resisting bodies and there was not going to be much more of this conversation. Sophie and Dorothy were near, Sophie not looking at anyone, silent, possibly tearful, Dorothy clutching a leather handbag that might have held a baby's cricket-bat and pads and wearing something of which it could be said with certainty only that it was lime-green and that she had made it herself. Charlie backed Peter into a minor angle of the stonework and gave a muted yelp as his ankle hit a boot-scraper.

'Er . . . there's something it would be good if you'd say to Rhiannon if you get a chance to talk to her alone.'

'Yes?' said Peter, pretty sure he knew what it was, his mind still on the events at Garth's.

'You know Victor and I are doing the reception, well for one reason and another we want to charge her the full rate on paper, so to speak, but she'll get a rebate in the post next month which she needn't acknowledge, okay?'

'Oh, marvellous,' said Peter, laughing a good deal at the imaginative poverty of his guess. 'Absolutely spiffing.'

'I mean Victor, we thought it might come better from you. If you would.'

'I'll make a point of it.'

'Cheers. See you there.' Charlie reached for a passing lapel and was gone.

Alone for a space, Peter had time to look without much engrossment at the dozens of people hanging about on the well-kept lawn and paths, searching for one another with heads raised or drifting uncertainly away, William standing with friends of his, Rosemary with friends of hers, younger couples being pulled this way and that by children, older couples consisting usually of a more or less apathetic old boy and vigilant, questing old girl with glasses and hat – yes, hat, nothing to do with the wedding as like as not, just part of the uniform – solitaries wondering what on earth had possessed them to come, Rhiannon in grey with white collar and cuffs along by the gate next to Alun's very fat and unsmiling brother who had come down from London to give the bride away, and hemmed in by Breconshire aunts and cousins and such, but at the moment speaking hesitantly into a microphone held out by a squat man in a white raincoat while a photographer circled round her – all this, as far as it went, Peter contemplated, until a well-known voice was heard.

'Tell us now, when's the baby coming then?' Although Garth's voice was quite well known in some quarters he sounded at the moment more like a Welsh comedian than usual.

'There isn't one, I mean not yet as far as I know,' said Peter, wishing he could drop easily into character like Charlie and the others.

'Awh! Reely! Well, there's posh for you.'

'There's *swank*,' corrected Tudor Whittingham at Garth's side. Tudor had somehow managed to shed his followers for the time being and kept looking round to make sure they stayed shed. His amazing lack of surplus flesh allowed full visibility to the spare, narrow frame that had stood him in such good stead as a squash player in the remote past. Its narrowness was extended upwards to his skull, which all generations had pronounced inadequate for an adequate amount of brain without compression of some sort. He had been Tudor Totem-Bonce in the form above Peter at the Grammar.

'Posh or swank, same difference,' said Garth. Then his manner changed abruptly and he went on to Peter at reduced volume, 'Tarc was saying last night he hoped you'd come in today for a bit if you had the time. You haven't been in much since poor Alun went, have you?' He rolled a mournful bardic eye at Peter.

'No. No, I suppose I haven't.'

'No, well we miss you there, Peter. I know Tarc does particularly. He feels rotten about that evening still, throwing us all out neck and crop. It's not that he feels responsible at all for . . . what happened later; I think I've talked him out of that. It's more that it grieves him that he and Alun parted for the last time on such bad terms. Was that your impression, Tudor?'

'No question. No question whatever.'

'Of course he never seriously meant we should take all our gear away. Temper, that was. He as good as admitted it when I went round the next morning. Perhaps I told you.'

Addressing Peter, but obviously reproaching Garth for the omission as well, Tudor said, 'I thought it was a lovely service and the young people looked absolutely radiant and I hope they'll be very happy.'

'Oh yes. Oh yes.' Garth intimated that between him and Peter that side of things was taken for granted. 'Yes, old Tarc really respected poor Alun. I reckon everybody did. Mind you, there's not a man who's ever walked this earth who didn't give those around him something to put up with. But taking him for all in all he was the best of fellows really, wasn't he?'

Somebody has to say it, thought Peter. 'Yes, I suppose he was.' The words drew a look of puzzled incredulity from Tudor.

'Actually,' Garth went on, 'actually not everybody did respect him if the truth were told. Remember that article in the *Western Mail*, that so-called appreciation? Nasty. Curmudgeonly is what I'd call it. Thoroughly curmudgeonly. Oh, and did you see that reference in a *Times* review, was it, the other day? Oh yes – wait a minute.' His hand moved towards his breast pocket but stopped before it got there. 'No, I've filed it. Er . . . he could be called a follower of Brydan if that were not taken to imply a certain degree of strength and vital . . . something. Very nasty. I'll get it copied and send it you.'

Tudor said with some determination, 'William and Rosemary going away for a bit, are they?'

Though ready and willing with a reply Peter never gave it, being instantly hiked off to be photographed. He hoped Tudor thought he was getting his money's-worth out of having dumped his family.

There was a line-up in the sunshine with backs to the church wall. Peter had been for sidling into his place at the end next to Muriel, but embraces were called for, not of course with the unsmiling brother, who unsmilingly nodded and that was that, nor with Muriel. She smiled, though, but not for long, which was just as well. He was not going to start digging all that over. There was one thing to be said at any rate: neither he nor anyone else could have done anything about it, probably ever. Who had used almost those very words to him not so long ago, and about what or whom?

For some minutes three or four photographers, one a

woman or girl, all showing in their clothing and hair structure what some might have seen as an unhealthy disrespect for stuff like weddings, huddled the six principals together with no result, spread them apart again, brought some forward, waved others away with sudden backhand sweeps. Nor was it lost on Peter that advances in science meant they took ten times as many photographs as would once have been found necessary and shaped up to take twice that number. It was easier for them like that, he inferred, more fun too, licitly buggering a set of strangers about. Quite understandable. Do it himself if he had the chance.

Eventually the consensus emerged that it would be unnecessary or perhaps futile to prolong the photographic session, which faded away without anything being said on either side. Soon afterwards removal to the Weaver house was set going, a matter of a couple of hundred yards on foot. As if the manoeuvre had been organized beforehand Muriel drifted across, thrust one arm through William's and the other round Rosemary's waist and seemed to swing them both through a semicircle towards the gate. With an advance six or more abreast pretty well ruled out, Peter found himself in a second rank between Alun's brother, said on their very brief first meeting the previous night to be called Duncan, and his suddenly manifest wife, who had glasses and a hat with the best of them and very red lips and abnormally long teeth thrown in.

On the far side of the gateway Rhiannon was with an aunt or cousin or so and Peter was stuck, irremovably as it turned out, with these in-laws of hers. He had always thought of himself as a cool head in a situation like that, not for the life of him to be driven into speaking first. Nevertheless after four minutes of total silence, the last three of them spent standing in a row at no particular point on the pavement, there he was asking the wife whether she and, er, Duncan proposed staying over until the following day or whether, on the other hand, they would be returning to London that same evening.

She turned to face him hungrily. 'Oh, we've got to get back, no two ways about it,' she said in an accent from somewhere not very nice in England. 'I tell you, it took all of everybody's time getting him to come away for just the one night.'

'Business responsibilities, I suppose.' Peter dimly remembered something about a finance company or building society.

'You're joking. They're a thing of the past, they are, it's getting on for four years now,' she said with gloomy relish. 'No, it's just he won't be moved if he can help it. What he's doing now, Mr Thomas, he's giving them a chance to get settled where we're going, you see, so he can just sneak in there without any of them saying anything to him.'

'Quite,' said Peter, turning his eyes but not his head towards Duncan, who was making rhythmical puffing noises and rocking to and fro where he stood.

'Or so he thinks to himself. He doesn't like being spoken to because people expect him to say things back. That's why he doesn't look very friendly. I tell him he wants to wear a hearing-aid, everybody knows better than try and talk to a person wearing one of them, but he won't. Just draw attention, he says.' She turned back her gold-inwoven cuff. 'Christ, that's long enough to get your grandmother and Mrs Brown settled.' Facing her husband now, she said in a tremendously loud voice with a lot of facial activity, out of sight from Peter but audible enough in her speech, 'We'd better get moving, Dad. They'll be wondering where we've got to. Come on, old boy. There.'

She did plenty of pointing into the middle distance while

she was saying this. Duncan nodded and got moving. The three of them crossed the road to the corner of the lane that led to their destination.

'I don't know why I still shout at him like that. Just habit. The nerves have gone, you see, both sides, so whatever you do he'll never hear anything. Virus, I think they said. Oh yes. Rhiannon did tell you, did she?' Duncan's wife mispronounced the name without any suggestion that it was unfamiliar to her. 'I mean she did mention it.'

Like enough, indeed. 'Yes,' said Peter.

'There's not a fat lot he can get up to if you follow me. He can't face learning the lip-reading and that sign language, everyone does it different, he says, no rhyme nor reason to it. There's the subtitles though, on TV. He likes his food all right, as you can see from his . . .' She paused for the first time but went on firmly, 'You know I feel a pig dragging him all this way and running him into all these people he doesn't know, but I'd go potty if I didn't get a break once in a while.'

'Of course you must,' he made himself say. 'That's quite reasonable and normal.'

At Rhiannon's front gate they halted again, Duncan prompted by his wife's hand on his shoulder. She said, 'Take my advice, Mr Thomas, and don't go deaf. Well, it's been nice talking to you. He's a lovely boy, that William. Now you go off and enjoy yourself. We'll be along in a minute.' Duncan gave a not quite unsmiling nod of farewell and thanks for not having said anything to him.

Inside the house the first person Peter saw was Gwen, her head at an offensive angle as she listened to whatever some tall, dignified old ninny in an injudicious green suit might have been trying to tell her; a cousin of Malcolm's, perhaps. It was easy to imagine her frowning and leering interestedly over the account of the conversation with

Duncan's wife she was never going to be given. Peter looked round for Charlie, failed to spot him and made for the bar, a trestle table with a really seriously snowy white tablecloth spread over it and loaded with bottles, an astonishingly high proportion of which seemed to hold soft drinks; not all of them, however. The ruddy-faced girlish youngster from the cocktail bar at the Glendower was doling out the stuff, with great efficiency as it proved. Another class of youngster sat round-shouldered on a folding metal chair against the wall. His face was not at all ruddy and his collar was undone. Good going for the time of day, thought Peter.

His only slightly delayed arrival had in fact given time for a large part of the crowd to get settled here or there, dozens of them in the garden all exclaiming at the warmth of the day and knocking back their drinks at a speed that, if maintained, would quite quickly stretch them out in the herbaceous border. He observed the scene from the step outside the french window and very soon picked up Muriel's rear view by her stooped head and clumping gait. With a couple of William's presumed friends, who stood not less than thirteen foot tall between them, she was strolling along the edge of the lawn and, just as he noticed her, she half turned to run a superior eye over what was growing – nothing very much, perhaps – in the nearby bed. She let her gaze linger, making quite sure things were as bad as they had looked at first glance, then snatched it apologetically away, both in a style he felt sure he would have recognized with an inward yell of loathing at ten times the range. Seeing it, seeing it unseen, catching the old bitch out even on such a puny scale, was as good as a stiff one.

He was turning away to refill his glass, which in the last minute had mysteriously emptied itself, when he caught sight of Rhiannon not far off, nearer than Muriel had been.

She was one of a group of a dozen women and some men apparently in a single noisy conversation, glances switching from one speaker to another, all briskly absorbed. Sophie was among them, Siân too, and a couple more he knew by sight, but who were the others? Well, for God's sake, who do you think they are, you bloody old fool – *friends of hers*, see, he notified himself carefully. What else would they be? But why should it need realizing? Because he had forgotten, if he had ever begun to understand, how small a part people played in others' lives and how little they knew about them, even if they saw them every day. Between Alun's death and this morning he had thought many times, several times anyway, about Rhiannon and her life, about how she managed for company with Sophie, Siân, Gwen, Dorothy, Muriel for Christ's sake – none of them exactly her type, he had thought since much longer ago – and no doubt with more besides, her daughters, London friends. What he was looking at gave him some idea. Not much even now. He would have said he had forgotten about love too, but just for the moment he would have had to admit there had been a few weeks once when somebody else had played a very large part in his life and he had known a great deal about her, until the rest of the world came swimming back.

He had to wait a minute or two at the bar, where Victor now presided, while a wave of refills was dealt with. In the interval he saw a man with a moustache nudge a man with a wholly different moustache and pass the word about himself, a word that must have left out the information that he was the sort of old buffer you could just go up to and say hallo to like that and, you know, that would be fine. Before it came to his turn, Victor reached over someone's shoulder and passed him a major Scotch and water with a flourish that said any possible Alun-related bygones were indeed bygones, and oh by the way don't forget that little message to Rhiannon. The unruddy young-ster had departed but he was soon accosted by a different one in the shape of the bridegroom.

'Dad, where have you been hiding?'

'Out in the open. Too big to be seen.'

'Come on, come and meet the blokes.'

The blokes were not far away, about five strides from the drink, in fact, and Peter felt he did pretty well with them, considering. He was touched and impressed by the unobtrusive production William put into this event, letting him feel he was meeting all or most of them while nursing him through with a couple of talkative reliables. After a time William said to him, with no fear of being overheard in the ambient uproar, 'She's a marvellous girl, you know. Or do you know? She says she's hardly seen anything of you over these weeks, I mean before today.'

'Yes, well, there sort of hasn't been a hell of a lot of, er . . .'

'No. Anyway she is. I expect you've heard it said that it's absolutely marvellous when somebody's very difficult to get to know and to get on with at first, and then when you do get to know them it's somehow much better than, well, if it hadn't been like that. Eh?'

'Yes. I mean I have heard it said.'

'So have I, and I suppose it might be right, but I must say personally it sounds pretty fair balls to me. Anyway, the point is that's exactly how it wasn't with Rosemary and me. Absolutely no snags or problems of any kind at any stage right from the start. My God, I've just realized it was love at first sight. Doesn't that sound ridiculous?'

'No,' said Peter.

There was a short pause while William took a considered sip of champagne instead of alluding to his parents' marriage, then or now. 'Anyway, she's a marvellous girl. You'd better find her quick if you're going to. We're nipping off right after the speeches. Don't want to get caught up with all these drunken bastards.'

'No, you certainly don't want to do that.'

'I think I might be a bit pissed myself actually. Look, we'll see you as soon as we get back. Really we will. I'm sorry I haven't done anything about it before when I said I was going to, just before I first met Rosemary, do you remember?'

'Oh, was that that day?'

'That was rather the point I'm afraid, meeting Rosemary I mean. It sort of drove everything else out.'

'Yes, I know the feeling. Well, I expect you're –'

'How are you, Dad? I've hardly seen you all this time.'

'I'm all right. I'm better. Those pains I mentioned seem to have, well, I'm keeping my fingers crossed.'

'I gather you were there then, well, when he went off.'

'Yes. It's an awful thing to say in a way, but I absolutely sailed through that bit.'

'Must have been a shock at the time, though. Pretty horrible.'

'It was a rather raw occasion all round.'

William extended his arm with military smartness to present his glass to the circling champagne-bottle. 'Well, at least I shan't have him to deal with.'

'He didn't need a lot of dealing with. Not if you weren't married to him.'

'Well, yeah. Frightful shit, wasn't he? I hardly knew him, of course.'

'I suppose so. The longer I go on the harder it gets to say that about anybody. Himmler, well certainly. Eichmann, that type of chap. Of course he did leave a certain amount to be desired in the way of friendship, Alun, I mean. Bloody Welshman, you see.'

'You really are okay, then? There's really nothing wrong?' asked William, looking hard at his father.

Peter returned the look. 'Nothing whatever, I promise you. Now you're quite right, I'd better track down your wife while there's still time. Have a word before you go finally.'

'Last time I saw her she was in the garden with my mother-in-law. Jesus Christ.'

By now they had moved to the dining-room, where there was an extensive spread of cold ham, veal-and-ham pie, English-style sausages and Continental-style sausage. Also on view were bowls of unadventurous salad and, more to the purpose, an array of pickled onions in three colours, pickled walnuts, pickled gherkins in two sizes, pickled beetroot, four kinds of chutney, three kinds of mustard, six kinds of bottled sauce, in other words a meal plumb in the middle of the genuine Welsh tradition, remarkably complete too barring only the omission of tinned fruit. Banks of sandwiches and uncountable cheeses stood in reserve and most flat surfaces within normal reach carried at least one opened bottle of Victor's special-price red or ditto white. Either or both of these would go down a treat after a few quick glasses of champagne and four or five large gin and tonics and in company with salami, mustard pickle, garlic bread, corona-sized spring onions and water-cress. Victor himself stood at the head of the table dealing out plates and cutlery and trying to awaken some sense of order in the talkative rout that had started shambling up to be fed.

After pushing past and through them Peter made his way as indicated to the garden. The general drift towards food had reached back as far as here and the last few figures were slowly converging on the french window. Rosemary was one, but he sent her no more than a glance of apology before almost clutching Rhiannon at her side.

'Can I talk to you privately? I've got a message for you.'

'Nothing awful, is it?'

'No, not in the least. I just want to talk to you for a couple of minutes.'

When they had moved thirty or forty yards away from the house she turned and faced him, smiling but still uneasy.

'Charlie asked me to tell you he and Victor are charging the full price for today but you'll get a refund they don't want you to acknowledge.'

She waited a moment and then said, 'Oh. What's that in aid of?'

'I can't imagine. Something to do with the office, probably. Some fiddle or other. I've no idea.'

'Oh. That's not all, is it?'

'No, it isn't, there's another message. This one's from Alun. No, it's all right – not awful at all, I promise you.' When she just stood very still he went on, 'Immediately before he died, in those few seconds, he said something, only a couple of words, but quite clearly. He said, "Little thing". Charlie must have heard too but I doubt whether he understood, but I feel I did. Alun was thinking of you, he was speaking to you.' Peter wanted to take her hand, but lacked confidence to do so. 'He was sending you his love before he died.'

'Might have been,' said Rhiannon. 'Perhaps he was. He used to call me . . .' Her mouth and chin moved in a way that recalled her youthful self to him more sharply and unexpectedly than anything he had yet seen. Then her eyes steadied on him. 'That's still not all, is it?'

371

'It's all I've got about him, but if you wouldn't mind just . . .'

'Hang on a minute. Stay there.'

He watched her hurrying back up the lawn to where Rosemary and another young woman still stood near the windows. After a moment he realized this must appear inquisitive of him and quickly turned his head away. The movement brought his eyes to a triangle of grass the sun had missed and left apparently still damp with dew. Beyond it, in the sunlight, a dishevelled brownish butterfly was clinging to the boundary fence and stirring feebly. Much further off, woodland flecked with thin greenery ran from one side to the other and out of sight.

When Rhiannon came back she said, staring over Peter's shoulder and speaking in a monotone, 'Thank you for telling me that. Don't mind if we don't say any more now. Can't really talk about him properly yet. But it was nice of you to tell me.'

She waited again and it dawned on him that he had almost no idea of how to start or where he wanted to get to. 'You are staying on here, aren't you, are you? Or are you . . .'

'Yes, for a bit anyway. I'll probably have to find somewhere smaller in the end. Round here, though. Rosemary and William'll be moving to London, but I don't –'

'Really? When? He hasn't said anything about it to me.'

'Perhaps he doesn't know yet. In the autumn. It's for the Bar, you see, for Rosemary.' Rhiannon's expression appealed to Peter not to question her about the Bar.

'Of course. But wouldn't it make sense for you to move there too? You've lived there for so many years.'

'Not now I'm back here. Now I'm here again I want to stay. You probably think that sounds silly – I've heard you go on about the awful –'

'It may sound silly but it isn't. You can't explain it.'

'Not to anybody who isn't Welsh you can't, or even talk about it.'

'Not to the Welsh either. Not to them, of all people. Wales is a subject that can't be talked about. Unless you're making a collection of dishonesty and self-deception and sentimental bullshit. That's all you ever hear.'

She said hopefully, 'But it makes sense when you think about it, to yourself. It's all right then.'

'Yes it is. Indeed it is, but only then.'

'M'm. So you think it's quite sensible on the whole to hang on. You would if you were me.'

He hesitated. She was looking at him in another special way of hers, affectionate, attentive, troubled, the way she had looked at him just before he told her that final abject lie, that there was nothing wrong between them and she was still the only one for him. Over her shoulder now he saw Rosemary, no doubt under orders, step out and head off the nearer approach of one of the hatted females from indoors, stacked lunch-plate at chest level. In sudden agitation he asked himself how long it would take a particular hatless female to miss him and Rhiannon from the party and scurry to find and fuck up. He said in something of a rush, 'Well, that's really what I wanted to talk to you about. Muriel says William getting married means she can leave Wales as she's always wanted, or does now, I don't know, and go back to Yorkshire. When she said that, she hadn't heard he was off to London either or she'd certainly have mentioned it. Well, I'll have to go too, to Yorkshire. I don't want to, I don't want to leave any more than you do, I've lived here all my life. And it's more than that, as you say. But I just can't think of anything else to do. The house and everything else all belong to her and I haven't got a bean. A pension that would keep me in cornflakes.

373

It doesn't sound very high-minded, I know, but it's a bit of a struggle being high-minded when you're hard up and pushing seventy.'

'But you wouldn't be able to stand it,' she said in open dismay.

'I'll have to. It's not sort of uniformly appalling. Some of the time we struggle along more or less all right. Six of one and half a dozen of the other.'

'Oh, really? Funny, I've never known anything to be that. It's just a thing people say.'

'To sound decent. Yes.'

Rhiannon shook her head impatiently to recall herself to the point. 'She'll change her mind. It's a big step at her age.'

'No she won't. Not after saying it the way she did, with dates and things. I know her. Take it from me, there's nothing for it.' He said with great emphasis and finality, 'I hate everything about it, but I'll have to go.'

'But you can't. I mean I thought we were going to start seeing each other again. You'd said you'd ring me up but you never did.'

'I did mean to but when it came to it I couldn't face it. Me, not you.'

'But I thought by about now you might be thinking it would be all right to. With the children getting married and everything. To each other, I mean. I was so hoping you would.'

'After everything I've done? After the way I treated you?'

'Yes. It was losing you I minded. The other didn't matter really, not after a bit. Didn't I tell you that time, we'd been to the Golf Club party? You can't have been listening. God alive, perhaps I didn't really say it. Anyway, I meant to tell you you'll always be . . . I can't say it now either.

It used to be so easy. Now, it's like talking about Wales.'

Slowly, to give her time to back off if she felt like it, and furtively, so that Rosemary and the others should not see, Peter reached out his hand. Rhiannon gripped it. Furtively again, he looked at her and saw that she was trying to look at him. Yes, she had changed: not the direct confident glance now.

'Let me try. Though you might well not think so,' he said with care, 'and there was certainly a time when I forgot it myself, I've always loved you and I do to this day. I'm sorry it sounds ridiculous because I'm so fat and horrible, and not at all nice or even any fun, but I mean it. I only wish it was worth more.'

'Ring me up. This time.' With her back half turned she said, 'I'm sorry, but I can't talk any more now.'

'I've got so much to tell you.'

He again watched her retreating, moving hardly any faster than earlier, certainly not running. One of her distinctions from other females had always been that she only ran to catch buses and such, not to let the world know about her wild free spirit or alternatively the coruscating wave of emotion that for the moment enfolded her. At her approach Rosemary released a foolish-looking black dog whose collar she had been holding. It jumped up at her in an ungainly fashion, half fell over itself on landing and followed her into the house.

Peter did the same at a greater distance, feeling very much drunker than he had ever felt in his life before, or something. By the time he got to the food most of it had been swept away, the main body of it at least, but back-ups were still in place. He found the sandwiches excellent, especially the cheese-and-pickle and the egg-and-tomato, more especially still with plenty of Vin Rouge de Pays to help them past his teeth, and he silently undertook never again to underrate Victor, as he was conscious of having done in days gone by. But he commented aloud on the merit of the sandwiches.

'First-rate sandwiches these,' he said. 'Especially the egg-and-pickle.'

'Don't seem to have come to those yet myself,' said Garth.

Peter had started on Dundee cake and Founders Reserve port when the word came that the speeches would begin in five minutes. Instantly, as intended, all those with elderly bladders, or as many as were capable of responding, made for the toilets. Others went or were there too. From among a small crowd round the one outside the kitchen Peter identified Percy Morgan.

'Marvellously happy occasion,' he told him.

'Oh, I should just about think it is, boy.' Percy was perhaps a little startled to hear this from Peter about anything. 'Seems very nice, your new daughter-in-law. I've seen a bit of her, you know, with her mother. No nonsense about her, oh no by George. Never took to the father, I tell you frankly. Never much cared, myself, for people who laid it on thick about the Welsh heritage and all that. I don't know whether you agree with me, Peter, but as I see it that kind of thing is, well it can be a trifle embarrassing, you know, if it's overdone.'

'Oh absolutely, I was saying just now –'

'I'll stay for the speeches, of course, and then I think I'll be cutting along. It certainly takes you back, this lot, eh?'

'You mean the –'

'Well, queueing up for a piss. Takes you back to nights out after rugger. Takes me back, anyway. She went off it in a week flat after one chat with Dewi.'

There had been so little apparent pause between this remark and the previous one that Peter wondered whether he might have passed out on his feet for a few seconds. 'Oh yes,' he said, doing his best to smile encouragingly.

'Liver,' said Percy. 'Another couple of months the way she was going and –' he passed the edge of his hand across his throat and gave a loud palatal exhalation. 'Of course, her being off it, I'm glad for her, but it leaves me a bit up in the air. I used to be the bloke with this impossible wife who was bloody magnificent about her, that was what I did, so what do I do now she's possible again all of a sudden?'

'Yes, I can see that. I think I'll try upstairs.'

Upstairs Peter found waiting Siân Smith, Duncan Weaver and another man he was nearly sure he was supposed to know, had even perhaps invited. It seemed to him reasonable, and also enterprising, to go up a further flight to the top floor. Here a passage ran the width of the building, at the far end of which he was just in time to glimpse a half-naked white-haired female with a garment or two over her arm dashing across and out of sight. A door shut and a bolt clicked. After a moment another door opened and the face of old Vaughan Mowbray peered out and turned in his direction, and after another moment, occupied by mutual astonishment, drew back again. On the whole Peter felt he might as well go back to the floor below.

He found the situation there unchanged, except that Siân had moved over to the landing window and was leaning across the sill, presumably in quest of fresh air. He presumed otherwise when he was near enough to pick up the noises she was making. Duncan Weaver also had his eyes on her, more casually though; with his deafness he had no call to shift from the fresh-air presumption. Simultaneously the second fart of Peter's day rang out – from Duncan it had to be, unless the other man's start, glare and forceful rattling at the door-handle were the work of a consummate actor. Peter contemplated briefly the strangeness of a world without sound.

There was still a queue near the kitchen, though with different people in it, but now he came to think of it there was a little cloak-room place by the front door which he had not yet tried. In mid-transit he was again perfectly placed to catch old Arnold Spurling and the best man quite turbulently hustling the Levantine-moustached Tony Bainbridge along the hall and out of the house. Before the fellow was lost to view Peter saw him mouthing curses and shaking his fist in an old-fashioned way.

The speeches came and went. Drinking continued until suddenly there was nothing to put in your glass, not even wine. Victor was having the whole lot collected, stowed in cartons, carried out to a small off-white van. One moment Peter was in a group, the next alone with Rosemary – Rosemary Thomas, as she now was and as he addressed her a couple of times.

'I gather you're going to be seeing something of my mother,' she said. Her ears had fuller lobes than Rhiannon's.

'Am I? I mean of course I am, but how do you know?'

'She told me.' Rosemary looked him in the eye and said not altogether seriously, but quite seriously enough, 'Now you behave yourself, right?'

'What? How do you mean?'

'I mean don't misbehave.'

'What? How could I do that?'

'Any pal of Alun's could find a way. On today's showing – no problem. No, I mean severely misbehave. Like let her down. If you do, William and I will kill you, okay? Oh Peter, I don't think you've met Catriona Semple, also reading law at Oxford. Catriona, this is my father-in-law.'

Ten – Malcolm

'How's she getting on up there?'

Gwen turned one of the neatly written pages. 'Oh, having a whale of a time, it appears. Dinner-parties every night, house never empty, weekends in the country. Country? What country?'

'It's quite a big place, actually, the size of here. She must still know a great many people locally, some of them pretty well off I shouldn't be surprised, even in these days of industrial havoc.'

'Muriel never kept up with them much as far as I heard. Anyway, there she is. The theatre, what's she talking about? In Middlesbrough? It can't be the theatre as *civilized folk* think of it. Racing? Is there a course somewhere in that region?'

'Sorry, no idea,' said Malcolm, smiling and spreading his hands. 'Not my department.'

'No, I realize that, no, I just thought you might happen to know. Whippet-racing perhaps she means.'

'Well, it's good to hear that she seems to be doing reasonably well.'

'It says something for her pride that she exerts herself to give that impression.'

'I'm afraid I'm not quite with you.'

'If you want my opinion, she's protesting too much. Life's not turning out to be much fun, how could it in a hole like that, but she's buggered if she's going to let anyone think she's made a mistake. Very roughly.'

'Maybe, I suppose.' Malcolm tried to sound about half convinced. 'What does she say about Peter?'

'Nothing very much. She's surer than ever she was right to make the break when she did, exactly what she said before, er, oh and if you see Peter tell the lazy sod to drop her a line. Underplaying it there, you see.'

'She must miss him a lot in spite of everything.'

'It's not him she misses, for Christ's sake, it's having a husband as a social seal of quality. And then, well, she doesn't like him not being there in another way, because he still belongs to her really. Some women don't like parting with anything on their inventory even when they've no further use for same.'

'You're amazing, the way you see things. I'd never have been able to penetrate that far into her motives.' He missed the sharp look these remarks drew from Gwen and went tentatively on, 'But you don't visualize her coming back.'

She gave a restrained sigh and said, 'Peter's more likely to go there than she is to admit she was wrong in letters nine feet high, and that's it. Mind if I take first knock in the bathroom?'

'You go ahead.'

Left alone, Malcolm poured a last cup of tea and lit his daily cigarette. Putting aside the *Western Mail* for later he noticed a section headed 'Welsh News', a mere quarter of a page or less, and that in the daily newspaper of the capital of the Principality. That, he considered, was coming out into the open with a vengeance. But it was hard to go on feeling indignant for very long, especially after having just spent a good ten minutes reading about a police scandal in South London and not much less on the prospects for England's cricketers on their Australian tour.

As strongly as ever before, the conversational dealings at his breakfast-table had reminded Malcolm of those at another, the one at 221B Baker Street. There, as here, the first party regularly offered well-meaning provisional explanations of bits of human behaviour and the second party exposed their naïvety, ignorance, over-simplification, non-virtuous unworldliness. But there, unlike here, the exposures were sometimes softened with a favourite-pupil tolerance or even varied with an occasional cry of 'Excellent!' or 'One for you, Watson!' Nor was it recorded of Holmes that half of what he said came in aural italics or bold or sanserif. Had Gwen started piling this on recently? Or had she only started doing it so's-you'd-notice recently? Well, they had been married a long time.

He picked up Muriel's letter. The firm, spacious hand, which he could not remember having seen before, impressed him and made him wish, vaguely and momentarily, that she had made more of herself than she had. Scorning the small change of inquiries after health or other sociability, the text launched itself *in medias res* with a fully dramatized but not very lucid account of some visit to somebody somewhere. The more factual stuff came later. Among it Malcolm noticed a piece of information, or supposed information, that Gwen had not passed on: in alliance with two friends and the daughter of one of them, Muriel proposed to open and run what she called a coffee-shop in a suburban shopping-centre. The way she talked about it sounded to him quite unlike part of a brave or overdone attempt to hide boredom and loneliness, whatever bloody Sherlock might say.

Malcolm cleared the table, loaded the dishwasher and set it going. Of late the steady humming it made had been reinforced by an irregular drumming and it shuddered violently every few seconds. With no one repairing anything any more the best plan was probably to let it run until it blew itself up. *Western Mail* in hand he strolled to the cloakroom. Some delay, but no real bother there, in fact all was well – as far as he knew. No, all was well. He had started telling people who asked him how he was keeping that he was all right as far as he knew, and then stopped when he realized that that was as much as was meant by just saying you were all right. As if it mattered.

Gwen had about finished at her dressing-table, squirting anti-static fluid on her tinted lenses and preparing to follow with the impregnated cloth. He thought the movements of her hands made them look slightly fat.

'All right if I take the car? You'll be looking in at the Bible, will you?'

'Might as well, I thought.'

'If Peter's there you could give him Muriel's message, perhaps.'

'Eh? Oh yes. Actually he hasn't been in for a week or two.'

'One can't help wondering . . .' She sat facing him on the oblong padded stool, her spectacles held up to the light. 'Has he ever said if he hands over any cash for his bed and board? Makes any contribution to the household?'

'Well no. Nobody's asked him, not even Garth. Putting up at Rhiannon's for a bit is what it's called.'

'For quite a bit – what is it, three months? Fascinating. In Wales. Under the same roof as an unprotected female in Wales. And her a widow too. You'd think you were in the twentieth century.'

'Good luck to them is what I say.'

'Oh, do you really? It's certainly what I say. I also say it to or with reference to the representatives of the younger generation. I imagine the lad can practise his trade no less profitably in London than hereabouts. Anything to get out of this dump.'

'You can call it that if you like,' said Malcolm. 'Personally

I feel that any place where two people can manage to fall in love can't be as bad as all that.'

'Meaning who? Meaning who?'

'Well – William and Rosemary.'

'Ah. Well, of course. Malcolm dear, I was just – I meant that's how William might think of it, as a dump to get out of. I'm very nicely set up here, thank you.' And she smiled at him.

'Sorry,' said Malcolm. He had forgotten to include sonic inverted commas in his run-through of Gwen's special voice-effects.

She got to her feet after that and brushed down her chequered front. 'Well. Give my love to Charlie.'

'I will if he's there. He hasn't been in for a bit either.'

'I'm worried about Charlie, I really am. That evening at Dorothy's, you noticed nothing out of the way but I thought he looked awful. Awful.'

One of Gwen's things was not only to know better in general but to know better than you did about the people you were supposed to know better than she did in particular. Or so it had more than once seemed to Malcolm, who now said, 'He told me he hadn't been sleeping well for a year or more.'

'Right, I'm off. Smarty-pants Eirwen could do with some critical comments on the exhibition of alternative Welsh culture at the Dafydd ap Gwilym Arts Centre' – some system of tonal notation would obviously have to be developed to handle stuff like that – 'and then it's coffee and perhaps a glass of lemonade at Siân's. See you.'

Malcolm went and brushed his teeth in a glancing style, an even less demanding exercise than formerly, now that the lower-jaw one with a hole in it had fallen to pieces on a mouthful of ham at the wedding in the spring. While he shaved he thought about the fact that since the moment when he had brought her the news of Alun's death Gwen had not mentioned him in any way. At first he had put this down to shock or other temporary state, but it had long since been too late for that. For months he had been able to close a conversation with her by an oblique reference, or would find he had done so, not that he had much use for such a weapon. What kind of punishment or self-punishment her silence was meant to inflict he had very little idea, but if she had wanted to remove any doubts he might have been trying to hang on to about whether she had had some sort of affair with Alun – well, she had pulled that off in fine style. He had not quite lost the hope that one day a casual pronouncement of the name would touch off an equally casual allusion to that affair, and he could tell her that that was of no consequence and never had been. But he judged it very unlikely. And it was odd how a taboo on a single, less than all-important subject had seemingly turned out to impose a blackout on so much else.

When he had finished in the bathroom Malcolm fetched his jazz records from the sitting-room, where they had been lying about for ages, and put them back in the white cabinet in his study on the first floor. Before settling down at his work-table he glanced out of the window. What he could see of the sky past various roofs was overcast, promising rain, real Welsh autumn weather. He had an hour or more, before leaving for the Bible, to work on his translation of a long poem by Cynddelw Mawr ap Madog Wladaidd (c. 1320–?1388), *Heledd Cariad* – more of an adaptation, actually, for among other adjustments he had altered the physical characteristics of the central figure to correspond with Rhiannon's. If she had found love with Peter he was glad, because he had nothing to give her himself. But she had given him something. The poem, his poem, was going to be the best tribute he could pay to the only woman who had ever cried for him.